Plague Land

Plague Land

S. D. Sykes

PEGASUS CRIME

NEW YORK LONDON

PLAGUE LAND

Pegasus Crime is an Imprint of
Pegasus Books LLC
80 Broad Street, 5th Floor
New York, NY 10004

First Pegasus Books hardcover edition February 2015

ISBN: 978-1-60598-673-9

10 9 8 7 8 6 5 4 3 2 1

Printed in the United States of America
Distributed by W. W. Norton & Company, Inc.

For Paul

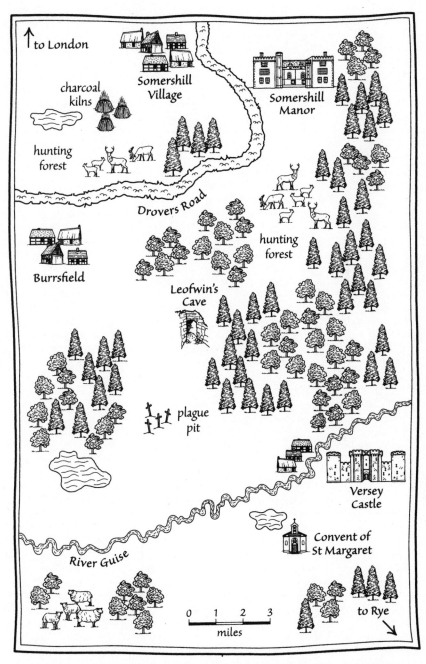

Somershill and its environs, West Kent circa 1350

The bubonic plague reached London in the autumn of 1348. Carried in the digestive tract of rat fleas, the Great Mortality went on to kill half the population of England in the following two years.

A Disputation betwixt the body and worms

Take heed unto my figure above
And see how sometime I was fresh and gay,
Now turned to worm's meat and corruption
Both foul earth and stinking slime and clay

Medieval poem
Anonymous

Prologue

Somershill Manor, November 1350

If I preserve but one memory at my own death, it shall be the burning of the dog-headed beast.

The fire blazed in the field beside the church – its white smoke rising skyward in a twisted billow. Its odour acrid and choking.

'Let me through,' I shouted to their backs.

At first they didn't respond, only turning to look at me when I grabbed at their tunics. Perhaps they had forgotten who I was? A young girl asked me to lift her so she might see the sinner die. A ragged boy tried to sell me a faggot of fat for half a penny.

And then a wail cut through the air. It was thin and piteous and came from within the pyre itself – but pushing my way through to the flames, I found no curling and blackened body tied to a stake. No sooty chains or iron hoops. Only the carcass of a bull, with the fire now licking at the brown and white hair of its coat.

The beast had not been skinned and its mouth was jammed open with a thick metal skewer. I recognised the animal immediately. It was my best Simmental bull, Goliath. But why were they burning such a valuable beast? I couldn't understand. Goliath had sired most of our dairy herd. We could not afford such waste. And then a strange thing caught my eye. Beneath the creature's distended belly something seemed to move about like a rat inside a sack of barley. I tried to look closer, but the heat repelled me.

Then the plaintive call came again. A groan, followed by the high-pitched scream of a vixen. I grasped the man standing next to me. It was my reeve, Featherby. 'How can the beast be calling?' I said. 'Is it still alive?'

He regarded me curiously. 'No, sire. I slaughtered him myself.'

'Then what's making such a noise?'

'The dog-headed beast. It calls through the neck of the bull.'

'What?'

'We've sewn it inside, sire.'

I felt nauseated. 'Whilst still living?'

He nodded. 'We hoped to hear it beg for forgiveness as it burns. But it only screams and screeches like a devil.'

I grabbed the fool. 'Put the fire out. Now!'

'But sire? The sacrifice of our best bull will cleanse the demon of sin.'

'Who told you this?'

'The priest.'

These words might once have paralysed me, but no longer. 'Fetch water,' I shouted to those about me. Nobody moved. Instead they stared at the blaze – transfixed by this spectacle of burning flesh. The ragged boy launched his faggot of fat into the fire, boasting that he was helping to cook the sinner's heart.

I shook him by the coarse wool of his tunic. 'Water!' I said. 'I command it!' The boy backed away from me and disappeared into the crowd, only to return sheepishly with a bucket of dirty water. And then, after watching me stamp upon the flames, some others began to bring water from the dew pond. At first it was only one or two of them, but soon their numbers grew and suddenly the group became as frenzied about extinguishing the fire as they had been about fanning it.

When the heat had died down to a steam, we dragged the sweating hulk of the bull over the embers of the fire to let it cool upon the muddy grass. As we threw yet more water over its rump, their faces drew in about me, both sickened and thrilled as I cut through the stitches in the beast's belly to release its doomed stuffing. It was a trussed and writhing thing that rolled out in front of us – bound as tightly as a smoked sausage.

As I loosened the ropes, the blackened form shuddered and coughed, before gasping for one last mouthful of air. Then, as Death claimed his prize, I held the wilting body in my arms and looked about me at these persecutors. I wanted them to see what they had done. But they could only recoil and avert their eyes in shame.

And what shame. For the face of their sacrifice is stitched into my memory like a tapestry. A tapestry that cannot be unpicked.

But this is not the beginning of my story.

It began before. After the blackest of all mortalities. The Great Plague.

Chapter One

It was a hot summer's morning in June of this year when I first saw them – advancing towards Somershill like a band of ragged players. I would tell you they were a mob, except their numbers were so depleted that a gaggle would be a better description. And I would tell you I knew their purpose in coming here, but I had taken to hiding in the manor house and keeping my nose in a book. At their head was John of Cornwall, a humourless clenched-fist of a man, whose recent appointment to parish priest rested purely upon his still being alive.

My mother bustled over to me. She had spied the group from our upstairs window, despite her claims to be practically blind. 'Go and see what they want, Oswald,' she said, digging her pincer claw into my arm.

I had been trying to decipher last year's farm ledgers, but the reeve's handwriting was poor and he had spilled ale upon the parchment.

Mother poked at me again. 'Go on. It's your duty now.'

'Yes, little brother,' said my sister Clemence, from the corner where she skulked with her sourly stitched embroidery. 'Though I'm surprised you allow such people to approach by the main gate.'

'I'll send Gilbert to deal with them,' I said, determining not to look up from my work.

'You can't. He's attending to the barrels from the garderobe.'
I had my back to Clemence, but I sensed she was pulling a face.
'You sent him there yourself, Oswald.'

'Then I'll send somebody else.' I looked to Clemence's
servant Humbert, a boy the size of a door who was holding
both of his enormous hands in the air so that Clemence might
wind her yarn about his fingers. His boyish eyes never leaving
his mistress's face.

She laughed. 'You can't have Humbert either. He's too busy.'

Abandoning the ledgers, I descended to the great hall where
one of the visiting party was now knocking at the main door
with intensifying boldness. Lifting the heavy latch I found the
culprit to be John of Cornwall, though he quickly dropped his
wooden staff on seeing my face and not that of a servant's on the
other side of the threshold. I might have reminded him that such
a wooden staff should have been deposited at the gatehouse, like
any other potential weapon, but seeing as our gatekeeper was
now employed as our valet, I did not challenge him.

'A girl has been savaged in the forest,' John of Cornwall told
me, without so much as a formal greeting.

I hardly knew what to say to this announcement and must have
let my mouth hang open a little too long.

A man with the skin of a cankered apple then bowed. 'The girl's
dead, my lord. Gored by a wild animal.' When I continued to
remain silent, the man looked about uneasily at his companions.

I found my tongue quickly, as they clearly thought me foolish.
'Was it a wolf attack?' I asked.

The man shook his head. 'No wolves left in Kent, sire.'

'But perhaps they've returned? Nobody has hunted the creatures since the outbreak of the Plague. As far as I know.'

John of Cornwall pushed the man aside. 'My lord. It is another
creature responsible for taking the girl's wretched life.' His
entourage groaned before falling silent and looking to me again
for a response.

'What sort of creature?'

Cornwall dropped his voice to a staged whisper. 'The Cynocephalus.'

'The what?'

'The dog-headed beast, my lord.'

So this was his notion. I nearly laughed out loud, even though it was hardly a fitting reaction given the news of the girl's death. 'That sounds unlikely,' I said.

Cornwall's lips pursed and his eyebrows rallied to a frown. 'There's no question. It's the work of the Devil.'

How tempting to tell him that I found the Devil to be as improbable as God, but I had the sense to suppress the urge. Instead I asked the girl's name and was told she was called Alison Starvecrow. It was not a name I recognised.

'Where's her body now?' I asked.

'We left her in the forest,' said a boy with boots too big for his feet.

'Why?'

'We thought you'd want to see her, sire.'

I shook my head. 'Me? No. You should inform the constable. Surely?'

'But the Constable's dead, sire.' The men looked at each other again, only just disguising their scorn.

'What about the Coroner?' I then immediately held up my hand. 'Yes. He's dead too. I knew that.'

Cornwall cleared his throat and fanned his robe. 'I have assumed the role of Chief Tithing-Man, my lord.'

'But you're a priest.'

He puffed out his chest. 'Indeed. But we must each suffer new burdens since the ravages of the Plague.' The man had tried to disguise his Cornish accent by adopting French pronunciation, but the colour of his true voice seeped through his speech like dye in a washtub. I found myself listening to the cadence of his words, rather than to the meaning of them. Sensing my mind was wandering, he coughed. 'In the absence of a constable,' he told me, 'we believe that you, as Lord of the Somershill estate, should take responsibility for the investigation.'

I hesitated. Was this the case? Was this really my responsibility? But if not me, then who else would take on this unwelcome duty? 'Yes. I . . . suppose that's—'

But suddenly there was a hot and breathy voice at my ear. 'Did I hear somebody say the Devil has murdered a girl?' It was my mother, peeking around my shoulder like a curious child at the door.

'It was not Satan himself, my lady,' replied Cornwall, pleased to find an attentive audience at last. 'It was his emissary. The Cynocephalus.'

My mother gasped. 'The dog heads? Here?'

Cornwall nodded gravely. 'They've been here for two years,' he said. 'Did you not know, my lady? They carried the Great Mortality to us from the Orient.'

The mention of the Plague was enough to provoke an even more fervent reaction from Mother. She clasped her hands to her cheekbones, fell against the doorpost and made a great show of fainting at Cornwall's feet.

With Mother providing the finale to this performance, the others in Cornwall's company were prompted to act out their own parts. The canker-faced man crossed himself feverishly. A tenant I recognised as our pig-herd, Hugh Gower, fell to his knees and prayed with an ardour I had never witnessed him display in church. And a youth with buck teeth muttered garbled words in concocted Latin, whilst pressing a piece of blackened wood to his lips. No doubt it was a fragment of the True Cross.

I had seen enough. When Gilbert returned from emptying the barrels into the moat, I sent for my boots and demanded to be taken to the girl's body.

Our shadows fell westward as we crossed the common pastures towards the forest. The dew was steaming and a host of finches chattered in the hedges. My home, Somershill Manor, rose behind us like a long knoll – the curtain wall of the old fortress now missing from the front of the house, revealing the great hall my grandfather had built. I looked back to see its large windows glinting in the morning sun, wearing their extravagant glass like a set of jewels.

Cornwall made it plain that he would lead the party to the girl's body, although it soon became obvious he didn't know the way. I couldn't entirely blame him, I suppose. The estate had been neglected for nearly two years – already the paths were overgrown with brambles, and the fields were full of foxgloves and ragwort. We came across sad, forsaken places, where only months ago we had driven off the wild dogs and ravens as they scavenged the bodies of the dead. I watched my step through the long grass, for fear of treading upon something that the dogs had missed.

When we reached the forest I tried to push to the front, since my father would have led our group, but Cornwall deliberately outpaced me at every attempt, or blocked my progress with the swing of his cloak. The forest was dense and dark, and resisted our attempts to penetrate, even though we walked along identifiable paths and trails. Beard lichen hung from low branches like cobwebs and tried to cling to my face or stick to my hair as I passed. Brambles scratched at my arms and hooked their barbs into the wool of my hose. Strange shapes seemed to dart in and out of the trees, but only ever at the periphery of my vision, so that when I turned to catch them, they had disappeared.

It was dark and lonely in this place – once the domain of hunting parties with their dogs and hawks – and suddenly I felt the urge to run home and find refuge in the open fields and sunlight of my meadows. But that was hardly how a lord should behave. Even one as young and inexperienced as I. So I continued to follow Cornwall around and around the same glade of willows until he finally accused me of being unreasonable in expecting

him to lead the way. After all, he argued, he hadn't been the one
to discover the girl's body.

I should have rebuked him for such perversity, but instead I
put Gower in charge and said nothing more. At least we now
made some progress, walking new paths until we reached a ridge
of yew trees where, at last, I recognised our location – on the
main drover's road to Burrsfield.

Not long after, we stopped by a standard oak that was said to
be near the dead girl's body. I took some ale from my leather
bottle, as much to improve my mood as to quench my thirst, and
then Gower led us to a thicket of nettles in a small hollow where
the girl still lay, face down in a carpet of leaf mould. It was a dark
and dismal place, even by the standards of this forest. The watery
sun failed to reach its banks, where pale cow parsley looked
ready to set seed.

I bent down to look a little closer at the girl's body, lifting
back her coarse woollen hood while the others in the party
backed away behind some holly. They pulled faces and shielded
their eyes, evidently repulsed by the sight of death, even though
they had spent the last two years engulfed by its stink. Personally
I was more disgusted by the pieces of food I had seen in Cornwall's
beard that same morning. But then I was accustomed to dead
bodies. As a novice in the infirmary I had regularly dressed them
for the grave.

Even so, the dead of the abbey hospital had never come to
their end through this door. They had been killed instead by old
age, bad luck, or contagion. Not by another living person.

I put aside my gloom to examine the girl with clear eyes, and
immediately noted the clean wound to her neck. There was no
blood beneath her body, nor anywhere else in the hollow. Nor was
there the acute stench you might expect to attend a corpse, which
suggested the body had been buried almost immediately after
death. Her limbs were flaccid, cold, and tinged with blue, which
led me to believe that she had been dead for at least three days.

The skin was not yet slipping from her bones. Her mouth, eyes, and the open wound to her neck were already infested with the tiny eggs of the blowfly, but we were not yet gazing upon a sea of writhing maggots.

Taking her delicate skull in my hand, I twisted it slightly to look at her face, but the girl was unknown to me – or so was my first impression. Then I couldn't be so sure, for there was something about her blonde hair and pale face that now appeared familiar to me. I looked again and tried to catch the thought, but the recollection slipped away.

Replacing her hood I asked Gower, 'How did you find her body in such a hidden spot?'

'It wasn't me that did it,' he said, backing further into the holly.

'I wasn't suggesting you did.'

'It was my pigs, sire. I brought them here to find carrot roots, but they sniffed her out. I had to beat them off her, you know. A sow'll have anything.'

His story was credible. If he had killed the girl himself, he could easily have left the body here and she might never have been found. And given the bite marks on a slender arm, it was obvious the poor girl had only just avoided the last indignity of being eaten by pigs.

Looking about the hollow for her original burial place, I soon found a depression in the earth beneath a wilting dog rose. This had to be the spot, confirmed by a thin skein of wool that had snagged on a thorn just above the hole. The wool matched the cloth of the girl's cloak and proved that her body had once been in this part of the clearing. But I could tell nothing more, other than that this grave must have been hastily excavated, since it had been shallow enough to allow a herd of pigs to unearth her corpse.

As I stepped about the area in search of more signs that might help to solve this mystery, the men edged cautiously over to the girl's body. When they thought I wasn't listening, the tallest pointed to her neck and whispered to his companions. 'See how she's been bitten. It must be the work of a dog head. Just as Father John says.' The others bobbed their heads like a row of chickens, clucking their approval of this fantastical story.

Wanting to put a quick end to this nonsense, I beckoned for them to draw near while I pulled back the girl's hood to reveal the cut to her neck. 'Look at this wound,' I said. 'Dog's teeth couldn't make such a perfect incision into soft flesh. It must have been a knife.'

They peered in and the clucks changed a little in tone, but before I could say another word, Cornwall caught me roughly by the arm. 'Don't ask the men to gaze upon the work of the Devil, my lord,' he said. 'They will become tainted.'

I laughed and pulled away from him. 'I don't think so.'

However, any amusement at this statement was mine alone. Cornwall rose over me and tilted his head forward to fix me a stare, his arms folded. Once again I should have rebuked him for such insolence, but he had unnerved me. The clearing was airless and grim and I wanted to be away from the place as soon as possible. So I didn't argue any further and instead asked Cornwall to remind me of the girl's name.

'Alison Starvecrow,' he told me. 'Daughter of your tenants William and Adeline Starvecrow. Both deceased in the Plague.'

'Does she have any living family?' I asked quickly, since I didn't recall the Starvecrow family, nor their purpose on my estate.

I sensed Cornwall relished my discomfort, since a contemptuous smile crept across his lips. 'The dead girl has one sister. Matilda,' he told me.

'Has this girl been informed?' Cornwall nodded. 'Then we should take her body back to the village and bury her properly. After that we can raise the hue and cry.'

Cornwall shook his head at this suggestion. 'No, my lord. There is no need to pursue the offender. It's better we pray for deliverance.'

For the third time that day I felt the urge to laugh out loud – as what had praying achieved in the last two years? The Great Plague had killed without discrimination. Saints and sinners. Those who pleaded with God like gibbering fanatics, and those who couldn't be bothered to put two hands together.

But impulsiveness should be guarded against. My tutor at the monastery, Brother Peter, had taught me this much. And what harm would praying do? It is an undemanding pastime. Physically that is. If my tenants and villeins wanted to pray for forgiveness, at least they were not wasting their scant energies on a hunt about the countryside.

And what realistic chance had a hue and cry of finding the true murderer anyway? I had witnessed such search parties before. Usually nothing more than noisy mobs who rounded up the nearest misfit and hanged the poor soul, whether proved guilty or not.

Alison Starvecrow was dead. Nothing would change that.

It was a mistake to let Cornwall have his way, however. To slap him foolishly on the back, as if we might become friends. 'Very well, Father John,' I said. 'I suggest you organise some prayer.'

He bristled at my touch. 'I was planning to,' he said.

Chapter Two

It was August 1349 when the Plague finally knocked at the door of our remote Benedictine monastery. We had thought it would not find us. Not after a year of stepping its feet upon English soil.

But plague does not move like a man. It is a poppy seed that blows on the wind and carries to every corner of the field.

The first of our order to die was not a lay monk, nor even an old priest in the infirmary, it was the abbot himself. The other brothers whispered that it was a rightful punishment, since the abbot was not a devout man. But in my opinion his end was as commonplace and ordinary as any peasant's death. He had not been singled out by God in any way. Instead he had allowed himself to become infected by stupidity, in sending for new gowns from London – even though we had been warned to keep our monastery sealed from the outside world. The abbot blessed the garment and claimed it could not taint him, but the contagion is said to linger in clothing for weeks and seems not to obey holy instruction. Within days he was lying in his bed complaining of a stiffness to his limbs, while scratching at a strange mark upon his leg. It could almost be described as a bite, but once it grew into a black pustule Peter banned me from the room.

And then, as a fever took hold of the abbot, Brother Peter washed his body in vinegar and rose water, but would not bleed him, though the man begged. And just as we had heard would happen, the buboes swelled in the abbot's armpits and groin until they were the size of duck eggs. Such was the blackness of his sores and the vileness of his appearance that I felt compelled to sneak into his dank bedchamber and take a look, despite the warning to stay away.

The abbot lived only until the next morning, even with Peter's best efforts to save his life. And then our brotherhood was without its leader and did not know how to act, for the Pestilence would now surely pick us off one by one in our small and isolated confinement of stone. Monasteries were a favourite haunt of the Plague, and many of our communities had been destroyed completely by its speedy appetite.

We talked of abandoning the abbey, if only for a few months, though some brothers spoke soundly against this plan. It would be God's will who survived and who did not. Those without the strength to face this test of faith were weak and heretical.

But Peter did not want me to endure this examination. Not by his God. He knew my faith would be found lacking. So he suggested I run away and only return to the abbey when the danger of the Plague had receded – a sin that would be forgiven by the other brothers because of my youth and the standing of my family.

My plans to flee were only interrupted by the receipt of a letter. Left at the gate by a messenger who rode away in terror – as if the Plague might swoop down from the walls of the monastery and catch him in its claw. Opening the roll I found it to be from my own mother, with the news that both my father and my two older brothers were dead. All three of them had contracted the Pestilence in Rochester and had died within days of each other.

I felt faint at these words and had to ask Brother Peter to read the remaining part of the letter. But, if I had expected sadness and sympathy from Mother, I was to be disappointed. This was purely a factual and instructional missive.

I was not to take holy orders as planned. I was not to become a Benedictine. Instead I was to return home immediately. For it seemed, at the age of eighteen and against all expectations I was now Lord Somershill – the keeper of more than a thousand acres in Kent. The owner of a village, whose inhabitants owed me servitude. And the master of a grand house complete with hunting forests, cellars, and a stable of fine horses.

It was an extraordinary turn of fate. But bittersweet. I had no deep fondness for my father and brothers, but it still grieved me to think of their lives so shortened. And I also knew of the burdens that the role of lord carried. The keeping of countless documents. The accounts, custumals and tenurial surveys. The fines, appeals and squabbles of the manorial court. The collection of the king's taxes, and the provision of men to fight the king's wars. The work had whittled my father into little more than a stub-end of a man. Hardened, pugnacious and difficult to please.

In truth, the news terrified me.

Confiding my fears in Brother Peter I even suggested, momentarily, that I might answer Mother's letter and decline the offer, proposing that there might be some distant cousin more suitable for the role than I. But Brother Peter would not hear a word of such cowardice. He urged me to consider the good to be done with my new powers. The wounds that might be healed. The injustices that might be remedied. And if this prospect did not appeal to me, then to consider how this news provided me with an excuse to leave the abbey legitimately.

I set out for Somershill the next day. I didn't have to persuade Brother Peter to join me.

When I returned from visiting the location of Alison's corpse, Mother had recovered from her fainting fit and was waiting anxiously in the great hall to speak with me. Her usually pale face was now flushed with anticipation. A strand of wiry hair had escaped from its netted crespine and was now hanging between her veil and her cheek. She would normally have poked this away, since she didn't consider it polite for a married woman to show her hair outside the bedchamber, but her adherence to manners had been forgotten in the expectation of some rare drama.

She was therefore rather irritated when I passed on the very briefest of details concerning Alison Starvecrow before retiring to the library to speak with Brother Peter. Mother went to follow me into the room, but hesitated at the threshold, remembering women had been banished from the library by my father – and though the man had been dead for nearly nine months, she still found it difficult to defy him.

I shut the heavy door behind me, not only to keep out Mother's prying eyes, but also to guard against the ears of my sister. Clemence was a keen eavesdropper, particularly eager to scrape up any morsel of tittle-tattle regarding Brother Peter – a man for whom she kept a special vial of spite. She continually pestered me to send Peter back to the monastery now that the Plague had receded, saying that he ate too much food and was a drain on our cellar. But I would not part with Peter. Not yet. He was my only friend.

I found Peter at his work, illuminating some text on a square of vellum he had brought with him from the monastery. It had been a hasty departure some eight months previously, and I soon discovered many unexpected items had found their way into our cart, though Peter insisted they were borrowed, not stolen.

That afternoon he worked beneath the large window, catching the evening sun before it abandoned the room. I peered over his shoulder to see that he was illustrating the patterns on a large letter 'P' that edged ever further across the page, leaving little room for any text. A thorny creeper twisted up the ascender of the letter, while a boil-faced demon peeped through the bowl. Armed with a fork, this demon was waiting to stab the wretched peasant who begged for mercy at his feet.

Peter had been a scribe before infirmarer, so his work was detailed and skilful – but of late it had become increasingly macabre, dominated by gape-faced corpses or mobs of hooded skeletons. I had hoped his spirits might improve with the longer days, but his mood remained as stormy and unpredictable as the summer.

'I'm designing a text on the Great Mortality, Oswald,' he said as I gently touched his arm. 'It's in English. I want children to understand the dangers of contagion.'

'And you think they don't?'

He banged the small trestle table. 'It's not a corrupted atmosphere that spreads the danger. They must understand that.' He cleared his throat, embarrassed at his sudden outburst. 'It's close contact, Oswald,' he said, more softly this time. 'Even touching the clothes of the sick is dangerous.'

I stepped back from his shoulder and sat down on a nearby bench, noticing he was already paying special attention to the tapestry on the wall opposite.

'I've come to ask what you know of the dog heads,' I said. 'Have you heard of such creatures?'

Peter put down his quill and let out a rare chuckle. 'The wicked men of the Orient. Flesh-eating creatures with the body of a man and the head of a wolf? What do you want to know about them for?'

'Cornwall's convinced this murder is the work of such a monster.'

The smile left Peter's face. 'What murder?'

'Surely you heard the commotion early this morning? John of Cornwall and some men came to the house with the news.' But I had forgotten. Peter rarely roused himself from bed these days before mid-morning. 'The dead girl was called Alison Starvecrow. They found her body in the forest.'

'But murdered? Are you sure?'

'Yes. Do you know her?'

Peter crossed himself. 'No. Though I believe she called at the house a few days ago. The afternoon I was reading to your mother in the solar.'

'Alison Starvecrow called here? Why?'

'I don't know, Oswald. She wanted to speak to my lady.'

'What about?'

He shrugged. 'Your mother wouldn't see her. You know how contrary the woman can be.' He paused, pulling at the mole on his neck and twisting its fleshy outcrop of skin between his fingers. 'Who discovered the girl's body?'

'It was Gower. His pigs unearthed her beside the road to Burrsfield.'

'And she didn't die of the Plague? I've heard of new cases in Rye. There is always a second, even a third wave in such a contagion.'

I shook my head. 'Her throat was definitely cut.'

He sighed and made for the tapestry, lifting back the image of an embroidered sea-serpent to reveal an alcove where a glass bottle and a solitary pewter mug were hidden. 'A murder. After all this misery. I sometimes wonder what Our Lord will throw at us next?' He held his hand up to me. 'And no, Oswald. I don't want to hear your opinions on the Almighty. Not today.'

He poured himself a mug of liquid that smelt strongly like brandy. Noticing the look of disapproval upon my face, he said, 'I keep it here in case of unpleasant surprises. The brothers didn't need it.' He downed the first cup, and quickly poured another. 'Have you raised the hue and cry?'

'No. John of Cornwall wants us all to pray for deliverance. He says the dog heads not only murdered this girl, but also carry the Plague. So we are all in danger.'

'Who cares what John of Cornwall says? He's nothing but a lowly parish priest.' He came over to me and took my hand. 'You are Lord Somershill. Not he.'

I pulled my hand away. 'It's not that easy, Brother. The men listen to him.'

'But Oswald. There is no such creature as a dog head. I'm
surprised you even allowed Cornwall to propose such a notion.'

'He's a priest. I didn't expect him to blame a monster.'

Peter snorted. The brandy was taking effect. 'There's always a
monster to blame. According to men such as him. No doubt he
will use this opportunity to sell more of his relics and indulgences. The man is no better than a common pardoner.'

'What should I do then, Brother?'

Peter caught my arm. 'Find the true murderer, of course.'

'But—'

'Show some courage. Investigate the crime.' He began to dig his
fingers into my skin. 'God has given you Somershill, Oswald. So you
might be a better lord than your father. A man who would have
ignored this crime. Just because the victim was a poor village girl.'

I looked at my feet to avoid his stare, and remained silent.

Peter leant over and peered into my face. 'Is it not convenient?
Is that your problem?'

'You don't understand, Brother,' I muttered, as sullenly as a
spoilt child.

'Understand what?'

I continued to avoid his eyes. 'My crops are rotting. The hedges
need scything, and de Caburn won't return my sheep.'

He banged his pewter cup onto the bench beside him, sending
a good quantity of the precious liquid into the air. 'I see. Not only
are you a coward, you are also indolent!' I would have argued
this accusation was difficult to suffer from a man about to spend
an afternoon with a bottle of brandy, but before I had the chance
to disagree, he renewed his attack.

'Don't you care about the Starvecrow girl?' he asked me.

'Of course I do.'

'Then find her murderer.'

'But—'

He held his hand up to silence the end of my sentence. 'Just
go, Oswald.'

'You don't—'

'Get out of my sight.'

Reaching the door, I heard the hasty footsteps of satin slippers across the rushes of the hall. Just as I had suspected. Clemence had been listening.

It is unsettling to disappoint a person you love. And I did love Peter. He had been my tutor and protector since I was seven years old, and had made abbey life at least tolerable for me. Keeping a promise to Mother, Peter had ensured there was always food in my bowl – even when kitchen supplies were low and the novices were the last to receive supper. I was not expected to join the lay brothers in the fields – even when I had broken the abbey rules. And when the abbot prowled at night, it was not my bed he disturbed.

Without Peter's care and guardianship it's difficult to say how I would have fared at the abbey, for I had not been prepared for monastery life. As the fourth surviving child in my family I was often little more than a lap dog to be indulged and fussed over by Mother. How she loved to comb my blond curls and sit me upon her knee. And how my sister Clemence would scowl as she watched jealously from the other side of the table, wincing as Mother sang to me and fed me spoons of honey.

But Clemence was not my only sibling to despise me. Once, when Mother was confined to bed with one of her headaches, my brothers William and Richard burnt the ends of my hair with candle wax, and then dunked my head into a bowl of brown walnut dye. Mother was incensed when she saw me, but since Father was rather amused by my likeness to a Saracen, she did nothing to censure their behaviour. Soon after this incident I left for the abbey, and at each subsequent visit, Mother would feel my hair and sigh in disappointment at its growing coarseness and darkening tone.

I soon learnt that Mother's love was as fickle as the blondness of my hair, whereas Peter remained steadfast in his care. And although he could not provide the honey that I had demanded with tantrums and a pair of stamping feet when first taken to the abbey, he was able to show a more enduring affection, which turned me from a spoilt child into a quiet and thoughtful boy.

So I could not let Brother Peter's low opinion of me persist, but how does a boy begin an investigation into murder?

My first idea was to question Mother about Alison Starvecrow's visit. But Mother denied any knowledge of the event – even though Peter had told me it had happened but four days previously. When I pressed Mother on the subject, she dredged up a vague recollection of a girl with the same name who had called to speak with her. She claimed to have sent the girl away since Brother Peter's reading of the scriptures had given her a headache, and she did not therefore care to receive visitors.

My next step was to question our servant Gilbert, since he must have opened the door to Alison, and it was possible she had mentioned the purpose of her visit. I found Gilbert in the kitchen where he was hanging a skinned rabbit from an iron hook. The kitchen cat purred at his feet, never taking her eyes from the pink and slippery carcass that was suspended above her. A stew bubbled in the copper pot over the fire, and some rye bread cooked in the embers.

I asked Gilbert to recall Alison's visit, but found him to be his usual impenetrable self. Not only was he cross at being interrupted whilst cooking supper, he also remained irritated that Alison Starvecrow had knocked at the main door to the house, when she should have called at the back porch like any other villager. The fact that the girl had been subsequently murdered gave no rise to a softening of his heart.

Since returning from the abbey, I had come to notice that servants were often more haughty than the family they served.

Gilbert could at least recall one important fact. Alison Starvecrow had initially requested to speak with me – but since I was away at Burrsfield, she had reluctantly asked for an audience with Mother. When Mother had refused to see the girl, Gilbert had sent Alison back to the village, with a warning not to return. It seems, however, that the girl took little notice, since half an hour later Gilbert chased her away from the porch by the chapel.

Alison was then seen to head off across the meadow in the opposite direction from the village. I suggested she might have been hoping to meet me on the drover's road, but Gilbert just shrugged his heavy shoulders. He assumed she had come to beg for money or a favour, like any other churl from the village.

So my initial investigations, such as they were, led nowhere. And by nightfall I had convinced myself that a lord is often called upon by his villeins and tenants – so Alison's visit to the house and subsequent murder were nothing more than coincidence. There were some enquiries I could make about the village, but they were unlikely to prove fruitful. In fact, the whole investigation was probably pointless, regardless of Brother Peter's sentiment. I did not see my role here as part of any divine plan. Somershill had only come to me by chance.

I sought some diversion in Father's copy of Roger Bacon's *Opus Minus*, but was unable to concentrate on Bacon's words of supposed heresy, because my obstinate mind returned continually to the murder. I tried to distract myself by thinking about geometry or the position of the stars in the night sky. But nothing worked. Not even the memory of the girl I had once seen washing in the river. My mind was stuck in a circle of thought that soon led to a sweating panic and then, most unfortunately, to the urge to open my bowels.

Retreating to our small garderobe, I hoped for some peace, but found no calm in this supposed place of privacy. Clemence kept walking past the door and complaining loudly of the smell. And Mother, fearing I needed to rid my body of corrupt matter, prepared a purgative of linseed oil and vinegar, which she slipped under the wooden door and insisted I drink in one gulp. I accepted the foul-smelling concoction to appease her and then poured it straight down the hole in the wooden seat, so that it dripped down a chute on the exterior wall of the house with the rest of the ordure, before piling up in a stinking barrel. If only my grandfather had invested in a latrine when the house was re-built. We had such a facility at the monastery, where our waste and its foul vapours were flushed away with running water.

With a sore stomach and a tender arse, I went to bed early – but found my night was no more peaceful and free of Alison. In my dreams I kept the girl in a caged enclosure, but then forgot to feed her. When at last I remembered my duty, I forced myself to look inside the cage, where her shrivelled body was curled in a corner like that of a starved animal. I wanted to look upon her face. It was as compelling as the urge had been to spy upon the plague sores of the abbot. But as I crept towards her lifeless body, she opened a pale eyelid to reveal a grey and sunken eye.

I woke with a start, taking a few moments to shake off the terror before Brother Peter's snoring reassured me of reality. We slept together in the only bed in the men's chamber, and once I was awake there was little chance of returning to sleep, since Peter snorted and wheezed like a sow at the trough.

I looked into his familiar face as he slept and felt both guilty and ashamed. I had disappointed him. But he was wrong. In one respect, at least. I might be a coward, I might even be indolent, but I did care about Alison Starvecrow.

And I would find her murderer.

Chapter Three

I woke the next morning with the intention of raising the hue and cry. I would round up the men of the village and search out Alison's attacker. We would be pursuing an offender with the head of a human.

I mounted my horse and rode into the village. It was now a short ride from the manor, but not so long ago the villagers had lived in a huddle around the house, before my grandfather had replaced the old Norman castle with our new residence – a house grand enough for the king himself to visit. He had removed their homes from the sight of the family, not wanting to look out of his new windows upon the untidy gardens and ragged children of his tenants and villeins. Now their ramshackle cottages clung about the parish church instead, and were only visible from the manor if you climbed the remaining north-west tower, and stood upon your toes.

The village had become a gloomy place in the last two years. Deserted cottages lined my path – their roofs stripped of timbers, while brambles and nettles pushed in at the doors like unwelcome guests. Anything of value had been looted, and soon these dwellings promised to be nothing more than skeletons of wood.

I will admit it was not only the lost lives that came to mind as I looked upon these shells. Half the village had died, but the dead pay no rent. And new tenants were impossible to find, not even with the more attractive terms and lower entry fines I had been forced to offer. And, if this were not bad enough, my surviving tenants were suddenly demanding higher wages to work on my demesne fields, with even the lowest villein and cottar now asking to be paid for their services – when their labour was bound to the tenure of their land and had never been waged before.

As Father often said, a poor harvest pushes up the price of grain.

Of course we had a local ordinance law to prevent wage increases, which I had heard would soon be reinforced with a parliamentary statute. But I doubted this new law would be any more successful. What was to stop a desperate lord from offering higher wages than his neighbour to keep his fields in crop and his cattle fed? The cottars and villeins might have to stay where they were told – but the tenants were free men and could go where they pleased.

And then I began to wonder if I should have written to Mother after all and declined this position? As cowardly as that might seem. For the monastery might have offered me more than this. With the nobility of my birth and the death of so many other brothers, I could have risen quickly to become abbot. Instead I was given Somershill – a gift that had smelt as sweet as the bloom of a rose, but which, on closer inspection, was barbed with thorns.

On reaching the centre of the village, I went to call on my reeve Featherby, but found his cottage to be as deserted as the rest of the street. Tying my horse to a post, I noticed a small boy creep out from a cottage and then begin bashing at a cartwheel with such dogged concentration, it was hard to determine whether he was trying to mend the wheel or simply destroy it.

I called to the boy, but he didn't look up. So I approached and took him by the arm, causing him to jump. When I asked where everybody was, he just stared back at me with cautious eyes and a face full of pitted scars. At my third repeat of the question, he finally pointed towards the parish church and then returned to his work.

Nearing the graveyard I could hear Cornwall's words, seeping through the stone walls like a poisonous vapour.

'Repent of your sins and the Cynocephalus will be gone. Beg for the mercy of the sweet Virgin Mary and the host of Heavenly saints. Pray to the bones of St Augustine and to the holy water of Bethlehem.' His voice was forceful and impassioned, calling upon every holy relic that had ever crossed the borders of our parish, and plenty of those that hadn't – rounding off each supplication with the threat of damnation or the promise of eternal life. His strange and contrived accent made the whole entreaty sound faintly comical, though I could hear that nobody was laughing.

I waited for him to end, with the intention of entering the church to speak with the village. But Cornwall's lungs were as strong as the bellows of a furnace, and worked without rest. When would he finish?

Peeping through the door for an opportunity to interrupt, I noticed immediately that there were no women or children in the church at all. Only men – whose large and bulky backs confronted me like an army of hostile faces. The only person to spy my presence was the wooden Virgin at the rood screen. Her arms outstretched and empty – as she looked about imploringly for the small Christ child that somebody had stolen from her many years ago.

My resolve now began to weaken at the idea of addressing this many men and wilting down onto the stone of the step, I hoped the ghost of my father were not watching me from behind a tombstone. He wouldn't have hidden in the porch like a leper. He would have marched into St Giles and demanded every man get to their feet and do his bidding. It wasn't a Sunday, so what impertinence was this to be wasting time in a mass? I wished I could have summoned the strength to follow his example, but at every new approach to the church door my legs refused to cooperate and soon I found myself unable even to look inside.

I am not an unreserved coward however. I didn't yet possess the courage to interrupt Cornwall, but there were other matters to attend to while the sermon droned on. Given that the women were not in mass, I decided to use the time to visit Alison's sister, Matilda.

Returning to the boy with the cartwheel I asked him where the Starvecrows lived, but once again he stared at me blankly. Now I spoke slowly and purposefully. 'The Starve . . . crows. Mat . . . hilda. Starve . . . crow.'

His large blue eyes wandered around my face, and then moved to my ear. I touched the side of my face in case there was something hanging from it, but found it to be perfectly clear. Now losing my patience, I shouted at the boy for an answer, but my tone was too harsh causing him to drop the mallet and bolt inside the cottage.

I cursed out loud and was turning to leave when a woman's voice called to me. 'Is that you out there, sire?'

'Yes. Who's there?' I approached the doorway and pushed aside some rough cloth to reveal a room full of silent women and children, their faces regarding me distrustfully. A small girl began to cry and buried her head into her mother's chest.

'Why are you all hiding in here?' I asked. The room was dark and airless.

Nobody answered. Instead they shuffled aside to reveal an old woman wrapped in a grey woollen shawl. Her body was as still and lumpish as a heavy sack of flour.

'Good morning to you, sire. I'm Eleanor. I was once your mother's lady's maid.' I didn't recognise the woman, but thought it rude to say so. 'Step into the light and let me see you.' I obliged and moved a little to the right, causing her to gasp. 'So tall now. And your hair still so fair. But where to goodness is the flesh on you? You should eat goose fat, sire. Goose! It fattens the arms, not the belly.'

I had been fed on a diet of goose fat since the age of seven, and it had achieved no effect upon my physique other than to give me spots and indigestion.

I repeated my question. 'Why have you all huddled in here?'

Eleanor clasped her hands together. 'To keep safe, sire. From the murderous beast.' The women then mumbled into their dirty veils and pulled their shawls about them, as if this supposed beast might be a draught of cold air. They were the last remains of the village, with faces so grey and exhausted they might almost be mourning their survival. A thin baby mewled, its skin loose against its cheekbones.

'You must return to your homes,' I told them. 'We'll find the true murderer.'

'Indeed, sire. The men are praying for deliverance with Father John.'

'Why didn't you join them?'

Eleanor shook her head. 'The women will stay inside their cottages until the beast is caught. That way it cannot bite our throats or taint us again with its pestilence.'

'There is no beast,' I said. 'The murderer is a man.' But this statement of fact did not reassure the women in the manner I had hoped. Instead a clamour arose. 'Is Matilda Starvecrow here?' I asked in an attempt to distract them from crossing themselves or sobbing into their surcoats. They didn't hear me at first, so I shouted. 'Matilda Starvecrow?'

Now there was an abrupt silence.

'The girl isn't here, sire,' Eleanor told me.

'Then how do I find her cottage?'

Eleanor shooed the other women out of the way and stood up slowly with the use of a stick. 'Let me speak with you privately, my lord,' she whispered, as the murmuring recommenced. 'Leave these poor souls to their prayers.'

She was unsteady, so I took her arm and we made our way outside the cottage so she might sit on the rough bench by the door. The small boy followed us and resumed bashing at his cartwheel, even though I asked him to stop.

Eleanor touched the boy's shoulder and put her finger to her lips. 'Don't be cross with him, sire. He's been deaf as a dor beetle since the pox. He suffered as a baby.'

She then settled herself down and bade me sit next to her. 'It's a shame I can't tend to your mother no more. But I'm full of the dropsy.' She poked a swollen foot out from under the shawl. 'See that? You can press your finger in there and make a pit.'

'How awful for you,' I said, declining the unpleasant invitation. 'Have you taken a draining tonic?'

She waved the idea away. 'Never off the piss pot after one of those things.' Then she took my arm affectionately. 'But tell me about my lady. Are her humours settled?'

'Mother is well at present, thank you.' I paused. 'Now please. If you would tell me how to get to the Starvecrow cottage.'

But she ignored my request completely. 'And how is she coping after your father's death? And those of your poor sweet brothers'?' She shook her head and sighed. 'And dying in Rochester. Not even in their own beds.'

'It was a shock to us all. But then, no family has been—'

'And I heard your father had to carry the bodies of William and Richard to the pit himself. What an indignity! It'll be what finished him off, you know.'

I shifted away from her so that she was forced to drop my arm. 'Eleanor. Please. I need to find the Starvecrow cottage.'

She wrapped her shawl about her. 'You sure you want to go there, my lord?' She then shivered, though I felt it was an exaggeration. Probably an affectation she had learnt in my mother's service. 'Some say the girl is cursed.'

'I don't believe in curses.'

'Perhaps you should?'

I shook my head firmly. 'No. I never will.'

Then she laughed and took hold of my arm again. 'Very well then, sire. But you shouldn't need me to give directions to the Starvecrow cottage. Ask your own feet to take you. They've taken you there enough times before.'

'No. I've never been to the place.'

She laughed again, but this time it developed into a hewing cough and it was a while before she had composed herself. 'But sire. You were nursed at the cottage by Adeline Starvecrow. Alison and Matilda's mother. Don't you remember?'

I shook my head. 'That can't be right.'

'She nursed you until you were three. Always running to her tit you were.'

'You must be mistaken. Mother would have employed a nurse-maid to come to the manor.'

'No, no. Your mother sent you to the village. You upset her humours with all your screaming.' She laughed again, but this time stifled the cough. 'Begging your pardon, sire, but you were a shrill and tiresome baby.'

'The Starvecrow cottage?'

Her smile dropped. 'You were better off farmed out to a village wife. That was the truth of it.'

'Eleanor!'

'Follow the path by the standard oak. It's through the coppice and down in the valley.'

I found the Starvecrow cottage at the bottom of two banks, next to a stream that plunged its way belligerently through the under-growth. The smell of the place was sickening. I don't just mean the usual scent of farmyard that attends the poor. There was an additional layer of dankness here – the odour of damp cellar or a woollen vest left too long in the washtub. Mother would never have sent me to such a place as an infant, so I dismissed Eleanor's story as a wandering of her mind.

At the bottom of the bank I climbed over an apple tree that had fallen into the stream and was now re-routing the water through a hog hole. As my boots sank into the mud, a young girl appeared at the door of the cottage.

'Are you the boy with no eyes?' she asked me. Her face was lucent and impassive, like the effigy of a saint.

'No,' I said. 'I can see perfectly.'

'Are you sure? I've lost one eye. Now it's a pebble at the bottom of the sea.'

I scratched my head. 'Is this some sort of riddle?'

'I still have my own eye,' she told me. 'But there is another. A half-eye that looks at the sky.'

It seems I had progressed from conversing with a wandering mind to a lost one. 'Are you Matilda Starvecrow?' I asked. She didn't answer, preferring to gaze at the swallows that swooped about us in search of flies. 'I said, are you Matilda Starvecrow!' Something cold and slimy was seeping into my boots, and squelching between my toes.

'Yes. I'm Matilda,' she answered at last.

'I need to speak to you.' I pulled my feet from the mud. 'We should go inside. The horseflies are biting me.'

The cottage was no more than a single chamber without windows. As Matilda opened the door I could see a crude wooden bed, a cooking pot, a fire pit, and an axe. The floor was laid with rushes that looked clean enough, but the room was smoky and confining. A small fire smouldered in spite of the warmth of the day.

I should have felt pity for the girl, having to live in such an ill-favoured place, but there was something sly in her manner. She had not curtsied to me yet. Moreover she had allowed the decrepit door to swing back in my face when I entered the house, and had not apologised. I rubbed my nose and left the door open

to let some air blow into the place – but only succeeded in allowing the stench from outside to invade the chamber.

'My name is Oswald de Lacy,' I told her.

'I know who you are.'

Her pale blue eyes stood out in the gloom, and suddenly I
recognised something about her – just as I had when looking
upon the face of her dead sister. Fine hair framed a thin, dainty
face. It was an unpleasant recollection, so I looked away, but
found it no more comfortable to be glancing about the room,
where elongated shadows formed eerie shapes in the rutted
daub of the walls. The door opened and closed in a sudden gust,
which ignited the embers into a few short-lived flames.

'I'm sorry about your sister Alison,' I told her. 'But I will find
her murderer.'

She smiled somewhat scornfully at these words and then
started to hum, meaning I had to cough to get her attention. 'I
need to ask you some questions, Matilda.'

'Why?'

'Because it would assist me in solving the crime.'

Now she laughed at me.

'Don't you want to help?' She only cocked her head and stared
at something beyond my shoulder. I persevered nonetheless. 'I
understand your sister recently came to the manor house to see
me. Do you know what she wanted?'

Matilda sat down on the floor. 'Why ask me? When you know
the answer?'

'Because I don't.'

She played with the rushes between her fingers. 'Are you sure?
I never saw my sister again. Not after she visited you.'

'But I didn't see Alison. I was away at market.'

Now she pushed aside the rushes and drew the outline of an
eye in the dust of the floor. 'Half an eye. Looks at the sky,' she
sang as she began to sway to and fro.

'Please stop doing that,' I said.

'Half an eye. Looks at the sky,' she continued, now louder – blowing herself into a frenzy. I tried to lay a hand gently on her shoulder to see if this might pacify her, but the rocking had increased with such violence that it was impossible to get near her. I gave up on this interview and turned to leave when, in a moment, the storm seemed to blow itself out.

Now she had calmed herself to a shallow gust, I tried again. 'I need to know why your sister came to see me, Matilda. Do you think you can remember?' She swayed and whispered and didn't respond to my question. Her eyes were distant and glassy, and a faint smile curled upon her lips.

Once again I was struck by the familiarity of this face. Had I seen the girl about the village? Did she sometimes work at the house? I endeavoured to make the connection, but my memory would not oblige.

Instead I took her hand and whispered softly. 'Was there something Alison wanted to tell me? Please try to remember, Matilda. It would be very helpful to know.'

'Oswald. Oswald. Half an eye. Oswald, Oswald, looks at the sky.'

It was futile. When she resumed her rocking I turned to leave, but now she lunged forward and snatched the tail of my cloak.

'Your father liked to visit my mother,' she said, her eyes suddenly focussing.

'What nonsense is this?' I tried to pull my cloak away from her, but she wouldn't loosen her grip. I pulled again, but she was resolute.

'Father, father. Eye of a lover,' she sang.

'What do you mean about my father? Stop it!'

'Liked to visit over and over.'

Each time I succeeded in dragging one corner of my cloak from her, she caught hold of another part – her hands clinging to me like the tentacles of a sea monster. When I had finally removed her from my clothing, she then attached herself to my feet.

'Let go,' I said.

'Father, father. Eye of a lover.'

'Get off me.'

'Liked to visit over and over.'

'Get away from me or I'll strike you!' I didn't mean it. I don't even know how such a threat crossed my lips, except that this pale-faced girl had terrified me.

It must, however, have appeared rather differently to the woman who came forward from the shadows. A woman with a still and stony expression. I had neither seen her enter the room, nor could be sure her grey face was not that of a ghost's. This place was so strange and ill-omened that anything was possible.

She did not seem shocked by my harsh words to Matilda, or indeed by my raised hand. Now that I looked at her again, I would almost say that guarded amusement was the most accurate term to describe the expression carved across her hard features.

I should have asked her name, but instead attempted to defend my actions. 'I wasn't going to strike the girl,' I said nervously. 'But she wouldn't release me.' The woman only continued to stare. 'She made insulting allegations against my father,' I added. But the silence endured until I lost my nerve completely and rushed away from the cottage, running up the bank only to slip over, face-first into a bush of stinging nettles. Rubbing at the painful rash that soon appeared on my cheek, I turned to see whether the silent woman had witnessed my indignity.

Thankfully there was no sign of her at the door, but then I noticed the slightest flicker of movement back into the shadows, and realised she had seen the whole pathetic episode.

I should have returned to the church to assemble the men for the hue and cry, but instead I rode straight home to search out Brother Peter.

I found Peter in the great hall with Clemence and Mother, seated at the long table beside a pile of rabbit bones. The air in the room smelt meaty and sharp, as if the rabbits had been left too long on the hook.

Mother was sunning her face in a shard of light, her skin as lined as a puddle of dried mud. On her lap she petted her small dog Hector – an animal I had repeatedly banished to the court-yard but who persistently found his way back inside the house. Clemence was hunched over her tapestry and welcomed me with the rebuke that I was cutting out her light, whilst Peter slept with his head on the table, his lips fluttering at each snore.

Angry at my approach, Hector leapt from Mother's lap and ran at my ankles.

His shrill bark woke Mother with a start. 'I didn't know Hector was inside,' she blustered. 'The naughty little boy must have crept in.'

Clemence called her servant Humbert over from the fire and ordered the boy to deal with the small dog, who was now making enough noise to be heard in Rochester.

Humbert put down the square of Clemence's tapestry that he had been tenaciously unpicking, scooped up Hector in his great fig-leaf hands and then dropped the dog's squirming body into the stairwell to the solar, where the spiteful little creature contin-ued to yap and growl at us through the gap at the bottom of the door. Humbert returned to Clemence and awaited his next instruction, before she imperiously waved him back to the stitch-ing without even looking up.

I shook Brother Peter's arm gently. 'Brother. Wake up.'

Peter opened an eyelid. 'What is it?' He tried to focus on my face.

I leant down and whispered into his ear. 'I need to speak with you, Brother. Alone.'

I was trying to be discreet, but unfortunately my words were in range of Clemence's accomplished hearing. She pulled a face and stabbed her needle ever more viciously at her cloth. 'God forbid a simple woman should hear what you have to say, little brother. My ears might crumble.'

Peter tried to raise his head from the table and settle his chin onto the palm of his hand, but he missed and fell against Mother.

'Leave the poor man alone,' said Mother, pushing Peter away from her. 'Can't you see he's ailing?'

'Ailing?' said Clemence. 'The man's been drinking since daybreak. He's pickled to the pips.' Then she clapped her hands, and Humbert reappeared at her shoulder. 'Cut this thread for me,' she commanded. The boy coloured as if she had asked him for a kiss.

Sensing a moment's opportunity I shook Peter a little harder, but still he didn't respond.

'Why are you pressing Brother Peter for an audience, Oswald?' asked Mother. 'Can't it wait until he's rested? We opened some Madeira and it has made him a little fatigued.'

'Or why not tell all three of us?' suggested Clemence. 'I'm sure our delicate minds can endure it.' She cocked her head at me and a sly smile crawled across her lips. 'Or is it one of those secrets only you men from the monastery can divulge to one another?'

'Do be quiet, Clemence,' said Mother. 'You're as cross as a wasp today. Are you bleeding again?' Clemence gritted her teeth and returned to her sewing.

'If you must know, I've just been to visit Matilda Starvecrow,' I told them both, 'and now there's a matter I need to discuss with Brother Peter.'

'Who have you been to visit?' said Mother, squinting and holding a hand to her ear.

'The sister of the murdered girl,' said Clemence over-loudly. 'You didn't miss an engagement.'

'Thank you, Clemence. I am not deaf,' said Mother. She turned back to me. 'Why were you visiting this girl, Oswald?' Then she clasped her hands together. 'Have you found the dog-headed beast? Is that why?'

I heaved a sigh. 'No, Mother.'

But her enthusiasm was not dampened. 'I had a thought this morning, Oswald. Perhaps we should let the wolfhounds out?'

'We haven't owned wolfhounds for two years.'

'Haven't we?'

'We could always release Hector instead,' said Clemence. 'I'm sure he would savage them to death.' My sister then smiled at her own wit. And seeing some amusement light up Clemence's usually fractious face, Humbert quickly joined in with a guttural noise I took to be laughter.

Mother turned her back on Clemence and then caught my sleeve. 'Talking of the Starvecrows, have you discovered why that girl wanted to speak to me?'

'No,' I said. 'Though it seems she actually called to speak to me.'

Mother frowned. 'You? Are you sure, Oswald?'

'I wasn't at home. That's why she asked for you.'

'I see.' Now she seemed affronted. 'Who told you that?'

'Gilbert.'

Mother shook her head. 'No, no. I'm sure the girl wanted to speak to me. I am the lady of this house.'

'I don't know why you're squabbling over such a foolish matter,' said Clemence, biting through a skein of silk with her teeth, since Humbert was struggling to use the scissors. 'It wasn't the queen coming to call. It was just some village girl.'

Her conceit riled me. 'A village girl who was then murdered.'

Clemence only huffed. 'Her type is always knocking at our door, little brother. Wanting a favour here, or a penny there. You'd do well to follow Father's example. He had no time for such people.'

'Is that so?' I said. 'Because I understand Father rather liked the company of village girls. I believe Alison's mother was once a favourite.'

As soon as the words left my lips I regretted them. Mother choked upon her Madeira and a heavy silence fell about the room. Clemence glowered.

'I expect your father was collecting rent,' said Brother Peter making a sudden and welcome interjection, as I had thought him still asleep. 'Or perhaps he was inspecting the Starvecrows' pigs.' He bowed his head to Mother. 'Lord Henry especially liked pigs didn't he, my lady? Particularly if they were ready for the spit.' Peter then attempted to lift the mood by laughing at this thin joke, though Humbert was the only other person to find any amusement in it. The boy quickly became silent when Clemence shoved him in the ribs.

Mother muttered some platitude regarding the price of hog meat before standing up to leave. 'Oh dear,' she said, holding her hand to her forehead. 'This heat is so perplexing. I may have succumbed to a fever.' Then, moving her hand quickly from her forehead to her breast: 'I can barely breathe.'

She left the room gasping for air, but was healthy enough to lift up her little dog as she passed through the door into the stair-well. 'I'm putting Hector back into the courtyard,' she lied, as she climbed the stairs to the solar and bedchambers.

When we were certain the upper door had closed, Clemence turned on me. 'Well done, little brother. Why don't you now really humiliate Mother and invite some of his bastards for supper?'

'What?'

'I think we should retire to the chapel, Oswald,' said Brother Peter, taking me by the arm.

I shook Peter away. 'No, Brother. I want to hear what Clemence has to say.'

But Peter took my arm again, more firmly this time and propelled me towards the other end of the hall.

As we neared the door, Clemence called after me. Her eyes now shining with malice. 'You really were closeted away in that monastery, weren't you, little brother?'

'There's no need for this my lady,' said Brother Peter. 'Please don't say anything more.'

'I don't take orders from you, priest.'

'Indeed my lady. But perhaps it—'

Clemence threw down her embroidery. 'Perhaps it is time Oswald knew what his own father was really like.'

'I knew Father just as well as you,' I snapped, though it wasn't true.

She put her hands upon her hips. 'Then you shouldn't be surprised to hear he has a dozen bastards about the estate?'

'Bastards?'

She smiled at me. 'Yes, Oswald. Children born to whores.'

'I don't believe you,' I shouted back at her. 'You're lying!'

'That's what lords do, Oswald. And one day it will be you.'

'It will not!'

And then, Peter pushed me through the door, before I could say another word.

The chapel was cool and silent, with only my ancestors and the saints for company. When Peter refused to discuss Clemence's accusations any further, I lay against the carved filial of a bench and breathed deeply with my eyes shut – a practice I had developed at the monastery to prepare myself for the long and tedious hours of prayer. With enough concentration it was possible to remove myself to a place where calmness and peace held sway. It was neither exciting nor boring, but allowed interminable masses to pass without desperation.

I thought about Father as I lay there. Could he really have a host of children about the estate? My memories of him were as a contrary and unfriendly man, and I had been unable to kindle anything other than a guarded affection for him. But he had been kind enough to me as a young child – particularly when he discovered I could read more proficiently than my older brothers – boys more interested in crossbows than books. Father gave me dried figs when I read aloud to him in the library. He had even wiped away a tear when I left for the monastery.

However, I saw very little of him from the age of seven. He

wrote strange, disjointed letters to me occasionally. Hurried messages, which on the one hand encouraged my intellectual education, urging me to learn Greek and Syriac, and then on the other hand proudly boasted about how many more hours' labour he had succeeded in exacting from our villeins. When I read the letters to Brother Peter, he had always sighed, making pointed comments under his breath. But I had caught his drift well enough. Peter thought my father a cruel and greedy tyrant.

Did the man really have bastards about the estate? I could not be sure. Clemence's grand accusations could be nothing more than mischief, as she was the sort of person who liked to throw fat into a fire, just for the pleasure of watching it burn. I probably shouldn't trust a word she said.

I slumped further against the filial of the bench, now trying to ignore the horsefly bites from my visit to the Starvecrow cottage. They were itching, and though I scratched them persistently, the prickling had become so intense that I called for Brother Peter. He was kneeling at the altar in prayer, his lips moving silently but feverishly with the words of his catechism – his brow furrowed with concentration.

I didn't like to disturb him, but he wasn't angry with me when I did.

He left the chapel to fetch some medicines from the cellar in the main house, but returned so quickly I wondered if he kept some supplies in the porch. I didn't remark on his speed since the bites were now red and swelling, and I was simply relieved when he pasted a potion of salt, honey and crushed onion onto my ankles. The smell was strong but not unpleasant – a clean and natural odour after the stench of the Starvecrow hovel.

I let the balm slowly cool the inflammation. 'I need to talk to you about my father,' I said, as he wrapped a bandage around my ankle.

Peter sighed. 'Why, Oswald? Your father's sins are not worth worrying about. Don't concern yourself with them.'

'But I should know the truth about Father. Particularly if everybody else does.'

'It's just gossip. And let me tell you. Only one tenth of village gossip is ever true.'

Then he accidentally dropped the coil of lint and we watched it roll along the floor, unravelling on its way across the slabs marking the dead of my family. Huffing, he bent down to pick it up again. 'It won't be easy for you to step into your father's shoes, Oswald. The man was like a beech tree. He cast such deep shade that nothing could grow beneath him. You will be a much better lord than he, but you must give yourself time.'

'What time is there?'

'Plenty. You are young.'

'William and Richard would have been ready.'

Peter sat up again. 'I don't think so. From what I knew of your brothers, they were as unprepared for this role as you are. At least you had some years at the abbey. It gave you the chance to grow in your own light.' He took my hand and smiled. 'They were good times, weren't they, Oswald? Before the Plague.'

I knew Peter's tactics of old. He was trying to change the subject. 'Does my father have bastard children about the estate?' I asked him again. 'Please tell me the truth.'

He dropped my hand and sighed. 'Most probably, Oswald. Though only Our Lord knows for sure.'

'Do you know their names?'

Peter bristled. 'Of course I don't! And take care to whom you ask that question, or face every scoundrel in the village claiming to be your sibling.'

'Were Matilda and Alison Starvecrow his children?' Peter looked away. 'Matilda said such strange things to me, Brother.'

'What type of things?'

'Nothing that made sense exactly.'

'That's because the girl is possessed. You can't believe a word she says. If I were her priest, I would cast out her demons.'

'But is it possible she is my half-sister?'

'I don't think so.' Then he took my hand again. 'Listen to me, Oswald. I knew the Starvecrow family quite well, as I was often here, copying manuscripts from your father's library. In my opinion Alison and Matilda resembled their own father well enough. I never heard anything to the contrary. And don't forget I sometimes took confession at the parish church. Village gossip will reach a confessional quicker than a fly smells blood.'

'Really?'

'Yes, Oswald. Really.'

Despite Peter's conviction, I continued to run over the events of the day until I felt wholly exhausted. I had always admired, if not loved, my father, but now his character was being unpicked like one of Clemence's tapestries. I tried to rediscover my quiet place of calm, but the more I attempted to dismiss my thoughts, the more they took hold of me.

As I climbed into bed that night and pulled the linen sheet over my head, an agitation came upon me. Images flickered across my eyes, and answers to the riddle of this mystery formed and then drifted apart like faces in a cloudy sky. It was a hot and still night, the type that threatens thunder, but we could not open the windows in the bedchamber as the panes of glass were fixed into their lead fittings.

At this time of year I sometimes envied the villagers and their airy homes. Unable to afford glass, they simply covered a square in the wall with shutters – shutters that could easily be opened to the sky in the heat of a stifling night. (I am told, however, this arrangement is less agreeable in winter, when a person will often wake from sleep with ice upon their eyelashes.)

My bedfellow Peter was less understanding than usual about my restiveness, and kept telling me to go to sleep. At my repeated turning, he finally offered me a sleeping draught, which I accepted. So, instead of lying in bed determining that tomorrow

I would make more progress with the investigation, I drifted off to sleep – wondering how far away the stars were from the earth, and why the moon waxes and wanes. Not even the imaginary howl of a distant wolf disturbed me.

I woke the next day feeling relaxed and calm, but it was not to last.

There had been another murder.

Chapter Four

Gilbert roused me with the news, and I thought I might still be dreaming – his words nothing more than a trick of the mind. But the roughness of Gilbert's hand upon my arm and the foul smell of his morning breath soon pitched me into reality.

I pulled back the sheets. 'Are you sure? I saw Matilda yesterday afternoon.' I still felt giddy, since the sleeping draught had not fully drained from my head.

Gilbert grunted something and then added, 'Mind you, they haven't found her body.'

'So how can we be sure she's been murdered then?'

'I'm told there's blood all about the Starvecrow cottage, sire. Looks like a slaughterhouse.' I jumped out of bed and Gilbert helped to lift my leather kirtle over my shirt. 'Those dog heads must be getting bolder,' he said. 'Coming up to the village. We should set the fires tonight.'

'There are no such creatures, Gilbert. Nobody in this household is to say so.'

Gilbert recoiled a little at my abruptness. 'As you like, sire.'

I went to apologise, but stopped myself since I had noted Gilbert distrusted courtesy, especially from me. Instead I told him to saddle my horse.

'Where're you going, sire?'

'To the Starvecrow cottage.'

When Gilbert had left the room, I tried to roll Brother Peter onto his side and wake him, since I needed his advice. But the man slept as deeply as a dormouse and would not be roused.

The air that morning was still, and no stiller than in that damp pocket of land that the Starvecrows inhabited. Even the stream, which had previously beaten its path so brutally through the nettles, now slipped silently down the hill like melted butter.

Looking down at the cottage in the hollow below, I wondered what new horrors awaited? But then a wave of hope washed over me, as the story could well be an exaggeration. Brother Peter was accurate in his assessment of village gossip. It was quite possible that Matilda had simply wandered away from the house, and this supposed 'slaughterhouse' might amount to nothing more than a few drops of blood upon the floor.

I had expected to meet a crowd at the cottage, but instead found myself to be completely alone. After tying my horse to a tree, I descended the damp bank of angelica and buttercups towards the cottage, making certain this time not to fall over.

Not only was there an absence of people about the place, but the pigs that had roamed about the garden yesterday were now nowhere to be seen. No doubt a neighbour had taken the beasts before anybody else had the opportunity. And then, shamefully, I found myself wondering who would actually inherit the possession of the Starvecrow property, if Matilda were actually dead? This land belonged to the manor, so there was only the livestock to be passed on — other than the ragged bits and pieces that furnished the cottage. And who would pay my rent, since nobody would choose to live in this place, when better quality plots were vacant? And lastly and most shamefully of all — I wondered who would pay my death heriot? As the owner of this land, there was at least one pig due to me.

I walked on and put these matters out of my mind, but nearing the cottage I could hear noises from within, and realised there was another person here after all. Treading silently towards the door, I wanted to spy upon this opportunistic thief. Peeping through a gap in the wood, it was the most unexpected person I saw inside the place. A man on his knees, feeling about in the rushes of the floor.

I would have watched him for longer, but the sun breached the clouds and threw my shadow across the room, revealing my presence. He turned to look at me. It was John of Cornwall. As surprised to see my face as I had been to see his.

For once I had the advantage of the man.

He stumbled quickly to his feet as I opened the door fully. 'My lord. I was looking for the footprints of the beast. There are some outside.'

I ignored this claim and walked across the threshold. 'I'm told Matilda Starvecrow is missing.'

Cornwall nodded.

I looked about, but it was difficult to see very much inside this gloomy abode. The smell overcame me again, and I took some mint from my belt – a bunch that I had picked on my way down the slope in expectation of the unpleasant stench. Crushing a few of the leaves, I inhaled their fresh and sharp scent, prompting Cornwall to look at me with such scorn that I dropped the leaves to the floor.

'I can't see the blood they speak of,' I said quickly. 'Where is it?'

Cornwall pointed to an area near the one and only bed. 'It's here,' he said. As my eyes became accustomed to the dark, I could see the bedclothes were indeed stained with spots of blood – though the marks were difficult to make out against the dirty grey of the woollen blanket. Looking closer I saw a viscous puddle of blood beneath the bed frame, its surface peppered with soil and dirt.

'I covered her blood with dust,' boasted Cornwall. 'To prevent the flies from causing a nuisance.' He pronounced the word 'flies' with a long and peculiar drawl that I imagined he thought sounded refined.

Kneeling to study the puddle, there was more blood than I had originally supposed. It had pooled into a small raised mound, bound together with the dust and dirt of the floor. 'You may have destroyed some evidence by doing this, Cornwall,' I told him.

'It was simply blood, sire. You could tell nothing more from it.'

'Maybe.' I studied the bed frame for a while. 'I think Matilda must have been attacked while she was sleeping.'

He nodded. 'That sounds likely, my lord. The beasts will creep up upon their victims while they sleep and bite their throats.'

I looked up at him. 'Randomly?'

'Sire?'

'I just wondered why these creatures targeted two sisters, that's all? When they could have attacked anybody in the village?'

Cornwall huffed. 'There's a simple explanation for that. The sisters did not attend mass regularly.'

I sighed and stood up. My hands felt sticky and hot. 'I visited Matilda yesterday and there was a woman here. She didn't wear a wimple, though she was certainly old enough to be married. Do you know her?'

I would tell you Cornwall gave a flicker of recognition at my description, but the light was too dark to draw any conclusion. 'She doesn't sound familiar to me,' he said blankly. 'But she cannot be connected with this crime.'

'How so?'

'Because the girl was killed by the beast.'

I was beginning to lose patience. 'What is your substantiation for such a story, Cornwall?'

My tone was discourteous and he visibly inhaled at my words, his chest rising through his cape. 'I believe you will find this proof enough.' He led me to the door and pointed to some footprints in the mud – though it was impossible to narrow this spurious evidence down to anything more specific than an animal with padded feet.

'I thought these creatures only carried the head of a dog,' I said. 'So why are we looking at paw prints?'

Cornwall fixed me with his eyes, light blue and cold. 'They are shape changers, and can take any form between man and dog.'

I raised an eyebrow. 'Really? I don't remember learning about such phantoms at the abbey.'

'Then your education remains incomplete, sire.'

'Perhaps so. We concentrated upon the gospels and the learning of Latin and Greek. So there was little time for fairy tales.'

Cornwall sucked his teeth. 'This is not a fairy tale. It is the work of the Devil. And I pray to Heaven for salvation.'

'But will Heaven care?' He flared his nostrils, but I didn't regret my candour. He had riled me with his imaginary nonsense. A creature that could take any form between man and dog was a vague and illusive quarry – only suited for terrifying a group of simple villagers. People who had only just recovered from the horrors of a plague.

The argument might have continued, but the door blew open and a shard of sunlight suddenly illuminated a pathway to the area under Matilda's bed, picking out a collection of bright dots scattered about in the rushes and dust. Leaning down, I quickly collected each one of them while the light still shone upon me, finding the objects to be ten small red beads.

'Look at these,' I said, opening my palm to Cornwall. He leant forward to take a bead, but I pulled away my hand and looked at him quizzically. Suddenly I had the suspicion that the rest of the beads were in his pocket.

'I'll keep them safe,' I said. 'The sheriff will want to see them.'

He snorted. 'The sheriff?'

'Yes. This time we will raise the hue and cry.'

'But—'

I put my hand on his arm. 'You are Chief Tithing-Man, are you not?'

'Yes, sire.'

'Then gather the men outside the manor house. Without delay.'

The men came mostly on small ponies, but Cornwall arrived in their midst on a fine destrier, and my first thought was to wonder how a priest could afford such a war horse? Not wanting to be overshadowed by the man, I foolishly asked our stableboy Piers to saddle up my father's black stallion, a horse named Tempest – the most capricious and unpredictable mount in the stable. Piers baulked at my request, as nobody had ridden Tempest since Father's death and I was the least likely member of the household to end his spell of freedom from duty. I was fortunate therefore that the horse was in an amiable mood that particular morning and did not buck me off in front of the men.

Drawing the crowd together, I informed them we were not only searching for a murderer, but also Matilda's body. I then described the stone-faced woman from the Starvecrow cottage, asking if anybody knew her identity. My request for information was met with vehement shakings of the head and exaggerated shrugs. When a young boy tried to raise his hand to answer my question, he was soundly shoved by his neighbour.

It was a mistake not to press the boy further, but Cornwall's horse was now pawing at the ground as if trained to cause a diversion. With the attention of the group now wandering from me and settling upon the priest, I cantered grandly around the men before setting out across the meadows towards the forest. It wasn't long before Cornwall chose to ride ahead of me. Digging my heels into Tempest, I tried to regain my position, but suddenly my horse lost interest, and soon I was riding along-side the old men on their small mules and ponies. As we reached the forest path I even kept pace for a while with an ancient man on a donkey, who told me he had only joined the search party since he refused to stay at home and listen to the wittering of the women.

As we spread out amongst the coppiced chestnuts, Cornwall contradicted my instructions to the men at every turn – and soon it seemed we were not looking for a murderer, nor even a body. Instead the men spent most of the morning searching for the signs of evil, though Cornwall was none too specific in his description of what these might be. Not that this lack of clarity concerned the men, as they were utterly taken in by Cornwall's story – his premise only further supported by the small group who claimed to have heard the howls of dogs the previous night, their calls advancing and retreating about the village like the roll of thunder. It was scarcely possible to argue with these tales, since the men were so convinced by their authenticity that each had a more dramatic account to tell than the last.

Gower had slept with the fire alight and an axe by his bed. He had barricaded the door to his house with a bench and a trestle table. When John Penrice claimed to have taken the very same measures, Gower then boasted he had even corralled his stinking pigs into his home, to keep them safe. The smell and effluent of these creatures within a small cottage must have been astounding, and demonstrated the true evil of Cornwall's fairy tale. Gower still had a small child alive, and this poor boy had spent the night in the company of pigs, merely because his father had been hoodwinked into believing that dog-headed devils were roaming our estate.

When I questioned their stories further, it seemed more than coincidence to me that these were the same men who had also been drinking late at the tavern. Though they protested heartily, I doubted a single one of them had heard the milk-souring howls they claimed to have. More likely it was the screech of an owl or the squeal of a fox.

When we had failed to find any evidence of Cornwall's evil in

the forest, I took the opportunity to repeat my more practical
instructions to the men. Look for anything out of the ordinary. A
hiding place. Newly made tracks or newly turned soil. Blood-
stained clothing.

The curl of a sneer crept across Cornwall's face as he listened
to my words, but I was determined to give reason and logic a
chance to solve this crime. Why should his wild superstition and
delusions have all the answers? My approach was far more likely
to produce a perpetrator than his mad visions of devilry. I just
needed time to convince the men.

At first it seemed I might be succeeding. They began a method-
ical search, keeping their eyes to the forest floor and their mouths
shut. But when a young boy stumbled across a tree adorned with
the skulls of small animals, my work was immediately undone.

Cornwall rounded up the men to look upon the boy's discovery. 'It is an altar to Satan,' he announced.

The bones were weathered and I was able to pull a clump of
fur from a fox tail that hung from a branch.

'Don't touch it, sire,' said Cornwall. 'The Devil has cursed
this place.' I groaned. Anybody could see this shrine was nothing
more than a pathetic attempt to pray to the full range of deities
– from the gods of the wood to the God of Israel. It had been
here a long time and was, in all likelihood, the work of a desperate soul during the days when the Plague had flooded through
this valley like the waters of a winter storm. I noticed Cornwall
failed to draw anybody's attention to the crudely formed crucifix
of stones that also lay beneath the tree.

After this unfortunate discovery, I suggested we split the
group into two. Cornwall would continue to search the forest,
whereas I would take a band of men towards the next village,
Burrsfield. Cornwall claimed he needed the larger of our two
groups, since he might come across a pack of dog heads at any
moment and need the men to defend him with pikes or crossbows. Surely his words of prayer and the sight of his crucifix

would be of more assistance in this situation, I suggested? He could scarcely argue, but suddenly there were more volunteers to go with me than were prepared to stay with him.

Despite this unexpected and sudden enthusiasm I picked only five men – a group whose company I found agreeable.

As we parted, the rain clouds opened and droplets of water quickly pierced the canopy of leaves, so that even with our hoods raised, we were soon wet to our skins. The summer had been like this for many days. The sunshine was ever short-lived, building to a bout of intense humidity and then followed by a storm. The forest still smelt of fungus and leaf mould, when it should have been sweetly scented with elderflower and honeysuckle. The dew ponds were overflowing and the mud of the tracks was thick and sticky.

The place felt as sinister and dank as the crypt of the abbey, and we hurried to be away from its shaded menace.

On reaching Burrsfield, I dismounted quickly and led Tempest to the stream, when a well-dressed man with a well-supplied belly limped across the path to greet me. He bowed to me awkwardly given his crooked leg and I recognised him as Geoffrey Wallwork, a local yeoman farmer who rented eighty acres from me. We exchanged greetings, and when I explained our purpose, he was insistent we join him for a warming bowl of pottage. Given the dampness of my clothes and the dejection that had suddenly descended on the men, I accepted his offer.

Wallwork's home was set back from the village by the length of two strips, and was a grander house than any of his neighbours', with jetties forming an overhang above the small windows of the ground floor. There was no reason to increase the space in the upper chambers in this way, since the constriction of city life was not suffered in this small village – so Wallwork could only have added the projecting overhangs to show off his wealth. I noticed that these follies only existed along the frontage of the house in order to be fully admired from the road. At the back of the house, the walls were flat from the ground to the roof.

Entering the hall I remembered having been here as a young child. The air was dark and smoky, and laced with the salty-sweet odour of the hams that hung from the high beams of the open hall, hoping to catch the smoke that rose from the open hearth and then seeped through the roof tiles. Wallwork called a girl from the shadows and she set up a trestle table and a bench for us next to the fire pit. While I warmed myself, my men were sent to the other end of the house to be seen to by a servant in the makeshift porch that served as the Wallworks' kitchen.

'Do you remember my daughter Abigail?' asked Wallwork as the girl laid two pewter bowls upon the table.

The girl was as fat and pink as her father. She smiled at me coyly and swept back her loose hair. 'Good day to you, sire,' she said, bending low to pour me a drink – her large breasts wobbling like two bowls of freshly curdled cheese.

'Abigail was to marry John Mortimer, weren't you, dear girl,' said Wallwork, taking the girl's arm and leading her into a patch of light, so I might view her beauty to greater effect. 'It was a very good match. He rented a good number of acres near Westford. But of course Abigail is able to read, and we farm eighty acres, so he would have been equally blessed.'

The girl repeated the unnerving grin at me. Wallwork continued. 'The unfortunate fellow died last year and poor Abigail is left without a marriage prospect. In the prime of her life. Healthy as a heifer in a bull field, aren't you, dear girl.' Abigail giggled and curtsied to her father.

'There's not a man around here worthy of her,' he continued, his face beginning to redden. 'Of course I've had many suitors at the door. But I tell them to go back to their families with their offers of marriage. I shall only find the best husband for my precious girl. And she's the only child I have left, sire.'

'We've all lost so many of our loved ones,' I said, and then quickly changed the subject. 'Now, Wallwork. I need to know. Have you had any trouble in the village? Has anybody raised your suspicions?'

'Is this to do with the Starvecrow murders?' I nodded. 'So you think the murderer might have come from Burrsfield?'

'It's possible. But it could equally have been a stranger, or a traveller.'

'There haven't been any strangers here lately, sire. We don't trust a soul we don't know. Not since the Plague.' Then a smile spread across his pink face. 'It was the pilgrims who carried it here, you know. On their way to Rochester to pray for salvation. A lot of good that did them!'

The irony tickled him, but when I didn't laugh, he stopped promptly. 'I'm sorry, sire. I just think they would have fared better by staying at home.'

He then leant forward to speak to me quietly, even though the room was empty apart from his daughter. 'Now, if you ask me, those Starvecrow girls were probably done in by a *certain person* in Old Ralph's family.'

'Which *certain person?*'

'Most likely Joan Bath,' cut in Abigail. 'She's an old biddy bitch and no mistaking.'

Wallwork coughed. 'Thank you, Abigail.' Then he laughed again and slapped my leg. 'These young girls? Full of earthiness.' I think he may even have winked at me. I stood up instinctively.

'Please, sire. Sit down. Abigail will get you some pottage, won't you, girl? And bring the silver spoons. Lord Somershill would like to see them.'

'I'm quite happy with this horn spoon, thank you, Wallwork.'

'But my silver spoons bear the leopard's head hallmark, sire. They are the best quality.'

I sat down again, but further along the bench. 'I'd like to know what makes you suspect this woman,' I said. 'I recognise her name.'

'There's plenty who know her name,' said Abigail, but Wallwork glared at her before she had a chance to continue.

'Go and get the spoons, girl,' he said, though she still didn't move.

Wallwork then edged towards me, but shifting away from him any further along the bench would have meant falling off the end. 'The Starvecrow girls were left orphaned,' he told me. 'After the Pestilence. But they have some hogs and possession of the land near a stream. Nothing like my family of course.' He puffed out his chest. 'I have eighteen hogs and four dozen ewes.'

'Joan Bath?'

Wallwork laughed. 'Of course, sire. Joan Bath is Old Ralph's daughter. You must know him? He's a tenant of yours in Somershill.' I nodded, though it was doubtful I could pick him out from the young Johns or old Geoffreys. 'She was married to John Bath.'

Abigail laughed. 'Though not for long. She quickly did for him.'

Wallwork glared at his daughter again. 'He died of the flux, girl. There's no proof Joan killed him. Now go and get that pottage and those silver spoons!' As Abigail reluctantly sloped out of the room, Wallwork smiled at me. 'Young girls will get such ideas into their heads.' He patted my knee. 'She needs company, sire.'

I drew back, though Wallwork hardly seemed to notice and patted my knee a second time.

'Let's return to Joan Bath, shall we?' I said quickly.

Wallwork's face fell a little. 'Yes. Of course, sire. What was it you wanted to know?'

'Please tell me why you suspect this woman?'

Now Wallwork cheered up a little. 'Well. It's like this. Joan's father, Old Ralph, took a fancy to the Starvecrow hogs. So once Alison's parents were dead, he hatched a plan to marry the girl. And she couldn't do much to object. Not having any family to see him off.'

'Surely she was too young to marry?' I said, thinking back to the fragile corpse we had discovered in the undergrowth.

'She was fourteen, sire. More than ripe for the marriage bed.' He winked at me again. 'I expect you, being of noble and more refined blood, like a girl to be a little more mature. My Abigail is seventeen you know.'

I ignored this comment. 'Alison Starvecrow was fourteen? Are you sure? She looked only ten or eleven when I saw her dead body.'

Wallwork sighed. 'Ah yes. Those Starvecrow girls were a sickly pair. Alison was stunted like dwarfed rootstock. And Matilda has a head full of demons. Not that it's put off Old Ralph. With the older girl dead he'll marry the sister. That's if you can find her alive.' He winked at me and whispered. 'He likes them young.'

We were interrupted by Abigail who had returned with the pottage and silver spoons, which to my surprise, were finer than most of ours at Somershill. The years before the Plague had been good to yeoman farmers, many of whom prospered as greatly from farming as a lord could from renting out his land. I dipped the spoon into the pottage and found it to be full of fresh peas and tender hoof marrow.

I ate it quickly, and as Abigail leant over me to ladle a second helping into my bowl, I caught her arm. 'Tell me some more about Joan Bath.' I watched her pink cheeks redden to a deep crimson.

'Go on, dear girl,' said Wallwork, pleased at my sudden, if belated interest in his daughter.

'Joan is Old Ralph's daughter by Maggie Wide-legs,' she told me.

'That was Margaret Furlong, sire,' said Wallwork quickly. 'Maggie Wide-legs is just a silly name some of the rascals gave her when she was alive.' He coughed. 'She had dreadful problems with her hips.'

I suppressed an urge to laugh. 'Why do you think Joan is involved with Alison's murder?'

'She didn't want her father marrying that girl, did she?' said Abigail.

'Why not?'

''Cause Joan was going to get Old Ralph's house and land when he dies. And he's got no teeth.'

'No teeth?'

'Boils on his gums, sire. Don't reckon he's long to go. His breath smells like a dog's arse.' I dropped her arm.

Wallwork scowled, but quickly changed the expression on his face to an obsequious smile. 'Old Ralph can smell a little stale, sire. That's all she means, don't you, dear girl.' Abigail nodded nervously. 'Young ladies will get bawdy when they haven't a husband to tame them.' He leant over and took my leg again. 'Now, if you were to think about taking a wife, sire.' He nodded towards Abigail and she giggled.

I stood up as if this would somehow extricate me from this awkward situation. 'Thank you, Wallwork. That is a thoughtful suggestion. But I'm not looking for a wife at the present time. My situation is too . . . demanding.'

Wallwork was not as discouraged by this announcement as I had hoped. 'That's quite understandable, sire.' He then joined me by standing up to whisper in my ear. 'But if you would like to taste the pie before purchase, then I'm sure that Abigail would be amenable to such an arrangement. With certain assurances, I would make no moral objections to such youthful exuberance. After all, it is the summer. And the birds are nesting.'

Abigail had heard every word of this supposedly private conversation, and she smiled, as if being peddled by her own father were just a foolish but amusing embarrassment. I thought of my own father. No doubt such an arrangement would have suited him. But it did not suit me.

'No thank you, Wallwork,' I said. And then seeing the girl's face fall, and in an attempt to alleviate her humiliation I added, 'It is a very tempting offer, but I believe my mother is looking into my matrimonial options. And I wouldn't want to upset her.'

Wallwork sighed. 'Perhaps then, if you need a little diversion in the meantime. Abigail's as ripe as the cherry on the tree, and ready for picking.' He winked again. 'You wouldn't have to marry her, sire. Just relax my rent a little. I'm sure that her services would more than please you.'

'No thank you, Wallwork.'

His eyes narrowed to a frown. 'But the harvest is bad this year, sire. I'll struggle to pay my rent.'

'Please, Wallwork. Let the matter drop.'

'I only have one farmhand left to collect all the grain. So I was thinking we could come to an arrangement. And Abigail's taken a liking to you, sire. I can tell.'

I looked at the poor girl, who had backed into the shadows with her face to the floor. 'Wallwork, please stop this. We're not at the horse fair.' He went to object, but I held up my hand. 'The girl is your daughter!'

His head drooped. 'As you like, sire.'

I dusted down my tunic, thanked him for his hospitality, and then asked to be directed to Joan Bath's house.

As I rounded up the men in the kitchen, I heard Wallwork call his daughter a foul-mouthed slut.

Chapter Five

Joan Bath lived a way outside the village of Somershill, on a north-facing slope where the lands of my estate started to rise towards the forests of the weald. Nobody else inhabited this area – since the ground was damp and boggy from the waters that drained from the hills. Joan was a cottar with only a small curtilage of land about her cottage, paid for by her services to the manor. But, according to the men, Joan never turned up to labour in the fields herself. She always sent her sons.

The cottage itself was humble but not dilapidated. No weeds grew from the thatched roof, and the timbers were not rotten, though they rested in the soil without stone foundations. The cottage sat in the middle of the narrow strip of land that was divided between a densely stocked vegetable patch and a small orchard. A bony cow chewed at some long grass while a pig stretched out beneath one of the apple trees, but there was no stench of animal dung hanging about the place. Instead I had seen a pile of decomposing manure further down the path, next to a mountain of crumbling soil that was dark and sweet smelling.

As we rode towards the cottage we saw two boys picking peas and collecting them in a wicker basket. They looked up at our group suspiciously, as a skeletal dog ran out to greet us with a set of bared teeth.

'Call off your dog,' I shouted, as the snarling creature edged towards us. The boys turned to the house and looked for instruction, where a tall woman now leant against the door-post and watched us with her arms folded. I pulled on Tempest's reins, for this was the same woman I had seen at the Starvecrow cottage. Her black and glossy hair still uncovered. Her face still grey and stony.

Gower rode up beside me and pointed to the boys. 'That's all Joan's got left, sire. Out of six sons. And each one a bastard.'

'Do you know her well?' I asked. Gower looked away and bit his lip. 'Oh no, sire. She's nothing to me.'

And then I recalled why the name of Joan Bath had been famil-iar. She was the widow of a Somershill villein, but since her husband's death had continued to produce a string of illegitimate children – despite the childwyte fines she received at the mano-rial court. It was now obvious to me why the men had been reluctant to identify her before. She was the village whore.

In the daylight Joan appeared only slightly less sinister than she had in the gloom of that cottage, and I found myself wondering how she made such a success of her trade, given that there was little to admire in her face other than its severity. Clearly the paying public of this part of the county were not too fussy. Or perhaps it was simply that Joan had the whole market to herself? But then I am a young man and no judge of true beauty, often drawn to girls with the faces of kittens. As Mother has frequently warned me, a pretty foal will make an ugly mare.

'Here, dog!' Joan called to the growling beast, which then slunk back towards the house with its tail between its legs, only reviving its spirits after she offered her hand to nuzzle. The dog settled down beside her, watching her face intently for her next instruction. And it was not the only creature expected to obey this woman, for she quickly shooed the two boys into the cottage and then shut the door on them.

We dismounted and tied our horses to the apple tree near the door.

'What can I do for you?' she asked as we approached. The five men who had accompanied me to this interview looked at their feet. 'I only see gentlemen one at a time. You should know that, Gower.'

Gower snorted and turned to me. 'I don't never visit this woman, sire. She makes things up to tease us. To make trouble.' He turned back to Joan. 'It's 'cause she knows that no man would take her as his wife. Dirty whore!'

At these words of insult Joan took a stone from a pile by the door and hurled it towards Gower. I had the feeling these small missiles were kept on a ledge for such occasions as these.

'You pigs!' she shouted. 'There isn't one wife in this parish who could give birth to as many sons as I have.'

Gower picked up the stone from the ground and went to return fire, but I held back his arm. 'Put it down!' I said, though he struggled against me. 'Do as I command you!' As Gower reluctantly let the stone fall, I turned to Joan. The woman had resumed her indolent lean against the doorpost and was looking straight at me. 'I'm here to discuss the Starvecrows with you, Mistress Bath.'

'What about them?'

Gower resumed hostilities. 'Show respect to Lord Somershill.'

Joan smiled at his words and curtsied to me mockingly. 'What about them?' She hesitated a second, 'sire.'

Her sarcasm provoked Gower to rush upon the woman and seize her roughly by the arm.

'That's enough, Gower,' I said. 'Let her go.'

The dog growled but Joan only laughed. 'That's his problem. He can't let me go. Can you, Hugh Gower? Always up here, he is.'

'That's not true,' said the man, his face now red and sweating. The dog was now tugging at the wool of his hose and would soon bite into the skin of his leg.

'Most probably made this one for me,' she said, patting a flat belly with her free arm.

'You're not with child!'

'That's what you say.'

Gower dropped her arm. 'She's lying, sire.'

She patted her belly again. 'Hope he's not as stupid as his father. Then again, I could do with a pig herder.'

The men behind us sniggered and Gower turned to confront them with a thunderous face. Now afraid that this rancour could quickly escalate into hostility, I insisted that Joan call off her dog and then speak with me in private. She was reluctant, but seeing as there were six men at her door, one of them her lord, she had little choice but to admit me to her cottage.

She left the dog outside, where the scabby creature maintained a steady growl by the door.

I had seldom spent as much time amongst the poor as in those few weeks, and in truth it had shocked me to see how they lived. While the churches and monasteries were filled with grand windows and tapestries, it seemed most people in England lived in hovels not much finer than the stall of an animal. And with only a lantern hole at one end of a low ceiling, these structures quickly filled with smoke and smelt as strong as a charcoal kiln.

Not that Joan's home was dirty. In fact, compared to the Starvecrow cottage, the place was orderly and clean. But it is difficult to shine a floor of mud, or polish a wall of wattle. It is still a hovel.

Bending my head to miss the low door lintel I saw her two sons were now sitting at a bench and shelling the peas they had just been picking. The windowless chamber was as dark as any of the other cottages I had been in recently, with an area screened to one end of the room by a hanging blanket. This, I assumed, was where Mistress Bath entertained her customers. As my eyes became accustomed to the light, I noticed a wooden stool in one corner that was laid with a mixture of offerings, from the petals of a dog rose through to the skulls of small animals. A crucifix sat alongside a dusty corn maiden.

Joan saw my interest in the corn doll. 'It's just something my son made last harvest. It's nothing but a toy.'

I picked it up. 'You should remove it, in case Father John comes here. He would denounce this as unholy.'

She grinned. 'Father John of Cornwall doesn't come to visit. Whatever makes you think that?' Her crude suggestions were beginning to grate upon my nerves.

I passed her the doll. 'What do you know about the Starvecrows?'

She shrugged. 'Nothing much.'

'But you do know Alison was murdered? It seems Matilda as well.'

'But you haven't found Matilda's body. So the girl could be fooling you.'

'Why would she do that?'

'Because she was to marry my father.' Then she smiled deviously. 'But perhaps she disappeared after the beating you threatened yesterday? Matilda's a sensitive girl. Apt to run off when she's upset.'

'I didn't touch her. She wouldn't let go of my cape.' Thankfully we were distracted from continuing the conversation by a muffled whine.

'It's just the dog,' said Joan quickly, though the creature was separated from us by the door. She then shouted for the animal to be quiet, which only made it whimper for its mistress even more loudly. Inside the cottage, the boys suddenly broke into song. Their voices were low and melodic.

'I ask them to sing when they're shelling the peas,' Joan told me. 'If I hear a tune, I know that they're not eating.'

Since the boys were now singing so loudly, I raised my voice. 'Why were you at Matilda's cottage yesterday, when I called upon the girl?' But evidently I was not loud enough.

'What was that?' she said, holding a hand to her ear.

'I said, why were you—' But it was hopeless, so I turned to

the pea-shellers and shouted, 'Will you please be quiet!' And to my surprise they stopped immediately and suddenly I found myself wondering how I might reproduce this commanding tone of voice in the future.

With silence established, I was now able to make myself heard. 'Why did you call upon Matilda Starvecrow yesterday?' I asked Joan.

She shrugged. 'That's no great mystery. I wanted to stop her marrying my father.'

'Why?' She pursed her lips and looked away. 'So you wouldn't lose your right to his land, perhaps?'

Now she laughed. 'I see you've been talking to the village gossips.'

'Are they right?'

'No. They're not!' A ball of spit hit my cheek.

'So why did you want to stop the marriage?'

'Because Matilda is thirteen and he's an old pig of sixty.'

'That's a cruel way to describe your own father,' I said.

'He's a cruel man.'

'Who would leave you disinherited?'

Her grey cheeks flushed, and for the first time I saw some colour in her face. 'My father would rather leave possession of his property to the village fool than me.' And then the energy and spite left her. 'I went to see the girl out of pity.'

'Pity for her? Or for yourself?'

'For her, of course. She's of no mind to marry an old man.' She paused and rubbed her eyes, but I could not be sure they were real tears she wiped from her face. 'I offered to take her in,' she told me. 'They might call me a whore, but I'm nothing like the monsters in this parish, who would see such a wretched girl married to a toothless pig.'

'And was Matilda interested in coming under your care?'

Joan shrugged. 'She was too disturbed to decide anything. I promised to return the next morning for her decision.'

'And under this arrangement, what was to happen to her pigs and her land? You were to take care of them as well, I suppose?'

'I gave it no thought,' she said – but it felt like a lie. 'My only concern was to stop my father taking one more girl before he leaves this earth. Is that so unbelievable?' Her brow was puckered and now the tears seemed genuine. But I knew better than to be affected by a crying woman. It was a ploy Mother often used when cornered in an argument.

'Did you return to the Starvecrow cottage this morning?' I asked Joan.

'No. I heard the place was found empty.'

'Do you know where Matilda is?'

'Of course I don't.'

'But you suspect she's still alive?'

She wiped her eye. 'I hope so.'

'So how would you explain the blood found about the cottage?'

She straightened herself up and now regarded me crossly. 'I'm not the constable. I wouldn't try to explain it.'

I took the ten beads from my belt pouch and held them out to her. 'Do these belong to you? I found them under Matilda's bed.' She feigned disinterest, but I pushed my hand under her nose so that she was unable to ignore me.

Joan grimaced at first, as if being asked to study the entrails of a chicken. But when she looked at the beads properly her face broke into a smile – and fleetingly she seemed handsome. Her teeth were straight and white. Her features were strong and symmetrical. Drawing me close, she whispered, 'They are red coral, sire.'

'What of it?'

Her eyes now glinted with mischief. 'If I owned such a necklace, sire, do you think I would be earning a living with my cunt?'

'Do they belong to Matilda then?' I asked, quickly returning the beads to their pouch to alleviate my embarrassment. Joan merely raised an eyebrow at this foolish question. 'So, do you know who they belong to?' I asked.

She folded her arms. 'No. I don't.'

The boys continued their work silently, dropping the peas into a square wooden bowl and the empty shells into a wicker basket. A fly buzzed about my ear, and the dog was now pawing and scratching at the wooden planks of the door. And then, suddenly, the door flew open and the dog sped in and began lunging at the pea pods greedily with its long pink tongue. The boys kicked the dog away, whereupon it disappeared into the screened end of the room and began to growl.

'What's behind the blanket?' I asked Joan.

'Nothing.'

'What's the dog growling at then?'

'Just an elderly man of the parish,' she answered. 'He's unwell so I've taken him in to restore his health.'

'Which old man?'

'You wouldn't know him, sire. He's a traveller.' She seemed nervous for the first time in this interview.

I saw her hand was trembling. 'Pull back the blanket,' I told her.

'That's not a good idea. He's sleeping.'

'But I'd like to meet him.'

'He's just an old peddler, sire. You wouldn't find him agreeable. He can hardly speak.'

'Pull it back, Mistress Bath.'

'I will not!'

I went to do it myself, but when she stood in my way I called for the assistance of Gower and Wycombe. As the men burst into the cottage, Joan's two sons tried to obstruct them – but the two skinny boys were no match for burly farmhands and were soon despatched to the floor alongside the crumpled blanket.

An old man was revealed in the alcove, bound tightly with dirty ropes and a gag about his mouth. He wriggled urgently like a worm in the beak of a blackbird, and when Gower released his gag, the man coughed until he was nearly sick.

Gower looked to me in disbelief. 'It's Old Ralph. Her own father.'

I leant over the old man, trying to hear his words – but he only panted a sequence of garbled noises. I turned to Joan. 'Were you trying to kill this man, Mistress Bath?'

'I would happily see him rot and die.' Her words were hot and vengeful.

'Is this what happened to the Starvecrow sisters?' I asked.

She spat at me. 'No!'

'Did they meet this same fate at your hands?'

Now she screamed and lunged forward, scratching me across the face – her nails scoring my skin and drawing blood. I backed away, but as she made a second attack the men pulled her from me and threw her roughly to the floor alongside the boys.

I wiped the blood from my face. 'Take them to the gaol house.'

Joan's sons may not have been the physical match for Gower and the other men in a fight, but they were faster and more agile. They dodged their pursuers easily, making their escape from the cottage with the scrawny dog loping along behind them.

'Run, boys!' their mother shouted. 'Run!'

Gower ordered her to be quiet, though she continued to scream after her sons until Gower went to kick her.

I pulled him back. 'Stop this, Gower. Now!'

He shrank away from me, seemingly disappointed he was not allowed to assault Joan with my blessing. 'Sire?'

'Just take the woman into custody,' I told him. 'She's charged with murder.'

Chapter Six

I may be a lord, but I do not hold land from the king himself and I cannot attend parliament. My family has but one manor, held from the king's tenant-in-chief, Earl Stephen. In return for the possession of this land we must provide service to the crown, sending men to fight the king's wars.

In the spring of 1350, however, I had received an unexpected letter from the earl, suggesting he would commute this obligation to a money payment. He even had the cheek to imply he would be doing me a favour with this new arrangement. But how was I to obtain more funds? The estate was struggling already.

I had yet to reply to this letter – though it constantly nagged at me like the sharp edge of a broken tooth.

I could not leave Old Ralph in his daughter's remote cottage, so I instructed the men to find a village woman to care for him. I would speak to the man when he had recovered. But such was his fever, it seemed more likely that Old Ralph would die before that opportunity could arise.

With the men attending to Old Ralph, I was grateful for the opportunity to ride alone back to Somershill that evening. But as I made my way along the purlieu land at the edge of the forest, I was suddenly forced to take shelter under an oak tree that had escaped felling – to avoid a hail storm that now bombarded the hills with its icy missiles. As the hail hammered down upon the leaf canopy overhead, I took Matilda's beads from my pocket and studied them more closely. If only they could whisper to me and tell me how to find the girl's body. For I knew she was dead. There had been too much blood under her bed to suggest otherwise.

Once, at the abbey, I had assisted an inexperienced brother with the amputation of a man's leg – as Brother Peter had been too drunk to attend to the patient. The man, an Italian merchant, had been an important customer for abbey fleeces, so the abbot was insistent we keep him alive – particularly as he was known to drive a poor bargain. But the Italian had suffered from a swollen vein, which had ruptured only to become infected – and then his whole leg threatened to succumb.

We cut the bone below the knee, but his blood surged relentlessly despite the tourniquet we had applied. It seemed we had not tied the binding tightly enough for, despite our best efforts, the poor man soon lost consciousness and died. My lasting memory from the incident was the small amount of blood loss needed to cause death. It had been less in quantity on that occasion than I had found pooled under Matilda's bed.

The hail eventually stopped, but was replaced with rain. Cold, autumnal rain – even though we were still in June. Water blew into my face and soaked my woollen cloak and I regretted not wearing the sleeved cape that my father used in bad weather. I had cast it aside, though it was waterproofed in tallow, because it smelt as unpleasant as a frying pan.

When the rain finally abated, I moved off – but Tempest held back his ears and slugged along the path as dolefully as a bear in chains. The weather did not agree with his constitution and he might even have thrown me from his back, had this not involved a modicum of effort. Every few steps he turned his head to check I was still in the saddle. There was something in the curve of his glassy eyeball that suggested he did not like what he could see.

And then, suddenly, the rain gave way to a fan of sunlight that pierced through the clouds to form a rainbow in the crook of the path. Childishly delighted by this sight, I dug my heels into Tempest's flanks and chased after its colourful arch, only for the vision to disappear as effortlessly as it had formed. Once galloping, Tempest was not minded to stop, and we carried on at speed until my grip on the horse's slippery flanks failed, and I fell into a swathe of bracken.

The landing was soft, my bones were not broken, and I couldn't help but laugh out loud. After all the misery of this year it was a release to be joyful, if only for a few moments. But I wasn't the only person to have found this spectacle amusing. Drawing myself up onto my elbows I realised a girl was watching me from behind a tree. She held my horse by his reins, while he nuzzled her hand as tamely as a pet lamb.

'Are you injured, sire?' Her face was beautiful. Her eyes dark brown and her skin the colour of honey – not in the least like the pale-skinned maids my mother had picked for both my brothers to marry.

'I slipped from my horse's back,' I said unnecessarily, as no doubt she had seen the whole episode. 'But I'm not harmed.' I made an attempt to jump up from the bracken athletically to impress her, but only slipped back and landed on my elbow. She disguised a snigger and tiptoed forward to offer me her hand, which I reluctantly declined in the spirit of chivalry. Instead I stumbled inelegantly to my feet.

As she passed me Tempest's reins, I couldn't help but notice the shape of her body beneath her loose tunic. 'What's your name?' I asked her.

She caught me looking at the sway of her breasts and quickly covered her chest with her arms. 'Mirabel.'

'Mirabel. A creature of wondrous beauty.' I don't know how such foolish words slipped out. Mirabel looked at her feet. 'Sorry. I didn't want to embarrass you,' I said. 'I was simply translating your name from its Latin origin *Mirabilis*. It means—'

'Thank you, sire. I don't know any Latin.'

'Would you like to learn? I could teach you some basic words.'

'I can't read.'

An uncomfortable silence followed my awkward suggestion.

'Your horse seems a little lame in his front leg, sire,' she said, to change the subject.

'Tempest just pretends to be lame. It's because he doesn't like me very much.'

Her smile returned a little. 'Pick him some dandelion and meadowsweet. Then he'll like you.'

'I'll try that. Thank you.' She curtsied to me and then slipped away towards the trees.

'Where do you live, Mirabel?' I called after her.

'In Somershill, sire.'

'Whereabouts?'

But she had disappeared.

Distracted by my daydreams, I didn't see Brother Peter until passing Tempest back to Piers in front of the stable. Peter was digging by the wall – a defence that had once run in a square about the old castle. Now its crumbling stone only remained along the north border – the other three sides having been demolished and used for building the new house. Before I was sent to the monastery I used to climb along this high crenellated wall and throw apples into the moat on the other side. In those days the moat had still been full of water – but now it was clogged with willow and bulrushes. No longer a line of defence, it had become a drain for the house – full of effluent, animal bones, and rotting kitchen waste.

I watched Peter drive a spade into the earth. The ground was soft from the recent rain. He pulled at a clump of thistles and threw their clod of roots to one side.

'What are you planting?' I asked him.

'Herbs. My stocks of medicine are low.'

'Are you going to grow any meadowsweet or dandelions?'

Peter looked at me quizzically. 'This will be a herb garden, Oswald. Not a patch of weeds. Why are you asking such foolish questions? '

'It was just something I heard. I wanted Tempest to like me.'

Peter stopped work and leant upon his spade. 'Are you feeling unwell? You look a little flushed. And what's that scratch on your face?'

I waved the question away. 'Have you heard Matilda Starvecrow is missing and probably dead?'

He returned to his digging. 'Yes. Your mother gave me the sad news this morning. I understand you raised the hue and cry.'

I nodded. 'For what good it did me.'

'So nothing was discovered?'

'We didn't find any dog heads, if that's what you mean?'

Peter frowned and struck the soil again with his spade. 'I need more lavender, and parsley. There's some lovage by the barn, but I haven't found any sweet cicely. There must be some on this estate. Perhaps I'll look down by the pond.'

'I've taken a woman called Joan Bath into custody,' I told him. 'It was she who scratched me.'

Peter looked up again. 'Into custody for what?'

'For the murders of course.' He drove the spade deeply into the soil and then folded his arms. 'Joan has good reason to want the girls dead,' I continued, despite the look of doubt that was creeping across his face. 'Her father had planned to marry one or other of the Starvecrow sisters.'

'What of it?'

'In the event of such a marriage, Joan stood to lose her claim to his land.'

Peter now grimaced. 'It seems a rather circumstantial argument. What proof do you have?'

'I found Old Ralph bound and gagged in Joan's house. She meant to kill him. Her own father.'

'But does that mean she murdered the Starvecrows?'

'I think it does.'

Peter cocked his head to one side. 'Maybe.' He then resumed his digging, although this time he was just scratching at the surface of mud. 'Joan is the village whore, Oswald. Did you know that?'

'Yes.'

'She's unlikely to receive a fair trial.'

'If she murdered two girls, then she deserves to hang.'

'If . . .' He looked up from his digging and fixed me with a glare. 'It's convenient you've solved the mystery so speedily.'

'I thought you'd be pleased. You told me to investigate.'

He raised an eyebrow. 'I'm pleased you're making an effort. Of course. But you must not rush to conclusions, Oswald.'

'I'm not.'

He dropped the spade and took my arm. 'I've known the Bath family for many years. Joan is a sinner, but she has been sinned against. By those closest to her.' Then he whispered, 'I cannot reveal the secrets of the confessional, but you must believe me in this regard.'

I shook his arm away. If we were discussing convenience, then nothing was more convenient to sway an argument than a priest alluding to a secret he had heard in confession. 'What manner of sins?'

He frowned. 'I cannot say, Oswald. I am bound by my oaths.'

'Then don't drop such hints.'

'I merely want you to think the matter through. To make some allowances for the woman's behaviour. The crime against her father might have nothing to do with the murders of the Starvecrow sisters.'

'Why do you care so much? What is the village whore to you?'

Now he pointed his finger into my face. 'That's enough, Oswald! Christ taught us to love our neighbour, even if she is a harlot. Have you forgotten everything you were taught at the monastery?'

I shrank away from him. 'I still think Joan is guilty,' I said softly.

'You *think*?' He snorted. 'What good is that? You must be *sure* if you are to send a person to the gallows.'

We didn't speak for a few moments and I considered leaving, but it upset me to argue with Peter – so I took the beads from my pouch and held them out on my palm, hoping to appease him by seeking his opinion. 'What do you think of these, Brother?' I asked.

Peter screwed up his eyes to look closer. His near sight was poor. 'They're red coral. Where did you get them?'

'I found them under Matilda's bed.'

He took a single bead in his hand and held it to the light.

'Have you seen such beads before?' I asked.

'Yes. On a paternoster rosary.'

'Could it belong to Cornwall then?'

'Why do you ask that?'

'He was acting strangely in the Starvecrow cottage. As if he had lost something.'

Peter frowned. 'I doubt it. Only a bishop or baron would own such an item. Coral paternosters are very valuable.'

'Did our abbot own one?'

'No. I don't believe so.'

'I just thought I'd seen it before.'

Peter smiled. 'I expect you saw a similar rosary when the Bishop of Rochester visited.'

I shrugged. 'Do you think Cornwall could have stolen it?'

A shadow now crossed Peter's face. 'More reckless accusations, Oswald? We might not like Cornwall, but the man is still a priest.'

'Then what were prized beads doing under the bed of a peasant girl?'

'Perhaps Matilda is your thief?'

'But who would she have stolen them from? I doubt she knew any archbishops or barons.'

I held out my hand for Peter to return the bead, but instead he closed his fingers about it. 'I've heard Brother Thomas still lives,' he told me. 'He's staying in Cowden before he returns to the abbey. I could take the beads to him and ask his opinion? He is an expert in devotional jewellery.'

I hesitated, feeling strangely reluctant to pass over the remaining nine beads. They were such perfect little spheres of red and I suddenly felt covetous of their beauty and value.

But I was being foolish. 'Of course, Brother. Ask Thomas. It would be helpful.'

I gave him the beads, which he dropped into a pouch. 'And will you think again regarding Joan Bath?' he asked me, as he tied the pouch to his belt.

I sighed. 'I don't know.'

'Please, Oswald.'

'But I'm sure she's guilty.'

The next morning I visited Old Ralph, to see if it were possible to rouse a little more sense from the man. He was being cared for by his sister-in-law, Mary Cadebridge – a local woman known for her good deeds and willingness to embrace any opportunity to improve her standing with the Almighty.

Gilbert often told the tale of how Mary had welcomed a group of wandering flagellants into her home when news of the Plague first reached Somershill. She hoped their devotion to pain might dust her family with the grace of God. But the flagellants were not part of the famed group from Flanders. And instead of reflecting her in their piety, they turned out to be a group of swindlers, who made off with her supply of wine and the virginity of her daughter.

When I informed Gilbert that Old Ralph was staying at Mary's house, he raised a rare smile. 'Mary used to deny they were even related,' he told me. 'Though the man was married to her own sister.' Then he chuckled. 'If Ralph doesn't die of

being tied up by his own daughter, then he'll die of being
prayed to death.'

Mary's cottage was grander and more neatly kept than many
others in the village, but the noise of Ralph's moaning and the
wailing of Mary's newly born grandson reminded me of the
Bankside stews I had once seen on a visit to Southwark cathedral.
Noisy brothels that clustered along the banks of the Thames and
paid such good rents to the Bishop of Winchester.

I knocked at Mary's door and enquired after Ralph, but was
told he still ran a fever and was too unwell to speak to anybody
but God himself. Mary assured me she was praying for his soul
and was certain he would either be delivered back into the fold
of his family by the next morning, or transported into the next
life surrounded by those he loved. Mary then cursed Joan for
subjecting her own father to such degradations, and hoped to see
the witch hanging by the throat at the very earliest opportunity.

Walking away from Mary's house I began to wonder if Mary
herself stood to inherit the possession of Old Ralph's land in the
event of his death, with Joan removed from the line. She seemed
suddenly so interested in justice for her brother-in-law – a man
she had previously refused to acknowledge.

My next port of call was the gaol house. I would tell you this
building was an impenetrable fortress modelled upon the White
Tower itself, but a modest room with bars at the window was a
more appropriate way to describe it. It did at least have a gaoler,
Henry Smith, though, as his name suggests, he also worked the
village forge. I believe he had secured the position as some-time
keeper by offering my father a deal on the manufacture of the
studded doors.

I passed a few pleasantries with Henry, informing him that
Piers the stableboy would be sent to Rochester to notify the
sheriff of the crimes. I was unable to try murder in the

manorial court, so would have to wait for a royal judge and the Hundreds court to come to Somershill. It was impossible to predict how long this would take. Justice was known to be a slow-moving cart, but since the Plague its wheels seemed firmly stuck in the mud.

It soon became clear that Henry was not hoping for a quick trial, since he would receive a small stipend for his duties guarding Joan. And Henry was a man in need of a stipend, since his business at the forge had reduced sizeably in the wake of the Plague. It seemed few cared to shoe their horses or mend their tools when a dead neighbour's goods could be had for nothing.

I found Joan Bath sitting in the corner of the one and only cell. Henry had supplied her with a small chunk of bread and a mug of milk, though I had not requested him to do this. She did not stand up to greet me.

'I need to find Matilda's body,' I told her. 'The girl deserves to be buried.'

She shrugged at me insolently and carried on chewing her bread. 'I don't know where the girl is.'

'There's no point lying to me, Mistress Bath. Matilda must be dead. There was too much blood.'

'If that's your conclusion. Then she must be dead.'

'So where's her body?'

'I don't know!' she said again. I stepped back quickly, as she looked in the mood to assault me once more.

Henry opened the door a little. 'Are you all right, sire?'

'Perfectly. Thank you.' He closed the door again, though stood just the other side of the grille.

Joan then looked up at me in the way my brothers might have, both confident and defiant – the very opposite of the usually demure village woman. Perhaps this explained her appeal amongst the local men.

'I've just been to visit your father,' I told her. 'But I couldn't speak to him as he's gravely ill.'

'Will he die?' Her tongue savoured the word, so I chose not to give her the pleasure of knowing his proximity to death.

'Just tell me where Matilda's body is, and I promise your sons will keep your cottage.'

'My sons can look after themselves.'

'Can they?'

For a moment she looked unsure of herself. I thought she might open up to me, but her face soon took flight to its well-defended keep and she would say nothing more.

I was wasting my time.

Leaving the gaol house I felt grubby and contaminated, as if I were a linen rag beginning to soak up the filth of this affair. I had also developed a raging thirst, but did not care to call in at the tavern and drink alongside the village men. What would I talk to them about? Instead I headed through the woody glade above the village to the Holy Well, where the waters rose from the rocks beneath the shrine to St Blaise. The water was clean enough, if you could stand the leaden taste.

It was still light, but there was nobody else on the path – my only company the strange whirr of the goatsucker bird as it called across the forest at twilight. The last rays of sun slanted obliquely through the canopy and illuminated the arching leaves of the ground ferns. Thin strands of light glinted from the piles of pine needles in the growing nests of wood ants. It seemed a peaceful and benevolent place, but then I had the unexpected sensation of being watched.

They say the god Pan lurks in forests and spies upon you from secret places. Stand still and you can feel his eyes upon the back of your head. His breath upon your skin. But turn to catch his face and he is gone – leaving only the echo of his laughter and distant patter of his hooves. I pulled my cloak about me and carried on. I was too old to believe in such stories.

As I reached the well, the wooden effigy of St Blaise loomed above me – his beady black eyes staring at something on the horizon. He might be saint to the traders of wool, but would he look kindly upon my efforts at sheep shearing? I doubted it. But then he had done nothing to save my shepherds from the Plague. Perhaps I believed more in the powers of Pan?

Turning my back to the effigy, I climbed down the steps to an underground chamber where the water bubbled up from a spring in the rock face and fell in a lethargic flow into a deep stone trough. When this trough became full, the water then slid over a shallow lip and into a land drain. Where it went then was anybody's guess.

The water had an odd salty flavour and was the colour of rusting iron. Amongst the wonders ascribed to its holiness were the promise of relief from colic and melancholia. More widely known was its power to have a bride with child within a month of the wedding night. All these cures and small miracles were claimed for its waters, but in my experience its foremost effect was to send a person straight to the nearest latrine.

I drank from my hands and splashed my face in the stone basin, waking myself from the stupor of the day. As the water settled again, a face seemed to appear, just below the surface. Cold blue eyes watched my own. Pale skin glowed from the blackness.

It was Matilda.

I jumped back in terror, nearly winding myself against the rock of the wall behind me. Here was her missing corpse. Submerged in a well.

Taking a deep breath, I crept forward again, but this time saw nothing in the water at all. Now I panicked and plunged my arms into the basin, feeling about desperately in its depths. But my hands found only smooth stones and a forgotten ampulla, left here by a pilgrim.

I waited for the water to settle once again and stared into its darkness. And as the surface calmed to a glassy standstill, somebody stared back at me.

It was a person with Matilda's blonde hair and Matilda's thin face. But it was not Matilda. It was my own reflection.

And then I knew for sure. The Starvecrows were my sisters.

I ran back to the village and didn't stop until reaching the church-yard, coming to a standstill by Alison's recently dug grave. Looking down at the wooden crucifix that marked the end of her short life, I wished I could pray for them both. For Alison and Matilda. But I couldn't. My faith was too pale and feeble.

Instead I spoke to Alison. Kneeling down and putting my face to the ground, I whispered into the wet and cold soil. I told her Joan had been arrested for the crimes, and that the woman would prob-ably hang. Of course Alison didn't answer, although I was fanciful enough to put my ear to the grave and listen for a response.

When I promised to find Matilda's body, the ground sighed.

Chapter Seven

I would keep my promise to Alison and Matilda, but my duties on the estate were beginning to poke at my skin like the bristles on a sack vest, and I could ignore them no longer.

June is the month to shear sheep, or so my reeve, Featherby, had informed me – a man with a looming gait and hair so tightly curled it looked as if his head were covered in worm casts. I had nodded knowingly, but in truth had little idea what he was talking about since my eldest brother William had been destined to become Lord Somershill, not I. My life had been spent in a monastery since the age of seven, where the lay brothers had taken care of the abbey farm, leaving the novices to spend their time in mass, class, or silent contemplation. My only practical skills were setting arms, draining wounds and shaving the other novices' heads.

But that was an old, forgotten life, to which I could never return. I knew that. And as I looked myself over in the mirror that morning I made myself stand a little taller than before. I even looked back down my nose at my own reflection. Why shouldn't I be Lord Somershill? I might be young and inexperienced, but I had as much energy as my older brothers, and certainly more education.

There was no reason to be afraid.

* * *

I was eating my daybreak bread and cheese with Mother in the great hall later that same morning when Clemence joined us. I should have been pleased to see my sister, since Mother was talking without stopping for breath. But Clemence's brow was already twisted into her early-morning grimace – a temporary flaw that, with age, was hardening into a permanent warp.

Clemence took her bread and cheese, looked me over, and suddenly cheered up. I was wearing a leather tunic that had belonged to Father and which smelt of mildew and horses. I had purposefully chosen to wear it that morning, since it looked agricultural – having organised to oversee the sheep shearing – but the unpleasant aroma was not the tunic's only deficiency. It drowned my slim frame, and although I had tried to roll up the cuffs, the leather was hard and resisted being turned over, so that only the ends of my fingers poked out of the sleeves.

Clemence squeezed up to me on the bench and smiled. 'I hope you're not stampeded by the rams today, little brother. We wouldn't want to lose our new lord.' She then lifted the baggy sleeve of my tunic and pulled a face of mock dismay when she found it so loose. 'Heavens. Is there an arm in there?'

I went to push her away, but she dodged my hand just in time.

'No fighting please,' said Mother, her mouth full of rye bread. 'It makes me choleric.' We ignored her. If she wasn't choleric, she was phlegmatic – her humours rarely in balance.

'It's the ewes being sheared today,' I told Clemence. 'Not the rams.'

Now she laughed at me. 'I'm surprised a little monastery boy like you would know the difference. All that time spent with the rams of the abbey.' Her face had crinkled into an ugly smile, as she helped herself to some bread from my plate.

'I find a ewe as easy to identify as any man does,' I said, grabbing her hand and squeezing it to make her let go of the bread. 'It's the mutton I find more difficult to notice.' She tried to wriggle her hand away, but I pressed more tightly. 'But no doubt, Clemence, you've discovered most men suffer from that problem.'

My sister freed her hand and went to strike my face, only deciding against it at the last moment. Instead she stood up, bowed her head to Mother, and left the room in tears.

'I do wish you wouldn't goad her,' said Mother, as Clemence climbed the stairs back to the solar and slammed a distant door. 'Her womb is suffocated with her own seed as it is.'

'Find her a husband then. At least we'd be free of her.'

My mother huffed and dipped her bread into her pot of warm beef lard, letting the honeycombed dough soak up as much of the rancid swill as possible. 'I would love to make a match for her, Oswald. But what am I to do? She's twenty-six, and practically winter feed.'

My mother still had the mouth of a cowherd, causing me to feel a sudden wave of sympathy for Clemence, and now regret my taunt. My sister's last two betrothals had ended with the suitor dead before the wedding – meaning Clemence hadn't even achieved the status of a respectable widow. And she had only narrowly avoided the convent of St Margaret by Father's reluctance to pay a dowry to Sister Constance. Through a combination of bad luck and avarice, Clemence was stuck at Somershill, like an apple going bad on the tree.

Thankfully my conversation with Mother was ended by Gilbert, who lumbered wearily to the table to announce my reeve was at the back porch. I stood up, attempted to smooth down the bulging tunic, and went out to greet Featherby, finding him fidgeting with a horsewhip and uncharacteristically shrinking against the wall rather than seeming about to pounce upon me. A light rain blew into our faces.

'Are we all ready for the shearing then?' I asked, clasping my hands together as if excited by the prospect of the day ahead. 'Are the men assembled?'

Featherby shifted awkwardly from one foot to the other and wouldn't meet my gaze. 'I only have the two men, sire. John Penrice and young Wilfred.'

'Where are the others?' He didn't answer. 'I presume you told them to be here at daybreak?'

There was a long silence. 'They're at church, sire.'

'Why?'

'It's these dog heads. The men are uneasy.'

I rolled my eyes. 'But I've arrested Joan Bath for the murders.'

'It's the word of Father John, sire. He still says the dog heads did it.'

'Well they didn't. Tell the men they have obligations to me on the demesne.'

'They won't listen to me, sire. I even threatened to whip them, and that didn't do any good either.'

'You mustn't do that!' I said, and then quickly added, 'We need them to be fit to work.'

Now he began to loom, so I stepped back. The rain was drawing the scent of horse hair and matted dung from his clothing.

'What should I do then, sire?' I noted his arms were folded and his head cocked.

'Wait here!'

I returned to my bedchamber, threw the stinking leather tunic onto the chest and changed into my best hose, tailored cotehardie, and finest cloak. This time I wouldn't cower in the porch. I would get past the church door and speak to the men. I would be their lord.

As we reached St Giles, Cornwall's familiar bellowing could be heard echoing about the gravestones. But I could bellow myself, if adequately provoked. And Cornwall had provoked me. The village must surely know by now that Joan Bath had been arrested on suspicion of the murders, so why was he persisting in his scaremongering?

I threw open the heavy door, and Cornwall's words trailed away to silence. This time there were both men and women in the congregation, and as they turned to look at me, they appeared as uneasy as a herd of cows regarding a stranger in their field.

Cornwall's cheeks were suddenly patched with red.

'I have an announcement to make to you all,' I said, striding through the nave towards the chancel. Turning to address the congregation, I suddenly felt self-conscious, but it was vital not to falter though the wooden Virgin peered at me, still holding out her empty arms, devoid of the Christ child. I took a deep breath and held my nerve. 'As you do not seem to have heard, I have arrested a woman for the murders of Alison and Matilda Starvecrow.' My words were met with murmuring and whispers. The villagers then rotated towards Cornwall.

'Whom have you arrested,' said Cornwall, and then remembered to add, 'sire.'

I cleared my throat. 'Her name is Joan Bath.'

This time the faces broke rank from their uniform movement and turned in all directions to speak to a neighbour or a friend behind them.

Cornwall raised his voice loudly to be heard above the uproar. 'What makes you so certain of this woman's guilt, sire?' The faces fell silent again. They knew it was insolent of Cornwall to question me so openly.

'I am more convinced of Mistress Bath's guilt than I am of the existence of dog heads.'

Cornwall spread the wings of his cloak. 'My lord, I would remind you I have prayed to God for the answer to this mystery. And He has informed me the agents of Satan are to blame.' A few elderly heads nodded at Cornwall's words. The others remained perfectly still, unsure which breeze to catch. 'I suggest that you think again,' he added and then pointed a finger at me.

This was the final provocation. I could tolerate this man no longer. 'Then I suggest *you* round up your dog heads for trial,

Father John,' I told him. 'The Hundreds court will visit the estate shortly. Then your suspects can answer to the crime in the same court as Mistress Bath.' Some muffled giggling broke out, which Cornwall was unable to stifle with the swing of his cloak or the flare of his nostrils.

A local wit called out, 'They can bark for mercy, sire!' The crowd burst into laughter. And soon other jesters joined in, with suggestions of tails wagging at the verdict or arse sniffing in the dock. I couldn't help but raise a smile despite the crudity of their comedy, because Cornwall and his ignorance deserved to be laughed at. The Plague had wrung the spirit out of England. These people needed hope, not more tales of damnation.

But Cornwall would not easily be quelled. 'The beasts can only be judged in Heaven by God himself,' he called over the merriment. 'You must all continue to pray for deliverance.' But, for once, the priest was ignored – and though he tried repeatedly to regain his position at centre stage, it seemed his flock had abandoned him and his nonsense.

Finding his words were drowned, he strode past me with fanned robes and only the most cursory of acknowledgements. But I cannot claim to have felt entirely triumphant at this moment, for my victory over Cornwall was pyrrhic. I knew that. We had been opponents, but it seemed we were now enemies.

Even so, I must admit to feeling rather pleased with myself.

Once the clamour had subsided I sought out Featherby at the back of the church beside the doom painting – a vivid depiction of Hell that had been painted on the lime plaster many years ago by an artist who had given Beelzebub a pair of cross eyes and the buck teeth of a rabbit. Featherby was leaning over a young woman who seemed relieved by my intervention, for she seized the opportunity to escape from his overbearing attentions and scamper away to her mother. I told Featherby to organise the shearing immediately on the demesne now that the drama was over, and for once he didn't offer me any objections or unsolicited advice.

And then as I watched the villagers leave the church, bobbing their heads or muttering their respects to me, a sideways smile caught my attention. It was Mirabel, her head covered modestly with a hood.

I bowed, causing her to giggle and then curtsey. It seemed my encounter with Cornwall had impressed her. I would even say she liked me.

But there was a boy behind Mirabel who seemed not to like me at all. He was tall and broad, with hair as orange as a weasel's. Not that he looked like a weasel. I might even have called him handsome, had he not barged through the crowd to take Mirabel's arm before throwing me a look of hostility.

I was pleased to see that she shrugged him away.

Returning to Somershill I found Clemence standing by the main door waiting for the rain to stop. She wore a fine velvet riding cloak – an outfit I had not seen since before the Plague. I could smell she had been chewing cardamom to sweeten her breath. Her devoted servant, Humbert, lurked behind her, staring at the elaborate braids and jewelled pins in her hair without blinking.

'You look elegant, Clemence,' I said, mindful of my insults to her at breakfast. 'Are you expecting guests?'

She eyed me suspiciously. 'In my riding clothes?'

'Are you making a visit then?'

She snorted and pushed past me. 'None of your business.'

'Clemence,' I shouted after her. 'I'm sorry about earlier. I didn't mean to upset you. I wish we could be friends.'

I waited for a reply, but she was gone.

Piers returned in only two days from Canterbury with a letter from the sheriff. The date for the next Hundreds court would be the seventeenth of July, assuming a royal judge could be spared. This gave me just over a month to prepare my case against Joan

Bath. A case that, even I had to admit, currently lacked sufficient evidence to convince a jury.

Needing to find Matilda's body, I sent men out to search for Joan's sons in the hope they could be persuaded to reveal the location of her corpse. But the boys remained elusive, probably hiding in the forests and living by their own stealth and ingenuity. This was not surprising, as they had been raised by their mother to be hardy, self-reliant children, and Kent is a large county to hide in.

I interviewed the villagers about Joan in order to understand her character a little better. But it seems she kept to herself, and soon it became obvious that the only people willing to talk about the woman were the disgruntled wives of her customers – and they shed no light on this particular crime whatsoever. My progress was frustratingly slow, but in truth I was wasting my time.

For, if my first mistake had been to let Cornwall have his way, then my second was to have my own. I squeezed what information I had gleaned into a story that suited me, but was truly only conjecture. In truth, the facts fitted into my case as badly as I fitted into my father's leather tunic.

The signs were there. With care and attention I might have seen them. But I became distracted, as a new storm blew across my path.

And suddenly I was caught in its eye.

Chapter Eight

It was a few days later and I was enjoying a rare hour of peace in my bedchamber, reading a text on geometry to try to stop thinking in antitheses. One moment I was concerned with the dark fate of Matilda Starvecrow, only to lurch into lustful thoughts about Mirabel and the way her breasts moved to and fro beneath her tunic. My mind was rather fixed on Mirabel's breasts when Mother burst into the room like a blizzard, and I quickly had to hide my embarrassment under a bed sheet.

Not that she noticed. 'I've just heard the news, Oswald. Clemence and de Caburn! At her age as well.' She whipped the book from my hand and flung it onto the bed. 'Our two estates linked. How clever of you to arrange it.'

'What are you talking about?' Mother's dog Hector had raced in behind and jumped onto the bed covers. He, at least, seemed to understand what I had been up to. 'Get off!' I said, trying to push him back onto the floor.

Mother did nothing – even though Hector was now trying to wriggle under the sheets. 'I do hope you haven't agreed too much of a dowry,' she said. 'Our income is a little fragile at the moment. And the ceremony should be a simple affair. I will insist on that much.'

'Mother. Please listen to me,' I said, trying once again to push the dog from the bed. 'I haven't the slightest idea what you mean.'

'And we shouldn't invite too many guests to the wedding. Clemence may be something of a boiling fowl, but we wouldn't want to make a spectacle of her. But, if we're too secretive, the gossips will say she's with child. And that sort of news would fly up to court like a—'

'I think you have dreamt this up, Mother. The story is nonsense.' Hector was once again attempting to burrow under the bedclothes. 'For God's sake get this damned creature off me!' I shouted.

'Never mind the dog, Oswald. I want to talk to you about Clemence and de Caburn!' Her voice was suddenly shrill, and caused Hector to shoot off the bed, as if he were fleeing thunder.

I sat up fully now the dog had gone and spoke calmly, so Mother couldn't misinterpret my words. 'I don't know what you've heard, but I have not arranged a marriage between Clemence and de Caburn. Do you understand?'

She frowned. 'You haven't?'

'No.'

'Oh.' She sighed. 'But Clemence has just told me the news herself.'

'She has?'

Now Mother pulled a face. 'Yes. Why do you think I rushed in here, Oswald? I'm not the Delphic Oracle.'

'Clemence herself? Are you sure?'

'Yes. How many times? Oswald? Where are you going?'

I got out of bed. 'To find Clemence.'

There was a tale often told in taverns about my neighbour de Caburn – that he was a man who loved his horse more than his wife. I don't suppose the two unfortunate women who had married him found this story entertaining, the latest dead from birth fever. She might have survived, but de Caburn had refused to send for the physician on the grounds that she looked healthy enough to him. More likely, in my mother's opinion, it was to punish the woman for producing another daughter.

The baby died within days, also without the attendance of a physician, though I heard from his bailiff that de Caburn did summon a surgeon only a week later, although this time it was for himself, as he needed somebody to sew up the fistula that was hanging out of his arse. Too much time in a wet saddle, joked the bailiff. But I didn't laugh. I wished de Caburn's whole backside had become infected, so he could never get in a saddle again. These days he rode his horses over my land a little too often.

It wasn't difficult to locate my sister. When Clemence wasn't tormenting some piece of linen with her needle, then she was usually to be found in the stables with her stallion, Merrion — the only beast she considered worthy of carrying her noble personage about the estate, regardless of the fact that he was every bit as unpleasant as my own horse Tempest, and as likely to buck my sister off as he cared to discharge any other member of the family.

It should come as no surprise that my sister was so devoted to such a crabby and haughty creature, however. And her attachment was certainly fortunate from the horse's point of view, since no servant, not even Piers, the stableboy, was keen to see to him. After Merrion had drawn blood by biting Gilbert's shoulder, our servants had more or less refused to groom the beast, so Clemence had taken it upon herself to perform the function, boasting about the shine of his coat, or the sway of his mane.

I opened the stable door to find her singing to the horse, as if that might temper the creature's bile. As ever, Humbert waited but an arm's length from my sister, his hands full of summer hay and his eyes constantly focussed upon his mistress.

'Clemence. I need to speak with you,' I said.

She was startled by my words, evidently lost in some sort of daydream. 'Don't creep up on me, little brother.' Her scowl returned. 'You'll unsettle Merrion.' The horse whinnied obligingly. 'See what I mean.'

Humbert now stood in my way, and as I attempted to push him aside, I found his chest to be surprisingly firm, when I had expected him to wobble like marrow jelly. When Humbert still refused to move, Clemence reluctantly waved for him to let me pass.

'I've heard a distorted story from Mother,' I said, when our eyes were finally able to meet. 'I need to clarify a matter with you.'

She curled her lip and returned to sweeping the horse's glossy flank with her iron curry comb. 'What sort of story?'

'That you are to marry Walter de Caburn.'

'And why should that be distorted?'

'It's true then?'

She put down the comb. 'Yes, it's true. We are to marry by St Swithin's day.'

I felt a swell of nausea rising in my stomach. 'You can't marry de Caburn, Clemence. I can't believe you would even contemplate it.'

She laughed. 'Why ever not?'

'He's a monster. I forbid it.'

'You're in no position to forbid me anything.'

'With all respect, Lady Clemence, you will need the permission of your brother to marry.' We turned to see Brother Peter standing at the door. In his arms he held a bunch of coltsfoot and elderflowers. 'I've collected these herbs to treat Merrion,' he said, passing the greenery to Humbert. 'It should clear the beast's cumbersome airways.'

'Take your witch's weeds away,' said Clemence, grabbing the herbs from Humbert's large hands and throwing them to the floor. 'That is twice you have exceeded your rank with me, Priest. I will not tolerate it again.'

'Brother Peter is correct, Clemence,' I said. 'You do need my permission to marry, and I won't give it.'

'You can't refuse me,' said Clemence, now gritting her teeth. The horse began to twitch and fidget and she struggled to hold onto his tether. 'I will marry Walter, whether or not you give me permission.'

'Then you'll receive no dowry,' I said. 'Think of the shame that would cause you.'

Clemence pulled Merrion down and whispered soothingly into his ear. 'What is shame any more? Who is to care what I do?'

'The world has not changed so very much,' said Brother Peter. 'The king's court still listens to gossip and scandal. The Pestilence did not destroy protocol and etiquette.'

Clemence turned on him. 'What do you know about such things? You're nothing but a farmhand with a set of rosary beads and a book of herbs. What would you know about protocol and etiquette?'

'Brother Peter was infirmarer at the abbey, Clemence. He has a respected position,' I said.

Clemence laughed. 'Respected? By whom?'

'By me.'

She pointed a finger. 'You may refuse me, little brother, but it doesn't matter. I don't need your permission. Nor your dowry.'

'I'm not sure de Caburn would agree.'

She laughed again. 'That's where you're wrong. Walter expected such a reaction from you and is happy to marry me with neither.' She took a stool from the side and stood on it to mount Merrion.

'Hold his tether,' she instructed Humbert, as she lifted her skirts and climbed into the saddle. 'I shall be visiting Walter at Versey Castle. Don't try to stop me.' Clemence pulled at the reins and Merrion shied fretfully, almost flattening Brother Peter against the wall of the stable. She then dug in her heels and was gone, galloping across the field with her cloak waving behind her like a battle standard. Humbert gazed after her, until she had become just a dot on the horizon, before turning back to the house pathetically, like a swan that has lost his mate.

Brother Peter took my arm. 'You must stop this marriage, Oswald. It's a dangerous union.'

'I agree. Look at the fate of de Caburn's last two wives. Why should Clemence fare any better?'

Peter shook his head as if I were the most dull-witted boy in his class of novices. 'I didn't mean that.'

'What do you mean then?'

'De Caburn wishes to marry your sister and is not demanding a dowry. Does that sound likely?'

'Perhaps he loves her?'

'And perhaps the Devil drinks holy water?'

Peter picked up the elderflowers and coltsfoot Clemence had thrown about the stable floor, and crammed their wilted stalks and blossom in amongst the hay of Merrion's horsebox. 'The horse should eat these herbs. His lungs are laboured,' he muttered into his cowl. He then cleared his throat and turned to address me. 'De Caburn is marrying Clemence for her land, Oswald. That's why he doesn't require a dowry.'

'She doesn't have any land.'

'Not presently.'

'I don't follow you.'

Peter raised his eyes to the heavens. 'Clemence has no land now, but there is only one de Lacy between your sister and the Somershill estate. And that person is you.'

I stepped back. 'Clemence doesn't appear to care for me, Brother. But I don't think she would wish me dead.'

He shook his head and waved his hand in irritation. 'No, no. I don't see Clemence behind such a scheme.'

'Then what are you suggesting?'

'I have no doubt Clemence believes de Caburn to be in love with her. And even if she doesn't hold out such hopes, it is at least a marriage. And you know how she craves to be a married

woman. If only to escape the persistent goading she receives
from your mother.'

'You mean I should be worried about de Caburn?'

'Of course that's what I mean!'

'But he wouldn't dare to harm me.'

Peter shook his head. 'Don't be so sure, Oswald. I took confession in his parish when there on abbey business. I heard of de
Caburn's sins from his own tenants and villeins.' He took my
hand and whispered. 'You were right to call the man a monster.'

'So what should I do then?' I will admit to feeling irritated.
Peter was right to bring this matter to my attention, but I can't
say I felt grateful. 'Isn't running the Somershill estate and solving
the murder of the Starvecrow sisters enough?' I said, a little
sullenly.

Peter waved my childishness away. 'Never mind the murders
for the time being. It's more important that you stop this
marriage.'

'And how am I supposed to stop Clemence? You know what
she's like.'

Peter sighed and beckoned me to leave the stables with him. 'I
don't know.' He closed the door behind us. 'But I'll think of
something.'

There was a troublesome logic to Peter's argument. I didn't
really know de Caburn. I sometimes raised a hand to him across
a field, or shared a bench with him at a Michaelmas day feast. I
only knew enough not to trust him. My father would not even
sell him a sheep.

Peter and I walked back towards the house, through a wet
meadow of tufted vetch and creeping buttercup. A blackbird
sang to us, and honeybees buzzed about the flower heads with
their industrious drone. I wondered at how animals and plants
carry on with their lives, undeterred by the troubles of
mankind.

Peter remained silent for most of our walk and then suddenly clapped his hands together. 'You must write to de Caburn immediately, Oswald.'

'And say what? That we have uncovered his wicked plot?'

'No, of course not.' He drew me close to whisper, even though the only spies would have been a slippery grass snake or a garrulous robin. 'Tell de Caburn you have arranged for Clemence to marry somebody else. It's a contract you cannot break.'

'Who? De Caburn will insist upon knowing a name.'

'Yes, you're right,' he said. 'Forget that idea.' But there was only the briefest of pauses before the next scheme came rolling off his tongue. 'I know. You must tell de Caburn there is a codicil in your father's will.' His voice was quickening with agitated excitement. 'Yes, yes. This will work. In the event of your death, the estate will not accede to Clemence if she is married. Tell him it was your father's dying wish.'

'Is such a codicil possible?'

'I'm not sure.'

'So what use is it then?'

Peter waved his hand at me in frustration. 'I'm not an expert in law, Oswald. But neither is Walter de Caburn. He will not marry your sister without the sniff of personal gain.'

'But he'll consult a man of law and find out it's a lie.'

'Of course he will. But he won't find one still alive in these parts. He would need to go to the ecclesiastical courts in Canterbury, and that would mean delaying the wedding.' When I shrugged at this suggestion, he shook me. 'It will buy us some time to persuade Clemence to change her mind.'

'I don't think it will work.'

'I disagree. Clemence will tell everybody they are to marry by St Swithin's. But if de Caburn postpones the ceremony, it will humiliate Clemence. Your sister is a very proud woman, and we may find she refuses de Caburn a second time, once he has discovered our little story has no credence. It is at least worth a try.'

'But a letter seems rather weak, Brother.'

He caught me by the arm. 'What do you suggest then, Oswald? Riding to Versey and facing the man? He would kill you on the spot.'

'De Caburn wouldn't dare do something so foolish.'

Peter shook me again. 'Don't be so naïve. He might not cut you down with his own sword, but he would certainly poison you or even push you into his moat and then pretend it was an accident.' I went to answer, but Peter shook me a third time and I hadn't the wind to tell him how ridiculous his theory sounded.

Instead I turned from him like a scolded dog, but he gently pulled me back. Seeing he had caused offence, he suddenly stroked my forehead and pushed the hair from my eyes. 'I'm sorry, Oswald. I shouldn't have done that.'

'No. You shouldn't have. I am your lord as well, Brother.'

He bowed his head. 'But you will write to de Caburn?'

I sighed. 'Yes. Very well.'

Chapter Nine

The following morning I rose early with the intention of giving this promised letter to Piers to take to Versey. It had been written the night before — but not by me, rather by Peter. He had not even trusted me to put my own quill to the parchment. I cannot deny this had annoyed me — and now walking towards the stable with the rolled letter in my hand I suddenly had the impulse to disobey my tutor. I had seen off Cornwall by myself. Why shouldn't I do the same with de Caburn? I was not some skulking priest from the monastery. I was Lord Somershill.

My father would not have sent a feeble letter.

On reaching the stables, I ordered Piers to saddle Tempest. When he asked me where I was going, I told him to mind his own business.

What arrogance. And what stupidity!

Versey Castle is a half-day's ride from Somershill, through the hunting forests of the high weald. I've heard it said that bears and ferocious cats once lived in these wooded hills, but by 1350 there was nothing more dangerous in these glades than the shadows. Even the bandits kept away from its paths, as there was nobody to rob but poor charcoal makers or weary drovers. Even so, I did not linger at any point, not even to take a piss.

Riding in towards Versey from the north-west, the castle appeared to be surrounded by its own moat, although on nearing the place it became clear the masons had simply made use of the river Guise as it flowed along the bottom of this remote valley. The water moved languidly at this point in the river's path towards the Medway, but still it moved – unlike the green and stinking pools that encircled many moated manor houses.

The Normans had built Versey to daunt and dishearten, but its position for farming was less favoured, with its steep valleys and cold clay soil. It was often said de Caburn coveted my flatter pastures with my barley and wheat – as his tenants had to be content raising sinewy cattle that barely produced enough milk to feed their own calves.

The river Guise also gave rise to mists and fogs, which enveloped the castle and had beset the family with congested lungs and heavy coughs. It was Mother's oft-repeated opinion that the de Caburns should relocate the hall to a nearby hill, where their humours would be less assaulted by the damp of the river. But the de Caburns were knights, and Versey was built for soldiers. We might have scorned their coughs and colds, but they mocked our small endeavours and lack of battle glory. I've heard it said they laughed at us and called us farmers.

I dropped my pace to a slow trot as I reached the castle, and now found my resolve weakening. I had practised my codicil story repeatedly, but suddenly was unable to convince myself that it rang true. De Caburn was not Cornwall. What was I doing here? The man could assault me with more dangerous weapons than a priest's blustering rhetoric and the swing of his cloak.

And then, as if another reminder of de Caburn's menace were needed, I sighted some sheep in the distance, which were not the small, wiry-coated Cotswolds that de Caburn kept for his own use. They were the larger Lincolns we farmed at Somershill for their wool. Turning Tempest, I was intending to inspect the sheep

at closer quarters, but the stupid animals scattered into the
nearby forest leaving only their piles of dung and the reverbera-
tion of their idiotic bleating for company.

I should have followed them into the trees and escaped this
place while there was a chance. Yet my bubble of pride had swollen again, and suddenly the idea of returning to Somershill and
admitting my mistake to Brother Peter did not appeal. Instead I
turned back towards the castle and approached the drawbridge,
where a ragged boy jumped out at me and waved a small wooden
sword, causing Tempest to rear.

'Keep away from my horse,' I shouted. 'He'll throw me off.'

'You should be better at riding then,' said the boy.

I was not accustomed to being spoken to in such a way. 'Who
are you?' I demanded to know.

'I'm Mary. Who are you?'

'You're a girl?'

'Yes. What of it?' Her face was filthy with mud, and the arms
of her doublet swung down well past her wrists. 'Who shall I say
is calling?' she asked.

'Where's the gatekeeper?'

She smiled. 'Dead. I tell Father who comes and goes.' She
waved the sword again and then performed a perfect advance
lunge at Tempest's legs.

'You're Mary de Caburn?'

'Stop asking me questions.'

So this was how the man treated his own daughter. Dressed in
the tattered clothes of a boy, she was working as his house
servant. But she was not alone in suffering neglect, as the whole
place wore the air of defeat. A tree had fallen into the moat and
was gathering debris about itself, with the effect of becoming a
dam. A wooden farm cart was decaying by the bridge, and crows
circled over the bony carcass of a dog.

'I'm Oswald de Lacy,' I told the girl. 'Lord Somershill. Please
advise your father I'm here to speak with him.'

The girl ran off across the drawbridge to announce my arrival, quickly joined by another blonde-haired child who must have been hiding in the beams under the bridge like a water rat. I wondered if this child were also a daughter of the house? She was certainly dressed as badly as the first.

As I waited to be admitted to the castle, the sun made a brief appearance through the clouds, and my mood felt fleetingly lighter. I looked about me. This place was uncared for, but it was not the damp purgatory of Mother's stories. Perhaps Clemence could be happy here, and I was wrong to prevent the marriage? She would become a lady, with her own castle, husband, and a pair of feral step-daughters to rule over. It might suit Clemence's character and disposition. In turn, the girls might end up with dresses and manners.

As I stared into the distance, a sudden ball of shimmering blue shot along the river just above the water surface and disappeared into the trees like an enchanted orb. I must have been transfixed by its beauty since I did not notice a man approach.

'It's a kingfisher, de Lacy,' he said. 'Don't you have them at Somershill?' He slapped me resoundingly on the back and nearly winded me.

I turned to find the girl with her father, Walter de Caburn – his striking face framed by grey curls. 'I believe we have a few, my lord,' I said, and then immediately regretted using the epithet.

My mistake was not lost on de Caburn. He smiled furtively. 'Please. Call me Walter. Now we are going to be related by marriage.' He slapped me again, but this time I had braced my ribcage and was prepared for the blow.

'It's the marriage I needed to speak with you about,' I said. But just as I was about to launch into my prepared speech, the ragged girl poked me with the tip of her sword, which turned out to be a blade of rusty metal and not the wooden toy I had previously supposed. As I dodged the second stab, de Caburn took his daughter by the back of her tunic and held her over the edge of the bridge. The girl quaked with terror but didn't utter a word.

'That's not how to treat an honoured visitor, is it, Mary?' he said, as she dangled in the air. The girl shook her head. 'Want to end up in the moat with the shit witch, do you?' He lowered her a little further.

The girl suppressed a sob. 'Please forgive my error, Father. I am at fault.' She spoke the words with the fluency of a mumbled prayer, giving the impression that this was a sentence she was often made to repeat. But by now she had controlled her trembling. Only her left eye twitched.

'We know what it stinks like down there, don't we?' De Caburn shook his daughter again.

It was uncomfortable to watch the girl being so tormented. 'Please don't punish Mary on my behalf,' I said. 'The girl was only playing. I'm not offended.'

I laid my hand on de Caburn's arm and for a moment it seemed he might push me roughly away. But then he thought better of the action. Instead he dropped Mary onto the wooden planks of the bridge.

Now he laughed. 'We were just having a little merriment, weren't we, girl?'

Mary picked herself up, glanced at me with a look I took to be gratitude, then made a break across the meadow with her sister, evidently to avoid any further opportunities for *merriment*. Their blonde heads bobbed for a few seconds through the grass before they disappeared from sight amongst the elder and chestnut.

De Caburn watched them for a while and then sighed. 'They need a mother, de Lacy. A woman to instil some discipline. Can she do it?'

I went to nod – for Clemence was nothing if not a disciplinarian. But my purpose in coming here was to prevent this marriage, so I quickly turned my nod into a circling of my neck.

De Caburn regarded me curiously, then led me across the drawbridge and through the inner ward of the castle to his great hall, which was cavernous compared to our own. A dirty servant lay asleep next to the central fire pit, and dogs barked and scratched from behind a heavy wooden door. From the timbre of their howls I decided they must be large deerhounds, the type of dog a man only keeps for hunting. The place smelt strongly of wood smoke and dog hair, but at least the height and width of the hall allowed for frequent draughts to alleviate the stale odour. The heads of stags and boar pigs peered down at me from every wall, like the faces of gloaters at a hanging.

De Caburn nudged the servant with his foot, though I suspected he usually roused him with a kick, as the man instinctively recoiled into a ball. 'He's a simpleton, I'm afraid,' said de Caburn in a whisper, in a mockery of caring for the man's feelings. 'Most of my servants have perished.'

We stepped up onto the dais at the far end of the hall and sat down at a table stretching the length of the platform. It could probably seat twenty – yet today it was only laid for one.

'I remember when this table was full,' said de Caburn, as if he had read my thoughts. 'But now we're such a depleted family.' He stared along the surface with such a look of melancholy that I suddenly felt equally cheerless. When he offered me a goblet of ale I forgot the warnings of Brother Peter about being poisoned and drank it down in one gulp before asking for more. My throat did not swell. My eyes did not give way to visions and my stomach did not twist itself into cramps. In short, it was simply ale.

Looking back now, it began as a pleasant afternoon. For the next hour or so de Caburn and I sat together at one end of the long table and discussed our neighbouring estates. The ale made it easier to converse with a man twenty years older than myself, and de Caburn was welcome company after the months I had spent cooped up with my mother and sister. He was not only well-informed about farming, but also knew much about the wider world – since he often travelled to London and dined with other knights and barons.

Or so he claimed.

And, of course, he had fought alongside Prince Edward at Cressy, which gave him every right to be welcomed at a nobleman's table, no matter how grand their birth. But then, such accidents of birth meant nothing to him. Or so he once again claimed. You must judge a man on his own qualities, he told me – but then proceeded to spew out a torrent of abuse against those not as grandly born as himself.

Because, worse than the pompous earls who declined to invite him to supper, were the merchants and traders of London. Though de Caburn farmed few sheep himself, he had taken against this rank of society due to their success at controlling the price of wool. He hated the way they huddled together in towns like pigeons, extending the upper storeys of their houses almost to touch the bedchamber of their neighbour's opposite. And he despised their wives – women who would openly flout the sumptuary laws of dress, wearing the furs and jewellery of a lady, when they were often no better than dairymaids. They had not been born into nobility, so they had no business pretending to be.

Yet he reserved his blackest bile for the newly empowered poor. The tenants, labourers, bondsmen and villeins. The people who rented our lands and worked our fields. His family had spent many years ruling over the Versey estate, and yet now there were pig-herds, shepherds and reeves, holding him to ransom over their wages.

The more ale we drank, the more attractive seemed his view of the world and its uncomplicated logic. He was a handsome man, despite his leathered and pitted skin, and it was easy to be charmed by him. If we allowed our peasants too much power, then their inexperience and lack of education would lead to chaos and starvation. They didn't possess the innate skills of the nobility to farm the land and feed the populace. I raised my pewter cup to this incontrovertible truth, though fully conscious, even in my drunken state, that our stableboy Piers would have better known how to plant a field of barley than I.

The gauze of alcohol masks the ugly, and for those hours I was the compatriot of de Caburn. We were brothers in arms. Knights and warriors, fighting a battle against the feeble minds of the peasantry. Even the carved faces in the arches of the hall looked down upon us and grinned.

And then we came to speak about my sister. I took a long swig of ale for courage and turned the conversation to Clemence. 'I have some concerns, Walter, regarding this marriage you're proposing.'

His face altered. 'What manner of concerns, Oswald?' It was the first time he had used my Christian name and it felt as out of place as dancing by a deathbed. 'Clemence will be well-cared for at Versey. If that's what worries you.'

'I'm sure she will be, Walter. But—' I tried to remember the words I had prepared on the ride here, but the ale had shuffled my memory and suddenly I felt unable to retrieve the right cards.

Muttering something, I turned to see de Caburn eying me suspiciously. 'You won't receive any better offer for your sister,' he told me. 'She is a little more saggy in the lower lip than most brides.'

I didn't care for this comparison of my sister to an aging horse, and my warm feelings towards de Caburn began to cool. 'I'm not sure I can give my permission for this match,' I said, perfectly clearly this time.

De Caburn slapped me roundly across the back. 'Of course you can. Your sister needs a new stable and a good ride.' He laughed as crudely as a scholar who has just drawn a phallus in the margin of a manuscript, and suddenly I noted that hairs grew from his nostrils. Now he didn't appear so handsome or charming.

'I'm not sure the union is in Clemence's interests,' I told him. 'There's the matter of my father's codicil.'

De Caburn sat up straight. 'What did you say, boy? You should speak more clearly.'

So – I was a boy to him, despite our pleasant afternoon of farm talk. 'There is a codicil in father's will concerning Clemence's marital state,' I said. 'It may not be in either of your interests to form this union.'

His eyes narrowed. 'What codicil?'

'Clemence will be cut out from inheriting the Somershill estate as a married woman.' I looked for a reaction from de Caburn, but none was forthcoming. Not even the twitch of an eye. 'If Clemence were married and then I were to die, the estate would pass to a distant cousin of my father's.'

'And if she wasn't married?'

'She would inherit the estate of course.'

De Caburn tipped his head to one side and leant forward. I noticed his hand unfurl on the table like the claws of a cat. 'And are you intending to die, de Lacy?'

'No. I'm not.' I coughed. 'Though we never know what the future has planned for us.'

I hoped he might nod in agreement. Instead, a cynical smile twisted itself across his lips. 'It's admirable you have such concern for Clemence's inheritance, but I imagine you're intending to marry and have offspring of your own?'

'I hadn't thought about it.'

De Caburn suddenly banged the table with his mug. 'For Christ's sake, de Lacy. Are you a sodomite? Is that it?' The clunk reverberated about the hall and even roused the dirty servant who had resumed his place by the fire. The dogs behind the heavy door scratched and whimpered.

'Of course not.'

'Even a sodomite can marry to produce an heir.' He leant forward and whispered. 'I know of many such men who poke their wives and keep their eyes shut. It gets the job done.'

'I'm not a sodomite. I intend to marry and have children.'

He sat back and rubbed his stomach with both hands. 'Then I cannot understand your concern. You mean to keep the estate in your own bloodline.'

'I merely think Clemence should wait until I myself have a wife, and a child is born. That's all.'

'When might that be? Do you have a bride in mind?' I shrugged. 'Then Heaven help your poor sister. She could be a hump-necked dowager by the time you get around to it.'

'I'm not sure that—'

'Come on, de Lacy! She might feel free to marry. But who would want her?' He paused. 'Is that fair to Clemence?'

I began to say something, but the words would not come out. This was nothing but a half-baked pie of a story, with only fresh air as filling. And I shouldn't have placed it on the table.

De Caburn held out his hand to me. 'Let's forget about this matter. It has no bearing on my intended marriage.'

I shook his hand. The skin was rough and calloused and his grip was crushing. 'Very well.'

I would tell you I felt satisfied with this result. De Caburn appeared to be marrying my sister for love – but somehow the merry mood of the afternoon had dissipated. My head was no longer warm with the glow of self-satisfaction and conceit. Now I felt sick – as if I'd eaten a whole side of pig fat. The dirty servant had stoked up the fire, and the flames were re-heating the stink of dog and rotten cabbage that seemed to hang about the hall.

De Caburn filled my cup and I drank some more ale in the vain hope it might rebalance my humours – but it only gave rise to the desire to vomit.

Then he laughed at me. 'Can't take your ale, eh?'

'I'm absolutely fine,' I said, as I began to heave.

I tried to breathe deeply, but it is impossible to keep a stomach still when it begins to roll, particularly if it is full of ale. I felt as sick as my first sailing on a Thames wherry boat. De

Caburn sent the servant for an empty half-barrel and then cheered each time I spewed into it. When this indignity was finally over, he bade me sleep off my troubles on a truckle bed in the anteroom to the hall.

It was an offer I should not have accepted.

I woke from my stupor later that afternoon, when a shard of light hit my face from the narrow arrow slit in the wall. My head was still giddy and my throat dry and cracked, but I forced my feet onto the floor, knowing I should return to Somershill before the night set in.

I brushed down my hose, removing flakes of regurgitated food from the woollen weave, only to realise that I had vomited the image of a fleur-de-lis onto my own leg. It raised a smile. I even considered showing my leg to de Caburn. Perhaps we could share a joke? But then I heard voices.

I went to the door and lingered.

The conversation was between two men. Their words were hushed and conspiratorial, but one of the voices was low and muffled and resounded from the walls like the boom of a bittern. Opening the door a crack I peeped out to see this voice belonged to a man who had not been in the castle earlier. In fact I didn't recognise him at all. The skin of his face was battle-scarred and as tanned as a ploughman's. As he spoke to de Caburn an uneasy feeling came over me and I chose to remain in the shadows.

Though this new man spoke quietly, the low tone of his voice meant his words travelled. 'Do you want me to do it now?' he said. 'While he sleeps?' De Caburn shook his head and ran a finger along the edge of his sword.

'But it has to be done before you marry?' said the scarred man. 'Or she doesn't get the estate.'

This time de Caburn nodded.

'I could do it as he rides back. People would blame bandits.'

De Caburn nodded again and then they turned to look at the

door to my room, giving me only a moment to dart out of sight.
My heart stopped, as it suddenly became startlingly plain to me
how ill-considered this visit had been. Far from protecting me,
the codicil story had only succeeded in placing my life in more
danger. De Caburn now believed I needed to be dead before he
married Clemence, or she would never inherit Somershill.

I had been such a fool.

I considered my options quickly. I could try talking my way
out of this corner by explaining the situation to de Caburn.
Perhaps we could laugh it off with a mug of ale and a dig in the
ribs – as I admitted to inventing the story in order to test his
resolve in marrying my sister. But somehow I doubted this would
work. The presence of his unpleasant-looking friend was enough
to convince me that escape was a better plan.

I peeked around the door again to see de Caburn and his
companion deep in conversation, but realised the only route out
of this place was to pass them – although only if I could keep to
the very edge of the hall. But this would be difficult to achieve,
as my creeping footsteps would doubtless rouse the dogs who
were currently silent behind their door, but who would sniff my
subterfuge without the slightest problem.

It may be difficult to force entry to a castle, but it is even
harder to break out. Mustering my courage, I crept from the
room, but within moments was greeted by the small and pale
face of Mary de Caburn. The girl had been loitering behind a
pillar, listening to her father's conversation and watching my
movements in silence. Now she stood in my path.

My heart thudded to a standstill and I nearly gasped out loud, for
I thought she would give me away. Instead she pulled my ear to her
lips and whispered very softly, 'Go back. I know another way out.'

I hesitated. Was trusting this ragged little girl a good idea? She
might be planning to lure me back into the room and then
summon her father. And who could blame the girl, as my entrap-
ment would no doubt raise her in his estimation.

But I had helped Mary earlier, and gambled that she wanted to return the favour. And, after all, what other options did I have? My plan to creep around the hall in the hope of not being seen was, at best, optimistic.

After we tiptoed back into the antechamber, Mary lifted back a heavy tapestry to expose a wooden door, which seemed as firmly shut as a portcullis. Once again I felt my heart stop. It was surely locked. But Mary poked her nimble fingers into the tiny crack between the rail and the frame – and slowly the door opened on its hinges without making a single creak. She then pushed me through the narrow gap into a dark void that soon revealed itself to be the bottom of a spiral stairwell. She motioned for me to follow her up the steps.

'I can't jump from the roof, Mary.'

'Just follow me,' she urged in a whisper.

And when we had climbed but one revolution, we came to a hole in the curve of the wall. This had once been an arrow slit, but stones had been pulled from either side of the opening in the way a chick breaks out of an egg. Now it was just wide enough for a boy of my build to squeeze through. Mary went first and dropped down softly onto the mossy bank below – a narrow strip of land between the castle wall and the moat. I followed, falling gracelessly onto the bank, and we stole around the outer bailey until we reached the drawbridge. Mary then pointed to my horse Tempest, who was fortunately still tethered on the other bank, before she disappeared into some long grass and I had lost my opportunity to thank her.

I wasted no time in crossing the bridge, mounting Tempest and galloping towards the cover of the forest – heading for the first gap between the trees, in the hope this path would soon meet up with my route home. And to begin with it seemed we were making good progress, but the path meandered in twisted directions, and soon I became disorientated, and panicked.

Stopping Tempest in a small clearing I looked about me and tried to take stock of the situation. The forest was humming with sound and movement. Buzzards circled overhead, and small birds flitted from bush to bush in the undergrowth. The floor of leaf mould steamed with the closeness of the day, and a veil of mist hung in the canopy. Large boulders watched me from behind the tree trunks like silent giants.

My heartbeat was slowing at last and my panic was receding. I was lost, but would be able to navigate north and westwards in the way Brother Peter had taught me. With concentration and a calm head I could get back to Somershill before nightfall.

Relief washed through me. I thought I was safe.

Then I heard the dogs.

At first they were distant and perhaps it was just my harried imagination – but soon the noise became louder and clearly discernible. It was the frenzy of barking – high-pitched and bloodthirsty. There could be no doubt about it. De Caburn and his hounds were on my tail. Tempest flicked his ears and tried to rear, since a horse dislikes hunting dogs as much as a fox or a stag, but I kicked his flanks before he had a chance to dislodge me and once again we resumed our gallop through the trees.

It is a strange thing to be pursued – an experience with which I was unfamiliar. The cellarer once chased me through the monastery for drinking his best port from the bottle, but on that occasion I had only been in line for a beating. Now it seemed I had carelessly placed my own head in a noose.

I cursed myself for coming here alone. For having the naïvety to take on a man such as de Caburn. I was a poor swordsman and an even poorer horseman, and easy prey to the men and dogs who were somewhere out there. In the dark forest.

At times I thought I had evaded them, only for the barking to return. And then, in the far distance I could hear their voices. Calling my name, as if I might be simple enough to answer. So I kept riding, until Tempest began to tire. His mouth frothed and white sweat clung to his neck and withers.

With the barking ever closer I rode up a narrow and steeply sided sandstone gorge in the hope of finding a passage to the next valley. But the path soon petered out in a clearing that was completely surrounded by rocks, and there was no way out other than to retrace my steps. I had trapped myself into a dead end.

And what a dead end!

An ancient beech tree grew from the rocks itself, and beneath its curling roots was a deep hole. I didn't need to look over the rim to see its purpose. I could smell it. It was a pit of the dead. A plague pit. And when I did muster the courage to look into its black depths I saw below me a layered cake of bones, clothes and hair. It was hard to tell these people had once been human at all – since the bodies had been disturbed and clawed at by wild animals. And although a rudimentary cross hung by the tree, it wasn't so much a mass grave as a rubbish heap. The stench made me want to vomit.

Tempest must have felt my revulsion. Rearing up, he threw me to the forest floor and then bolted back through the gorge. I called after him, but he was gone, and now I was left with only a pile of dead bodies for company – and they could hardly tell me what to do. Cursing loudly I climbed the rocks to try to escape from this confined bowl, but then caught the distant sound of the dogs and the galloping of hooves. Whoever had been on my trail was now following my horse – but it would not take long for them to catch up with Tempest and realise he had ejected his mount. And then they would know I was somewhere nearby, only this time on foot.

Despair was beginning to take hold of me – but his hands were still loose and slippery about my throat. I was not ready to die.

Now my mind worked at speed. I could climb a tree or dig a hole and hide in it. Or I could run to water, so the dogs would lose my scent. Except I hadn't passed a stream on this higher ground, and a hiding place would be easily sniffed out by the nose of a deerhound. As for climbing trees, it was not something in which I excelled.

And then the most disgusting idea revealed itself to me. I would hide amongst the dead.

I approached the pit of bodies again and breathed deeply. The noise of the dogs was fading. The air was still as oppressive as a kitchen full of steam and I felt faint. There was no need to do this. I could just run. Even without the speed of a horse, I might still get away.

The barking stopped. There was silence. But then, almost immediately it started again – except now the desperate, excitable calls were closing in. Soon the dogs would catch my scent and I would be murdered by de Caburn or his ugly friend, only to be left beside the road in the pretence of having been robbed and killed by bandits.

But this was not how I would die.

The corpses were no longer putrefying – as a body left to rot in the open air is soon reduced to bone, with only the occasional strand of desiccated flesh hanging from a rib or finger. But the smell of decay was still strong and I knew the foul scent would mask my own. Even if the dogs could smell me, I doubted de Caburn would approach the plague victims for fear of contamination.

I was only afraid of their odour, however, for I knew their sickness would never harm me.

I held my nose, slipped down the steep sides, and pulled aside the bones and dirty cloth to make a small hollow. As I dragged a coat over myself I disturbed a multitude of maggot shells, which only served to make me feel more nauseated. And then I lay there, totally still. Sinking into this creaking and bony mattress of death.

The dogs soon approached – their soft cantering paws thudding through the undergrowth. Their urgent barking stopped.

Instead they sniffed and whimpered in the way a dog will, when it is straining on a leash. I could see nothing but the lattice of fading daylight through the thin tunic of the man whose body rested on top of me.

And then I closed my eyes and kept them tightly shut. For how long, I cannot say. My breathing was fast and shallow, and choked my throat. My heart missed a beat. When I eventually dared to look, I saw only the shadow of something as it circled the rim of the pit. It was impossible to tell if it were a man or beast. I only knew it was looking for me.

I held my breath until there was silence. An intense and foreboding stillness. Where had the dogs gone? Were they still there? And then I no longer cared. Something seemed to wriggle inside my tunic. Thinking it was a maggot, I panicked. I would even have faced de Caburn and his dogs.

Pushing the tangle of bodies and clothing away from me, I scrambled up the slippery sides of the pit – rolling into the clearing to beat away the maggot shells that clung to my clothes. The light had now faded completely. The sky was dark and grey.

I was not of sanguine mind. I will admit that. I was both exhausted and disturbed. But I did not imagine what happened next. No matter what the others would say.

Something moved in the shadows, just yards away from me. I was being watched. Examined. Smelt. And then forms moved stealthily in the undergrowth, though in this light it was impossible to say if they were animal or human. I called for them to come forward. To show themselves. But they remained hidden in the cover of the bushes, content to wait and observe me.

I wanted to run, but my body was gripped with icy fear. Now sensing my paralysis they began to advance from the undergrowth, creeping towards me in the thick darkness. And then, just for a moment, the clouds parted to reveal a white and radiant moon. And in a fleeting beam of moonlight, I saw their faces.

It was only for a moment. But I know what I saw. The creatures had the heads of dogs.

I called for help. I prayed to God. I even called to de Caburn.

Suddenly a torch flamed in the clearing. The faces melted away into the shadows and somebody pulled me up by the hand. And then we ran.

Chapter Ten

As we fled, my champion was always ahead of me – picking a path through the trees, as a fox runs on his own tracks. I sensed he was a boy, but he kept his face hidden beneath a long hood. And though I tried repeatedly to speak with him, he remained steadfastly silent.

After crossing a low valley, we followed an outcrop of rock until the boy located a hidden gap. We then squeezed between two boulders to climb a steep path that rose above the tree canopy. A narrow ledge ran along the rocks at this level, along which we sidled with care before stopping by a recess in the stone. It was pitch black by now, but I could tell this was the entrance to a cave. A cold air emanated from the void.

'Go in,' he told me.

I hesitated. 'Who are you?'

He pushed me. 'Get in! It's not safe out here.'

Inside, the cave was as dank and chill as it had promised to be, until the boy lit a fire by the entrance. Then I could see that it was a home, of sorts. His home. Animal skins were spread across the floor. A crude bench was pushed against a wall, and knives and axes hung from hooks in the rock. The boy lifted a large copper cooking pot and lumbered it over to a trivet on the fire. Once the pot had warmed a little, the boy lifted the lid and gave the contents a stir.

Always he took care to keep his hood low so that I was still unable to see his face. 'You stink like a dead man,' he told me. 'You should take your tunic off.'

He was correct. I smelt as revolting as a vat of piss at the tanner's. But as much as I reeked, I did not feel inclined to wander about his cave in just my braies and shirt, so I shook my head.

'You can't stay in here smelling like that,' he said. 'I have some furs you can wrap about yourself tonight.'

Reluctantly I removed my tunic and he motioned for me to pass him the garment, so that he could place it near the fire in order to smoke out its foul odour.

It was at this moment his hood finally dropped, revealing his face. I gasped. For he was as misshapen as a galled tree. His head was long and thin with a pronounced forehead and jaw. His teeth were prominent and flipped over his bottom lip, and his eyes barely seemed to fit into their sockets. Long black hair grew patchily over his scalp and was drawn back into a crude plait. If anything, he had the head of an animal. I might even say a dog.

I shrank away from him. 'What are you?'

'And what are you? Smelling like a dead man. Lazarus?' He laughed bitterly and then began to whistle a tune as he threw me a sheepskin. It was a nursery rhyme.

My voice was unsteady. 'The creatures in the forest. Were they the same as you?'

He stopped whistling. 'What creatures?'

'The creatures you saved me from.'

He shrugged. 'I didn't see anything.'

'Yes you did. You waved a burning torch to scare them away.'

'It was dark. We needed some light.'

'You came there to save me.'

He looked me in the eye. 'No, I didn't.'

'So what were you doing there?'

He snorted. 'I could ask the same of you.'

'I was hiding.'

'Who from?'

I hesitated. 'Walter de Caburn.'

He snorted again. 'Never heard of him.'

'My family will be looking for me,' I said, in an attempt to scare the boy. 'If you harm me. They'll hunt you down.'

But my feeble threat was only met with yet a further shrug.

He stirred the pot again. 'You're not very good at hiding, are you?' He smiled but didn't look up at me. 'I saw you straight away.'

'I'd been in the pit before you got there. I'd just climbed out.'

This time it was the boy's turn to recoil. 'The pit?'

'Yes.'

Now he shuffled away from me. 'Why did you go into such a place?'

'I told you before. I was hiding from Walter de Caburn.'

'Then you'll die from the Pestilence.' I noticed sweat now beaded amongst the untidy hair of his upper lip.

'That won't happen to me,' I said.

'Why? Are you Christ himself?'

'Of course not.'

He backed away against the wall and drew a small knife. 'Then you'll taint me. You must get out of here. Now!' He brandished the knife, though I doubted he would actually attack me, given his fear of the Plague.

I tried to speak softly. To reassure him. 'I cannot poison you. You must believe me.'

He trembled. 'Yes you can. I heard what happened in the villages. Just one brush with a dead body is enough to kill a man.' Now he pushed the knife as close to my face as he dared. 'I shouldn't have brought you here. I should have let them take you.'

'Let *what* take me?' I grabbed the boy's hand and pushed him against the wall, but his wiry strength soon had the better of me, even though he was shorter by at least a foot.

'You must go,' he said. 'Leave me alone.'

I didn't want to stay in this damp hole. But then again I did not want to face what lurked outside. Noises reached us from the mouth of the cave. Furtive scuffling, then silence. The sound of something patient, waiting to take its prey.

'I cannot infect you,' I said again to the boy. 'You must believe me.'

'Why do you keep saying that?'

I took a deep breath. 'Because I have already suffered from the Pestilence.'

His face twisted in suspicion. 'That's a lie.'

'It's not. I cannot suffer a second time.'

'That's not true. Everybody dies.'

'No. It is possible to recover.' I sighed. 'Though few do.'

'But you will carry the contagion. And pass it to others.'

I felt angry now, since this ignorance was the reason I kept my secret. 'It's nine months since I was ill. I've infected nobody.' I looked him in the eye. 'I promise you.'

'I don't trust you.'

'Why else would I have hidden in such an evil place?'

He studied me cautiously for a while, still unsure whether to believe my story. And then he relaxed and slowly we returned to our places by the fire. Watching the flames in silence.

'What's your name?' I asked him in the end.

He hesitated. 'I don't have one.'

'Of course you do. Somebody gave birth to you and taught you to whistle that tune.'

He hesitated again. 'It's Leofwin.'

'Do you live here alone?'

Now he smiled at my question. 'No, I have a beautiful wife and three children. And sometimes the king comes to visit.'

We returned to silence, which was only broken occasionally by Leofwin stirring the pot. The carcass of a rabbit was boiling with onions and peas, and when it finally bubbled

Leofwin ladled a portion into a clean wooden bowl. 'Want some?' he asked me. As he passed the stew, I noted his fingers were fused together, giving him a large claw-like pincer rather than a hand.

He saw me looking. 'Wondering what I am, are you?' he said, thrusting his deformed hand at me. 'My mother was a devil and my father was a werewolf.' He then threw back his head and laughed, revealing more of his extraordinary teeth – teeth that seemed to grow at the oddest of angles from his jaw.

When I didn't respond to his joke, he spooned himself out a generous portion of stew and sat down next to me on the bench.

'Thank you for helping me,' I said. 'You saved my life.'

He shrugged and sucked some meat from a bone.

Around the cave were the skeletons of forest animals. I counted five skulls of various sizes. A pile of animal skins lay in the corner, but also a gown, sewn with fine embroidery.

'Why do you have a dress?' I said, pointing to this garment.

'None of your business.'

'I'm a lord, Leofwin. Don't speak to me in such a manner.'

'Are you?' he said, still chewing his rabbit meat.

'Do you know Somershill?'

He took the bone from his mouth. 'That's where you come from, is it? Is that where you're *lord*?' The word seemed to amuse him.

'Yes.'

He leant forward but avoided my gaze. 'Have there been many deaths there?'

'Yes. At least half the village died in the Plague.'

'I meant in more recent days.'

'Why do you want to know?'

He continued to suck the bone. 'It's just a question. That's all.'

'Since you ask, there've been two murders.'

He sat up straight and looked at me. 'Who?'

'Two girls. Alison and Matilda Starvecrow. Do you know them?'

He relaxed immediately. 'Of course I don't know them. I don't know anybody.' He went back to the cooking pot and ladled himself out a second helping. 'More?'

I nodded. The stew was good. 'Will you lead me back to Somershill tomorrow?' He hesitated. 'I'll pay you.'

'What with?' I showed him the silver ring on my little finger, but he pointed to the signet ring. 'I'll take that one.'

I felt the band of gold and amber. 'My father gave me this. You can't have it.'

'Find your own way back then.'

'Take the silver ring. It's valuable.'

He shook his head.

I sighed. 'Very well. But take me the back ways. We mustn't cross de Caburn's land.' He held his palm open, expecting me to drop the ring into it. 'I'll give it to you when we get there.'

He bowed with a mocking flourish. 'As you wish, my lord.' But then his face darkened. 'But you must never talk of me. Do you understand?' I nodded. 'I will only take you to the border of your parish. No further.'

Now we had finished eating, Leofwin rebuilt the fire near to the entrance and then threw me a second sheepskin to lie on. A blanket followed, which was of the finest wool. I wanted to ask him how he came by such sumptuous belongings, but I suspected the answer would be the same as for the gown.

'Tell me how you survived the Great Mortality,' he said, when I had settled down upon the sheepskin. 'How were you cured?'

I hesitated. 'I don't know. It must have been good luck.'

Leofwin huffed. 'You want to keep the cure to yourself? Is that it?'

'Of course not.'

'Then tell me your story.' He closed his eyes. 'I like stories.'

'I could tell you about something else.'

'No. I want to hear about the Plague.'

In some ways it would be a relief to tell this tale, since Brother Peter had sworn me to secrecy. He had feared my position as lord would be placed in jeopardy if the truth were known. So I had not told a soul. Not even Mother. Or perhaps I should say, especially not Mother. There would be some, like Leofwin, who would consider me tainted and at risk of spreading the contagion. But there would be others who claimed I had been cured by magic or witchcraft.

I sighed and pulled the blanket about my neck. 'It was September last year when the Pestilence finally reached our monastery. I was a novice and apprentice to the infirmarer.'

'I thought you were a lord.'

'Do you want to hear this story?' He grunted and I continued. 'I left the abbey with Brother Peter after the first of our order died. We thought we had escaped the Plague, but it seems it had come with us. I developed a fever as we travelled.'

'Was it as painful as they say?'

'Yes. At first you sweat, but soon you are trembling until your legs are too weak to bear your own weight. When I reached this state, we could not continue our journey.'

'So what did you do?'

'Peter found an abandoned cottage where he could nurse me.'

'He didn't leave you?'

'No.'

'But he risked death himself.'

'He wore a mask that protects a physician from the deadly miasma.'

Leofwin laughed. 'They don't work.'

'Once again that's not true,' I said. 'Peter tended to the abbot and did not catch the Plague. And he did not suffer after treating me, though he nursed me through the whole sickness.'

'So it was his treatment that saved you?'

I sighed. 'He cooled my brow with water and gave me infusions to drink. But it was not the potions that saved me.'

'What was it then?'

'The buboes grew in my armpits and groin. Bigger and blacker by the hour. Peter feared for my life, but he would not administer the last rites, even though I wanted to die.'

'But you didn't.' The boy opened his eyes. 'So it was sorcery?'

I shook my head. 'No. It was science.' The fire created shadows on the ceiling and somewhere outside an owl hooted. Thinking I heard scratching again near the entrance to the cave, I sat up. 'What's that? Is something out there?'

Leofwin waved his hand. 'It's nothing. Go on with your story. I want to know the end.'

I settled down again, trying to feel reassured. 'There is only one way to save the patient once the buboes have grown so large. But it's a dangerous cure that may kill the patient as quickly as the Plague. And it's hazardous to the physician himself.'

'Why?'

'It releases a poisonous vapour that spreads through the air and infects the lungs.'

'So what did he do?'

I thought back to that moment. Stuck in that dirty cottage with death at my shoulder. I hardly wanted to speak of it.

'What did he do?' insisted Leofwin.

'Peter lanced each of the buboes and drained them of their pus.'

Leofwin now pulled a face of disgust. 'Did it hurt?'

'Of course it did! It was the worst pain I have ever endured.'

'And what did it look like? The pus.'

These questions were beginning to annoy me. 'I don't know. Black, I suppose.'

'And did it smell?'

'Probably! I can't remember. I was dying.'

'But you didn't.'

I smiled to myself. For the memory of survival was still sweet. 'No. Once I was freed of the contamination, my fever began to cool. And then, after a few days I was able to walk again.'

'And then you were cured?'

'Yes.'

Leofwin whistled. 'He must love you. This monk.'

'He's a man of God. He wouldn't have abandoned me.'

'You're lucky to have such a friend.'

I caught his eye and for a moment we exchanged a look that might even have developed into a smile. 'I've told you about the Plague, so you must tell me about the creatures we saw earlier at the pit.'

Now Leofwin stiffened and his smile disappeared. 'I know nothing of them. I told you that before.'

'Did you see their faces?'

'No. It was too dark.'

'It seemed to me they had the heads of dogs.'

He stoked up the fire. 'I saw nothing like that.'

'But you must have seen something, Leofwin. Otherwise, why did you come to save me?'

His face darkened and I even would say he growled. 'Go to sleep.'

'But—'

'I told you. I saw nothing!'

The day had been arduous and the sheepskin was soft. I watched Leofwin secretly for a while. He had positioned himself with his back against the wall, sitting near to the fire in order to replenish it with wood when necessary. As he pulled his long tunic he rubbed an abscess on his leg, which was red and swollen and crusted by a scab the size of a beech leaf. Leofwin dabbed it with some ashes from the fire, but this would not cure the infection. When he caught me watching, he pulled down his tunic and turned away, telling me crossly to mind my own business.

It was my intention to stay awake, but my heavy eyes soon betrayed me and I fell into a restless slumber, dreaming of the shadowy creatures by the pit. At first light, I woke to find Leofwin treading down the last of the flames.

He scraped back the hair from his face with his awkward fingers. 'I can use a knife and shoot an arrow,' he said without looking up from the sooty embers. 'I don't need your pity.'

'I don't pity you,' I lied. 'But the abscess on your leg needs draining.'

He stumbled forward and thrust his strange face into mine. 'It's not some plague bubo. I know how to drain a boil.'

'Do you?'

'I don't have my own devoted monk to nurse me, my lord. I treat myself.'

I ignored his sarcasm. 'How many times have you drained it?'

'Many times.' He backed away from me a little and dropped his hostility for a moment. 'But it won't heal.'

'Then some contamination must remain lodged under the skin. A small object you haven't removed.'

'What would you know about such things?' The words rolled off his tongue contemptuously.

'I was apprentice to an infirmarer. Remember?'

He scrutinised me for a few seconds and then slowly lifted his long tunic to present the abscess on the shin of his left leg. Perhaps he expected me to recoil from the red and swollen boil, as he had recoiled from the description of my plague sores? But I did not, even though his abscess smelt unpleasant and was oozing a thin trail of pus. His leg was hot to the touch, and when I pressed my finger into his skin he flinched.

'Do you have a sharp knife?' I asked him. 'If it is silver, all the better.'

He dropped his tunic again and walked away from me distrustfully.

'Leave it then,' I said. 'Wait for the corruption to spread into your bones and your blood. Nobody but the crows and flies will know you've died.'

He stopped, though he did not turn to look at me. Instead he shuffled about at the back of the cave and appeared to be searching for something under blankets or behind stones. When I realised he was looking for a knife, I also asked him to bring me some vinegar and honey.

'I don't have honey,' he said.

'Lard will do. And I need some linen. And garlic.'

He soon returned, clasping the items I had asked for. The knife was a whittle tang with a blade of silver and a handle of horn. I didn't ask how he had acquired such an expensive blade but he read my thoughts.

'I found it,' he said.

'And the leaf lard? It's from a sheep's kidney, isn't it?' Once again he was reluctant to answer me. 'Did you poach it?'

'The animal was nearly dead already.'

I placed the knife in the embers of the fire to warm it a little, while I washed down his abscess with some linen and vinegar. 'How did this happen?'

'I was shot in the leg. I thought I had removed all of the arrowhead.' His face grimaced as the acid of the vinegar stung at his skin.

'How long ago?'

'In the spring.'

'Did you see who shot you?'

He looked away. 'No.'

'Was it de Caburn?' He was silent. 'Did he catch you taking his sheep?'

'None of your business.'

I took the knife from the fire and blew the ashes from the blade. 'Do you have something to dull the pain? Brandy perhaps?'

He puffed out his cheeks and tried to laugh. 'Brandy? Who do you think I am? A Dutch merchant?'

'I thought you might have *found* some.'

He pulled a face at my words. 'Get on with it.'

I had perforated an abscess before, though usually under the supervision of Brother Peter. At the infirmary we had lancets to pierce the crust of the boil, and glass cups to draw the poison. We dressed the cavity with poultices of lavender and rosemary oil, and then we sprinkled the wound with dried yarrow to stem the flow of blood. But none of these herbs was available to me, so it was fortunate Leofwin was a brave and stoic patient.

I opened the sinus hole of the boil and allowed the pus to drain more freely until I could scrape away the dead matter, soon finding the small shard of arrow that lay embedded deep within his skin. He only screamed when I washed out the wound with vinegar, but the paste of lard and garlic formed a cooling ointment, and the intensity of his pain seemed to diminish. I could only hope the wound would heal, since I could not stitch it.

Leofwin then slept, but woke in a delirium. His fever was high. I left the cave when it was safe and found some willow bark for him to chew upon. His teeth were healthy enough, if not exactly in the conventional position in his jaw. He did as I bade him and slowly the fever broke.

While he was exhausted and bewildered I tried to converse with him. To find out where he came from and who cared for him. Who was the person who brought him flour, dried peas and sausage – all of which I found in a small alcove carved into the wall? He knew of Dutch merchants and of nursery rhymes and the Bible, so something of the outside world reached this lonely hermit hole.

Mostly I tried to draw him on the creatures that had surrounded me by the plague pit. He knew what they were, though he persistently denied it. I had previously given Cornwall's theory no credence, but during those lonely hours in this strange and damp cave, I began to wonder if I had been right to dismiss him so readily. Something lurked outside in the shadows and I made sure to keep a fire burning. Even in the daylight.

My schemes to coax information from Leofwin failed until, just as I was about to quit, he began to mumble a few words. I wiped his brow and spoke softly. 'Which beasts do you speak of, Leofwin?'

His face was hot and sweating. 'They will not find you. Nobody will hunt you. I will keep your secret.'

'What secret?' I squeezed his hand. 'Tell me.' But he would say no more, and drifted back into a restless sleep. And nothing else I said to him would induce an answer.

As Leofwin slowly recovered I had only myself for company, apart from the bats who roosted inside the cave, and the large eagles who liked to dive at my head every time I ventured out. At night I felt something watching me from the ledge outside. It felt sinister and menacing, and sometimes scuffled and scratched at the rock. I built the fire up to a blaze and did not sleep until daybreak.

On the second morning Leofwin sat up and asked for something to eat. His wound smelt clean and the skin on his leg had returned to a wholesome colour. I was unable to offer him anything but a thin pottage made with dried peas. I did not possess the boy's skills to survive in this forest, and after three days I was starving.

'Does your gown smell any better?' he said, pointing to my tunic, which was still hanging on a boulder near the fire.

'I think so.'

'Put it on and we'll leave.'

'Are you well enough?'

'Yes.'

I was pleased to be going, since Brother Peter would have search parties out for me by now. I put on my tunic, but it was still seasoned with the scent of decaying flesh – only now it was also tinged with the odour of bonfire. I considered being rid of the garment for ever, except I could hardly return to my estate in just my underclothes.

After finishing the remains of the pottage, we set off, but not before Leofwin insisted on blindfolding me. I tried to argue against this, but he was insistent. If I refused, he would simply drop me off in the nearest clearing and be gone, in spite of my success in treating his leg.

Before I let him tie the length of linen over my eyes, I tried one last time to ask him a question.

'Why did you help me, Leofwin?'

He considered this question at least. 'How old are you?'

'Eighteen,' I told him.

'So am I.' I hid my surprise, since I had assumed him to be only about twelve or thirteen. 'We deserve some more life, don't we?' he added wistfully, and that was all he would say.

We walked for maybe four or five hours. It was hard to keep track of time, but I was aware, despite the blindfold, that we were sometimes walking in circles. No doubt a deliberate ploy to disorientate me, so that I would never find my way back. We talked occasionally, but only for Leofwin to tell me we were about to cross a stream, or climb over a fallen tree trunk. I could scarcely have retraced my steps, but made a note of the sounds and smells of our route. The buzzing of the horseflies. The lemony scent of the last of the elderflowers, and the ugly stink of the first of the hogweed. The pull of the deep, sticky mud we encountered at every descent.

The day was becoming warmer and warmer, and Leofwin had no food or clean water with him. My stomach rumbled like a grinding millstone and I felt a headache brewing – the type that bores a hole into the back of an eye and disturbs vision.

Eventually we reached a point when we walked no further. My headache was intense by now and I felt sick.

And then, suddenly, I realised I was alone.

'Leofwin? Where are you? What's happening?' I called his name, but there was no response. Deciding to pull off the blindfold, the sun burnt my eyes and I could hardly focus. I panicked. 'Leofwin!' I shouted. By now I was dizzy and nauseous, and fell to my knees thinking I might vomit. Then somebody took my arm. 'Leofwin? Is that you?' I said.

Shielding my eyes from the glare of the sun, I discovered it was not Leofwin's face looking down at me. It was my servant's — Gilbert. Brother Peter and some other men were peering over his shoulder.

'Who's Leofwin?' said Gilbert.

'He's a boy,' I said. Then realising I had already broken my promise, I quickly retracted. 'I don't know who he is. I'm dreaming.'

Gilbert turned to Peter. 'He's not making sense, Brother.'

Peter took my hand. 'We've been searching for you for days, Oswald. Did de Caburn do this to you?'

'No, I ran away from him and hid in a plague pit.'

Gilbert and the other men looked at each other uneasily. Peter noticed their disquiet. 'Lord Somershill is feverish. Pay no heed to his words.'

'He smells like the Devil,' said one of the younger men, who was now fanning his nose with a hand.

'Be quiet, boy! And bring the cart.' Peter watched them disperse and then bent down to whisper in my ear. 'Say nothing more, Oswald. We will talk later.'

As I lay in the cart, holding my head and wanting to be sick again, I glanced down at my right hand. My father's signet ring was still there on my third finger, but my silver ring was gone.

Chapter Eleven

Once returned by the men to Somershill, I spent many hours in my bedchamber with a cold compress held to my head. I had suffered such headaches when younger, but they had never lasted this long. Mother had appointed herself my nurse, but was more concerned with interrogating me about my absence than she was with my health. Unfortunately it seemed my story was now the talk of the estate. At times I feigned sleep in the hope Mother would go away.

I must have dozed off, for the next thing Brother Peter was pinching my cheek to wake me. 'We must talk quickly, Oswald. Your mother and Clemence have ridden to the village.' I groaned, sensing a new round of questioning.

'I need to know exactly what happened to you,' he said.

'I told you earlier, Brother. When we were first alone. I was helped by a boy. His name was—'

Peter rolled his eyes. 'Yes, yes. Leofwin. A disfigured outcast who lives in a cave. On a ridge full of eagles.' He now applied a new compress to my temple. It was cold and smelt of spearmint and lemons. And it stung.

'It's true,' I insisted, but he ignored my assertion.

'You realise Cornwall has raised the hue and cry again?'

I pushed the compress away. 'Has there been another murder?'

'No. Of course not, Oswald. But you disappeared for four days. Cornwall has convinced everybody you were taken by dog heads.'

I wanted then to tell Peter of my strange encounter by the plague pit, but before I could speak, he started again. 'Of course, you've only made it worse. Saying the oddest things.'

'What sort of things?'

Peter pulled at the mole on his neck. 'Some delirious nonsense about strange forms in the dark.' He sighed. 'You said they had the heads of dogs. You can only imagine the effect of such words.'

'You see, there—'

He held up his hand. 'Please, Oswald. I only want to know what happened with de Caburn. No more foolishness.'

I quickly put the compress back onto my head. 'I told you everything earlier, Brother.'

'But you weren't making sense.'

'The plan to stop Clemence's marriage failed. What more is there to say?'

Hooves clattered in the yard below.

Peter looked out of the window and cursed. 'Bones of St Helena! It's your mother and sister. And they have that rogue Cornwall with them.' He took a small glass bottle from his belt pouch and swigged from it. 'He must be here to visit you.'

'I don't want to see Cornwall.'

'Pull up the sheets. I'll tell them you're too weak to receive visitors.'

I lay down under the blankets as Peter went to intercept my mother's party on the stairs. But he was too late, for moments later Cornwall strode into my bedchamber with all the swagger of an earl. As he leant over my bed, I noted his neck was draped with heavy chains and his velvet cap was new. It seemed the sale of his relics had been boosted by my disappearance in the forest.

Cornwall bowed, though not quite as deeply as he should have. 'Lord Somershill.'

I closed my eyes. 'What is it, Cornwall? I'm unwell.'

Mother bustled in behind him. 'See how Oswald has suffered piteously, Father John. You must pray for him.' She busied herself about my head, rearranging the linen of the compress so that it hung over my face like a woman's veil. I peeked through to see my sister Clemence now leaning against the oak of the door, with a smile fixed across her face.

'I will say a mass for Lord Somershill,' said Cornwall, 'to ensure he has not been tainted by his encounter with the Devil.'

I mumbled. 'How much will that cost?'

He pursed his lips again. 'It would be my honour and duty, my lord.'

Peter pulled back the veil and held his hand to my forehead. 'Lord Somershill didn't encounter the Devil. So there is no need to say a mass.'

'Then what happened to him?'

'He was bucked from his horse when returning from Versey Castle. See how pale his countenance is.'

Cornwall crossed his arms. 'But I'm told he has been mumbling in his sleep. Saying he was confronted by creatures with the heads of dogs.'

'Lord Somershill has simply been delirious. He had an injury to the head and nothing to eat for three days. A person may say many strange and fantastical things when in a state of senselessness. I have studied the mind under such conditions.'

Cornwall smirked. 'Yes. I have heard you're an expert on the state of senselessness.'

Clemence let out a guffaw, which Mother silenced with a stare.

I now opened my eyes fully, though the light in the room was strong and it was necessary to squint. 'Brother Peter is correct. I became disorientated after hitting my head against a rock.' I pulled the compress back over my eyes. 'Now please leave. I may be sick.'

Mother leant her face into mine. 'Are you quite sure, Oswald? There was no mention of hitting your head before?'

'I didn't want to alarm you, Mother. I know how easily your humours are disturbed.'

'Perhaps Father John could say some prayers for you?' she whispered.

'No! Not even a Hail Mary.'

'But Oswald—'

I drew Mother closer. 'Do not give that man a single penny. Understand?' These words were meant for her ears alone, but it was clear Cornwall caught them. He drew a deep breath and swung the corner of his cloak over his shoulder.

Mother sensed the slight and tried to make amends by taking Cornwall's arm. 'My son is still unwell, Father John. His nerves have been quite unhinged by this whole episode. Please, join me in the great hall.' She led him to the door. 'I have some sweet port you may like to try. Its heat is said to warm even the blackest of bile.'

'Thank you, madam.' His voice receded as they walked through the solar and then descended the staircase. 'But one mass may not be sufficient. I'm told Lord Somershill smelt of the abyss when they found him. I fear I may need to say at least four.'

I lifted the compress from my eyes completely to see Clemence had remained in the room. 'What excellent comedy,' she said. 'I could be watching a company of fools at the fair.'

'Your brother needs to rest, my lady,' said Brother Peter, pulling the curtains about my bed and releasing a bloom of dust.

Instead I sat up and pushed back the heavy damask. 'I need to speak to you, Clemence.'

She raised an eyebrow. 'What about?'

Her demeanour was hostile, but I persevered nonetheless. 'De Caburn tried to kill me.'

Now she laughed. 'What a fanciful notion.'

'He chased me through the forest with his dogs.'

'He was looking for you. You fool.'

'He was trying to kill me.'

Her brow now tightened into its familiar frown. 'Absolutely not. You disappeared from his home without bidding him farewell. Walter was concerned for your safety.' Then she smirked. 'I'm told you were very drunk.'

'That's not what happened.'

She crossed her arms and lowered her voice to a vicious whisper. 'I know exactly what happened, little brother. You went to Versey with lies about Father's will. Thinking to thwart my chance at marriage.' She then pointed at Brother Peter. 'No doubt it was his idea. But you've been found out. Both of you.'

'But—'

'Nothing will stop my union to Walter. Do you understand? Not you or your pathetic priest.'

Clemence drew up her gown and left the room, slamming the door behind her and rattling the thin panelling of the partition wall. A wooden crucifix fell from its alcove, and though Peter tried to catch it, it bounced profanely about the floor.

When it had finally come to rest, Peter picked the ornament up and then joined me on the bed, sighing so deeply his chin sank into his chest. 'You should have listened to me, Oswald. The letter might have worked.' His eyelids hung heavily and he needed to shave. He turned the crucifix over and over in his hands. 'You shouldn't have gone to Versey without me. You put your life in danger.'

I took his hand to stop this repeated fiddling. His skin was dry and cold. 'There's something I need to talk to you about, Brother. It concerns the Starvecrow murders.'

I felt his hand stiffen, but his eyes remained glued to the crucifix. 'We should be more concerned about attempted murder. Yours.'

'Please just listen to me. I did not become delirious in the forest. When I climbed from the plague pit, I *was* surrounded by strange creatures.'

Now he looked up, but said nothing.

I took a deep breath. 'It was dark, but they had the heads of dogs. I'm sure of it.'

If I had hoped for some understanding, it was not forthcoming. Instead Peter pulled away his hand from me and burst out laughing. 'Not you as well? This story is becoming as contagious as the Plague!'

'Don't mock me, Brother. I'm not imagining it.'

Peter stood up and paced across the rush matting of the bedchamber floor. 'Then what in the Lord's name are you talking about? I thought better of you than this.'

'The creatures would have attacked me. I was saved by Leofwin.'

Now he guffawed. 'Of course! You were rescued from a pack of dog heads by a boy with the face of a dog!' He leant over me. 'You don't think this story sounds in the least bit extraordinary?'

'No. It's what happened.'

He drew even closer. 'Are you sure you didn't eat some fly agaric mushrooms? It's easily done, if you're starving. They are red and spotted, and would appeal to an exhausted and fevered mind.'

I didn't care to respond to this ridiculous suggestion, so I pulled back the sheets and put my feet clumsily onto the floor. 'It was not a hallucination.'

'What are you doing now? Stay in bed.'

I pushed him away. 'Just leave me alone, Brother. I don't need your help.'

But he stood in my path and it was impossible to circumvent his wiry frame. As he took me in his grip his breath smelt of onions and beer, but the weave of his black gown was familiar and reassuring. He was right in one respect. I was exhausted. I was still feverish. Cold sweat dripped from my face and clung to my chest. I had managed to stand, but now only had the energy to rest my head upon his shoulder – though it was as bony as the backside of a dairy cow.

He patted my back gently. 'I'm sorry, Oswald. I know you're not a liar.'

'Then don't treat me as one.'

'But you must consider the likelihood of your story.' I pushed him away again, but now he took my hand. 'You put yourself through an ordeal. It was foolhardy to confront de Caburn. But it was still brave, and I do admire you for it.'

'It doesn't seem that way.'

'But think how such an ordeal will affect a person's mind. You were frightened and desperate. So desperate, you hid amongst the dead in a plague pit.'

'You believe that much then?'

'You have the stinking clothes to prove that part of the story.'

'It's not a story!'

He took my head in his hands and forced me to look into his eyes. 'Dear Oswald. Do you remember being in that cottage? When the Plague finally took over your body?'

I tried to look away, not wanting to think about it. The filthy straw bed. The flies. The clammy stink of prowling Death. But Peter wouldn't release his grip. 'You were delirious, Oswald. Talking of dragons and demons in the rafters, waiting to drop down and eat you. You even accused me of lancing your sores to drain the gold from your body.'

'I had a fever, Brother.'

'And you've had a fever for the last few days. Can't you see that?'

'I don't know.' My resolve was weakening.

'I'm sure it's what happened to you.'

'But—'

'Please, Oswald.' He released my face. 'Just think about it. For me.'

When I had recovered, I walked to the churchyard and sat beside Alison's grave. The weeds were not yet growing over her freshly turned soil, so once again I whispered my story into the earth.

Alison didn't find my tale extraordinary.

In fact, she said nothing at all.

The next day the marriage notice of Clemence and de Caburn was posted on the door of St Giles, and a betrothal ceremony was conducted soon afterwards by Cornwall. I was not invited to this ceremony and could only take this as a deliberate slight. After I searched out Clemence the same evening, she reluctantly agreed to speak with me. We took a walk into the orchard and sat on the bench beneath a tree heavy with green fruit.

Clemence folded her arms and wouldn't look me in the eye. 'I can't see why you feel snubbed. You oppose my marriage, so why attend the betrothal?'

'Because I'm your brother. I should have been there.'

'Then give me a dowry.' She scowled. 'Brother.'

I tried to touch her shoulder, but she shifted away from me. 'Please don't marry him, Clemence.'

'And stay here with you and Mother for the rest of my days?'

'But he's a cruel man.'

'No he's not.'

'Of course he is. Everybody knows how he treats his wives.'

She waved her hand in front of her face, as if she were swatting away a fly. 'They were green apples, little brother. Walter won't behave that way towards me. I wouldn't let him.' Then she stood up. 'Am I excused now?'

I insisted she sit back down again – a request to which she grudgingly complied. 'What if I were to expressly forbid this marriage? As head of this family, you still have to obey me.'

She smiled. 'You might be a lord, Oswald. But you're not related to the king are you?'

'Pardon?'

'I forgot to tell you. We have the blessing of Earl Stephen.' My expression of shock must have delighted her, since she only just suppressed a squeal.

'I don't believe you.'

'The earl has written to Walter and congratulated him. They have become especial friends. Would you care to see the letter?'

I thought of the earl, and put my head in my hands. I still hadn't replied to his request for a money payment rather than military service from the Somershill estate. It might be possible to ignore his letter until the autumn, but I couldn't ignore the man's wishes when it came to this marriage. He held Versey as well as Somershill from the king, and had vast lands that circled both mine and de Caburn's. Nothing could move in or out of our estates without passing along one of his roads, or crossing one of his bridges. Father had always kept the earl happy, but de Caburn had been less keen on diplomacy. When the king granted the earl a pavage tax on his road to Rochester, de Caburn drove his sheep across the fields to avoid the toll. The two men had feuded ever since. But now, inexplicably, it appeared they were friends.

The wheel of fortune was turning ever more treacherously against me. I asked Clemence to talk with me a little longer, but she refused. Instead she stood up, bobbed a curtsy, and left.

I pulled an apple from the tree and took a large bite. It was as sour as my sister.

As Mother readied the house for the wedding, I threw myself into work on the estate. Thankfully, my remaining men had tired of searching the woods for dog heads and were slowly returning to the demesne. The sheep were eventually sheared after a fashion, and the hay was scythed and collected. But, despite all my best efforts, it seemed nothing in the fates was prepared to assist me.

It continued to rain, making the hay damp and difficult to cut. My herd of sheep was thirty ewes down since the last head count, and my workforce grumbled about the quality of the food and drink that was provided for them by the house. My father was said to lay on a banquet after the hay harvest. Their earnest faces belied the blatant untruth of this claim. Even I knew that Father was loath to offer anything at harvest other than the toughest rye bread and most adulterated ale.

When I passed their complaints on to Mother, she told me she had no intention of wasting good food on a few ragged peasants, when she was stockpiling our scant supplies for the wedding feast. She didn't have long to amass this store cupboard, since Clemence and de Caburn were to marry in a matter of days — much sooner than the usual forty days between the betrothal and the wedding.

Brother Peter continued to warn me of the dangers this marriage would pose to my position, but what was I supposed to do? The earl had sanctioned it, and although it was not his family's name carved into the door lintel at Somershill, it might as well have been. Not only did I have to agree to the union in order to please him, now I was faced with offering the dowry to Clemence, which I had previously refused. I did not mention the earl's blessing on the marriage to Peter, since I could not bear to be counselled against yet another enemy.

In truth I had taken to avoiding Peter — as his advice was beginning to wear. The shapes by the plague pit had been an illusion – I had reluctantly accepted this story. Yes, I had drunk too much ale, been chased by de Caburn and his dogs, and hidden in the filth of the plague pit. Yes, my mind had been warped sufficiently to cause delirium. But I did not need to be constantly reminded of it. And then I wondered if I did truly accept this explanation? Peter's argument made more sense than my own account.

But who then had blindfolded me, if not Leofwin?

And who had taken my silver ring?

Around this time I began to suffer nightmares. My sleep disturbed by the same dream. I was in the dirty cottage where Peter had saved my life. His rosary hung over my head as my body arched in pain. And then he took his blade to me. It was cold and sharp against my hot skin. But when he made his first searing incision I woke with a scream, feeling at my armpits and groin, but finding no oozing sores. Only the ridged and tender scars of a tortuous ordeal.

During these few days my investigation into the death of Alison and Matilda Starvecrow progressed no further. There was no news of Matilda's whereabouts – which did not surprise me, since I never believed she had found her way to another village, being both penniless and mad. Equally, there was no sign of a body. I visited Alison's grave to apologise at my failure to find our sister, but the soil remained silent. Sensing the girl was angry with me, I returned to the gaol house on two more occasions to press Joan Bath for the location of Matilda's corpse, but the woman either continued to protest her innocence, or wouldn't speak to me at all.

Old Ralph, on the other hand, was pleased to speak to anybody. Having recovered from his fever, he was telling any soul who would listen to him that his own daughter should hang for the murder of the Starvecrow sisters.

He had been moved back to his own home, where I gathered he was bereft of visitors apart from myself and a neighbourly woman who left food outside his door before scampering away. When I did summon the courage to visit the old man, I found a distinctly unpleasant smell lingering about the cottage, which went over and above the usual stink of the man. His arm had become infected – a wound he had suffered after being tightly bound by Joan and her sons. I knew the smell instantly, but could not persuade the old fool that his limb was gangrenous.

I offered to bring Brother Peter, assuring Old Ralph that Peter was skilled at amputation and could even administer a potion to ensure he wouldn't feel his own arm being sawn off. But Ralph insisted he could cure the arm himself with a herbal concoction. Apparently it had worked on such a wound before. No matter how much I tried to convince him this was impossible, he would not believe me that a limb simply does not recover from gangrene. On all my subsequent visits, he would delight in showing me how well this ointment was working, only for me to see how a little more of his arm had been eaten away. With the date for the Hundreds court still more than two weeks away, I could only hope the man would survive long enough to be a witness.

The mood in the village was unclear with regards to Joan. There were a few goodwives pleased their husband's nocturnal activities with the local whore were curtailed. On the other hand, there was also a group of widowers who were missing Joan and her services. Two of the men started a fight needlessly at the hay harvest and had to be separated by Featherby. I thought back to my days amongst the novices and remembered what it is to have too many men cooped together without the company of women. They are like a cage of cock robins. Too eager for a fight. So, when I heard rumours that Joan had resumed trading at her new address, aided and abetted by Henry the gaoler, I did nothing to investigate.

On the Sunday before the marriage, I had decided to take communion at St Giles rather than at our own chapel. Not only did I need some respite from my mother, but in truth I was also hoping to see Mirabel again. And there was the question of Cornwall. I had also been avoiding the man since his visit to my sickbed and this weakness would not have gone unnoticed. Cornwall currently held the advantage in our quarrel, and I needed to wrest it back.

With the wedding only days away, Mother's hysteria had been building relentlessly. The blue cloth for Clemence's dress had been 'too muddy' in its tone, the ale for the feast was 'too cloudy', and the hogs 'too melancholy'. This was an unlikely problem, but still Mother insisted she could predict how a pig would taste just from looking at the expression on its face. There was no arguing with her.

Clemence, for her part, was less tolerant of Mother's quirks than ever, and had stabbed her fingers more than usual with her embroidery needle. Her tapestry was blotted with bloodstains. We had all noticed de Caburn's absence from the house, but dared not mention it to Clemence. The man was making no effort at all to court his wife-to-be. In fact, since the betrothal ceremony, he had not paid a single visit to Somershill. Not that it concerned me. I was quite happy to meet my tormentor as little as possible.

As I left for mass that morning, Brother Peter came running out after me. I wished then I had ridden, since he would never have caught up with me. His words of wisdom and constant fussing over my welfare were becoming suffocating.

'There's no need for you to join me,' I said. 'You've said mass already this morning.'

He ran along to keep up with me. 'It will be interesting for me. I want to hear Cornwall's sermon.'

'I don't. But it will give me the chance to sleep.'

Brother Peter laughed. 'I doubt it. The man is said to nearly blow the roof from the nave.'

As we entered the village, I once again regretted the lack of a horse. We must have cut a strange sight. A young lord, accompanied by a red-faced priest who could barely keep pace. The villagers bowed or curtsied as we passed, but it seemed more of a wearied reflex than a genuine act of respect. I looked about for Mirabel amongst their downcast and worn-out faces, but her lovely eyes were nowhere to be seen. Instead, a thin trail of brown-clothed people made their way towards St Giles, hobbling forward like a gang of captive soldiers.

I joined their meagre group and stepped inside the church. From the exterior it was a building of simple proportions with a square tower and plain glass in the arched windows. But inside it was gaudily decorated with icons, tapestries, and carvings.

'Look at this place,' I whispered to Brother Peter. A trestle table to the side of the altar was now laid with a selection of skulls, squares of cloth, and shrivelled pieces of skin.

Peter nodded. 'Cornwall has turned your church into a market stall.'

I took my place in the front bench, facing the rood screen, and watched Cornwall prepare for his mass. The man was every inch a performer, wearing a new yellow chasuble that could have been made for the part of Gabriel himself in a miracle play. He moved about his stage deliberately, as if every step he took were coated in significance.

As the poor prayed, crossed themselves and came to the rood screen for communion, Peter and I listened with increasing bafflement to the mass. Cornwall clearly had little grasp of Latin, and the further he mumbled his way through the liturgy, the worse it became. At one point I even stifled a laugh as he repeated the same invented words over and over again to accompany the blessing of the bread and wine. Hearing my snigger, Cornwall turned to look at me, his eyes meeting mine with the affection of a poisoned dart. Yet, throughout the mass, the other communicants carried on their devotions, ignorant of the gibberish accompanying their worship. Only the childless wooden Virgin seemed to notice – her sad face more troubled than ever.

When the mass was over we were treated to Cornwall's popular sermon, broadcast to the congregation in common English. Cornwall was clearly much more comfortable with this part of proceedings, stepping into the nave and wandering amongst us. With his ornate and copiously folded chasuble trailing along the floor and the large crucifix around his neck, he looked ready to perform the next act of his show.

For the second time that morning he fixed me with a stare, then announced his sermon would address the sin of bearing false witness. Hushed anticipation spread throughout the congregation.

Cornwall strolled between the benches. 'There are those among us who would lie to serve their own ends.' The anticipation in the church began to harden into fear. Were the sinners about to be named? I looked about me and saw prayers being hastily muttered. Chests being crossed. Brother Peter snorted, folded his arms, and deliberately looked out of the window.

'Is it you, Henry?' An oily-faced boy trembled in his seat. 'Or is it you, Catherine?'

An older woman shook her head vigorously. 'No, Father John. I am a true witness. I pray hourly to the heavenly saints. And I sleep with this lock of the Virgin's hair in my hand.' She showed Cornwall a coil of dark-coloured hair, which he inspected like a length of cloth at the market, before dropping it back into her lap. By the contemptuous expression on his face, this relic had not been one of his own sales.

Moving off again, he raised his voice. 'There is one among us who has come face to face with the Devil, but denies it. He knows where this Devil lurks, but will not name that place. Should we forgive that sin?' He loomed over a young girl, who shook in her seat. 'Should we?'

The girl didn't dare to look up and whispered something into her lap.

'That's correct, Ruth,' said Cornwall. 'We should seek the truth, and only then forgive.' Now he spoke softly. 'But perhaps also, we should understand why this person refuses to admit he's seen the Devil.'

'Is he in league with Lucifer?' said Mary Cadebridge – the woman who had first volunteered to take in Old Ralph.

'A question indeed, good wife,' said Cornwall, striding back towards the chancel. He turned to face us, raising the folds of his chasuble to resemble a great swan, before roaring as loudly as I have ever heard a person address a congregation. 'It might explain why he will not lead us to them! Why he repeatedly denies they exist!'

I went to speak, but Brother Peter held me back. 'Keep your peace, Oswald. Say nothing.'

Cornwall dropped his arms and strolled over to me. 'Sire? Is there a truth you would like to impart?' His voice was as smooth and deceiving as a spoon of boiling treacle.

'Don't be provoked,' whispered Peter. 'He will use your words against you.'

My heart thumped so heavily it might be punching its way out of my chest. I had seen the Devil in the forest. It wasn't a hallucination. I wanted to confess. But before having the chance to say a word, Peter had taken me by the arm and was pushing me towards the door.

'Lord Somershill has seen the dog heads, but denies them,' said Cornwall, standing in our way. 'Why doesn't he answer the charge?'

'Get out of the way,' said Peter. 'This boy is your lord.'

Cornwall raised his wings once more. 'If the boy won't answer me, then he must answer to the Lord of us all. The Lord redeemer. The King of Heaven.'

Peter whispered into my ear, 'Move. Now!'

At our last confrontation in this church it had been Cornwall who left in humiliation, but now it was my turn. As I was swept through the door by Peter, I caught sight of Mirabel at last. She smiled at me sadly and then looked to her feet.

We stumbled out into the bright sunlight and put a good distance between ourselves and St Giles before stopping. Peter was red in the face and breathing heavily. 'Why does that man feel emboldened to speak to you in such a way, Oswald? He is nothing but a country parson.'

I slumped down in some long grass. Wearied and defeated. 'I think it has something to do with the earl.'

'What?'

'The earl has taken sides with de Caburn.'

Peter frowned – the sunlight catching the deep lines across his forehead. 'How do you know this?'

'The earl has written to de Caburn and given his blessing to the wedding. Cornwall knows I'm in a weak position.' I sighed. 'Everybody is against me now.'

Peter sat down beside me. 'Why didn't you tell me this before?'

I laid my head on his shoulder. 'I thought you would become angry again.'

'Of course I wouldn't. Though you should have told me, Oswald.'

I picked a blade of grass and pulled my fingers along the stalk to release the seeds. 'I want to give up the estate, Brother. Let Clemence and de Caburn have it.'

'Don't be so foolish.'

'But I could go back to the monastery with you. Take my vows and return to the infirmary. It would be easier than this.'

Peter patted my head. 'No, Oswald. We will fight them.'

'I don't want to.'

'Of course you do.'

'But—'

'Somershill is yours.'

Chapter Twelve

I walked to the river alone and watched the heron fishing for trout. A corncrake made its rasping call from a nearby hayfield, as the bees worked tirelessly at the foxgloves and comfrey. What a simple life such creatures lived. There were no lords or villeins. No churches or courts of law. No arranged marriages and bastard children. I considered diving into that river and breathing in its watery air until it turned me into a fish. Then I could swim away and hide for ever under the lily pads. Recognising my bout of self-pity for what it was, I straightened up and made for the house.

Returning to Somershill, a curious sight awaited me. Brother Peter was saddling up a horse at the same time as Mother was trying to unsaddle the creature. A tug of war was taking place between the two of them, which made me smile for the first time that day. The horse was a tired old pony that we had more or less abandoned to the field.

Mother saw me and dropped her side of the saddle. 'Brother Peter is returning to the abbey. You have to stop him.'

'I'm making a short visit, that's all, my lady,' said Peter, now tying the strap of the saddle underneath the horse's flank. The pony, for all of her breed's supposed placidity, was shying away from Peter. She had been happier eating clover and buttercups in the field.

'Tell him he can't go,' said Mother. 'It's only a week to Clemence's wedding. He must be here to conduct the ceremony.'

Peter patted the pony. 'I'm sure John of Cornwall will be delighted to perform the ceremony if I'm not back in time.'

Mother threw up her hands. 'Father John? No thank you. That man knows as much Latin as this pony.' It seemed we were not the only ones to have noticed Cornwall's linguistic shortcomings.

I turned to Peter. 'Why are you going to the abbey so suddenly? Have you received a letter from the other brothers?'

Mother interrupted. 'He's free to go after the marriage. But I can't have the Ayres and Peverils listening to Cornwall's nonsense. They might think the marriage isn't legal.'

'I'll return within the week, I promise. Please stand aside, my lady. So I may mount this beast.' Peter tried to get a foothold in the stirrup, but missed.

Mother now stamped her foot. 'Oswald! You're the lord here. Do something.'

If only I had a silver coin for each reminder of my duties, I would buy a cog ship and sail to the land of Amazon. I took the reins of the pony, noting Peter's breath was more pungent than usual – which would explain his difficulty in getting into the saddle.

'Let me speak with Brother Peter alone,' I told Mother. 'I'm sure we can solve this problem.' Mother looked at me guardedly for a moment. 'I'll do my best to convince him to stay.' With a show of reluctance, she wandered back to the house.

When we were certain Mother was out of earshot, Peter drew me closer. 'I'm going to see the bishop. Not the abbot.'

'In Rochester?'

'Yes. I'm going to ask him to find Cornwall a richer parish.'

'Where?'

Peter threw up his hands. 'What do I care? All I know is we

can't allow Cornwall to remain here. Not after what happened in church this morning.'

'I could remove him myself, Brother. The lord appoints the parish priest.'

'That's true, Oswald. But now Cornwall has the protection of the earl, you might find it a little difficult. We are better to tempt him away to a more lucrative church.'

'But you can't just saunter in and make demands of the bishop.'

Peter coughed. 'The man is in my debt. And don't ask me why, because I won't tell you.'

'You really think this will work?'

'Yes, Oswald. Have faith.'

I helped Peter onto his mount and placed his saddlebags over the pony's rump. The bags were heavy and made a chinking sound as I moved them. 'I see you're taking some provisions.'

Peter reddened a little. 'The bishop isn't generous with his cellar. Also, I may need to get past a few men in order to speak with him.' He patted the bag. 'It's always useful to have something to bargain with.' He leant down from his pony and motioned for me to draw close. Placing a hand on my shoulder, he said, 'Promise me something, Oswald. It's very important.'

'What is it?'

'Stay away from Cornwall while I'm gone. And if he insists on confronting you about the dog heads, say nothing.'

'But Brother Peter—'

'Just do as I say, for once.' I heaved a sigh. 'Please, Oswald.' I nodded grudgingly and he moved away.

And then an idea suddenly struck me and I chased after him across the meadow. 'Brother Peter. Would you ask the bishop about the beads?'

He pulled the pony to a stop. 'Which beads?'

'The ones I found under Matilda's bed. You were going to show them to Brother Thomas. Remember?'

He screwed up his nose. 'But why would I show a handful of loose beads to the bishop?'

'Because you said they were likely to belong to such a man.'

Peter pulled a face. 'You want me to ask the bishop if he owns some jewellery that was found under the bed of a murdered girl?' Now he laughed. 'I fear we would not find him too cooperative after such a question.'

'I'll have them back then,' I said.

'Sorry?'

'You do still have the beads?'

He patted his belt pouch. 'Yes. Of course I do. But——'

I held out my hand. 'Thank you, Brother.'

Peter hesitated, then opened the pouch and let the beads fall into my palm like a cascade of tiny haw berries. I closed my hand about them tightly, in case he asked for them back.

Peter turned the pony and trotted away across the meadow. Reaching the gate, he called back to me, 'Tell your mother I'll return towards the end of the week.'

I watched him leave, seeing his image become smaller and smaller until it disappeared completely between the trees. And then, for all the times he had annoyed me, I suddenly missed him.

The week wore on, but it did not bring Peter back to us. The longer he was missing, the more Mother and Clemence blamed me for his continued absence. As if I had deliberately set out to ruin the wedding by denying them a qualified priest.

When the Peverils and Ayres began to arrive, Mother panicked that Brother Peter would never return. She then called upon Cornwall and demanded he learn the Latin marriage service by heart. There were rumours that the earl himself would attend the ceremony, so she did not want to be made a laughing stock by the inadequacies of our parish priest.

With my sister's wedding looming, the house was filled with clamour and cooking, stirred together with bad temper and tears. As a result I kept to myself as much as possible.

De Caburn was yet to make an appearance, and Clemence felt his absence keenly. She excused him with fibs and stories, but it was a slight even Clemence did not deserve. Not that anybody could criticise de Caburn in front of my sister. When Mother joked that her husband-to-be seemed so disinterested in the wedding, he might as well send one of his servants to say the vows at the church, Clemence almost stabbed Mother with a tapestry needle.

Clemence should have been blossoming as the wedding approached, but unfortunately the unpleasant atmosphere in the house reflected itself across my sister's face. The creases around her mouth had deepened, and her teeth seemed permanently clenched.

At least there happened to be one person, other than myself of course, who was content with the absence of de Caburn. I heard Humbert asking Ada if Clemence would really go ahead with the marriage – his tone childishly hopeful that she would not. Ada laughed at the boy's question and warned him to find a new mistress, since there was no chance he would follow Clemence to Versey Castle. Everybody knew de Caburn kept as few house servants as a common wool merchant. Humbert sloped away into a corner at these words, where he hid as dolefully as an injured animal.

Humbert had done well to find a quiet place in such a full house. I tried to read my *Summa Theologica* by Thomas Aquinas in the chapel, but was constantly interrupted by a small boy from the Ayres family, who wanted me to practise archery with him, or play hide and seek.

The Ayres were at least tolerable guests.

Not so the Peverils. They were my mother's family from Winchester, and liked to mention with predictable regularity that they were descended from William of Normandy. They rode into Somershill with an entourage of servants, and took my bedchamber, although they had not been offered this room. When I expressed my surprise at their number, Mother informed me the Peverils had survived the Plague by isolating themselves in the family castle with a year's worth of provisions and an armed guard at the door.

At our first family feast, a pallid young girl called Geraldine was made to stay sitting next to me at dinner, as one by one everybody else left. She was one of the Peveril party and about as good company as a hermit crab. When I also tried to leave, my exit from the hall was blocked by Mother, who more or less ordered me to resume my place at the table and make conversation with the girl.

I sat back down a little further away than before and attempted to do as instructed. As Gilbert and two of the newly hired servants from the village cleared the plates, I asked Geraldine's opinion on such subjects as the trajectory of Venus or the writings of Pope Pius. But she seemed to hold no opinions on these matters whatsoever. In fact, it was difficult to get her to say anything at all, such was her air of apathy and dejection.

After a few more attempts to converse, only to be answered by sullen mumbles and shrugs, I changed my line of attack and demanded to know if she knew the reason for us being so obviously left alone. My sudden firmness woke her from her stupor and I soon discovered she was my second cousin, aged thirteen, and that we were betrothed. By her demeanour she was as unimpressed with this arrangement as I.

When I looked up to see Mother spying at us from the squint in the solar, I beckoned for her to join me in the great hall. Before Mother descended, I suggested Geraldine take a walk to the stables and look at the horses, which she did without a fragment of enthusiasm or energy.

When Mother appeared, I dragged her to the cellar – which was the one place in the house we could be sure of being alone.

Once Mother had found a seat on a barrel, I closed the door. 'Have you organised a marriage between me and this girl?' I asked.

Mother played with the wire of her crespine nervously as the rush light threw shadows across her sallow skin. 'Don't you like her?'

'No. I don't.'

'She's a little pale, I'll grant. But that's because she's bleeding. I've seen her rags.' She seemed not to notice the look of disgust on my face. 'I'm sure by Sunday she will have assumed a rosier tone.'

'Have you organised a marriage?' I said. 'Yes or no?'

She took my hand. 'It's a good match, Oswald. The girl is a Peveril. Directly from William himself.'

'From his bastard son, you mean.'

'What does that matter? William Peveril was still the son of a king. The line is good.'

I pulled my hand away. 'I don't want to marry that girl. Now please reverse the arrangement.'

She stood up and crossed her arms. 'What's wrong with her?'

'I don't like her.'

Mother puffed. 'She isn't the most handsome of girls, but she'll get better with age. As I've always told you, Oswald, don't judge a girl too soon. A pretty foal will make an ugly mare.'

'I didn't mean Geraldine's appearance. I tried to converse with her, but I might as well have been talking to the wall.'

'What did you ask her about?' Then she rolled her eyes. 'Not the writings of Pope Pius, I hope?'

'She wasn't interested in anything I like.'

'What does that matter?' Waving a finger in my face, she spoke sharply. 'Your only responsibility is to father children, Oswald. Whether you bother to speak to the girl is beside the point.'

'It's not beside the point to me. It's important she should share my interests.'

Now she flung her hands up, as if in despair. '*Interests?* Share your interests with Brother Peter. Or even your friends at the tavern. All you need to share with your wife is your seed.'

I groaned again. 'Why do you say such things, Mother? It's revolting.'

This almost seemed to please her. 'Let's drink a little of the wine Brother Peter hides away in here,' she said. 'Where is it?'

'It's behind the ale barrel. Unless he took it with him.'

She found the bottle and poured me a cup. 'You should marry the girl, Oswald. You'll need sons.'

I quickly downed some wine to ease the pain of this conversation. 'I can marry when I'm older.' I passed her the cup, but she waved it away.

'No. You need to get on with it. You could die at any moment.'

'That's encouraging. Thank you, Mother.'

'The girl won't last beyond a first child. She doesn't look as if she could spit out a walnut from those hips. But, at least if the boy survives, you'll have an heir.'

I took a second gulp from the cup. 'More words of encouragement?' The wine was taking immediate effect. 'You're such a beacon of hope.'

'You're not a child any more, Oswald. I want the estate to succeed to a de Lacy. Not a de Caburn. Do you understand me?'

I stared at her blankly.

She poked a finger into my arm. 'If you don't hurry up and produce a child, then de Caburn or one of his offspring will have this place.'

I snorted. 'At least it would be Clemence's child. She's a de Lacy.'

Mother huffed and waved her hand at me. 'Clemence won't bear de Caburn a child. She's too old.'

'She's only twenty-six. You gave birth to me at forty.'

'But my bleeding was regular, Oswald. Clemence is like the river Guise. She either floods or dries out. It's no good for planting a seed.'

This conversation was nauseating, drunk or not. I stood up to leave, inventing some task that needed doing. 'I must inspect the plough heads with Featherby. I promised him earlier.'

'Why? You won't be ploughing again for months.'

'Featherby must be confused,' I mumbled.

'I doubt it. He was your father's reeve for years. But I find he stands too close, don't you? I can smell the fumes from his stomach.'

'I must go, Mother.'

'Will you at least consider marrying Geraldine?'

'No.'

I slept badly again that night, but my dream was different this time. I was not lying in that filthy cottage waiting for Peter to lance my skin. Instead I dreamt of the marriage that Mother proposed.

It was the night of my wedding. Geraldine called me to bed, where she lay naked upon sheets stained in blood. I wanted to run away but she bade me kiss her, as Mother and Lady Peveril watched us through the squint. Her body was as scrawny and bony as a street donkey's, and though I resolved to do my duty, she smelt unpleasant and sickly, like the marzipan sweets I had once been given by an Italian merchant. As Geraldine opened her thin, broomstick legs, a host of small silver snakes slipped out from within her and slithered across the sheets towards me, their tongues flicking and their heads flexing from left to right.

Waking from this horror I sat bolt upright, not recognising the room about me. Then the moon crept out from behind a cloud and shone through the window to illuminate the ladies bedchamber where I had recently been forced to sleep with Mother and Clemence.

Mother nudged me and smiled. 'You called Geraldine's name, Oswald. Were you dreaming of her?'

'No, Mother.'

She nudged me again and I heard Hector growl. Evidently we were disturbing the dog's sleep. 'Are you sure, Oswald? It sounded pleasant.'

'It was a nightmare. And no. I will not marry her.' I pulled the sheets over my head and turned my back.

Having considered my decision on this marriage arrangement to be unequivocal, the next day I was astounded to overhear Mother scheming with Lady Peveril. Their plan was crude and disagreeable, and involved a hunting party organised solely with the intention of abandoning Geraldine and myself in the forest with only a flagon of wine for company. The thought of such an unpleasant outing was enough to provoke a quick escape from the house and a day in hiding.

I kept to the edge of the fields and near to the woods at a good distance from the house, in case Gilbert or any of the other servants caught sight of me. When I heard my name being called, I disappeared further into the trees. I even thought to visit Alison's grave, but the church was too busy with preparations for the wedding and I would surely be discovered. But there was one place where nobody would find me. The deserted Starvecrow cottage.

As my feet found their way to the small valley where Alison and Matilda's home was situated, I decided to take another look about the cottage with the vague idea of seeking out some evidence that I might have missed on previous occasions. The sky had clouded over and a silver rinse seemed to have washed the colour from the world. Once again I had the impression of being watched, but dismissed the feeling. My mind was tired. I hadn't slept properly for days, and perhaps I was even in danger of suffering another bout of hallucinations.

The grass and nettles around the cottage had grown even higher, and the fallen apple tree was now diverting the stream across the vegetable patch as well as through the hog hole.

Managing to stay upright, I descended the steep bank to the cottage. My descent was made easier because the long grass appeared freshly trodden.

Once reaching my destination, I found the cottage to be as pitiful as before, hiding away in this lonely hollow, like a dog waiting to die. Wedging the door open I ventured inside, but the place felt different. The wooden bench had been removed, which was only to be expected I suppose, since a neighbour had probably taken a liking to it. But it was more than that. The cottage felt somehow occupied.

I pushed around in the wood ash of the fire pit with my foot, and something immediately roused my suspicions. Kneeling down, I felt the embers with my hands. They were warm.

And then, behind me, the door slammed and I jumped – for I had made sure to fix it open. It was now dark and eerie in the windowless cottage, so I went briskly to re-open the door and shed some light back into the room, only to find it was stuck fast. I pushed with all my strength, but the wood would only budge a little, and not nearly enough for me to squeeze out through the gap.

Then, hearing the rustling of legs through the long grass outside, I kicked at the wood ferociously until it gave way. Now free, I could see somebody had jammed a forked branch against the door in order to keep me trapped inside.

I ran up the bank to follow the footsteps and soon found myself enclosed by woodland. The smooth grey trunks of beech trees surrounded me like the stone pillars in the crypt of Rochester Cathedral, enveloping the silence into a circle of soft and heavy air. In the distance a woodpecker drummed against a tree.

I called out. 'Who's there? Is it you?' But nobody answered. 'Come out! Show yourself!' But nothing happened.

It was a lost opportunity, and as I dragged my feet back towards the cottage, I cursed myself for not catching up with my assailant. Then, as I looked to the ground with some dejection, I noticed the footprints in the damp mud. They were only lightly trodden into the soil, but were freshly made and could only have been made by the person I had been pursuing. Who else would come to this lonely and damp spot?

The footprints led me further into the wood, ending in a basin where they circled and ended. A small stream cut through this shaded dell, but its waters were muddy and shallow and of little use to anybody, when cleaner water could be found nearer to the village. There seemed no reason why a person would come here. I looked about the dell, catching my face in the silk threads of a spider's web. Pulling the sticky gauze from my hair, I noticed an area of disturbed soil beneath the holly.

It was a rectangle of earth. Just the size of a young girl's grave.

I knelt down and put my ear to the soil as if the clay might give up its secrets, but could only hear the beating of my own heart in my ears – thumping in anticipation of my next task.

I had no choice.

I pulled at the soil with my bare hands, though the clay was sticky and cold. After excavating a small hole to the depth of a foot I found nothing, and it had taken me nearly an hour. The earth was still recently disturbed, so I knew the hole went deeper, but a spade was needed to finish this appalling job.

And then I felt something upon my neck. A breath. I turned. Shadows danced between the trees. Eyes watched me.

'Who's there?' I called again, but once again nobody answered. A twig snapped. Light flickered. Leaves rustled. A cold breeze brushed against my skin.

I was terrified. I picked up a heavy stick and rushed into the undergrowth, hoping to flush out this demon – only to disturb a squawking blackbird and its dull-brown mate. They had been looking for worms in the leaf cover. I put a hand to my neck again and discovered the ghostly breath had been nothing more than the tickle of a spider.

I dropped her leggy body to the ground and might even have laughed, except this was hardly funny.

I returned to Somershill and sought out Gilbert.

I found my servant in the kitchen – no more pleased to see me than he might have been to find a wasp in the honey jar. Clemence's wedding was taking place the next morning, and Gilbert was now busy skinning rabbits and cleaning the spits. His fingernails were black. I whispered to him through the kitchen window and kept my voice low, not wanting to alert Mother to my presence, as she was said to be furious with me following my disappearance.

Gilbert made a show of resentment at being pulled away from his many tasks in the kitchen, so I thought about asking Piers instead. But this was not a job for a stableboy. I needed a man with Gilbert's strength and Gilbert's stomach. Reluctantly the burly servant fetched two spades and followed me back to the wooded glade, though he muttered the whole way about being on a fool's errand.

We dug for a further hour to the accompaniment of Gilbert's complaints that we would find nothing more than a dead dog or a rusty kettle at the bottom of this hole.

I wish he had been right.

The first part of her body to be exposed was the blackened skin of a small and decaying foot. The flesh was bloated and already slipping away from the bone. Gilbert crossed himself and was unwilling to continue unless we called upon Father John to join us – but Cornwall was the last person I wanted at this exhumation. The body was clothed in a simple woollen gown and immediately the scent of her corpse attracted flies. She had been dead for maybe three weeks, given the progress of the putrefaction.

A surge of nausea rose through my stomach as I waved the bluebottles away. 'Let's quickly unearth her face and we can be certain of her identity.'

'But surely it's the Starvecrow girl, isn't it, sire?'

I sighed. 'I expect so.'

We removed the soil from her chest and arms until we reached her upper body. Her neck was gored and mutilated, but as we dug further into the grave, we found no head attached to it. It seemed it had been removed completely.

I let out a groan and this time could not prevent myself from emptying the contents of my stomach into a nearby bush. Gilbert crossed his chest and fell to his knees. 'Jesus Christ. The creatures have eaten her head.'

'Be quiet, Gilbert.'

'Where is it then, sire?'

I splashed some water from the stream onto my own face and swilled a handful about my mouth to remove the taste of bile. I then held my nose and looked down into the grave at this wretched sight. A bloated and rotting body with a mutilated stump instead of a head. 'Is that you, Matilda?' I whispered.

Gilbert struggled back to his feet. 'What should we do now, sire?'

'Cover her back with soil.'

Gilbert frowned. 'But she should be buried in the churchyard. Head or not.'

'Of course. But I want to leave her here for a little while longer.'

'Why?'

'That's my business.'

'But sire?' His face was now furrowed.

I hesitated to tell him the truth, but Gilbert was not a simple man. He should not have been shocked by my answer. 'I want Brother Peter to examine her body before she is properly laid to rest. There may be some information to be gathered from her corpse.' I put my hand upon his muscular arm. 'You must keep this quiet. Do you understand?'

Gilbert crossed himself. 'It seems ungodly to me.'

'Please.' He still did not look convinced. 'Think of the distress this would cause before the wedding, Gilbert. Let's at least wait until Clemence is married.'

He sighed. 'As you like, sire.' Then he muttered under his breath, 'God forgive us.'

That night I sneaked back to the graveyard to tell Alison that our sister was found. It was still and quiet as I whispered into the soil.

Did I hear her sigh?

Or was it just the slither of a snake in the long grass?

Chapter Thirteen

If the eve of Clemence's wedding was marred by the discovery of a murdered girl, then the morning of the day itself was no more auspicious. The rain, which had kept away for a week, arrived in a fierce deluge, with so strong a downpour that a loose tile gave way on the roof of the great hall, causing water to fall onto the fire.

Mother insisted Gilbert climb up and replace the tile despite the heaviness of the rainstorm. He scrambled across the roof cursing and blaspheming, while the Peverils sat below on a bench, looking as disgusted as a row of Mother Superiors. Had they never heard the coarse language of a servant before? Mother assured me their sneers were testimony to the nobility of their French blood, and reminded me of this breeding were I to marry into the family. But one look at Geraldine's conceited face was enough to convince me I would never take this girl as my wife. No matter how superior her family claimed to be.

After the tile was replaced, Mother retired to the solar to soothe my sister's brain by combing her hair. Clemence was said to be suffering from a headache, but given the screams and scolding that could then be heard about the house, it was evident Mother's treatment was neither gratefully received, nor working. The rest of us waited in the great hall, uneasy and embarrassed.

To avoid conversing with my aunt Hillary, a woman who liked

to grill me in Latin gerunds, I made for the kitchen to watch Gilbert preparing for the wedding feast. The smell of wheat bread slipped out from the ovens and filled the room with a warm sweet aroma, which put me in mind of previous feasts held in the great hall – particularly the lavish banquets given by my father. They had been great celebrations of our family's status and wealth. The tables spread with spiced meats, peaches and pears, cakes decorated in elaborate sugar creations, cheeses from every corner of England, and wines from France and Italy. Now the most exotic offering to our guests was white bread.

I might have wanted to hide away in the kitchen, but I was not welcome there. Not only was my presence distracting for the servants, but Gilbert had not forgiven me regarding the grave in the forest. He threw me hostile glances and crossed himself repeatedly until I left the chamber and went instead to wait by the gatehouse, in the hope that Brother Peter would miraculously return in time for the wedding.

The shadow of the headless body hung over me like a pall, and it was impossible to uphold the pretence of joy at Clemence's union that Mother had firmly instructed me to maintain. My previous night's sleep had once again been disturbed by the same nightmare. The filthy cottage. The knife at my skin. The rosary over my face. I wished Peter would return. I was tired and frightened and felt bereft without him.

De Caburn finally made an appearance at Somershill around noon, though he had been drinking heavily and had not changed his tunic for a clean over-kirtle, despite this being his wedding day. At the arrival of his noisy party, I slipped into the cellar to avoid seeing him and his unpleasant friends – one of whom was certainly the man with the battle-scarred skin. I did not see his face, but knew him to be the same person – since the low boom of his voice rattled the bottles on the cellar shelves.

De Caburn and his entourage did not stay long at the manor, as Mother soon shooed them away to the village with warnings of the bad luck they would bring upon the marriage should they see the bride before the ceremony.

I am told they gladly left and went straight to the village tavern.

When absolutely certain they were gone, I wandered into the garden. The rain had ceased for a while, although the sky was still as grey as a muddy puddle. And then, on an impulse, I picked some roses for Clemence from the Damask bush – an old rose that grew against the warm wall of the chapel. Mother said it came from Persia and had been sold to my grandfather by a crusader, who swapped it for enough money to buy a new pair of shoes. Each year we thought the rare and precious rose might die, but then its ancient fist of wood gave forth a new crop of green shoots, which sprouted up as vigorously as if the bush were only just planted.

I reached for one of its crimson blooms, and though the petals were dotted with rain drops, its scent was as heady as ever. Picking a number of stems, I ran to give them to my sister as she passed through the great hall. She took the posy from me with some grace, but then threw it back and cursed. A thorn had pierced her finger and blood had seeped onto her gown.

As the rain continued to pour, Clemence de Lacy was married to Walter de Caburn in the porch of St Giles church, as was the custom. The ceremony was hastily conducted in front of the whole village by Father John of Cornwall, the priest with little Latin. Thankfully the earl did not attend.

When the vows were finished, the village onlookers made their customary exclamations in praise of the beauty of the bride and the dignity of her new husband. But their words were a sham. The rain had leached Clemence's rouge into pink stripes. And de Caburn, far from being a chivalrous knight, looked more like a guttersnipe who had stolen a barrel of ale and drunk it all himself. For my own part, it was impossible to feel any joy at this union, and as petals were thrown into the newlyweds' path, I stepped back to avoid catching Clemence's eye.

The Peverils were even more disgusted by the appearance of my sister and her new husband than they had been by the missing tile. But at least the bedraggled bride and groom diverted attention from Cornwall's Latin – though it was clear he had been practising, since his rendition of the vows was more passable than the mass I had attended. Nevertheless, it was still a hopeless cobble of incorrect vocabulary and poorly declined nouns. I noted Aunt Hillary's exasperated puffs at each of his grammatical errors.

With the ceremony and blessing completed, there was just one more obligation to fulfil before we could finally think about the wedding feast. A progress to the well of St Blaise, to take holy waters with the bride.

The well was only a short walk from the church, but I still heard de Caburn protesting, especially as the visit involved drinking something as dreary as spring water. But Mother stood her ground with him. The de Lacys always took the well water after a marriage. Indeed, she had sent Gilbert to the well that same morning to cover the shrine in flowers. When de Caburn continued to complain, Mother pointed her finger at her new son-in-law and advised him to think of his heirs. If Clemence drank the waters of the well she would produce a son within the year. It seemed this promise, if nothing else, persuaded de Caburn that the visit was worth the effort.

We progressed up the woodland path towards the spring, and then gathered about the entrance to the well – waiting for Clemence and de Caburn to descend the stone steps, take the first cup and then invite the other women of the estate to join them in drinking the miraculous waters. They were gone only a few moments before we heard a high-pitched scream, followed by the sight of Clemence bursting from the cave, accompanied by her new husband and Mother.

'What's the matter?' I grabbed Mother's arm, but for once the woman was speechless.

I pushed through and ran down the steps towards the well, but found nothing immediately terrifying. I wondered whether Clemence had been spooked by her own reflection, as I had been at my last visit, so I leant over the large basin and looked into the water, but saw only my own face. It was the same as last time — my own blond hair and pale blue eyes looked back at me.

But then something caught my eye, for my likeness was not the only inhabitant of this water. There was something else lurking beneath the surface. I looked closer. But it was not a smooth stone, nor even a pilgrim's ampulla. It was a globe of blackened flesh, surrounded by a halo of floating golden hair.

My heart thumped, but this time I did not back against the wall. Instead I took a few deep breaths before putting my arm into the trough and trying to lift the head out by its hair. The hair was fine and slippery and difficult to grasp, and when I did pull it from the water, it came away in a mat, leaving the rest of her skull behind.

I felt sick.

Now I could hear Mother shouting for me at the top of the steps, so I called for her to stay where she was. I then plunged my hands into the water a second time, and now scooped out the whole of the head. Large maggots had burrowed into the slit across her neck and wriggled in my hands.

I quickly wrapped the head in my cloak and turned to find Gilbert's face behind me. His face was as grey as the walls of the cave.

'It's Matilda, isn't it?' he said.

I nodded.

'At least we can bury the girl now.'

Leaving the well we found Mother and a noisy crowd had gathered at the top of the stairs. Cornwall pushed his way through their shocked faces. 'So, the beast has attacked again.'

I ignored the statement and told the villagers to step back and let me pass. But instead they pressed forward.

'Sire. Is it true you have the head of Matilda Starvecrow?' Cornwall asked me, pointing at the small package that I cradled in my arms.

'Yes, it is. Now let me through.' Nobody moved.

'This is a bad omen,' said Mother. 'Clemence's marriage is cursed.'

'Be quiet,' I said, hoping Clemence had not heard her own mother's words. Thankfully my sister was slumped under a tree a few yards away, whilst being fanned by Ada. De Caburn and his friends were gathered not far from her and seemed to have found the whole incident amusing. The battle-scarred man caught my eye and waved.

'It's not a curse,' I said quickly. 'Matilda's head was left here by her murderer.'

'The head wasn't in the well this morning,' said Gilbert. 'When I put flowers on the shrine.'

'Has anybody else been up here since?' I said, looking about me.

Most shook their heads, but a boy found his tongue. 'We've all been at the church, sire. Except for Old Ralph.'

'And his daughter,' said a woman, with breasts the size of whole cheeses.

'Old Ralph has advanced gangrene in his arm,' I told them, 'and Joan Bath is locked in the village gaol. Neither of them could have put Matilda's head here.'

'Then you agree this is the work of the dog heads?' said Cornwall, keen to re-establish his place at the centre of this drama.

I was sorely tempted to reply to this statement, but remembered my promise to Brother Peter. Instead I held my hands up to address the crowd. 'You should all proceed to the wedding feast.' There was a slight movement at the mention of food, but nobody seemed eager to leave apart from the Peverils. I soon saw their fine clothes disappearing through the trees.

'We must bury this head immediately,' said Cornwall. 'Though not in the churchyard.'

'Why not?'

Cornwall crossed himself solemnly. 'Because we do not have her whole body.'

'I don't see why that should—'

'Lord Somershill and I know where the rest is,' Gilbert suddenly announced. 'We found it yesterday.' I glared at my servant and rolled my eyes to show him my displeasure at making this revelation.

Cornwall turned to look at me. He was momentarily confused rather than accusatory.

'Is this true, Oswald?' said Mother.

I sighed. 'Yes. It is. We found a headless body buried in the forest.' A wave of dismay ran through the crowd. 'We believed it was the corpse of Matilda. Unfortunately we now have the head to prove it.'

Mother went to say something, but Cornwall spoke over her. A vein throbbed at his temple. 'Then the girl should have been buried yesterday, sire. Why did you not summon me?'

I hesitated, knowing any response would be greeted with scorn — so was grateful when Gilbert stepped in to answer Cornwall's question. He must have felt guilty for previously blurting out our secret. 'Lord Somershill asked me to fetch you, Father John. But it was late last night and I decided not to rouse you.'

'Why ever not?' Cornwall turned on my servant.

'You had the wedding mass to say today, Father. I thought the burial of a headless corpse might upset your humours.'

Cornwall glowered. 'It is not for you to decide such matters. I am perfectly capable of conducting a funeral and a wedding within a day.'

I quickly intervened. 'Gilbert behaved correctly, Father. Such news would have disrupted my sister's wedding.'

Cornwall sucked his teeth and then I would say he almost smiled. 'Instead it has been disrupted by a head in a holy well.'

The crowd broke up slowly after I had sent Gilbert and two other men to exhume the other part of Matilda's body. Avoiding any further confrontation with Cornwall, I quickly took Matilda's head to the gaol house for Joan Bath to look upon. I had hoped such a grisly sight might shock the woman into some form of confession, or even to reveal her accomplices. But she simply repeated her denials, before crouching in the corner of the cell with her hands over her face.

Leaving Matilda's head at the gaol house, I belatedly made my way back to the great hall at Somershill for the wedding celebration, but was met by a glum scene. The bride and groom had already left for Versey Castle. The Peverils had also departed in haste, believing Matilda to have been killed by the Plague. And the tile had once again fallen from the roof so that the roasting pig was being doused in rainwater.

Mother sat alone on the dais, gnawing at a bone. Behind her, in a dark corner, sat Humbert, holding a square of my sister's embroidery to his cheek and looking as bereft as an orphan at his parents' grave.

Mother waved a rib at me. 'Have some pork, Oswald. It's rather fatty, but it shouldn't affect your phlegm. As long as you eat some onions afterward.'

I dipped a pewter cup into a barrel of ale, picked off a piece of bone and sat next to Mother, attempting to ignore the way she was dislodging pig meat from her teeth with a strand of her own hair.

'Well, I'm glad that's over,' she said.

'So am I.'

'But the wedding went well, don't you think, Oswald?'

I choked on the rib. 'Apart from finding the head of a murdered girl.'

She laughed. 'Oh, that. There were *two* men murdered at my wedding feast. And my cousin lost an eye.'

'In that case, Mother, Clemence's wedding was a great success.'

Having finished with the wedding feast, I made my way back to the gaol house with the intention of examining both parts of Matilda's corpse before she was buried – to ensure, if nothing else, that we were making a correct match between her head and body. But on reaching my destination, I was met by the shame-faced gaoler Henry Smith, who informed me that Matilda was now being buried. Demanding to know on whose authority he had released the corpse, Henry admitted that it was Cornwall's.

By the time I reached the churchyard of St Giles, Matilda was already beneath the soil, lying alongside her sister Alison. Onlookers gathered about her grave, shedding their false tears – the very same people who would have seen this pitiful girl married to Old Ralph. A man four times her age.

Old Ralph himself had somehow staggered to the burial, although those about him were giving him and his arm a wide berth. It was little surprise to see he was near death and that his herbal ointment had failed to cure the gangrene.

I interrupted Cornwall in the middle of his prayers. 'I did not give you permission to bury Matilda.'

Cornwall kept his eyes shut and continued his words.

'I wished to study her body. And you've ruined that possibility.'

The mourners caught their breath at my words. What fools! Dead bodies were routinely examined at the monastery. I was not intending to despoil or dissect her in any way. But since my last comments were clearly offensive to some present, I had the sense to add, 'I simply wanted to collect more information concerning her death.'

Cornwall opened an eye. 'We all know who is responsible. No further information is needed.'

'It was my daughter, Joan Bath,' shouted Old Ralph from the

back of the crowd. 'It was her that did it. Hang the whore!' He looked about for the others to endorse his condemnation, but they only edged further away from the man and his appalling stink. 'Hang the whore!' he repeated nonetheless.

'Joan couldn't have killed this one, could she, Ralph?' said Woodcock, a peasant farmer with skin the colour of a cobnut. 'She's been in the gaol house since the beginning of June.'

'Joan Bath is still under suspicion,' I quickly told them. 'Given the decay in her body, Matilda was murdered at least three weeks ago. Before Mistress Bath was taken into custody.'

'Then who put her head in the well this morning, sire?' said Woodcock.

I hesitated. It was a good question. 'She must have had an accomplice.'

'But why would they have cut the girl's head off?'

I did not appreciate being cross-questioned by a farmhand, so I told him sternly that I was investigating all possibilities. But the subsequent expression across his face did not portray any confidence in my powers of detection.

'Matilda's body was freshly wounded,' said Cornwall. 'Her neck was still bloodied.' His conclusions were met with nods and amens from the crowd.

I crossed my arms. 'And you're an expert on bodily decay and fatal wounds, are you, Cornwall? Perhaps you're a physician, or a barber surgeon?'

'I'm guided by the Lord, sire. I pray for answers, and they're given to me.'

'How expedient. Does the Lord agree with everything you propose to Him?'

He glared. 'I am merely the tool of the Almighty. I am His obedient servant and His mouthpiece.'

At this nonsense I nearly demanded they exhume Matilda's body a second time. But I stopped myself – not because of my promise to Brother Peter, rather because I could not have gleaned any more information from the cadaver since I did not possess the skills required for such an examination. And I would not have demanded Matilda's dead body be kept above ground until Peter returned, since we had no idea when that might be.

But perhaps more than that, it just felt cruel to disturb Matilda again. Her fragile body had finally been laid to rest, and should remain so.

Then, just as I turned to leave, another commotion unfurled. Following his exertions in attending the burial, Old Ralph had collapsed and was barely breathing. I've heard it said that country life is uneventful, but in my experience the opposite is true. A woman slapped Old Ralph about the face as I tried to rouse him with some oil of Hartshorn. But even its pungent, piss-like aroma would not wake the man, since the poison in his arm must have spread to his heart.

With Old Ralph so near to death, I demanded Cornwall administer the last rites, as the gutless fraud was already backing away from the dying man like a child from a harvest spider. With so many witnesses, Cornwall was obliged to cooperate, although he kept his distance from the stench of Ralph's gangrenous limb.

Minutes later, the old man died. Since we were already in the graveyard I gave the order to bury Old Ralph immediately. Cornwall suggested we lay his body with the Starvecrow sisters, as the ground about their grave was freshly dug. But here, at last, was something I could do for Matilda and Alison. I ordered Old Ralph to be buried at the other side of the graveyard.

He would not lie with them.

Not while I was their lord.

Chapter Fourteen

I left at first light while Ada was sweeping the rushes from the hall and Gilbert was feeding the chickens. Gilbert nodded his head to me, but did not bother to ask where his lord was going at such an early hour of the morning. And I wouldn't have answered him if he had.

This was a journey I should have undertaken two weeks earlier. Instead, I had allowed cowardice to stand in my path and cloak my inaction with his soft robe of excuses. Two girls lay dead in the churchyard. They were my half-sisters. I was certain of that. But I could no longer be certain their murderer was locked in the gaol house.

The sky was grey and low and reflected its cold dullness onto the millpond as I made my way towards the forest. A few souls were working their own strips of land, hunched over fields like snipe birds wading through the reeds. They paid no attention to me, as I was on foot and cut no particular sight – only stopping to tie a bootlace or to take a drink from my leather bottle. A bottle I had made sure to fill with ale.

Once in the forest I followed Gilbert's instructions to head south-west and not to deviate. I had described the ridge of stone to my servant and asked him if he knew such a place. Gilbert had nodded, but did not ask why I wanted to go there. I think he was nervous of becoming caught up in my affairs again. And what would I have told him, if he had asked? That I was searching for a boy who lived in a cave. A boy who could tell me where to find creatures with the heads of dogs.

The forest was quiet and dark – absorbing my footsteps into its verdant world. Sometimes I caught sight of the spotted rump of a fallow deer, as the secretive animals glided silently through the oak and willow. The shrill call of the yellowhammer pierced the air. Squirrels leapt from branch to branch in the high canopy – chattering and hissing at my presence.

But I kept walking. Just one foot in front of another. Finding paths through the trees and undergrowth, always maintaining the south-westerly direction Gilbert had advised me to keep. Every so often I would stop to look up at the sky to locate the position of the sun. Once, when the canopy was too dense, I climbed an oak tree, only to find the clouds were still low and white. But I kept going. Determined to reach my destination.

When I finally came upon the outcrop of rock, fear took hold of me. Not the fear of meeting Leofwin again, nor even the fear of the shadowy creatures with the heads of dogs. I was afraid, instead, that Brother Peter had been right. That the episode I remembered so clearly had indeed been a dream. An illusion caused by a fever. When I looked about me, however, I knew for certain that I had been here before. The ledge along the rock face was familiar, as was the call of the eagles – their cries unnatural and sinister. I walked slowly and cautiously, for if these birds saw me, they would announce my arrival by diving at my head from their high eyries.

I positioned myself below the ridge near the entrance to the cave. It was exactly as I recalled, though at first it seemed to be just a gap in the stone – as dark and uninviting as any cave might appear. It did not appear inhabited and it now struck me that I would have to venture inside this gloomy-looking hole to reassure myself that Leofwin had ever existed. Then, thankfully, a thin trail of smoke spiralled out from the cave and before I could get to my feet, Leofwin appeared from the entrance. As he stepped out onto the stone ledge, the light caught the ridged bone of his forehead.

I stifled a gasp. The boy's face was still astonishing.

But I didn't call out his name – deciding instead to watch him for a while. To see him come and go from this cave, when he thought nobody was looking. He let the sun warm his skin for a few moments, then disappeared inside and reappeared almost immediately with a hessian sack. This sack looked heavy and bulky, and its underside was stained in red. I now felt uneasy.

Leofwin threw the sack over his shoulder then climbed down the rocks towards me with the ease of a wild cat, and suddenly I crouched down behind my tree, fearing he had discovered my hiding place. He passed within yards of me, but did not turn to look. Flies followed him, landing on the liquid that had seeped through the loosely woven hessian and now formed a dripping trail of red behind him.

I knew then, for certain, what the sack held. Something that was dead.

With my heart in my mouth, I followed Leofwin through the forest, but made sure to keep my distance – although, every so often, he would turn on his heels, as if he sensed somebody was behind him. When at last he seemed to relax, I heard him whistle the same nursery rhyme as before. His thin legs were as bandy as a baby's, but his stride was as upright and confident as a knight's – whereas I now felt full of foreboding. Had I been wrong to befriend this boy? Had my pity for him coloured an obvious truth?

After a while we came upon a familiar place – the clearing where the plague pit lay beneath the shade of the beech tree. Vomit rose in my throat as I once again caught the stench of this place.

Wiping my mouth clear of the bitter bile, I looked back into the clearing to see Leofwin untie the sack. I now had the dreadful feeling that he was about to empty the dead thing he carried into the pit alongside the other bodies, where he thought it would lie undetected in its bed of bones. But instead he lifted the sack and dropped its contents upon the ground. Now I almost didn't want to look, half expecting to see a body. The corpse of another murdered girl?

But this was not a human victim. Instead it was a butchered sheep. Skinned, bloody and hacked into pieces.

I let out a sigh of relief, but it was short-lived. For then faces emerged from the trees at the edge of the clearing. Black skulking forms. Strange and sinister creatures, with low, prowling bodies. They crept warily towards the meat, glancing nervously from side to side and tentatively sniffing at the air.

It was then that I realised that Peter had been right all along. I had indeed been fooled the last time I came here by exhaustion and terror. It had been a delusion. I almost laughed at my mistake. For these were not dog-headed beasts. They were simply wolves.

I then stepped a little too far forward and slipped down the leafy bank, announcing my presence to Leofwin and his lupine friends. But only the smallest wolf looked up from the meat and growled at me, baring his long white teeth. The others were too interested in their feast.

Leofwin was angry to see me. 'What are you doing here? You swore not to return.'

'Why are you feeding wolves?'

'None of your business.' He then looked anxiously over my shoulder. 'Have you brought others with you?'

'No.'

Leofwin scanned the clearing nervously. He didn't believe me. 'Then what are you doing here? Leave us alone!'

'Why didn't you tell me it was wolves who circled me that night? You let me believe it was evil phantoms.'

He threw back his head and laughed, revealing his peculiar teeth to their full glory. 'Why do you think?'

'I've no idea,' I said innocently. The small wolf now advanced towards me, and suddenly the others in his pack began to take interest.

'Because you would return to hunt them,' he said.

'But they're dangerous animals, Leofwin. Look at them.' I watched their lithe frames stalk towards me. Their eyes were cruel and yellow. 'The king has decreed they must be eradicated from England.'

Leofwin reddened at my words. 'Who cares what the king says. Not me!'

'But wolves attack people.'

'Only when they've been threatened themselves.'

I instinctively drew my dagger as the creatures began to circle. 'Call them off.' I edged towards the boy.

Leofwin smiled. 'Stay still and drop your knife.'

'But—'

'Just do as I say.'

I took a deep breath and obeyed. The wolves regarded me a while longer.

'Look to the ground and remain still,' Leofwin told me. 'Don't stare them in the eye.' I followed his instructions and slowly the wolves lost interest, retreating to an easier meal.

I spoke softly now and kept my eyes upon the muddy forest floor. 'You put your life in danger by doing this.'

'They won't harm me.'

'You can't be sure of that.'

I looked up to see he had reddened again. 'But if I don't protect them. Who will?'

'Surely they can look after themselves, Leofwin? They are wolves.'

He took me by the arm. 'They are killed when they go near villages. I feed them to make sure they stay in this valley.'

'But why?'

He turned his back on me and wouldn't answer.

'Why, Leofwin? They're wild animals. Vicious and pitiless.'

He whispered, 'Just leave us alone. You don't understand.'

'No. I don't.'

'They are hunted down and killed if they stray outside of this forest.' His teeth sounded gritted. 'They are the same as me.'

'Of course they're not.'

'Yes. They are!' Now he raised his voice. 'Don't you see? There is no place for us in this world.'

We stood in silence with only the sound of teeth on bone.

Leofwin took my arm. 'Do you want to go now?'

I nodded.

'Will you return with hunters and poison?'

'I came here to find dog heads, Leofwin. Not wolves.' I took his hand, gripping his strange webbed fingers. 'I will not return. I give you my word.'

My arrival back at Somershill that evening coincided with Brother Peter's return from Rochester. I was tired, but seemingly not as tired as he. Watching him unsaddle his pony, I noticed the veins across his cheeks had deepened to a spider's web of purple. The whites of his eyes were now as yellow as buttermilk.

After the most cursory of greetings, I followed him to the cellar where I lit the candle and sat myself on a bench, waiting until Peter had poured nearly half a bottle of the honey-coloured liquid into his mouth. With the wine still glistening on the hair of his top lip, he drooped down beside me. The bench creaked a little at his landing.

I would tell you I was concerned about Peter's drinking, but experience had taught me there was no sense in worrying. I had pestered him enough times in the past after the occasional drunken bouts that had nearly ended very badly – such as treading on the abbot's robe at the Easter vigil, or almost amputating Brother Mark's healthy arm.

Brother Peter was past giving up his drink, and now, far from killing him, it seemed to keep him alive. And at least he wasn't an unpleasant drunk, such as Father Luke – an old crab apple of a priest who drank cider until he vomited, and then started all over again.

'How was your visit to the cathedral?' I asked, when Peter finally opened his eyes.

He sat up a little straighter, rubbed his face and rearranged his black Benedictine habit. 'Not so good, I'm afraid, Oswald. The bishop can't help us with Cornwall.'

'Oh. I see.' I attempted to sound surprised, but in my opinion this plan had always been lacking in chances of success.

'The problem is, he has nobody to replace Cornwall.' Peter took another slug of the wine. 'There's hardly a soul left at the cathedral. The bishop has lay monks mixing herbs for the hospital, and altar boys saying mass.' He laughed softly. 'Some might call it sacrilege.'

'So you couldn't call in your favour?'

He frowned. 'Favour?'

'You said the bishop would have to cooperate with you. Remember?'

He waved his hand at me. 'Of course I remember. But the world has turned inside out since the last time I saw the bishop. Old debts are no longer recognised.' He puffed his lips and sighed. 'I don't know what to make of it.'

'So we are stuck with Cornwall,' I groaned.

'It appears so.' He offered me the bottle. 'Here, Oswald. Cheer yourself up with some of this. It's a sweet Malvasia.'

I took it from him, examining the neck and deciding not to drink from it. A small leather cup lay on the floor by a half-empty sack of rye flour. It hadn't been washed since its last use and a sticky residue had fastened itself to the bottom surface. Wiping the cup out with my sleeve, I dislodged a dead fly.

'You know Matilda Starvecrow's head was found in St Blaise's well?' I said, pouring myself some wine.

Peter nodded solemnly. 'The toll keeper told me. Such sad news.'

'It's given Cornwall a whole new wind.'

'Was the girl's throat mutilated?'

I nodded.

Peter took a deep breath and turned to look at me. For the first time ever I noticed his eyes were not symmetrically positioned on either side of his nose, and the hairs growing on his chin were red rather than black. He needed to shave.

He cleared his throat. 'I wanted to speak with you regarding the Cynocephali, Oswald.'

'Oh yes.'

Now he coughed. 'I consulted with the bishop on the matter, and I was quite surprised to hear his opinions. You might be interested to hear that he believes they exist.'

I crossed my arms and frowned. 'Well I know they don't.'

He looked at me quizzically. 'So sure now, Oswald? Not a month ago you claimed to have seen them yourself. By the plague pit.'

It was on the tip of my tongue to tell Brother Peter about the wolves, but I decided against it. I had made a pledge to Leofwin to keep their existence a secret. This time I would keep my promise to the boy. 'I imagined them, Brother. You were right all along.'

'But that's just it. Perhaps you didn't?' His hand was shaking a little. 'If the bishop is certain they exist, then perhaps we should give the story some credence?'

I could hardly believe this turn-around, and must have let my mouth hang open.

'He's a bishop, Oswald. A learned man.'

'So, he's no longer a jackass in a cope. Isn't that what you used to call him?'

'I did not.'

I tried to stand up, but Peter pulled me back down again. 'We must at least consider the possibility, Oswald.'

This topic of conversation was beginning to irritate me. 'Why? It's nonsense. And always has been.'

'But others don't feel that way, Oswald.' He paused a little and then sighed. 'I wish it was not me to tell you this.'

'Tell me what?'

He pinched at the mole on his neck. 'As I was returning from Rochester, I met Cornwall in charge of a pilgrimage. The whole village was with him.' His voice was soft. Almost apologetic.

'That can't be right. The men were harvesting today. I told Featherby to organise it.'

'No, they're weren't, Oswald. They're walking to St John's in the marsh to pray for deliverance.'

'From what?'

'The dog heads of course!'

St John's in the marsh was twenty miles away, meaning this pilgrimage would interrupt work in my fields for at least three days. I stood up again, this time dodging Peter's attempt to grab me. 'I can't allow this to happen. Cornwall didn't ask my permission. I'll have to catch up with them. They can't just leave Somershill at this time of the year.'

Peter jumped nimbly to his feet and put up his arm to block my way. 'No, Oswald. Let them pray for deliverance. Let this whole episode blow over. You have made enough of an enemy of Cornwall.'

'But—'

'Let him sell his pardons and pieces of saint bones. And let him organise his pilgrimage. Your men will be back to work in a couple of days. By then I guarantee they will be bored of the whole matter.'

'Let me pass.'

He pushed me back violently. 'No! Do as I tell you.' I kept

back in the shadows. The candlelight made strange shapes across the damp walls and illuminated the red hairs of Peter's chin.

He took a number of deep breaths and held his chest. 'I'm sorry, Oswald. I've failed you. I encouraged you to investigate these murders. I encouraged you to confront Cornwall. I even travelled to the bishop to try to remove the man. But my interference has only hindered you and made your task here more difficult. I beg you, Oswald. Let this matter lie.'

'But I know the Starvecrow sisters weren't murdered by dog heads. I'm ashamed I ever considered the possibility.' I looked into his tired eyes. 'And you feel the same, don't you, Brother? Regardless of what the bishop has to say.'

He turned to avoid my gaze. 'We must both learn to do what is expedient, Oswald. Otherwise we won't survive. The world outside the monastery is base and brutal. We can no longer afford our high principles and morals.'

'So, now you *want* me to believe in dog heads? Is that what you're saying?'

He stepped forward and took me by the hands. 'What I'm saying is this. Let the villagers have their dog head story. It harms you more to fight it. Release Joan Bath and be done with this matter.'

'But what if she's guilty?'

Peter dropped my hands. 'You've had her locked up in a gaol house for weeks, Oswald. How can she be guilty?'

He reddened a little. It was hot and stuffy in the chamber now, and the candle was giving off the unpleasant odour of burning hair. I noted pearls of sweat across Peter's forehead. He flopped back down on the bench and mopped his brow.

'Don't let's argue. Please.' He patted the bench, motioning for me to sit beside him. I refused, but he held out his hand to me. 'Please, Oswald. We only have each other.' Reluctantly, I joined him.

'Let's examine the evidence against Joan Bath,' he said. 'How do we explain the head in the well? You must concede Joan couldn't have done this.'

'Perhaps her sons did it? The two boys who ran off when she was arrested.'

He nodded. 'It's possible, of course. But why would they do such a thing? With a dead body, Joan can no longer argue the girl has run away. So why would her sons exhume Matilda, remove her head and place it in a holy shrine? It doesn't make sense.'

I stuttered, 'I don't know. But she could still be guilty of the murder of Alison.'

'I disagree. I think both murders were committed by the same perpetrator. The attack at the neck is the main indication.'

'But they were attacked in different ways, Brother. Alison's neck was cut cleanly, whereas Matilda's neck appeared to be hacked away at. And I'm certain her head was removed a long time after her death.'

'What leads you to that conclusion?'

'The maggots on her neck were as large as in a newly made wound.'

'But her corpse had been in the soil. This could have delayed putrefaction.'

I shrugged. In truth I knew too little about the decay of the human body. Particularly once a person had been buried.

'And are you sure Alison's neck was cut?' he asked. 'Not assaulted in some way?'

I thought back to the shaded glade where we first saw Alison Starvecrow's body. The memory was fading, but I recalled thinking of a blade and not a set of teeth. 'I think so,' I said.

'How was her body placed when you found it? Could it have had ritual or pagan meaning?'

'I can't say. She'd been disturbed by Gower's pigs.'

We sat silently for a short while, while Peter drummed his fingers on his cheeks. A mouse scurried across the floor, then stopped perfectly still by the sack of rye flour, thinking if it didn't move, I wouldn't see it. Its heart beat visibly in its tiny chest.

Peter broke the silence. 'To me, these crimes bear the hall-mark of devilry. Particularly the manner in which Matilda's head was deposited in a holy well. It was not a random choice to leave it there.'

I found a cherry stone on the floor. 'When you say devilry, I take it you mean dog heads?' I threw the stone at the mouse, but my aim was poor. The creature wriggled under the sack, its long tail and bony feet the last parts of its body to disappear.

'I'm at least willing to keep an open mind on the matter.' I went to argue with Peter, but he held up his hand to me. 'No more quarrelling, Oswald. Please. I need to rest. My journey has been a long one.' He put one hand on my shoulder and then got to his feet.

No longer displaying the nimbleness of his earlier movements, he stretched his back and arms stiffly, just as the door opened and Gilbert lumbered in with a barrel of ale.

'You should announce your entry with a knock,' said Peter, shielding his eyes from the light.

Gilbert harrumphed. 'What you doing in here, priest? Always appearing and disappearing.'

Gilbert hadn't seen me as the sudden breeze had extinguished our candle. I stepped into the light. 'Brother Peter was with me. We were talking.'

Gilbert raised an eyebrow. 'Funny place to talk. It's as damp as a dew pond in here, sire.' He dropped the barrel next to the sacks of rye. 'Look at this flour. It'll be full of weevils soon.'

I shrugged. For at that moment, I didn't care.

I felt disturbed and irritated. Angry with Brother Peter for his volte-face, but also angry with myself. I had been undermined by a parish priest and his pilgrimage. And I had been a fool in so many other ways. My education had centred on rational argument and the study of empirical evidence. I had read Roger Bacon and Aristotle. And yet I had allowed myself to believe in monsters and shadows. I had even whispered words into the soil of a grave. There had been a good reason why Alison did not reply to me. She was dead.

The Starvecrow sisters had not been killed by devilry as Peter maintained, but neither had they been murdered by Joan. I had to admit that much. She could not have put the head in the well herself, and I doubted her sons would have come up with such a macabre scheme. It would neither help their mother nor have been an easy task for two young boys. Even two such resourceful young men.

I had been wrong to imprison Joan for so long.

At first light the next morning I went to the gaol house, but found the main door was locked. Wondering if Henry Smith, the gaoler, had joined the pilgrimage and abandoned Joan Bath to her cell, I banged heavily on the door until hearing some feet come running from the other side. It was Henry himself, looking rather sheepish and red about the face. When he opened Joan's cell, her dishevelled dress and the disturbed blanket gave away the reason for his embarrassment. Not wanting to listen to Henry's excuses, I asked him for the key and then told him to return home.

Joan turned her back to me and combed her hair, which was long and black – though a few lonely white strands had found a foothold at her temples. As she ran the comb along her shining tresses, she released the scent of rose oil and camphor. It was momentarily heady and appealing in this dirty and dismal place.

'I need to ask you some more questions,' I said. 'And you would be wise to turn and face me.'

'I've answered all your questions again and again, sire,' she said, taking three portions of the hair and forming them into a plait. 'I've nothing else to tell you.' She didn't turn around.

'I was considering releasing you, Mistress Bath. But if you continue to sit with your back to me, then perhaps I will keep you here a while longer.'

She shifted a little, but stubbornly wouldn't face me.

'Very well,' I said, walking towards the door. I was tired of her games, and the air in the cell had lost its scent of camphor and now smelt unpleasantly of naked bodies.

'Wait,' she said, as I reached for the key. 'What is it you want to know?'

She motioned for me to sit next to her on the bed, but I remained standing. 'Do you believe in dog heads?' I asked.

I expected her to leap at this opportunity to absolve herself. Instead, she huffed. 'No. Such creatures don't exist. Cornwall is a liar.'

'So, who killed the girls? Can you answer me that?'

'I have no idea, sire.' She wiped the comb and slotted it behind her belt. 'I was only trying to help them.'

Looking through the bars of the window, I could see Old Ralph's tumbledown cottage in the distance. It looked more like a pigsty than a home.

'Am I free to go then?' she asked, standing up and gathering her belongings about her. 'I'll have to burn these clothes. They're covered in lice.'

'Sit down again. I have more questions.' She returned to the bed reluctantly. 'Do you know why Alison Starvecrow wanted to speak with me? On the day she went missing.'

Joan nodded. 'I've told you this before, sire. She wanted you to stop her marriage to my father.'

'But is there anything else you can remember?'

'She claimed you would have to help her.'

This was a new fragment of information. 'Why did she think that?'

'She wouldn't say, sire.' Then she looked at me slyly. 'Are you sure Alison didn't speak with you?'

'Yes.'

'She didn't threaten to reveal a secret you would rather keep?'

I almost laughed. 'Are you suggesting *I* murdered her?'

She bowed her head. 'No.'

'I'm aware my father visited the Starvecrow house, if that's what you're implying. If Alison hoped to threaten me with such a story, she would have been disappointed. I'm told it's common knowledge.'

Joan nodded. 'Your father visited most houses. Particularly if there was a pretty woman to call upon. But at least he left the young girls alone.'

'So there is nothing else you can tell me about Alison?'

She folded her arms. 'No, my lord. There isn't.'

'Very well. You are free to go.'

We left the dankness of the cell together and as Joan stepped into the daylight she squinted, as if she had never seen the sun before. 'I hope it's to be public knowledge I'm innocent,' she said. Then she laughed. 'That will please the village gossips.'

'I'm sure Cornwall will be delighted to announce it in church.'

'Are my boys free to return?'

'Yes.'

'And will you continue to seek the true murderer?'

'Of course.'

She cocked her head to look at me. 'Indeed, sire?'

I looked at my feet. 'I've been advised to say the girls were murdered by dog heads.'

'And will you?'

I shook my head. 'No. I will not.'

She regarded me thoughtfully, then curtsied and walked away towards Old Ralph's cottage – the tenure of which she had now inherited. Watching her go, I wondered momentarily if the woman had duped me, for she was as artful as a vixen with cubs. I disregarded the thought however. Joan might be sly, but she was not a murderer.

When the villagers returned from their worthless pilgrimage I would question each one of them again. Somebody would be able to shine a light into the shadows of this mystery. People do not live in a village as small as Somershill for their whole lives and remain unknown to their neighbours. Secrets leak from thin walls and flow through the village as quickly as the flux.

I turned back to Somershill, but was surprised when Joan caught up with me. She was breathless and looked a little uncomfortable.

'What is it now, mistress?'

'There is something I should tell you, sire,' she said. 'It's about Cornwall's pilgrimage.'

'What about it?'

She took a deep breath. 'He's not taking the villagers to St John's in the marsh. They are going to the chapel at Versey Castle.'

'What?'

'After a short mass, de Caburn is to offer them higher wages to stay on his demesne. He means to take your labour.'

I could barely speak at first. 'Are you sure?' She nodded. 'And Cornwall has arranged this with de Caburn?'

'Yes.'

'How do you know?'

She reddened. 'Cornwall visited me in the gaol house, sire. To lecture me on my sins.'

I raised an eyebrow. 'But he's a—'

'A priest? Yes. He is.' She shrugged. 'But you'd be surprised who comes to see me. When the sun sets.'

I sighed.

'When he wasn't lecturing me, sire, he liked to boast. How he would become more powerful than the de Lacys. How he has important friends who will assist his rise.'

I took her by the wrist. 'Why are you helping me?'

She tried to shake me off, but didn't quite succeed. 'Because . . . you care about Alison and Matilda.'

I found this difficult to believe from a woman I had imprisoned for weeks. 'Are you telling me the truth?' I squeezed her hand, but she didn't flinch.

'Go to Versey yourself then, sire. If you don't believe me.' She shook me off. 'See your men working in his fields, when yours lie empty.'

'I will.'

Chapter Fifteen

The only practical means of reaching Versey Castle from Somershill is on horseback, but I hadn't ridden since my last visit to that place, having lost my confidence with horses since Tempest had thrown me off by the plague pit. Now I preferred to walk wherever possible. Even so, it didn't seem a good idea to confront de Caburn on foot and demand my men return. So I saddled up Brother Peter's pony – a beast with the spirit and energy of a caterpillar, but which could be relied upon to take me to my destination and subsequently return me.

Checking that my dagger was in its sheath, I realised Mother was watching me from the door of the stable – her mouth hanging open like a brown trout. She held Hector in her arms and stroked his bristly head.

'Are you off to murder somebody, Oswald?' When I didn't answer, she dropped the dog to the floor. 'Is there a raiding party coming?' Should we lock the doors and close the gates?' She pulled a small knife from inside the cuff of her gown. 'They won't take my honour.'

'What sort of raiding party are you expecting, Mother? The Danes?'

She gasped. 'Surely not?'

'God's bones! The Danes haven't invaded for four hundred years.'

She pulled a face at me, and returned the blade to its secret slot in her sleeve. 'You startled me, Oswald. I've not seen you arm yourself before.'

'I'm going to Versey Castle.'

'To visit Clemence?'

I belted my tunic and put on my leather gloves while Hector sniffed about my ankles, looking as if he were about to piss against my leg. I pressed my boot against his nose and pushed him away. 'It's not a social visit.'

'Then why are you going?'

'I've discovered Clemence's new husband is bribing our men to work at Versey.'

'Bribing our men? What with?'

'Higher wages, Mother.'

'That's disgraceful.' Her voice tightened enough to scare Hector into abandoning his attempts to urinate on my boot. He shot at speed under a nearby hay stall. 'Who do these labourers think they are? They can't just leave our estate when they please. You need to get them back, Oswald.'

'That's what I'm doing, Mother.'

'You should go straight away.'

'I am!'

I went to mount the pony, but Mother poked me in the arm. 'I'm not in the least bit surprised about de Caburn, you know. The man is vermin. You should have prevented the marriage, Oswald. I said so at the time.'

'What?' This was contrary, even by Mother's standards. 'It was only Brother Peter and myself who stood against the union. If I remember, you thought it was a wonderful idea.'

'Nonsense.' She leant down to coax her dog out from under the stall. 'Take Hector with you. He never liked de Caburn. Did you, sweet boy?' She held out her hand to the wiry-coated little goblin, who met her affection with a steady growl. 'See. He even objects to hearing the man's name.'

'I'm taking Humbert with me.'

'That big oaf? What use will he be?'

'More use than a small dog, Mother.'

Before she could continue this conversation, I got into the saddle and backed the pony out of the stable. Seeing Humbert waiting for me at the gate, I took a slow trot over to him, though Mother still managed to keep up with me, the dog now reinstated in her arms. Watching her scamper alongside me like a beggar at the city gate, I wondered what secret potions she drank to maintain her agility. For, despite her protestations of ill health, she was startlingly nimble for her age.

Humbert wore a detached smile across his face. He was hoping to see Clemence when we reached Versey, even though I had explained this would be an unpleasant visit and had ordered him to bear arms. But with a long dagger hung awkwardly from his belt, he looked about as menacing as a spring lamb. And I doubt he had any idea how to wield the weapon. For, despite being the largest boy in the village, his nature was placid and quiet. Sitting on his sturdy pony, his thick legs nearly reached the ground.

And then I thought of my father. He would have ridden to Versey with a company of men and demanded de Caburn return my farmhands. Instead, I was to approach the place with nothing more than a façade of courage and a simple-minded boy. But I could not give up on this venture. I might be afraid. But I was angry. How dare de Caburn take my men and women? It was a provocation that could not be ignored, no matter how weak my position.

There was also more at stake here. I was tired of Brother Peter's schemes and excuses. I was tired of keeping quiet and appeasing my enemies.

I must return to being a lord.

'Don't tell Brother Peter where I've gone,' I said to Mother, as we turned to leave.

'Are you sure?'

'Yes. He would tell me to write a letter.'

For once the sun was shining hard onto the wheat and barley, which enraged me further – the village should have been working in my fields, making the most of the brief opportunity the weather had provided. Humbert and I didn't pass a soul on the road. Not even a wandering knife-grinder or a stray dog. How empty and remote this place suddenly seemed.

'Why do you care so much for Clemence?' I asked Humbert as his face jolted up and down in time with his pony's trotting.

Patches of magenta formed on his pasty cheeks. 'She's kind to me.' This was as articulate as I had ever heard him sound. Perhaps because he was not looking directly at me.

'She's cruel to me,' I said. 'But that's because I'm her brother.'

He shook his head. 'She's not cruel.'

I laughed. 'She is.'

He stopped his pony and glared at me. 'She stopped them. Always.'

'Who?'

But now he wouldn't answer.

'Do you mean my brothers, Richard and William?'

He suddenly trotted on, and it was clear I had picked at the scab on an old wound. But I had that scar myself, though it was better healed than Humbert's. My older brothers loved to torment the weak and feeble, and I had been their favourite plaything until the age of seven. They must have looked around for a new victim at my departure for the monastery, and found him in the clumsy boy who had been dumped on the doorstep and lived in the hay barn.

Reaching the forest that separates my lands from those of de Caburn, our silent journey was interrupted by a distant howl. Thumping my ear, I wanted to make sure this was not some imagining inside my head. But it was definitely a canine sound. A repeated howling and barking. Even the faithful pony picked up her ears warily, and had to be encouraged to enter the woodland path by a sharp dig in her flanks. Within a few seconds the barking had ceased and the silence returned, only disturbed by the hooves of our ponies on the track.

'Wolves?' I said to Humbert.

He shook his head. 'Just dogs, sire.' We continued, but his assurances didn't entirely comfort me. It was humid and dark in the dense woodland, and although we kept to the track, I longed again for the open meadows and orchards of Somershill.

We had travelled on at a steady trot for nearly an hour when the barking began again, only this time we could hear voices in the distance – both male and female. A scream stabbed the air.

We stopped the ponies and listened. The sounds were coming from somewhere ahead of us, in an area of densely coppiced chestnut – trees with long saw-edged leaves that shielded the source of the noise from view.

Dismounting, we tied the ponies to an oak tree, and then I instructed Humbert to stay with the animals, whilst I crept towards the coppice with my sword drawn. The ground was wet, despite the warmer weather, and the sun had disappeared leaving a grey tone to the woodland, which only amplified the despondency of this place. The birdsong had ceased, and the carcass of a badger lay in my way, as if the path itself might lead to the underworld. Sweat beaded across my brow and my hand shook as I tried to master my fear.

Creeping closer and closer to the source of the noise, I listened for voices. Being an accomplished sneaker and creeper, I was practised in moving about unheard – as a nocturnal visit to the abbey kitchen had sometimes been the only means of a decent meal. Other novices were often caught, but not me. My feet trod as softly across the leafy soil that day, as they had at night along the stone corridors of the abbey. I did not snap the thinnest twig nor rustle the driest leaf.

Now close, I could make out muffled voices and screaming, followed by laughter. The dogs could smell my approach, since they growled and barked, but it was too late to retreat. Tightening the grip on my sword, I moved forward to pull aside a small branch in order to spy upon the scene.

I would tell you the Plague had deadened my heart. But it had not completely. What I saw that day was as repugnant as my first sight of maggots in a wound or the bulbous lesions of a leper's face. There, in a small clearing, I saw de Caburn with his doublet raised and his braies by his ankles. He was leaning over a girl with her gown hitched up to her waist and her legs forced apart. Three men stood behind. Two were dressed in the garb of servants and I did not recognise them. But de Caburn's third companion was well known to me. It was Cornwall. And by his face I had the impression he was waiting to take his turn.

And then de Caburn moved aside and I could see their victim. It was Mirabel.

There was no moment of hesitation, or contemplation of the best course of action. Instead I rushed from my cover with a raised sword. 'Get away from her!' I shouted.

But de Caburn was a knight and had served the king in France. I could not hope to frighten such a man. He swerved deftly as I swiped at him, causing me to stumble and fall. Getting quickly to my feet, I attempted another strike, but this time de Caburn kicked me easily to the ground and then booted me again and again until a fierce pain seared through my body.

When I was completely subdued, he placed the tip of his sword at my neck. 'Are you spying on me, de Lacy?'

I cried out for Humbert to come to my aid, but it was a mistake since this only caused de Caburn quickly to send his two servants into the forest to track down my companion. And then, as I looked through a swollen eye at Mirabel's trembling body, a terrible realisation came upon me. 'You've done this before, haven't you?' I said to de Caburn.

He only laughed at me.

'You and Cornwall. You murdered the Starvecrow sisters.'

Now he sneered. 'Who?'

I should have considered this possibility. I should have examined the bodies of my sisters further and looked for evidence. 'You raped them first. Didn't you?'

He kicked me again in the face, but I would not be silenced.

Blood trickled from my mouth. 'Cornwall invented the dog head story to cover your crimes.' I felt a tooth come loose. 'You're rapists and murderers.' The tooth dropped to the forest floor. 'Both of you.'

At these words, de Caburn resumed his attack, but John of Cornwall did not answer my accusation, nor join in my torture. He simply slipped away into the coppice and silently disappeared.

His desertion went unnoticed by de Caburn, as the man was too interested in trying to kill me. He even failed to notice when Mirabel picked up my fallen sword and crept up behind him. She should have used the opportunity to flee while de Caburn was occupied with my termination. But I am pleased she didn't. Her face was twisted into a knot of hatred and she might even have had the strength to fell our enemy – but I must have given her away, for just as she attempted to swing the weapon, de Caburn turned on his heels and pushed her to the ground. She screamed, calling him the foulest of names, but he just laughed at her.

There was indeed a monster in this forest.

Our only hope now was Humbert, but within moments he was also marched into the clearing by de Caburn's men – his face cut and his tunic torn.

De Caburn recognised Humbert immediately. 'Look. It's my wife's little boot-licker.' He sauntered over and poked his sword into the boy's groin. 'Did my wife leave you, boot-licker?' Humbert didn't look up, but his shoulders were beginning to shudder. De Caburn pushed the sword in harder and put his face right into Humbert's. 'You wanted to lick more than her boots, didn't you?' Humbert's tears now flowed. 'Isn't that right, boy?'

The two servants laughed at him. Perhaps it was de Caburn's taunts, or perhaps it was the recollection of my brothers' bullying, because Humbert screwed up his face and spat at de Caburn. I have rarely seen so much malice concentrated into so small a ball of spittle.

De Caburn screamed with fury. He wiped the spittle from his face and went to stab the boy, when a sudden radiance flared through the air, followed by a deafening boom that was as loud as a hammer breaking through the glass of a cathedral window. A strong burst of flame threw de Caburn and his men to the floor. The dogs broke free of their leashes and fled into the trees.

I had shielded my eyes instinctively, but Mirabel was dazed – her clothes and hair burnt. She was alive, whereas de Caburn and his men appeared lifeless and blackened, having taken the full force of the blast by virtue of being upright when it came upon us. Only Humbert remaining standing – like a pillar of scorched stone.

I took Mirabel's limp hand to try to rouse her. But then, through a cloud of grey and acrid smoke, a figure ran towards us, waving the fumes from his face.

It was Brother Peter.

He grasped me in a powerful embrace. 'Oswald! You're alive. Thank the Almighty. I thought I'd made a terrible mistake.'

'It was you?'

'Yes.'

'What was it?'

'I'll tell you later,' he said, pulling me up. 'We need to get out of here.' He turned to de Caburn and his men, who were beginning to groan. 'Quickly. They're coming round.'

I staggered to my feet and we lifted Mirabel between us. Her hair was sooty and her thin clothes were burnt away to reveal the blackened skin of her legs. I felt guilty, since Humbert and I had

been protected from the force of the blast by the leather of our
tunics and boots.

Brother Peter gave his cloak to Mirabel and we wrapped her
up like a small child against the wind. Then we carried her away
to the ponies, but we soon found my own mount was too small
to take the weight of both of us – so I was forced to use the horse
that Brother Peter had ridden in our pursuit. It was my beloved
Tempest, who seemed every bit as pleased to see me as I was to
see him. The flames and boom hardly promised to have settled
his mercurial nerves, but Brother Peter whispered into his ear
and stroked his neck, before sending Mirabel and myself on our
way. He and Humbert followed closely behind on the ponies.

In the distance de Caburn called my name.

His voice bore the vengeance of the Furies.

Gilbert was reluctant to wait upon Mirabel, despite her obvious
injuries, so I persuaded Mother to perform the duty – once we
had established Mirabel was neither my whore, nor a witch. She
was given a bed in the ladies' bedchamber, a draught of Brother
Peter's sleeping tonic, and was left to recover from the horror of
the day. Mother promised to keep a vigil at her side and to feed
her ale and honey if she awoke.

Once I had washed myself clean of the sooty residue, I sought
out Brother Peter in the library. He was consulting his books
on herbs, and writing some notes onto a separate piece of
parchment.

'Come in quickly, Oswald. I have your tooth here. If we
replace it now, it will grow roots again.'

My tongue found the empty gap in my front teeth. 'How did
you find it?'

'It was lying on the ground near where you fell. I have it in this
cup.'

He showed me a small white piece of bone floating in some
sour-smelling milk. 'Are you sure it's mine?' I asked.

'Of course it is, Oswald. I would recognise your tooth anywhere. Now sit down here.' He took my head in his hands. 'Open your mouth.' His long fingers tasted salty and rough as he pressed my tooth back into its cavity. But it wasn't painful.

'I suppose it was Mother who told you where I was going?' I said. 'Even though I asked her not to.'

'You know the woman can't keep a secret, Oswald.' He passed me a bottle. 'Here. Drink some of this to clear your mouth of corruption.'

The brandy was both fiery and soothing about my gums. 'Thank you for coming, Brother.'

Peter took the bottle from me and drank a little himself. 'Why did you do it, Oswald? It was very foolhardy.'

'De Caburn's taken all my men, Brother. I had to do something.'

'Then offer your men higher wages to return, Oswald. You can't use aggression against such a man as de Caburn. He is strong and violent. You must use your brains.'

'I had to confront him for once, Brother.'

Peter threw up his hands. 'But what good has it done you? The man nearly killed you.'

We sat in silence for a few moments. He tapped his foot upon the floor. 'I think I've solved the mystery of the Starvecrow murders,' I told him.

He stopped tapping. 'Oh yes?'

'It was de Caburn and Cornwall.'

He said nothing.

'They rape young girls and then murder them. The dog head story was an invention to disguise their crime.'

Peter now pulled at the wart on his neck. 'I see.' He sighed. 'Are you sure?'

'I'm going to write to the sheriff.'

Peter stood up and clasped his head in his hands. 'What? You can't do that!'

'Why not?'

'I told you to use your brains, Oswald! De Caburn is protected by the earl. And Cornwall is a priest.'

'But I have witnesses.'

'It doesn't matter.'

'So I should just forget about it?'

'De Caburn and Cornwall will be punished, Oswald.'

'But not at my hands. Is that what you're saying?'

'Let God deal with them.'

I raised my voice. 'No. Alison and Matilda will receive earthly justice. I will make sure of it.'

Peter took a deep breath and went to argue back, but stopped himself. The awkward silence returned as Peter sat down again and resumed the tapping of his foot.

I thought about leaving, but then remembered my purpose in coming to the library. 'So how did you make the flash and boom, Brother? Was it alchemy?'

Peter smiled weakly now. 'Alchemy? I thought you were sceptical of such notions, Oswald.' He stood up again. 'Let me show you.' He led me to the corner of the library where he lifted a blanket to reveal a pole of iron. It was as long as my arm and as thick as the trunk of a young apple tree. 'It was a gift to me from a crusader. It comes from Arabia, I believe.'

'Did you know it could make such a flare?'

'He told me it would. But I've never used it before.'

I touched the cold, grey shaft of the weapon and tried to lift it. 'It's so heavy, Brother. How did you wield it?'

'I propped it in the crook of a tree.' He pointed to one end of the pole. 'See. It's hollow. I placed small stones into it at this end.' He then pointed at a small slit drilled into the tube. 'Then I lit a piece of rope here.'

'But how would that cause the stones to shoot out with such force?'

He smiled again. 'Ever the inquisitor, Oswald? There is

another ingredient. It's a black powder that I placed into the tube before the stones. The burning rope ignites this powder and causes the flare.'

'And this powder made the soot and the smoke?' He nodded. 'Could you use it again?' I asked, suddenly imagining how I might punish de Caburn and Cornwall, and gain justice for my sisters.

But it seemed Brother Peter had read my thoughts. He took the weapon away from me. 'No. And I'm glad of it. The powder is the Devil's dust, Oswald. I only had enough for one blast.'

'Could you make some more?'

He flared his nostrils. 'I've no idea what's in it. And, even if I did, it would be a mistake. It's an ill-fated material. I nearly killed you.'

He covered the metal pole with the blanket. 'De Caburn will retaliate for this attack. He's been shamed in front of his men.'

I nodded, knowing with morbid fatality that this was true. 'So, what should we do?'

'We should pray, Oswald. God will provide an answer.'

I sighed. 'No, Brother. You know I don't believe.'

He touched my hair and stroked it gently. 'Please, Oswald. Take communion with me. If only to please an old man.' I looked up at his face. His eyes were red about the rims and his face thin and grey.

But he had saved my life and I loved him.

So, I followed Brother Peter to the chapel. I took communion with him and prayed. Barely two days later our prayers were answered, though not in the way we had hoped.

Chapter Sixteen

At first light a distant figure was seen walking towards Somershill. Piers had kept the night watch from the north-west tower, and on seeing the stranger emerge from the forest he ran into the great hall and bashed the copper cook pot, rousing the whole house.

Given the urgency of the noise, I was expecting to see a group of mounted knights from Versey Castle when I rushed to the window. But from the faint awkward image it seemed as if a cripple or leper were approaching the gate of the house. The solitary figure limped forward through the early morning mist, but not without determination and purpose. And there was something familiar in their gait.

It was Mother who noticed first. 'Look. It's Clemence.' She held her hand to her mouth in dismay.

'What! Where's her horse?' I said.

'Perhaps Merrion threw her off?'

Even from this distance, I could see my sister was not wearing her riding gown, so I pulled on my boots and ran out to meet her with Mother keeping to my shadows as if we were about to confront a wild animal.

If Clemence were not a wild animal, then she was an injured one. As she came fully into focus we saw a face caked in blood. Her dress was muddy and creased, and her sleeves were torn away – exposing a trail of ugly bruises that marked their path up her arms. She looked as exhausted as a camp follower returning from battle.

I rushed to embrace her, but at my touch she became as rigid as a rock. 'What happened?' I released her quickly from my unwelcome hold.

Her voice was weak and hoarse. 'I am sent to you from my husband.'

'De Caburn did this?'

She nodded.

Mother crept out from behind me and took my sister's limp hand. 'Did you provoke him, Clemence?'

Clemence snatched her hand away. 'No. I did not.' She pointed at me. 'He did!'

'Your husband meant to kill me, Clemence. I didn't imagine it would lead to this.'

I would have pressed my case further except Clemence was too weak for argument. She fell to the ground sobbing and would not be comforted by either Mother or myself. As we tried to lift her, we looked up to find Humbert pounding over from the house with the speed of a hen pheasant fleeing the hounds. He ran to Clemence and pushed us aside.

'Take me inside,' she said to him. 'And be gentle.'

Humbert scooped Clemence up in his arms and carried her to her old bed in the ladies' bedchamber, where Brother Peter administered a sleeping draught. When we were sure she was sedated, Mother sent Humbert away while we stripped Clemence of her dirtiest clothes and bathed her wounds in an ointment of rosemary and tar. Given the scratches and swelling about her body, it was clear she had been both assaulted and raped – though Mother and I did not speak of this openly.

We were about to leave her sleeping next to Mirabel, when I noticed Humbert in the shadows. He must have sneaked back into the bedchamber, ghost-like as a she-cat. I didn't have the heart to remove him, so pretended not to have seen the boy.

We ate a late breakfast in the great hall without speaking. Brother Peter chewed methodically upon his rye bread, while Hector snuffled about under the table, scavenging for crumbs. Even Mother was silent.

Suddenly, the great hall reverberated with Clemence's screaming. 'Get this whore away from me!'

Mother dropped a spoon into her pottage and scowled. 'Why must she shout so? This is not Cheapside market.'

'We should be forgiving, Mother,' I said, leaving the table to investigate.

Brother Peter wiped some pottage from his mouth and stood up to join me. 'Your daughter has been harshly violated, my lady. Kindness is required.'

Mother muttered something under her breath as we left the room, but we didn't wait to hear it repeated.

Opening the heavy door to the bedchamber we found Clemence holding Mirabel by the hair. Humbert stood between them, but his efforts to stop the fight were as ineffectual as a child with flapping hands trying to break up a pair of brawling dogs.

'What is this whore doing in my room?' said Clemence when she saw me. Her words were slurred by the swelling to her lip.

'Let her go,' I said.

But Clemence twisted Mirabel's hair more tightly, tugging it hard enough to make Mirabel squeal. I pushed past Humbert and forced Clemence to release the girl. 'Her name is Mirabel. And she's not a whore.'

Clemence snorted. 'I know who she is! Flaunting herself about Versey. In front of my husband.'

Mirabel sobbed. 'I never did, my lady. I wanted him to leave me alone.'

'Lies!'

I grasped Clemence with both hands. 'Mirabel was also attacked by your husband. You should have sympathy for her.'

Clemence broke free of me and slumped back down onto her bed. The energy of the fight had suddenly exhausted her, and tears began to stain her face. 'Is that why you tried to kill my husband, little brother? To save this whore?'

'I came across de Caburn and Cornwall in the forest,' I told her. 'They were attacking Mirabel. She was not the first of their victims.'

I sat down next to Clemence and stroked her forehead. She was hot, and the sweat ran greasily through her long black hair. 'Was it de Caburn alone who did this to you?' I asked her softly.

'It was just him,' she whispered to me. 'He would have killed me, but . . .' she almost smirked, 'he made sure to leave me the strength to return.'

'I'm so sorry.'

She opened her eyes and grabbed my wrist. 'What good is being sorry, Oswald? You must avenge me.'

Brother Peter interrupted. 'God forgive you, Lady Clemence. Do not incite your own brother to sin.'

Clemence turned to Peter, her face red and sneering. 'I would kill de Caburn myself, if I were able. And God would be pleased about it.'

'That is blasphemous talk.'

She burst out laughing, but it sounded as harsh as the call of a crow. 'You won't be so principled when he comes for you, priest. You and your precious Oswald.'

Peter remained calm. 'And Lord Versey plans to do so?'

'Of course he does. You burnt him. He won't let it pass.'

'What does he intend to do?'

'Don't ask me. How would I know his plans?'

She gripped her stomach and rocked to ease her pain. Peter then poured some more of the sleeping draught and attempted to feed her, but she pushed him away. 'No more of that poison,' she told him.

'It would help you to sleep, madam.'

'I don't care to sleep!' She was becoming angry again. Her teeth were gritted.

'I can dilute its strength if it would please you.'

'No,' she said. 'I must stay awake. Remain vigilant.'

I tried to take her hand, but she waved me away. 'You're safe now, Clemence.'

Peter fared no better when he tried to gauge her heat by feeling her forehead. She pushed him away with surprising vigour. 'I should inspect your wounds, my lady,' he said.

Now she sat up straight. 'No! Keep away from me.'

'But I'm an infirmarer. I've treated a woman intimately before. It really would be—'

'You're not treating me intimately, priest!' She shrank back into the bed and pulled the sheets about her.

'But you're running a fever. And your wounds may become corrupted.' Peter went to place a comforting hand upon Clemence's shoulder, but this time Humbert pressed himself in the way.

Seeing this approach was unlikely to succeed, I drew Peter back to a private corner of the room, where the others could not hear us. 'I think we should allow Clemence to rest, Brother. Let's approach her again tomorrow when she's calmer.'

Peter shook his head. 'Clemence must be treated today. She's been wounded internally.'

'But she won't allow you to treat her, Brother.'

'Then she risks a stronger fever. Perhaps worse.'

'Why don't we fully sedate her?'

He sighed. 'No. She resists too vigorously. And I will not tend to her wounds without her agreement. It would be a further affront to her dignity.'

'Then what are we to do?'

Peter looked about the room as if the tapestries or the bed curtains might answer his question. A flock of small birds landed at the window, pecking at the cobwebs on the external glass for flies and spiders.

Peter took a metal flask from the recesses of his tunic. 'Would you care for some?' I declined the offer since the wine had been warmed against the bare skin of Peter's belly and the thought of it was unpleasant.

He took his customary swig and then wiped the red dregs from around his mouth. 'Clemence must go to the convent of St Margaret. Sister Constance treats women who have suffered at a man's hands. She has special remedies. Clemence will allow another woman to help her.'

'Sister Constance is still alive?'

'I believe so.'

'But Clemence can't just arrive, unannounced.'

'I'll take her and make all the necessary introductions. I can ensure Clemence receives the correct care. '

'Is Clemence ready to travel?'

'We'll take her in the cart. I can give her a draught to numb the pain. If she knows the reason for taking the potion, then she might be more agreeable.'

'Why are you being so accommodating?' I whispered. 'You despise Clemence.'

He touched my shoulder for a moment. 'She has goodness in her heart . . . somewhere, Oswald.' He took a last gulp of the wine and placed it back into its hiding hole. 'I'll get the cart ready.'

'You must be careful not to travel near de Caburn's land. St Margaret's is close to Versey.'

'I know the back paths. Don't be concerned. Nobody will stop an old priest with a covered body in a cart. Especially if I suggest my load is suffering from the Pestilence.'

* * *

So, it was agreed. Clemence was changed into a clean gown and
cloak, and laid on the back of a hay cart like a sack of barley. But
she still would not take Brother Peter's sleeping draught, claiming that she would rather be knocked about on a rutted road,
than tricked into a delirium.

And she would not travel without Humbert. Equally the
boy would not be left at Somershill without her. So I gave
him my brother Richard's sword to earn his keep on this
journey and told him to guard Clemence with his life.
Humbert might not have been violent, but he had the capac-
ity to look so. The boy handled the weapon with some
trepidation – who knows what torments he had received at
the hands of this very same sword? But when I proposed
that Clemence needed protecting from de Caburn, he
gripped it as firmly as a crusader charging at an army of
infidels. He was Clemence's champion and would defend
my sister's favour to the end.

Peter would not let me help him load the cart, though he
struggled to lift a very heavy casket onto the back.

'More brandy?' I asked him.

He smiled. 'The abbess is as miserly as the bishop.'

'How long are you planning to be away? You must have a
supply in there to last weeks.'

'I will return as soon as possible.'

'You promise.'

He looked at me and smiled. 'Don't worry, Oswald.' Then he
whispered into my ear. 'Come with me, quickly. There's something I must show you. Before I leave.'

He led me to Father's library and shut the heavy door behind
us. Shards of light from the window picked out a thousand
dancing specks of dust in the air. Peter led me to the back wall.
'If you come under attack while I'm away, there is somewhere
you can hide.'

'In here?'

He nodded and lifted back the tapestry of the three-headed sea-serpent to reveal the alcove where he kept his brandy and solitary pewter cup.

'I can't hide in there,' I said.

'Don't be so foolish, Oswald.' He then pushed at a small carved angel in the back of the alcove and slowly a panel in the wall moved – rotating outwards in the manner of a door hinge. Its movement was entirely silent, and the heaviness of the wood did not make a single scratch upon the floor. I looked with wonder inside the cavity to see only darkness.

'It's an escape tunnel,' said Peter.

'Who built it?'

'Your grandfather. When he redesigned the house.'

'And how do you know about it?'

'Your father revealed it to me. Years ago. When I was copying manuscripts for the abbey. He used this tunnel to store his most precious books.' Peter coughed. 'Any text that might seem seditious or profane.' A damp and cold smell crept out from the opening.

'Where are the books now?'

'On the shelves in the library. This is no place to keep books, Oswald. They will only warp and rot. I removed them as soon as we returned to Somershill.'

Peter lit a candle and beckoned for me to follow him. 'Come inside and I will show you how to escape at the other end. You cannot stay too long in here as the air is fetid.'

The thin light of the candle illuminated a set of stone steps and a narrow corridor that sloped gently downwards into the distance. The walls were the work of master masons. Each stone perfectly carved into place in the lancet arch of the tunnel.

'Are there any other tunnels about the house?' I asked, as we made our way into the darkness.

'Just this one, to my knowledge,' said Peter. 'At least your father did not tell me of any others.'

'I wish he had told me about this place.'

'He didn't have the opportunity, Oswald.'

'Does Mother know of this?'

Peter laughed. 'Of course not. Your father wanted this tunnel to remain a secret!'

'And nobody else knows? Not Gilbert, nor any of the other servants?'

He shook his head. 'Not a soul.'

As we climbed the steps at the other end of the tunnel, we were met by another wall. Peter counted down seven stones and then pushed. This door was much heavier and smaller than the one in the library, and was made of stone. Once again it pivoted outwards, and as we peeped through the tiny aperture, I saw that we were now on the outer face of the high crenellated wall that ran from the north-east tower to the north-west. No wonder this part of the wall had been left standing, when the other three sides had been demolished. In front of us stood the stinking remains of the moat.

Peter pulled me back. 'Let's hurry back now, Oswald. There's no time to waste.' He showed me how to open and close both the doors from the inside of the tunnel and then we made our way back to the cart, where Clemence and Mother awaited us.

But Mother refused to see the party off – proclaiming she had never seen a de Lacy leave Somershill in a more degraded state, and was ashamed our servants should witness such a thing. It was lucky then that we had no more house servants than Gilbert, Ada and Piers the stable lad.

Before she left I held Clemence's hand and kissed her scratched cheek. 'I'm sorry this happened, Sister.'

'I know, Oswald.' Her voice was weak, but the next moment she squeezed my hand with surprising vigour. 'But he will pay.'

Under Brother Peter's instructions, we shut up the house as if preparing for a siege. He also persuaded me to write another of his letters – this one to the earl. I was to express my dismay at de

Caburn's behaviour towards Clemence and then to plead for men to aid my defence. I was to say nothing about the Starvecrow murders.

I was unconvinced, but Peter felt we must try to invoke old family alliances. The earl was known to be both mercurial and chivalrous. If I pleaded my case poetically, he might be moved to take my side. And if that didn't work, my agreement to commuting the military service to a money payment might also swing the argument in my favour. So, against my better judgement I sat down and composed the most emotional and florid of appeals, then despatched Piers to the earl's castle near Rochester.

Those of us left at Somershill took turns to watch from the north-west tower. For three days we feared the approach of de Caburn, but he didn't come. Instead I looked out morosely upon my fields of wheat and barley, which ripened in the unexpected sun, with nobody to harvest their crop.

At my second watch I saw Gilbert moving the dairy cattle and their calves about in the fields with a long stick. The sunlight gave him a vaporous quality, as if he were an illusion. I wished he would keep the herd nearer the house, but he refused, saying they needed the sweeter meadows of the pastures nearer to the forest and hence nearer to de Caburn's land. The next day he was gone for so long, we wondered if he had been captured by my enemy. But Gilbert returned at dusk, driving the cattle grumpily into the dairy barn and calling for Ada to help him milk the beasts.

Mirabel joined me on the third evening to watch an orange sun setting in a pale sky. Small bats flitted amongst us, and the squeal of a dog otter drifted up from the river. I looked at my companion. The warm light cast shadows across her beautiful face and lit up the velvet down of her skin.

'Do you think we will starve this winter, sire?' she asked.

'Of course not,' I lied. 'The villagers will return soon. The harvest will be a good one.'

I wanted to take her hand and hold her. But she had been distant since that afternoon in the forest, reluctant to say much at all. Mother had plans to train her as a lady's maid, but I was adamant Mirabel would receive care and attention rather than Mother's instruction. For even then I had formed ideas regarding Mirabel. Plans that would take both courage and luck.

On the dawn of the fourth day, Gilbert was driving the cattle out through the main gate when I called for him to bring them back. I had been watching the woodland, our most vulnerable point. My eyesight is keen, but I will admit that my imagination can sometimes be keener. Seeing something move in between the distant trees I first dismissed it as the wind, since the early morning was gusty and cold. But this was not air moving about between the oaks and ash. It was people.

I shouted again to Gilbert. 'Quickly, drive the cattle back!'

The man suffered from wilful deafness and held his hand to his ear. 'What's that, sire?'

'We're under attack, Gilbert. Bring the cattle back!' He seemed to hear me this time and began to round them up with a shrug, as if being under attack were a tedious nuisance. By the time I had run out of the tower to join him, the cattle had dispersed in all directions.

Gilbert looked into the distance. 'I can't see nothing, sire.'

'Over there!' We turned to look at the woodland, where some people were now emerging. They were moving slowly and to my mind stealthily. 'It must be de Caburn and his men,' I said.

Gilbert snorted. 'I don't think so, sire. They don't look so dangerous to me.' We looked again, and now they were closer we saw a trickle of people with their backs bent and faces to the ground. They were a string of peasants in dirty brown and grey tunics, followed by a gaggle of children.

I recognised them immediately.

'They've come back,' Gilbert shouted. 'That's the villagers, sire.' And indeed it was.

We ran across the field to meet them as if they were long-lost family. I even forgot to look angry – though once we caught up with their guilty faces it was clear they were expecting some level of censure from me, so I quickly dropped my look of joy and exchanged it for a frown.

'I understand you've been at Versey Castle,' I said. They looked from one to the other and then to the ground.

William the ploughman spoke first. 'We were on a pilgrimage, sire.'

'We wanted to be saved from them dog heads,' said Hilda, the ruddy-faced woman who sometimes worked as our dairymaid. 'Father John said we had to pray at the shrine of the Virgin.'

'That doesn't take a week.'

Again silence. It was the ploughman who braved an answer, though he muttered his words, half hoping I wouldn't hear him properly. 'Lord Versey asked us to take in his harvest.'

'There's a harvest at Somershill,' I said. 'Can't you see it? Rotting in the fields.'

'But he offered better wages, sire,' said a boy. 'Uncle got a farthing more per day.' The boy was quickly kicked by a man I presumed to be his uncle and told to be quiet.

'So why have you returned? If you were made such a good offer by Lord Versey?' More silence. A couple of women crossed themselves. The boy kissed his crucifix.

'Answer Lord Somershill,' said Gilbert, looking at them in turn. 'Come on. Satan cut your tongues, has he?'

The ploughman coughed. 'Lord Versey is dead, sire. Killed by the dog heads.'

'What are you talking about?' I asked. A general uproar broke out, and it became impossible to make sense of what anybody was saying.

I dragged the boy forward. He, at least, seemed able to speak the truth. 'De Caburn is dead. Are you sure?'

The boy shivered. 'I saw his body myself, sire. Hanging over the Virgin's shrine at Versey. We all went to look at it.' The others nodded and expanded on the story with garbled details and calls to the Almighty.

I told them to be quiet. 'What did his body look like?' I asked the boy.

'He was naked, sire. His throat was all mangled by the dog heads.' The boy's eyes were wide. 'But it wasn't just his throat. They'd chewed away at his face and his hands as well. And he smelt strange.'

'Dead bodies always smell strange.'

'No, sire. He smelt sort of . . . cooked.' Once again cries to the Almighty rang out.

'Cooked?'

The boy's uncle intervened. 'Tom has a bit of an imagination, my lord. I think it was just the scent of evil myself.'

Sensing this strand of conversation would inevitably lead into the direction of dog heads, I quickly grabbed the boy again. 'When was the body found?'

'Yesterday morning, sire. Elfric saw him first. He was going to the shrine to pray.'

I looked at Elfric, a youth whose eyes pointed in different directions, so it was a wonder he could see anything at all. 'And when was the last time Lord Versey was seen alive?'

'Don't know, sire,' said the boy. 'Lord Versey was always in his castle.'

'I saw him riding out alone the afternoon before,' said young Ralph. 'He was headed out on the road to Burrsfield.'

'Do you know where he was going?' I asked. They all shrugged. It was a foolish question anyway. De Caburn was hardly likely to share his diary of engagements with a group of villagers.

'And where's Father John?' I asked, suddenly remembering Cornwall. The boy was about to reply, but the ploughman interrupted him. 'He didn't want us to return to Somershill, sire. Thought we should stay and finish the harvest at Versey.'

'And why didn't you?'

The ploughman shifted on his feet, seeming more uncomfort-able than ever. I looked about at the other faces, but nobody would answer my question.

'Why didn't you stay at Versey?' I said again. The ploughman muttered something inaudible. 'Speak up, please,' I told him.

'We weren't sure who'd pay us. Now Lord Versey is dead.'

'And not just that, sire,' said Hilda. 'Versey is cursed.'

'Last week Somershill was cursed, if you remember!' I said.

'Oh no. It's much worse there,' said Hilda. 'Oh yes. First the girl went missing and then Lord Versey was murdered.'

'Which girl went missing?'

'My sister, sire,' said the boy. 'Mirabel Turner.'

'No. She is—'

But then somebody caught my eye. The tall, red-haired youth who had followed Mirabel in church with jealous eyes. At mention of her name, his face hung and his eyes studied the ground, and suddenly I felt angry. It was not for him to grieve over Mirabel. She belonged to me.

I should have told the whole village that Mirabel was still alive. Instead I asked her brother to accompany me back to the house, telling the rest of them to meet me later in the fields.

For once, there was no discussion.

Chapter Seventeen

The colour returned to Mirabel's face as she grasped her small brother and spun him about. It was such a joyful embrace that it provoked Mother to break up their reunion rudely, and demand the girl take their noisiness elsewhere. When they left the room, I realised Mirabel had been in the process of emptying Mother's piss pot.

'She's not your maid,' I said. 'I keep telling you that.'

Mother shrugged nonchalantly. 'Well. She's certainly not my houseguest, Oswald. She must earn her keep if she wants to stay here.'

'I want her to recuperate.'

Mother pulled a comb through her long, wiry hair and laughed. 'Recuperate? That girl is as greedy as a horse. If she stays much longer, she'll eat the whole winter store.'

'Don't speak about Mirabel that way. She'll stay here as long as I say so.'

Mother pulled a face and returned to combing her hair. Her tresses were still black and sleek about the back of her head, but the hair on the top of her head was white and bushy. Suddenly she reminded me of a badger.

'De Caburn has been found dead,' I told her.

She dropped the comb. 'Really?'

'He was murdered.'

She puckered her mouth into an oval pout and gasped. 'Goodness me. What a piece of luck.'

'Mother!'

'But that makes Clemence a widow. And a rich one at that.' She flapped her hands in excitement. 'She won't want to dawdle about in that convent now. We should send Piers to tell her the good news.'

'De Caburn was murdered,' I repeated, 'I would hardly call it good news.'

Mother raised an eyebrow. 'Really, Oswald?'

'Yes, Mother. He was draped over a shrine to the Virgin Mary.'

Now she smirked. 'So you're not in the slightest bit pleased de Caburn is dead?' I didn't reply. 'Even though we've barricaded ourselves against the man for the last three days. A man who stole our village and attacked your sister.'

'Very well,' I conceded. 'I won't mourn his death.'

She returned to combing her hair. 'How this tale has turned? De Caburn a victim of the Cynocephalus.'

I raised my eyes to the ceiling.

She ignored me. 'Perhaps these dog heads are not the agents of Satan, as Cornwall says. Perhaps they fight on the side of the angels? Picking out the evil and depraved among us.'

'Alison and Matilda were hardly depraved and evil.'

'Meretrices. Lupae.' This excursion into Latin took me by surprise. 'They were she-wolves, Oswald. Whores.'

'Says who?'

'I know about such matters.' She picked at the teeth of her comb. 'Evil must be punished. Sin must be castigated.'

'What evil? What sin? They were just young girls.'

She waved my question away. 'It must be God's will to punish them. The dog heads are doing His work.' I shook my head at this stupidity, which caused her to snort. 'Who is committing these murders then, Oswald? Tell me that.' I hesitated. 'See. You don't have an answer.'

'But—'

'Or when you do, it's wrong. First it was that Bath woman. Then you told me it was Father John and de Caburn. But how does your theory stand now? With de Caburn murdered himself?'

I sighed and sat down beside her. 'I'm not sure, Mother. But I shall ride out to Versey later and arrest Cornwall. He's involved in this somehow.'

She smiled and stroked my arm. 'Don't disturb yourself, Oswald. There won't be any more killings. I'm certain of it.'

'I wish we could be sure.'

'No, no. We can be absolutely certain. I've been studying the signs.' She lifted her piss pot and twirled around the contents like a pan of soup. 'There's no blood in my water. See.'

Declining the opportunity to study my mother's excreta, I left.

I had planned to take a party immediately to Versey, but put off my departure until the next morning so that we could take advantage of the fine weather and begin the harvest. But this delay was my next great mistake.

As I reached the fields that morning, the men were already working. A strong sun picked out the bristles of the wheat ears, while a soft wind swept over the field, moving the crop in gentle waves. It was a cheering sight for once. But then I saw my workers, and my cheerfulness was stubbed out.

I remembered the swathes of men who used to work the fields at this time of year. To my childish eyes they had always seemed like giants with scythes and pitchforks, working their way steadily across the field like an army of miner beetles. There were no giants today. Only the odds and ends of the village. The leftovers of the Plague.

Taking a scythe, I began to cut. My clumsy attempts at cutting the stalks appeared amusing to my reeve and a couple of his cronies, but I carried on anyway. My labour was needed, even if I was inefficient.

Further down the field a flock of woodlarks rose into the sky and flew back over us. I could hear the beat of their wings as they circled overhead, and then swooped down towards a copse of hazel at the edge of the field. The women put down their tools and pointed at the sky.

'Why have they stopped working?' I asked Featherby.

'They don't like disturbing the birds, sire. They think it's—'

'A bad omen?'

'That's right, sire. They do.' I went back to my scything and remained silent on the matter.

We worked for another hour or so, until my back hurt so badly I thought I might never stand up straight again. Tall weeds grew amongst the wheat, threatening a harvest of dandelion and dock rather than grain.

And as we worked we disturbed many more flocks of birds, causing the women to stop over and over again to pray – to deflect the bad luck that was certainly coming our way. There would be bad luck, that was guaranteed, looking at the quality of our pickings. It would come to those who didn't have enough food to eat this winter.

But I should have paid greater attention to the omens, and not dismissed them as fanciful wanderings. For, as we were sitting to eat some bread, there was a sudden commotion on the horizon. A thundering of horses' hooves. A billowing of brightly coloured cloth, and the call of a group of men.

The women jumped up and instinctively drew themselves into a circle – the older shielding the younger within.

'It's the earl's men,' said Featherby. 'I wonder what they want?'

'Piers must have delivered my letter.'

'Sire?'

'I wrote to the earl about—' I changed my mind about revealing any more to my reeve, though he loomed over me intently for an answer. 'It's no matter.'

Four young squires cantered towards me in the livery of Earl Stephen. Their horses were fine destriers, with coats as smooth as glass and legs so long a man could stand beneath their stomach barrel and not have to stoop. The young men in our group gasped at these magnificent beasts, but I knew better than to be impressed by such a spectacle. In my experience the most elegant of horse was likely to carry the most debased of man, and nothing here was going to change my opinion. The faces circling me were conceited and proud – carved from cruelty and privilege.

'Are you Oswald de Lacy?' the nearest squire asked. He rounded his horse, and it nearly knocked me over, though it was no accident.

'Yes,' I answered, trying to remain upright. 'I'm grateful for your visit, but we're no longer under attack.'

The squire swung a leg over his horse and dismounted. 'What attack?'

'I wrote a letter to the earl. But the problem is solved. You may return now.'

He eyed me suspiciously. 'I don't know anything about a letter.'

'I thought perhaps you—'

His black hair was as gleaming as the coat of his horse, and his face was cleanly shaven. There was something familiar about him that nagged at me. 'I have a warrant for your arrest,' he said.

'My arrest? What for?' The other three riders closed in around me.

'The murder of Walter de Caburn. Lord Versey.'

At last I recognised his face. His name was Godfrey, and once, when we were young boys, he had hidden a slug in my boots to amuse everybody at a family wedding. The smirk across his face caused me to recall the cold slime of the slug's body as it flattened against my toes and stuck to my woollen stockings. I had squealed until my father beat me.

'That's absurd. I didn't murder de Caburn.'

'It's not just Lord Versey.' He took a rolled document from his belt and read aloud. 'You are also accused of the murders of Alison and Matilda Starve . . . crow.'

'What? I didn't kill any of them. I'm not a murderer.'

Godfrey looked about at his companions and sniggered. What a victory for him over the small boy who had once taken his place on his mother's knee and eaten his candied violets. All because my young hair had been soft and white, whereas his was coarse and curly.

'Plead your innocence to the earl, in court,' he now told me.

'But surely I'll be tried by a judge?'

He shrugged. 'There's a gaol house here, isn't there?'

'Yes. But—'

'You are to be taken there.' He seized my arm.

I tried to shake him off, but his grip was firm. 'I will not!' I said. 'Get off me!'

My workers peered in through the legs of the horses, the better to see what was happening. Their faces were fearful, but also fascinated.

'It's the order of the earl,' said Godfrey, now taking a length of rope and attempting to wrap it about my hands.

This time I broke free of him. 'Then the earl is wrong,' I said. The crowd became noisy, causing the horses to twitch and struggle against their riders. A mounted squire took a whip to the nearest man and beat him back, prompting the other villagers to flee to a safe distance.

Godfrey now rounded on me, placing a hand on his sword. 'You are under arrest, de Lacy. Move.'

But I was a nobleman, not a villein or a beggar. He could not simply cut me down. 'I will walk to the gaol house. Do not tether me.'

As we progressed, I tried to keep my dignity, but could scarcely muster the energy to hold my eyes up from staring at the ground. A coil of bad fortune had wound itself about me in the last year, so surely I was due some slack? But no. For now I was to be locked in my own prison. Interrogated in my own court. And then, if found guilty, hanged from my own gallows. No better than a common thief.

I had not foreseen this turn of events. My legs felt unsteady and my heart thumped. It was unfair. I was innocent.

I was angry.

But more than that, I was terrified.

Mother visited me in the gaolhouse that evening, though I tried to dismiss her once she had passed over some bread and potted meat.

'How ever did you manage to slip out and murder de Caburn?' she whispered. 'We had the gate locked for three whole days.'

I hissed at the foolish woman. 'That's because I didn't do it, Mother.'

'Did you swim across the moat?'

'We don't have a moat.'

'Yes we do. At the back of the house.'

'No. That's a ditch that used to be a moat.'

'Whatever you call it. I'm surprised you survived. That water is infested with rats. And their scent can poison the lungs, you know.' She reached inside her pocket bag and pulled out one of her many vials of medicine. 'Can I give you some powders to sniff? They will cleanse your passages.'

I pushed the bottle away. 'If you want to help me, Mother, stop suggesting I'm guilty.' I looked towards the grate in the cell door, checking whether the young squire guarding me was listening – but there was no discernible movement. Usually he stayed outside, grooming his horse.

'Are you saying you didn't kill de Caburn?' Mother screwed up her eyes and knotted her forehead in confusion. The lines formed a neat criss-crossed grid in her skin.

'Yes, Mother. I'm innocent.'

'Why has the earl imprisoned you then? You must have done something.'

'No I haven't.'

She let out a slighted sigh. 'I see. If you don't want to confide in me, Oswald. Then I won't say another word.'

'That's because there is nothing to confide!'

The squire rapped on the door, since I had raised my voice. It seemed he was not outside with his horse after all.

A long silence followed, only broken by Mother's sorrowful puffs.

'Why don't you just go home, Mother?' I said in the end.

'But you'll be lonely, Oswald. I wanted to cheer you up.'

'I'd rather be on my own, thank you.'

Another sigh. 'That cunning little Delilah would come to see you. If I permitted it.'

'Mirabel?'

'She's baked you a pie, although Gilbert is furious. She used all of the saffron.' Then she huffed. 'But I know what you're like. Happy to confide in such a silly girl, when you won't say a word to your own dear mother.'

I thought of the four squires about the village, and imagined how vulnerable Mirabel would be away from the house. 'You mustn't let her come here, Mother. Not under any circumstances.'

'She's very headstrong, Oswald. Yesterday she would only clean my feet if I allowed her to wear a scarf over her nose.'

'You must say I don't want to see her, Mother. It's important.'

She suddenly smiled and tapped me on the knee. 'I agree. I wouldn't want to see the girl either. She's very dreary.' Then she frowned. 'But what about this foolish pie she's made you?'

'Eat it yourselves.'

Mother stood up to leave. 'Is there anything more I can do for you, Oswald?' As if she had spent the last hour comforting me.

'Just get word to Brother Peter at the convent. It's important he knows I've been arrested.' She hurried away, full of promises and with the glass bottles of her mobile apothecary chinking against one another in her pouch.

It seemed she would do as I asked, but after two further days spent in near solitary confinement, I began to wonder.

The days rolled into one another. My only visitor, apart from Gilbert, was Joan Bath, who insisted upon sweeping out the cell and giving me a washed blanket. I was surprised to see her, since I had not treated the woman fairly. She accepted my gratitude rather suspiciously, arguing that nobody had cleaned the room since her imprisonment, so she didn't like to think of me sleeping in her dirt and dust. She also brought some lavender and sage, which she suggested I rub occasionally to allay the stink of the cell – caused by the primitive latrine that emptied through a hole in the wall into a pit below the only window.

I tried to glean some news from Joan, but she was hurried away by the squire, who then negotiated an arrangement between the two of them. I could hear the whole conversation and noted Joan settled on twice the price he initially offered. At least somebody was profiting from my misfortune.

For three days I slept upon the hard wooden bed, with lice crawling at my back and ankles. But on the fifth day of my imprisonment my prayers were finally answered. Flustered and red about the face, Peter burst into my cell with news that the royal judge would be in Somershill by the following morning. He gave the squire some pennies to spend at the tavern and to leave us alone for an hour. We were then bolted into the room, with a bench jammed against the door in case we somehow managed to pick the lock.

Peter watched the squire go and then hugged me. 'Why didn't you get word to me, Oswald? As soon as you were taken into custody?'

'I tried. Mother promised to send a message to you.'

He huffed indignantly. 'That old nanny goat couldn't promise to remember her own name.' He checked the window again to make certain nobody was spying on us from outside, even though the pile of night soil from the latrine would deter even the most fervent of eavesdroppers.

'Who told you I was here?' I asked.

'The earl's men came to the convent looking for Clemence. They believe she's your accomplice, Oswald. Only the sanctuary of the convent has saved her from arrest.'

'My accomplice?'

'Yes. They think she sent a letter to de Caburn, requesting he visit her at the convent. They believe it was a trap devised by the two of you. She lured him into the forest, where you then murdered him.'

'But I didn't leave Somershill for three days, Brother Peter. I have witnesses.'

Peter pulled the flask from his belt pouch and took a gulp. It was brandy. 'I know that, you foolish boy. I don't suspect you.'

I felt panic rising. 'What about Clemence? Could she have done it?'

'She can barely walk, Oswald. She had to be—' He hesitated and shook his head. 'No. I won't speak of it.'

'But she has Humbert with her. He would do anything Clemence asked of him.'

He nodded. 'I wondered the same, so I confronted the boy. He insists upon his innocence.' He offered me the flask, but I refused. 'It's hard to know whether or not to believe him. The boy is as blank as a lump of limestone.'

'You know I'm accused of the Starvecrow murders as well?'

Peter sighed. 'Yes. That's Cornwall's doing. He's taken the opportunity to feed the earl all sorts of lies about you. And unfortunately there are coincidences that link you to both girls.'

'Such as?'

'For one thing, Alison Starvecrow came to speak with you on the day she disappeared.'

'But I didn't see her.'

Peter cleared his throat. 'We both know that. But others believe you granted her an audience. Only you didn't like what she had to tell you.'

I almost laughed. 'Of course. This great secret. Which nobody seems to know, apart from a dead girl.'

Peter threw up his hands. 'There's no great secret, Oswald. You know how a village girl's mind works. She probably wanted to accuse you of dancing naked with devils or making love to goats. In the hope you'd give her a penny to go away.'

'And Matilda? Why am I suspected of her murder?'

'You were the last person to visit her.'

'No. Joan Bath was there when I left the house.'

'We've discussed Joan Bath before, haven't we Oswald? And then there was the issue with Matilda's body. You found her head-less corpse but did not alert anybody.'

'But Gilbert was there as well. He can vouch for my innocence.'

'He's your valet, Oswald. People will accuse him of saying whatever you demand of him.'

I put my head in my hands. The skin of my forehead was damp, and my fingers smelt stale and greasy. I had never spent so long in such a filthy place. 'We could tell the earl the truth.'

'What truth?'

'That we found de Caburn and Cornwall in the forest. That they were about to rape and murder Mirabel.'

He sighed. 'It's still too much of a risk, Oswald. The accusation might rebound and send you even more quickly to the gallows.'

Gallows. Such a word. I felt sick and had to put my head between my knees. Peter comforted me and held my hand, but then the squire began banging on the door. We hadn't noticed him return from the tavern.

'Time to leave, priest,' he shouted through the grate.

Peter whispered into my ear. 'Listen to me, Oswald. You mustn't worry. I have an idea to save you.'

The squire had opened the door by now and was motioning for Brother Peter to leave. His words were slurred after his hurried bout of drinking. 'Come on. Get out of here, now. You've had your time.'

Peter waved him away and again whispered in my ear. 'I'll see you in court tomorrow, Oswald. Do not contradict anything I say. Do you understand?' I nodded pathetically. 'Promise me. Your life will depend upon it.'

I found it difficult to sleep that night – my dreams were strange and terrifying. I was not in the filthy cottage, waiting to die of the Plague. Instead I had become two persons within one body. One soul was good. But the other was an aberration. A monster, responsible for murdering my own half-sisters and de Caburn.

There had been such poor souls in the infirmary. Crouched in corners, speaking to company that didn't exist.

I woke from my doze with a start, as if somebody had come into the room and grabbed me by the foot. But nothing was there, except shadows against the walls – flitting shapes that could have been the ghosts of long-gone prisoners, leaching out from the stone. I returned to a fitful sleep, but woke again – this time hearing my name in a whisper. Now I would not even open my eyes – not until something small and hard hit my head. Looking out from underneath my covers, I saw a pair of small hands at the bars of the window.

I crept over cautiously. 'Who's there?'

'It's me. Mirabel.' I looked through the bars and saw she was standing in the overflow from the latrine, but was not tall enough to reach the sill. 'I've brought you some pie, sire.'

'It's not safe for you here, Mirabel. The earl's men are in the village.'

'They're sleeping at the inn. They have women with them.'

'Please. Go back to Somershill. Quickly.'

'But I baked this pie especially for you, sire. It has a special ingredient.'

I suddenly imagined that she and Brother Peter had baked a knife inside this pie and that now I was expected to murder the guard and make good my escape. Perhaps this was the secret plan to save my life? I hoped not.

'Did Brother Peter ask you to bake this?'

She seemed confused. 'No. It was my own idea. It has a special ingredient. Nobody else knows.'

'What type of special ingredient?'

'I grated a little of your Mother's bone of St Peter.'

I suppressed a smile, thinking of the sacred bone that Mother kept in a silver casket next to her bed. At best it was a fragment of a peasant's skeleton, but it could even have started life as part of a sheep or a cow. I knew the tricks the relic mongers played. Boiling up the carcasses to remove all vestiges of flesh. Dusting the bones with chalk and wood ash. But Mother would not hear of her own precious relic coming from such deceit. She prayed with it nightly – and would not have been at all pleased to hear it had been grated into a pie!

I looked down at Mirabel's beautiful face and wondered at her gentle compassion, but also her foolishness. 'Pass the pie up. Then you must leave.'

She held the pastry-covered dish to me, but there was no chance something so large would fit through the bars. So she broke pieces off and squeezed them one by one between the iron poles.

'I can stay with you for a little while, sire. Are you lonely?'

'Yes, Mirabel. I am.'

'Are you frightened?'

'No,' I lied. 'I'm sure justice will be served tomorrow.'

'St Peter will save you. With the dust of his bones.'

She put her hand through the bar, and I held it. It was small but strong – not the limp paw of a gentlewoman. I kissed the rough skin of her fingers, and she agreed to go.

After watching her melt into the shadows, I ate the pie, which tasted every bit as unpleasant as it had promised to be.

Chapter Eighteen

The galloping of hooves is seldom anything but the announcement of trouble. So, on hearing horses the next morning I was quick to jump out of bed and speak to my guard. He was cleaning dried mud from his boots and brushing dust from his over-kirtle. His face was shaven, and his hair was combed for the first time in days.

'Who's that arriving?' I asked.

He didn't look up at me. 'The earl and his knights. They are here for your trial.'

'Or to see me hang. So the earl can take my land.'

The squire looked up at me soberly. 'The earl can be a just man. Unless you provoke him.' Then he smiled to himself, and added under his breath, 'Just make sure you laugh at his jokes.'

I slumped back down onto the bed. Could any man who befriended de Caburn be described as a just man? I doubted so.

It was the day of my trial, but if I had hoped for a bowl of water to wash my face and a blade to shave my chin I was unlucky – for I left my cell feeling as sticky as a ripe damson waiting to be devoured by wasps.

Silent, gawping faces watched my progress through the village towards the place of my trial, which was to be the great hall at Somershill. I expected no less, since it was the usual location for the Hundreds Court, but it felt strange and jarring to be tried under my own tiles. Perversely, it almost made me want to laugh.

As we neared St Giles I noticed old Eleanor at the road-side – the woman who had once been Mother's lady's maid. Despite her dropsy, she had struggled out of her cottage to watch me pass.

'God bless you, sire,' she said, thrusting a bunch of St John's Wort into my hands. 'Wasn't your fault them dog heads corrupted your soul. It was the milk.'

'Milk?'

'Your nursemaid's, sire. Adeline Starvecrow's.' The guards pulled me away. 'Rub the leaves, sire. The Chase-Devil plant will ward off the demons.'

I tried to pass the small posy of yellow flowers back to Eleanor, but she wouldn't take it. 'The Devil stinks of the sewers. This will sweeten your nose.' I should have dropped this foolish talisman into the mud, but somehow it found its way into my pocket.

The disgrace of being led through my own gate under armed guard was shaming, and I looked to my feet to avoid meeting the eyes of Gilbert or Ada. Fortunately there was no sign of Mother or Mirabel. I then was dumped in the cellar without a candle, and left to contemplate my fate, while the hall was made ready for the trial.

In the velvet of the black, something moved. I was disorientated and called out, but nobody answered. The room smelt mustier than ever and, although my eyes were adjusting to the lack of light, the barrels and sacks seemed instead to be forms waiting to advance upon me.

Something moved again. I felt a breath upon my face. And then suddenly I saw faces in the shadows. At first I thought it was an old woman. Then a girl. Their cadaverous features materialised and then disappeared within moments. A rushed desire came upon me. I would scream out. Demand to be released.

For the first time in many weeks I felt the overwhelming need to shit.

The moment passed. I closed my eyes, took long and deep breaths and felt my way across the room to Brother Peter's secret supply of Madeira. Sure enough a bottle was hidden in a familiar place. Sitting down upon the step near the door, I pulled the cork from the neck and downed the warm and slightly vinegary drink. There were no ghouls or ghosts in this room. The darkness was nothing but a cruel kindling – stirring up my fear of the gallows and the injustice of being accused of crimes I had not committed.

Something brushed against my leg, but this time I was not startled. It was only the kitchen cat, stalking the cellar for mice and rats. I stroked her soft coat as she arched her back and purred, and somewhere on the other side of the heavy wooden door came the booming voice of a man. It could only be the earl.

Earl Stephen, in common with many noblemen, rarely spoke English. Preferring French, his speech was tainted with long vowels and an awkward emphasis on the second syllable of most words. In order to make himself understood in English, a language he despised, he believed it was necessary to shout. Perhaps he thought all ordinary Englishmen deaf or stupid, because each sentence, even the most modest of requests, was delivered with the boom of a battle cry.

'Where is the priest?' I heard him say. The reply was impossible to hear, being merely a sequence of low-sounding murmurs. 'What is his name? Con Wool?' Once again the reply was too indistinct to hear. '*Oui. Lui.* Cornwall. Don't sit him next to me. And where is that *femme*? That woman?' The muffled voice was flustered and appeared to be listing women, all of whose names were met with a petulant '*non, non, non!*' The earl raised his voice another notch. 'She is a *cadavre*. A skeleton.' Another pause. The earl's tone relaxed. '*Oui, oui.* Madame de Lacy. She must not attend the trial. *Elle parle trop.* She talks too much!'

The conversation now faded, though I could still hear Earl Stephen demanding to be served '*vin*' and '*viande*'. Moments later Gilbert burst into the cellar and knocked me from the step.

Flustered by his mistake, he picked me up and dusted me down. 'I'm so sorry, sire. I've to fetch wine. Anybody would think this is some sort of feast.' He then muttered some obscene remarks about the French, which I will not commit to this account.

'Is the judge here yet?' I asked, as Gilbert rooted around behind me, rocking each barrel in turn.

Gilbert stood up straight and sighed. 'Yes, sire. He's wanting ale.'

'I'm not guilty.'

'I know that. I've told them you never left Somershill when Lord Versey was murdered. But they don't believe me.'

'Where's Brother Peter?'

'I haven't seen him, sire. But you know how he comes and goes. Never sure where he's going to appear.'

'And my mother?'

'She's been banished to the solar, with all the other women.' He let a smile escape. 'The earl doesn't like all their talking.'

He picked the barrel up awkwardly and shuffled past me. 'I'd better go. They're wanting this wine as well. But I've prayed for you. The Lord looks kindly upon the innocent.' I thanked him for his words. I think he meant them.

The door slammed shut behind him and the chamber returned to darkness. Sitting back down again on the step a cold draught hit the back of my throat and the stone chilled my backside. The walls were damp in this underground chamber, and an ill-favoured miasma filled the room with its dank odours and cold bile. I took the St John's Wort from my pocket and rubbed it in my hands. The soft leaves gave off an oil – the same oil Brother Peter and I used in the infirmary to treat the bed sores of the oldest monks.

I sighed. Where was Brother Peter? What of his promise to save me?

In the late morning two squires led me from the cellar into the great hall to be tried in front of a jury of free men. But seeing their twelve faces was no consolation, for they were not the local men I had expected – instead my jury was to be a collection of the earl's knights and squires. Behind them a rabble of villagers vied for position, pushing and shoving each other in a desire to watch this mockery from the closest possible point.

Featherby loomed over his fellow spectators like a gallows tree, while behind him stood my tenant Wallwork and his buxom daughter Abigail. She did not look so keen to marry me now. By her mocking smile she seemed to be enjoying my discomfort, after the shame I had caused her at our last meeting. No doubt she saw this as a fitting repayment.

Three men sat at my dinner table. In the middle was the royal judge – a small and shrivelled man who didn't seem to fit into his own clothing. The scant hair he possessed was red, and his face was flushed with freckles. I had never met this man before, but from his appearance I knew him to be Deaf Ellingham – the judge famed for sending the wrong man to hang after mishearing his name.

Earl Stephen sat to Ellingham's right in a cape edged in ermine and a parti-coloured doublet of green and blue, as if it might be mid-winter. He was a tall man with the colouring of a Moor. His long arms spread out like the limbs of a grasshopper, resting indolently across the table as only a man of his standing feels able to do. To Ellingham's left was Cornwall, with his cloak spread wide revealing a glimpse of red satin. His hands lay upon the buckskin coat of a Bible – a manuscript that should not have left St Giles.

I pointed to the Bible. 'It's a pity you cannot read the words inside, Father John.'

'What was that?' said Ellingham. He cupped a freckled hand to his ear.

I cleared my throat. There was little point in being reserved. 'I was wondering why Father John has the Bible with him? When he knows so little Latin.'

An amused smile spread across the earl's face. He leant forward to stare at Cornwall, cocking his head to listen for an answer.

Cornwall reddened. 'Must I answer such a foolish question?' He spoke to Ellingham in a sideways whisper, but the judge merely wrinkled his nose to suggest he had not understood.

The earl answered for him. '*Bien sûr. Père Jean*. Answer. Please.'

Cornwall bowed his head elegantly to the earl, since he now had no option but to reply to my question, no matter how foolish he felt it to be. 'I'm a man of God, my lord. I always have the Bible with me.'

'But can you read Latin?' asked the earl. 'We want to know.' There was a moment's silence, and then the earl slapped the table and began to laugh. There was neither a witty pun nor clever insinuation in this comment. In fact there was nothing to find amusing in it at all, but this didn't stop the jury of leather-skinned knights and pimply squires quickly falling about in hysterics. Even Cornwall, who was the butt of this supposed joke, attempted to laugh, though his face was now blotched and sweating.

'I am only teasing you, *Père Jean*,' said the earl when the laughter had died down. 'You are not on trial.' He waved his arm at Ellingham as if he was shooing off a flock of geese. '*Alors*. Please. Continue. This is taking too long.' He then yawned like a baby.

Ellingham appeared to understand, and quickly straightened his papers. The volume of the earl's voice clearly had some advantages, if only to communicate effectively with a man who was hard of hearing.

Ellingham looked up at me. 'Lord Somershill. Oswald de

Lacy. You are accused of the murders of Alison Starvecrow, Matilda Starvecrow and Walter de Caburn, Lord Versey. How do you plead?'

'I'm not guilty,' I said with all the confidence I could muster. 'And I am outraged to be standing here. I don't—' My attention was suddenly drawn to the squint, from where Mother waved at me as enthusiastically as if she had just seen me take my first communion. The earl turned to see what had caught my attention.

'Your mother, eh?' he asked, pointing up to the small window where Mother's face and breasts were now squashed against the glass. 'Madame de Lacy?'

'Yes, my lord. I'm afraid it is.'

Earl Stephen once again slapped the table and dissolved into laughter. 'He is afraid!' His followers responded as before, each striving to guffaw more loudly than the next. '*J'ai peur aussi!*' Tears stained his cheeks and ran into the black hair of his beard. '*Votre mère est une truie ancienne!*'

He had called my mother an old sow, and I might have challenged him, except I didn't want to ruin his good humour.

'My lord,' said Ellingham after an acceptable pause, 'should we continue?' The earl made another of his goose-shooing gestures, and the trial resumed.

Ellingham peered across at me and, given the cloudy film across his pale blue eyes, I began to wonder if he were not also blind as well as deaf. The bright light of the room seemed to affect his vision, and he squinted. 'We will commence with the murder of Lord Versey.' An expectant hush descended. 'Oswald de Lacy. You are accused of luring Lord Versey to the Convent of St Margaret to visit your sister Clemence. As he travelled there, you ambushed and murdered him.'

'I was here at Somershill at the time of his death. I have witnesses.'

Cornwall broke in. 'Men who will say whatever he tells them to. Their testimony should be discounted.'

'What?' Ellingham cupped his hand to his ear again.

I spoke loudly to prevent Cornwall's answer being heard. 'I didn't lure de Caburn to the convent. You have no evidence to prove such a theory.'

'I saw the hand-written note,' said Cornwall, 'from your sister.'

'Where is it then? Who is to say it even existed?'

Cornwall folded his arms. 'I say it existed. And it smelt of evil.'

'You smelt the letter?' I hoped my exaggerated astonishment might ignite the earl's strange sense of humour, but he seemed more interested in picking his fingernails. I persevered. 'Did you smell the letter since you were unable to read it?' This, at least, raised a smile at the corner of the earl's lips, but still he did not look up.

Cornwall, always conscious of the earl's mood, saw his opportunity to pounce. 'It is my contention that Lord Somershill committed this murder for personal gain,' he said grandly. 'With his sister as Lord Versey's widow, he would hope to gain control of the Versey estate.'

Cornwall then flared his cloak to reveal a flash of red satin. What vanity to wear such expensive cloth, when it was usually the preserve of nobility. His mistake was not lost on the earl. He regarded the shine of Cornwall's gown and suddenly frowned.

Now was my chance. 'I think it more likely that you murdered Lord Versey, John of Cornwall. Your motive was fear.'

Cornwall clasped his hands upon the Bible. 'What nonsense is this now?'

Deaf Ellingham cupped both ears this time. He was struggling to follow any of the proceedings. 'What did de Lacy say?' he asked Cornwall.

Cornwall raised his voice to the boom of a sermon. 'Lord Somershill would debase himself so low as to accuse a man of God of these crimes. Crimes he himself committed. It proves his guilt.' Nods and murmurs from the crowd seemed to support his claim, but still Earl Stephen said nothing.

Only as the hubbub died down did the earl divert his interest from his fingernails and speak. 'Why do you say this, de Lacy?' He pointed at Cornwall. 'Why do you say *Père Jean* is guilty?'

I thought back to Brother Peter's warning about implicating de Caburn in these crimes – but what choice did I have? 'I accuse John of Cornwall of murdering Lord Versey,' I said.

The earl shrugged. 'Yes. But *pourquoi*? Why?'

'Lord Versey and Father John liked to rape and murder young girls.' Gasps were audible amongst the crowd.

'*C'est vrai?*'

'Yes. It's true, my lord. I only discovered their guilt recently.'

But the earl did not seem convinced. 'But why did *Père Jean* kill Versey?'

'With their crimes exposed, they either argued. Or more likely, Father John wanted to silence de Caburn.'

Cornwall threw up his hands. 'Listen to this false testimony. The boy would even accuse Lord Versey! Regard the evil of the boy.'

'Do you deny I caught you and de Caburn in the forest with a girl?' I asked the priest.

Cornwall turned to the earl. 'My lord. We should not countenance such defamation and slander. Lord Versey was your friend.' The earl rocked his head from side to side at this suggestion and then looked absently into the distance.

Cornwall was becoming irritated. 'The boy speaks against Lord Versey, my lord. You should not allow this. What say you?' The earl suddenly focussed and leant forward to stare at Cornwall, looking down the bridge of his nose with the full force of aristocratic condescension. An awkward hush fell upon the hall.

Cornwall pulled his cloak about him, shrinking into his seat and hiding the red of his satin lining. 'He has no evidence for this accusation, my lord,' he whimpered. 'De Lacy's attempting to trick you.' Still the earl said nothing. His lips puckered into a grimace.

I broke the silence. 'John of Cornwall. Do you deny I caught you and Lord Versey in the forest with a girl? You were about to rape her.'

'That is a lie.'

'Just as you and Lord Versey had already murdered the Starvecrow sisters?'

'Another lie!'

The earl now gazed at me and it was my turn to feel the burn of his sneer. 'I managed to save the girl, my lord. But otherwise she would have met the same fate as the Starvecrows.' I felt blood rush into my face. 'It should be John of Cornwall on trial. Not I.'

The earl heaved a sigh and stretched out his long grasshopper arms. '*Extraordinaire.*'

'My lord,' said Cornwall. Beads of sweat bubbled across his forehead like blisters. 'I am a man of God. These are blatant lies and—'

I interrupted before he regained his momentum. 'The girl will bear witness to Cornwall's crime. I can call her to the court.'

The earl sat up at my words. 'She is here? *Ici?*'

'Yes, my lord.'

'*Alors. Je l'écoute.* I will listen to her. Bring her into the—'

But his words were drowned by a sudden scuffle.

Through the mêlée I heard Brother Peter's voice. He was shouting. 'Let me speak. I have important information. I must be heard!' He shoved his way through the crowd, but I have no idea how he had gained entry to the hall, since the main door was locked, and I had not seen his face before this moment.

Peter bowed as deeply to the earl as his back would allow. His voice was breathless and agitated. 'My lord. I beg your indulgence, but I have news that will shed a new light upon this trial.'

The earl cocked his head to one side and stroked his beard. 'Who are you?'

'My name is Brother Peter, my lord. Of the Benedictine order. I am the infirmarer at Kintham Abbey.'

The earl turned to his entourage with a smile. 'A saw bones, eh?' The men began to snigger. 'Are you unwell, *Père* Saw-Bones? You sweat like a *cochon*. A pig.'

Peter ignored the gibe. 'My lord. I had the honour of treating your son two years ago.'

'*Lequel?* Gregory *ou* Hugh?'

'It was Gregory, my lord. He broke his arm hunting at Versey. I re-set the bone.'

The earl's face dissolved into a broad smile. 'Ah *oui*! I remember you. *Vous l'avez bien fait.* You did it well.'

Peter bowed again. 'I trust Gregory's arm is recovered. And that he may use it well again?'

The earl laughed out loud. '*Oui. Bien sûr*. His arm is recovered. And he uses it very well.' He made an obscene gesture to indicate how Gregory was exercising his re-set arm and looked back to the jury for the obligatory roar of laughter.

Ellingham waited for the comedy to subside, with a face not able entirely to disguise his weariness. 'Why have you disturbed the court, Brother Paul?' he asked. 'This is a murder trial. Not a meeting of old friends.'

'I have discovered the true murderer of Lord Versey and the Starvecrow sisters.'

Ellingham cupped his ear. 'What?'

Brother Peter shouted, 'I have discovered the true murderer. You must release Lord Somershill.'

Ellingham screwed up his face and waved a bony finger. 'You are wasting our time, Brother Paul. Please stand aside and let the trial continue.'

'But if you continue, you risk—'

'Stand aside, Brother Paul!' said Ellingham. 'I will not tell you again.'

Peter looked to the earl, but his new friend was once again

picking his fingernail and didn't care to respond. 'But the court should hear what I have to say!' Still no reaction from the earl. 'You have arrested an innocent man. And my name is Brother Peter!'

Ellingham beckoned to the guards to take Peter away, but as the two men went to seize him, Peter managed to shake them off. 'You must listen to me.'

'Arrest the man.'

'But I have discovered the dog-headed beast!'

The court became instantly silent. My heart missed a beat. 'What are you doing, Brother?' I tried to whisper to him. 'This won't help.'

But Peter ignored me. 'Give me some men, my lord. I'll lead them to the beast.'

'Stand aside,' repeated Ellingham. This time the two guards succeeded in taking Peter, but relaxed their grip, when the earl pulled the judge towards him. '*Non! Arrêtez!* I want to hear this man.' He then bellowed in Ellingham's ear. '*Frère Pierre* must speak!'

The judge held the side of his head and cried out in pain.

Peter bowed to the earl. 'Thank you, my lord.'

'*Alors.* Speak.'

'I came here to inform the court of my discovery. The Cynocephalus. The dog-headed beast.'

The earl snorted. '*Une bête?*'

'It is responsible for the murder of Lord Versey and the Starvecrow sisters.'

'A dog head? *Qu'est-ce que c'est?*'

'It is a sinful creature that has crept here from the east, bringing plague and pestilence to our lands. It has the head of a wolf and the body of a man.'

The earl pulled his chin into his neck and frowned. 'I don't know it.'

'Ask Father John, my lord,' said Peter. 'He was the first to identify the mark of the dog-headed beast on the Starvecrow sisters. He brought the creature to our attention and knows of its guilt.'

The earl leant forward to regard Cornwall. '*C'est vrai?*' Cornwall looked blank at his words, not understanding even the most simple of French. 'Is that true? *Père Jean?*' said the earl, now becoming irritated again.

Cornwall remained silent for a few moments as the wheels and pulleys of his mind worked quickly. He would appear a fool for accusing me of the murders, when he had previously cited dog heads. On the other hand, he risked being called a murderer himself – a charge I was having some success in promoting.

Cornwall opened his cloak tentatively. 'I am heartened to hear Brother Peter admit to the existence of such beasts, my lord. Both he and Lord Somershill have previously denied them.'

Peter put his hands together and bowed most obsequiously to Cornwall. 'I now regret my former intransigence. I most humbly beg your forgiveness, Father John.' I tried to get Peter's attention, but he steadfastly ignored me.

The earl beckoned his knights from the jury bench. They spoke softly in French, but since the earl's whispers were at the level of ordinary conversation, his words were hardly a secret. Anybody with the rudiments of his language could understand that he was asking his knights if they had ever heard of such creatures. There was a general shrugging and questioning of the story until one of his party claimed to have sighted a similar beast, in the forests of Gascony.

The earl then waved the men away and pointed to Brother Peter. 'You know where this dog head is?' Peter nodded. 'You can lead some men there?'

'Of course.'

'*Allez*. Go quickly. Bring the creature back. I want to see it.'

My heart began to drum against my chest. Peter's deception would be too easy to expose. I wished he had left me to pursue Cornwall rather than concoct this preposterous story.

Peter stepped forward nervously. 'I would be pleased to capture the dog-headed beast, my lord. But I shall need the assistance of your knights and squires.' The earl now looked uneasy. Perhaps this was Peter's plan? To draw the best men away from Somershill, so I might escape?

'You may take my squires,' said the earl. 'My knights stay here.'

'Thank you, my lord.'

'And take *Père Jean*.'

Brother Peter froze. 'That's not necessary, my lord. I have enough experience of dealing with devilry. I'm sure Father John would rather stay here.' Cornwall felt his cloak nervously, unsure whether it was a good idea to be part of this search party or not.

'*Non*. Take him!' The earl turned to his men. 'He can smell out the evil, eh?' The joke was as thin as when I had cracked it – but on this occasion it was met with great guffaws.

Then, like a child suddenly bored of a game, the earl signalled that he wanted to clear the hall. The jury headed for the tavern, Deaf Ellingham collected his papers, and the villagers filed out. Only I remained in custody. Taken back to the gaol house, from where I watched the search party leave on horseback.

The afternoon was dissolving into evening, and a low haze hung over the meadow outside my small window. I could almost smell autumn, and had I been a boy who believed in portents and prophecy, I would have taken its promise of dampness and decay as a bad omen.

I did not understand what Brother Peter was planning, and could not see how this hunt for dog heads would help me.

I felt damned.

Chapter Nineteen

The night was heavy and still, and the moon was bright. I lay awake watching the shadows on the wall again and listening to the snoring of the squire who had been left behind to guard me. I wondered if I would be hanged tomorrow, when, inevitably, they would not find a dog-headed beast. I was both tired and alert, so that every time I closed my eyes all I could see were flashing images. The more I tried to dislodge them, the faster they blinked and burnt, until they spun into a skewer of pain that bored relentlessly into the back of my eye.

As the sun began to rise, sleep finally found me, but it was only for the briefest of time. I was woken up by the sound of voices. Excited voices. Urgent, frightened voices. And there was a smell too. It was the true smell of autumn. Of wet wood smoking in the hearth.

I rattled the door. 'What's going on?' I shouted through the cracks.

The door was unexpectedly opened. 'They've found the dog head,' said the squire. His face was red and animated. 'You're free to go, sire.' He bowed to me. 'The earl says so.'

'What do you mean? What dog head?'

'They found it hiding, sire. They're going to burn it.'

I tried to leave, but found my progress blocked by the earl himself. His long and finely dressed arm crossed the doorway like the rail of a gate.

'My lord,' I said and bowed my head.

'You have heard the news, eh? A dog head.' He laughed. 'I have never seen such a creature. *Un visage comme un loup*. A wolf. You want to watch it burn?'

'I don't know what you're burning, my lord. But it cannot be a dog head. They do not exist.'

I went to push past him, but the earl pressed a hand against my chest. '*Non, non*. It is a monster, de Lacy. *Un diable*. I say it must burn!'

'But—'

He lowered his chin and raised his thick eyebrows. 'This is my verdict, eh?'

'But I think that—'

He clapped his hands. 'Enough!'

'May I go then, my lord?'

'*Bientôt*. Soon.'

He sniffed the air of the cell in disgust, waving to the squire for his bag of fragrant herbs. He pressed the bag firmly to his nose and then beckoned for me to follow him outside.

As I left the cell he put his arm around my shoulders. 'Stay a while, de Lacy. We are friends now, eh? I want to talk to you.'

'But I must—'

'I have something for you, de Lacy. *Un cadeau*.'

'A gift?'

'*Oui*. Of course!' He said this as if we often exchanged presents. I felt sweat begin to form in my armpits. 'I have decided you will have Versey. As well as Somershill.' He punched my side in jest, but his long limbs encased me like the legs of a spider, and his breath smelt sour.

'But de Caburn has daughters,' I said. 'And my sister Clemence is his widow. Surely they will inherit the estate?'

He snorted. '*Non, non*. Send her to a nunnery. I will not discuss my business with women. We are *voisins* now. Neighbours. We share interests.' He leant forward and feigned a whisper. 'De Caburn was a fool. *Non?*'

'A fool?'

'*Oui. Il riait toujours.*'

I must have frowned, giving the earl to believe I didn't understand his French.

'He was always laughing, de Lacy.' His face contorted. 'But why? It is very foolish.'

'But I thought you and de Caburn were friends?'

He squeezed me tightly. '*Jamais! Non*. And I am happy the Devil has taken him. He didn't pay his dues. *Vous comprenez?*'

I understood perfectly. I was younger, less experienced, and more easily bullied than de Caburn. And the earl had belatedly realised that he could exact more money from me.

I wriggled free. 'I must go, my lord.'

'*Oui. Allez.* Go to the burning,' he said, slapping me roundly across the back. 'But I will return in a month. We will talk more then.' As I sped away, he shouted to me, 'Remember, de Lacy. *Vous êtes Seigneur Versey*. I said so.'

I ran towards the smoke that rose into a pale sky. A noisy crowd was already gathered about its flames, and pushing my way through their backs I soon came up against two of the earl's squires as they dragged an angry and struggling woman away from the fire. It was Joan Bath.

She screamed with unhallowed fury. Her face was stained with tears and mud. 'Stop this!' she bawled. But the crowd about her only hissed and jeered. A small boy kicked at her dress, to which she responded by spitting.

And then she caught sight of my face and managed to pull herself free of the guards, clutching at my legs with the desperation of a child being separated from his mother. 'Stop them, sire.' She choked. 'Please. Stop them! It's not a dog head they are burning.'

I knelt down to help her, but she was soon peeled away from me by the heavy hands of the squires, and once again hauled off into the sea of people.

'The priest betrayed me!' she screamed, before disappearing into the uproar. 'It's he who should burn!'

Now I pushed my way to the flames themselves. 'Let me through,' I shouted.

At first those about me didn't respond, only turning to look at me when I grabbed at their tunics. Perhaps they had forgotten who I was? A young girl asked me to lift her so she might see the sinner die. A ragged boy tried to sell me a faggot of fat for half a penny.

And then a wail cut through the air. It was thin and piteous and came from within the pyre itself – but pushing my way through to the flames, I found no curling and blackened body tied to a stake. No sooty chains or iron hoops. Only the carcass of a bull, with the fire now licking at the brown and white hair of its coat.

The beast had not been skinned and its mouth was jammed open with a thick metal skewer. I recognised the animal immediately. It was my best Simmental bull, Goliath. But why were they burning such a valuable beast? I couldn't understand. Goliath had sired most of our dairy herd. We could not afford such waste. And then a strange thing caught my eye. Beneath the creature's distended belly something seemed to move about like a rat inside a sack of barley. I tried to look closer, but the heat repelled me.

Then the plaintive call came again. A groan, followed by the high-pitched scream of a vixen. I grasped the man standing next to me. It was my reeve, Featherby. 'How can the beast be calling?' I said. 'Is it still alive?'

He regarded me curiously. 'No, sire. I slaughtered him myself.'

'Then what's making such a noise?'

'The dog-headed beast. It calls through the neck of the bull.'

'What?'

'We've sewn it inside, sire.'

I felt nauseated. 'Whilst still living?'

He nodded. 'We hoped to hear it beg for forgiveness as it burns. But it only screams and screeches like a devil.'

I grabbed the fool. 'Put the fire out. Now!'

'But sire? The sacrifice of our best bull will cleanse the demon of sin.'

'Who told you this?'

'The priest.'

These words might once have paralysed me, but no longer. 'Fetch water,' I shouted to those about me. Nobody moved. Instead they stared at the blaze — transfixed by this spectacle of burning flesh. The ragged boy launched his faggot of fat into the fire, boasting that he was helping to cook the sinner's heart.

I shook him by the coarse wool of his tunic. 'Water!' I said. 'I command it!' The boy backed away from me and disappeared into the crowd, only to return sheepishly with a bucket of dirty water. And then, after watching me stamp upon the flames, some others began to bring water from the dew pond. At first it was but one or two of them, but soon their numbers grew and suddenly the group became as frenzied about extinguishing the fire as they had been about fanning it.

When the heat had died down to a steam, we dragged the sweating hulk of the bull over the embers of the fire to let it cool upon the muddy grass. As we threw yet more water over its rump, their faces drew in about me, both sickened and thrilled as I cut through the stitches in the beast's belly to release its doomed stuffing. It was a trussed and writhing thing that rolled out in front of us — bound as tightly as a smoked sausage.

As I loosened the ropes, the blackened form shuddered and coughed, before gasping for one last mouthful of air. Then, as Death claimed his prize, I held the wilting body in my arms and looked about me at these persecutors. I wanted them to see what they had done. But they could only recoil and avert their eyes in shame.

And what shame.

For the creature I cradled was neither a dog-headed beast, nor a devil that required to be purged of sin. It was a boy. Leofwin. His face distorted – not by a misfortune of nature, but by terror and pain.

I ran into the trees and wept, and when my tears were finally exhausted, I let my body shake and convulse until it settled to a weak tremble. And then I returned to the remains of the fire, afraid the boy's body would be further despoiled in my absence.

Now I found a new crowd gathered – with John of Cornwall at its core. Kneeling before Leofwin's limp and lifeless body, Cornwall feigned the seizures of an exorcist in the midst of an incantation. Struggling to his feet, he then turned to the crowd with his hands raised, as if he were Christ himself.

My fury was now complete. Snatching the pig herder's staff from Gower, I thrust the crowd aside and leapt forward to strike Cornwall soundly across his back. 'Get away from him. There is no devil here but you!'

Cornwall tried to protect himself by pulling his cloak about his head – but fine velvet would not save him from my rage. He called for the others to help, but they flinched away, afraid to be the next recipient of the wooden staff across their guilty bodies.

A madness came upon me. I will admit it. Cornwall was a liar, a rapist, and a murderer. He deserved to die. I struck him about the head until I found that I enjoyed hurting him. The crack of wood against his skull satisfied me. His calls of pain pleased me. The blood that surged from his mouth thrilled me. I felt elated, free of censure and restraint. I wanted him to die. I wanted to kill him myself.

I would have killed him.

And then I felt a gentle hand upon my arm. It was Mirabel. 'Please stop this, sire,' she said. 'Don't kill this man.' I stopped to look at her beautiful face. For a moment it tempered my fury, but the madness urged me to finish the job. I went to strike

Cornwall again, but she now grasped my arm tightly. 'Don't commit a mortal sin. Not for his sake.' She touched my cheek. 'Please, Oswald.'

She had said my name. She had touched my face. I lowered the staff. The lust to kill Cornwall had suddenly left me. I was exhausted. I would let him live.

Long enough to answer for his crimes in court.

As Cornwall was dragged away to the gaol house, I chose two large boys from the crowd and told them to carry Leofwin's body to the churchyard and then to prepare a grave.

They shifted about, uncomfortably. 'But it was a devil, sire,' muttered the shorter of the two. 'We can't bury it in sacred ground.'

I went to explain my request, but stopped. 'Just do it,' I told him. The boy hesitated, but I would not suffer such questioning any longer. I was their lord, and they would obey me. 'Do it!' I said. 'Or be thrown in the gaol house yourself.'

The air was still thick with the smell of smoke as I turned to leave. Then a figure came running towards the church. It was Mother. When she finally reached me, her voice was breathless and eager. 'Where's the fire, Oswald?'

'You're too late.'

'The burning is over?'

'Yes.'

She emitted a squeal and would have stamped her foot, had not half the village been watching her. 'Damnation!'

I had expected to find Joan Bath in the gaol house, but discovered only Cornwall – groaning in a corner of the cell with the lining of his cape held to his bleeding mouth. I was told Joan had been dumped outside her own home by the earl's men and told to stay away from the burning under threat of death.

I rode directly to Joan's remote cottage, where her two sons sat on the doorstep with their skinny dog. When they saw me, they ran inside to alert their mother, who soon appeared on the threshold – her face still swollen with tears. 'What do you want?' she said.

'May I speak to you about Leofwin?' I asked softly.

She wiped her eyes. 'How do you know his name?'

I dismounted my horse. 'I can explain. If you will let me in?' I looked at her sons with their hostile, grubby faces. The whole family seemed impervious to kindness. 'I'm not here to trick you.'

She hesitated again.

'Please.'

She sighed. 'As you like.'

I followed her inside. As last time, the cottage was dark and the ceilings were low, but the air smelt of sage and lavender without the usual fog of bonfire that inhabited these cramped and airless homes. The bedding was hanging over a low beam to air, and the floor was covered with fresh rushes. I sat on the single bench and insisted she join me, her body still shuddering to suppress her sobs.

'Why were you pleading to save Leofwin's life?' I asked her. 'Nobody else tried to help him.'

She took a deep breath and held her hands together. Her two sons were peeping around the doorpost, so I shooed them away.

'He was a boy. Not a beast.'

'I know.'

Her laugh was hollow. 'So, why didn't you stop them?' She sneered, 'My lord.'

'I was too late.' She looked away from me. 'He's to be buried in the churchyard. I've made sure of that.'

She didn't thank me for this gesture. 'How did you know his name?' she asked me again. 'Did your priest tell you?'

'Brother Peter?'

She gritted her teeth. 'Yes, Brother Peter. The betrayer.' She was now shaking as furiously as a lid on a boiling pan. 'I told him of the boy in confession. He pretended to be my friend. Praying for my sins. Said I reminded him of somebody. Some poor woman he had failed.'

'Which poor woman?'

'I don't know!' I took her hand and slowly she quietened. 'But he was no good Samaritan. He betrayed me.' Then she wiped a glistening tear from the corner of her eye. 'Though I never told him where to find the boy.'

Her face was drained of its strength, and for the first time she looked old. The boys were peeping around the corner of the door again, and this time she waved them away. 'Go and feed the chickens!' she said. 'And see there is water in the pig's trough.'

Her hand was cold and limp. 'Leofwin saved my life,' I told her. 'He rescued me from wolves and took me to his cave.'

She pulled her hand away. 'So it was you. *You* told them how to find him.'

'No.'

'Is that how you repaid his kindness?'

'No! I would never have done that.'

'So how did they know where to look?'

'I don't know,' I said honestly. 'I really don't.'

She buried her face in her hands. 'I've spent my whole life keeping him hidden away. To stop his persecution. And they found him anyway.' She sobbed loudly. 'And then they burnt him like a pig. My boy.'

'Your boy?'

'Yes. He was my son. What of it?' She had become angry again. Spittle foamed at her mouth. 'And his father was my father.'

I heaved a heavy sigh. So this was the sin Brother Peter spoke of. I offered Joan my hand once more, but instead she fell against my chest, her shoulders shaking. And then I held her in my arms until the force of her tears had subsided and only sorrow was left.

'Our sin was punished,' she whispered. 'Our son was cursed with the face of a beast.'

'But it wasn't your sin, Mistress Bath. You were just a girl.'

She shook her head. 'I had to hide Leofwin from the village. They would have called him a demon, but he was a sweet boy. A good boy. He should not have borne the punishment for my sins.' Her warm tears now flowed again into the wool of my tunic. 'My father wanted to kill the boy. His own son. So I hid him in the forest.' She let out a long sob. 'He was a sweet boy. A good boy. I only came back to the village when he was old enough. We needed money. But I took him food every week.' Her faltering sentences were now muffled. 'I never left him hungry.'

'I saw that.'

'He loved me. But now he has been stolen away. Murdered by priests. Burnt like a pig.'

She looked at the door, where the two boys had made their third, wary appearance. 'Get back outside, you little bastards. Go on!' she cried when they hesitated. 'This is none of your business.'

She turned to me and whispered again. 'I can never love them as I did Leofwin. But nobody would understand that. They would only see the boy as a gargoyle. A monster.'

I continued to hold her and offer soothing words, but my attempts at sympathy were inept and childish. In the end I rolled out her straw mattress upon the floor and bade her rest. She curled up into a ball and sobbed from her core.

Leaving the cottage, I passed the two boys, who were still sitting on the front step. They looked at me distrustfully.

'What's the matter with Mother?' the taller boy asked. He had such a dirty face, but his tunic was clean and his hair was combed.

'Be kind to her,' I told him. 'Stew some peas. Make her some supper.'

He shrugged at me in the way young boys will, so I caught him by the wrist. 'Are you listening to me? Your mother needs your help and understanding.'

He shook beneath my grip. 'I'm sorry, sire,' he bleated, so I released him — but not until I had stared a while into his pale and terrified eyes. 'Just be of assistance to your mother. Be quiet and undemanding.' He nodded to me, and the two of them scampered into the house before I could say another word.

Chapter Twenty

Iknew where to find Brother Peter. He would be drunk. But not in the cellar, his usual drinking hole. That secular square of damp would not assist his prayers to Heaven. He needed a holy place. A silent, sacred place, where he could speak directly to his God.

The door to the chapel was unlocked. The candles were lit at the altar, and Peter lay prostrate on the floor before the Virgin. Her lifeless eyes regarded him blankly, while her polished pink hands held the doll-like Christ child. Peter did not acknowledge my arrival. His eyes were shut.

'How could you have done it?' I asked him. 'You sewed a boy inside an ox and burnt him.' His eyes remained closed and he ignored me, continuing to mutter the words of his prayers as if his life depended upon it.

The urge to kick him came over me. 'Answer me. What drove you to such cruelty?' The catechism became louder and more urgent.

I pushed my foot against his face. 'Answer me!'

Peter trembled. 'The ox was Cornwall's idea. I couldn't stop him. The crowd were baying for blood.'

'But it was a boy.'

He opened an eye that was red with tears. 'I couldn't let them hang you, Oswald. You must understand that.' He held out his right hand to me, but I moved away from him. 'Help me stand up, Oswald. Please. I'm an old man.'

'No.'

'Please. You must forgive me.'

'I never will.'

At my refusal, he hoisted himself onto a bench awkwardly and wiped his brow with a sleeve. I noticed how old and muddy his habit had become, the folds of black woollen cloth too bulky for his ever-thinning body. 'I had to do it, Oswald,' he mumbled. 'I had to save you from hanging.'

'I didn't need your help, Brother. The judge and the earl were ready to believe in my innocence. You should have given me the chance to defend myself.'

'Against a man like Cornwall?' He shook his head. 'It wouldn't have worked.'

'But I had him cornered, Brother.'

'No, no. Cornwall would have tightened the noose about your neck with his clever arguments, and squeezed it further with every one of his lies. And now it would be *you* lying dead in a field and not that poor forsaken creature.'

'He was not a creature. Leofwin was a boy and you murdered him.'

'Don't you think I know that, Oswald?' He breathed out slowly and crossed himself. 'And may God forgive me.'

And then I noticed something about his hand. A red fluid oozed from between his fingers. 'You're bleeding.'

'It's nothing.'

'What's in your hand, Brother?' He didn't move. 'Show me!'

I grabbed his wrist and forced his palm open, revealing the silver blade of a whittle tang knife. Blood now flowed from a slice in the skin of his hand – but it was nothing more than a surface wound. I recognised the knife immediately, even though Peter had removed its handle of horn. I had used it to clear the abscess on Leofwin's leg. 'What are you trying to do, Brother?'

He held the blade out to me. 'Take it away, Oswald. Please. I thought I had the courage, but I don't.'

'You would have killed yourself? With this?' I hesitated. 'I don't believe you. You're peddling for my sympathy.'

He wiped his eyes with reddened fingers. 'That's not true, Oswald. I wish I could do it, but suicide is a mortal sin.' The blood from his hands smeared across his cheeks like paint.

'So is murder.'

Peter's lunged forward to hold me, but I dodged his advance. 'I had to turn them against the boy. You must understand that, Oswald.' Fumbling about in his belt pouch, Brother Peter found his flask of brandy, his hands shaking as he removed the cork.

As he gulped noisily, I turned the knife in my hand. 'You stole this from Leofwin.'

Peter's voice was hoarse, but muted. 'It was stolen already.'

'You can't be sure of that.'

'Such a creature doesn't own a silver knife.'

'Stop calling him a creature! He was a boy. The same as me.'

Peter took another gulp from the flask. 'No, Oswald. He was *not* the same as you. Our Lord doesn't hand out a face like that without reason. Now please, give me back the knife.'

'What? So you can pretend to cut your own wrist again?'

'No. That urge has passed. I will live with the sin and let it torment me. Does that satisfy you? The knife can go to the abbey.'

I put the knife under my belt. 'No. It belongs to Joan Bath. As she was Leofwin's mother.'

Peter froze.

'Don't pretend to be surprised, Brother. Joan told you of Leofwin in confession. Though you broke another vow by betraying her.'

He looked at me as a tear worked its way slowly down his cheek, forming a thin watery line through the blood.

'So how did you find Leofwin?' I asked. 'Joan didn't tell you where he was hidden.' He whispered something in reply. 'What was that?' I said. 'I can't hear you.'

He cleared his throat. 'It was you who told me, Oswald.'

'I did not. You wouldn't listen to a word of my story about Leofwin. You let me believe I had suffered delirium.'

'But you did tell me.'

'Stop lying.'

'You described the golden eagle to me.'

I felt my stomach turn. 'What?'

'You described their size and call.'

'No. That's not true. You're tricking me.'

'There are few such eagles left in Kent, Oswald. They only survive deep in the weald, on one solitary sandstone ridge.'

'How would you know that?'

'Because I sometimes go there. To collect the rare filmy fern.'

'The what?'

'I stew it to make a poultice, Oswald. You can use it to—'

'I don't care what you use it for!'

So Joan was right. I had been the one to betray Leofwin. Holding my head in my hands, I fell onto the bench.

Peter left me alone for a few moments and then sat down beside me, putting his hand upon my back. 'This is my sin, Oswald. Not yours.' He stroked my hair and drew so close to my ear I was forced to shrink away from the vapours of his breath.

'Dear Oswald,' he whispered softly. 'Dear boy. You mustn't blame yourself. You're alive. You must be thankful for that.'

I stood up sharply. 'Get away from me, Brother.'

'But, Oswald—'

'You disgust me.'

I did not see Brother Peter for the rest of that day. I believe he hid in the chapel, avoiding me in the hope I would soften. But that would never happen.

Instead I went to the churchyard and laid the poor scalded body of Leofwin to rest. I was not qualified to perform such a ceremony, but the only priests in the parish were both responsible for the boy's murder. Their evil would not taint his burial.

I had sent for Joan with news that we were burying her son, but Piers returned with the message she was performing her own ceremony to bless his parting and would not join us. So Leofwin was buried with just Gilbert and myself to pray for his soul. My prayers were probably useless. As for Gilbert's, I cannot say.

After that I returned to the gaol house, to speak to Cornwall. When Henry unlocked his cell, I found a deflated, defeated creature cringing in the corner. His face was bruised, and dried blood was matted to his hair. His velvet cloak hung about him like a torn sail.

'What do you want, de Lacy?' he said. 'Come to finish the job and kill me?' His voice had lost its French pretensions and now he spoke as softly and colloquially as any other Cornishman. He tried to laugh, but the skin around his mouth was purple and swollen.

'I've come to charge you with the murders of the Starvecrow sisters and Walter de Caburn.'

He laughed again, only this time he managed to complete the sound without holding the edge of his cape to his lip. 'You have no evidence against me.'

'I caught you and de Caburn about to rape Mirabel.'

'What does that prove? I didn't rape the girl, did I? And she's still alive.' He dabbed his gums. 'You've broken most of my teeth, damn you.'

'I also caught you at the Starvecrow cottage. Searching for the beads that she had pulled from your neck as you attacked her.'

'I was looking for footprints. I told you that before.'

'Will you keep to that story when your house is searched and we find the remaining beads in your possession?'

He shrugged. 'Go ahead. You'll find nothing.' He then began to laugh at me. 'You will look so foolish in court, de Lacy. More foolish than ever. You privileged little arse.'

I turned to leave, making certain to swing my cape. My gesture was not lost on Cornwall. He stumbled over to the grate in his cell door and shouted at me as the door was locked.

'Your time is nearly gone, de Lacy.' Henry told him to be quiet, but he shouted even louder. 'The Pestilence was a gift from God. And now the common man will rise against you. It is we who will inherit the earth!'

That evening I took a bath in the buttery next to the kitchen. Gilbert had warmed the water over the stove and filled the wooden tub until it was deep enough for me to sit in and stew. Needing to remove the stink of the fire, I asked Ada to bring me some of Mother's hard soap, although our servant soon returned saying Mother could not spare any.

An unpleasant and acrid odour lay on my skin and hung about my hair like sticky weed, so I sent Ada back to inform Mother that I would have the soap whether she could spare it or not. Ada returned with a small and well-used lump of mutton fat and wood ash, from which I had to pull one of Mother's black hairs. I would tell you the soap's sharp scent of rosemary and lime rid me of the smoke and soot about my body, but each time I put my fingers to my nose I could still discern the smell of a boy burning to death.

We searched Cornwall's cottage, but he had been right. We did not find the remaining red coral rosary beads, though we did discover a collection of whitened sheep bones, waiting to be sawn into relics. This did not surprise me in the least, but what did amaze me was Cornwall's collection of richly embroidered clothes and rare and expensive jewellery. Even a cape of weasel fur – which Cornwall could never have worn outside the confines of his private quarters. Such pelts were the preserve of nobility.

I then imagined him, wrapped in this cape – parading up and down the room as king of his own small bedchamber, irked that he could not wear such clothes in society for fear of breaking the sumptuary laws. Laws that prescribed exactly what a person should wear, according to their rank in society. It must have rankled with a man as ambitious and grasping as Cornwall, that no matter how rich he became in his life, he would never be allowed openly to wear such finery.

Perhaps the words he had shouted from his cell were prophetic? If the common man was to inherit the world, then we could all dress exactly as we pleased.

It was disappointing not to find the beads in Cornwall's home, but it did not deter me from believing in his guilt. I wrote to the sheriff that morning and requested the Hundreds Court return to Somershill. It would be the second request in so many months.

In the field near the church, a black circle of ash scarred the soil like a plague sore. Nobody went near, apart from Joan Bath, but she could not cleanse the bad ground with her tears, no matter how many she cried.

A week after Leofwin's burning, I dreamt about planting an acorn in this black circle, hoping to heal the soil where no grass would grow. But in my dream an oak sapling did not appear the following spring. Instead, a strange and ugly tree grew from the circle, its branches contorted into snakelike coils, its trunk swollen with cankers and patches of dead bark. And when it fruited, it bore a harvest of hard black acorns that were spread by the jays and poisoned the pigs.

I woke up and ran to the window, breathing the fresh air that seeped through the lead casement. Mirabel was feeding the chickens in the courtyard below, making this most common of chores seem as graceful as a dance. The birds followed every twist of her body, changing direction as often as she did in the hope of catching the next handful of seed.

Watching Mirabel, an idea now hardened to resolve. Brother
Peter had been right in one respect. After all the misery and
desolation of the past year, I should be thankful to be alive.

It was later that same morning when I caught Mirabel's arm as
she left the hall carrying a pot of my mother's piss to the moat.
Mother was refusing to use the garderobe, which expelled the
family's effluent down the wall of the house, claiming that exposing her arse at such a height had given her a frozen bladder. The
pot was dangerously full – the contents threatening to spill over
with each of Mirabel's careful steps. She was not altogether
pleased to see me, since any disruption to her balance might have
caused the foaming piss to spill onto her tunic.

'Why are you clearing the pots, Mirabel? That's Ada's job.'

'Your mother wants me to do it, sire.' As she curtsied, the piss
swayed dangerously close to the rim. 'I've never seen as much
water produced in one night.' Then she thought better of this
implied criticism. 'Though, of course I've never tended to such
a grand lady as your mother. I imagine a noble woman produces
more piss than a peasant.'

I suspected Mother of filling the pot to the rim with ale just to
make the task more difficult. But I didn't share this thought with
Mirabel. 'Take it to the moat and then come straight back. I need
to speak with you.' She bowed her head and I saw how thick and
dark her eyelashes were against the buttermilk of her skin.

I stood in the porch and watched as she walked away. The
morning sun threw shadows across the patches in her dress. She
was poor, but why should that deter me? I was the lord of two
estates now. I was my own master. Why shouldn't I be happy?

As soon as she returned I took her hand. 'Mirabel?' I felt
nervous and slightly ridiculous, being no practised seducer or
exponent of courtly love. I encased her small hands in my long
and awkward fingers and hoped my voice would remain steady.

'Yes, sire. What is it?'

I coughed. 'I wanted to know what you thought of me, Mirabel?'

Her hands trembled a little. 'I admire you very much, sire. You saved me from Lord Versey and Father John. I'm very grateful to you.'

I squeezed her hands a little tighter, causing her to look away. 'But do you feel anything else?' She bit her lip and withdrew her hands. I had embarrassed her.

'Because I love you,' I blurted out like a fool. Unfortunately my declaration did not seem to please her. In fact she looked concerned enough to run away, had I not taken her hands again and held them more firmly.

'I think you're the most beautiful girl in the world.'

She looked at me suspiciously. 'Do you, sire? Or do you just want to lie with me?'

'No, no. Please don't think that. My love for you is pure and untainted.' I hoped nobody was listening to this performance, since I must have sounded as genuine as a potions seller at the fair.

'Then what are you suggesting, sire?'

'I would like you to marry me, Mirabel,' I said quickly.

She laughed. 'Marriage?'

'Yes.'

She laughed again, emitting a strange whooping noise through her nose.

'I don't believe you'll have a better offer,' I said, slightly offended at her reaction.

She bit her lip and screwed up her eyes. 'But sire. I don't see how we can marry. I'm the daughter of a tenant farmer. You're a lord.'

'Which means I can do as I please.'

'But surely my lady has arranged a union for you?'

'Yes. But I rejected her choice.'

'Won't the earl want you to marry one of his daughters?'

'He hasn't mentioned it.'

'But it isn't usual for a lord to marry a servant.' She tried to pull her hands away again, but I wouldn't relax my hold. The amusement over, an ugly grimace now made lines across her brow.

I wanted her beautiful face to return. I wanted to convince and reassure her – so, speaking softly, I drew her towards me. 'Two years ago I was due to become a Benedictine, but then the Plague changed everything. It seemed like the end of the world, but now I'm glad of it. It means I'm free to marry you.'

'But I'm betrothed to Nicholas Carpenter, sire.'

I thought of the tall red-haired boy. Sometimes he came to the house to mend a door or patch a rotten roof truss in the chapel. I would not employ him again. 'Tell Nicholas you're no longer betrothed.'

'But I think my father made certain promises to the—'

I dropped her hands petulantly. 'Will you marry me? Yes or no?'

She looked about as if a jester might pop out from behind a wall and announce it was fools' day. Her voice was apprehensive. 'Yes, sire. I do wish to marry you. I'm just afraid it won't be possible.'

'I will make it possible. We shall be married as soon as I can sober up Brother Peter.'

She relaxed a little. 'Really?'

'I promise.'

'And it will be witnessed by your family? And the whole village? I don't want one of those weddings that nobody believes took place.'

'Yes. Then you will be Mirabel de Lacy. No longer cleaning out my mother's piss pots.'

She laughed again, but this time it was a pleasant peal of giggles, and we kissed. Her lips were warm and full – but most pleasant was the feeling of her breasts against my body. I wanted to slip my hand inside her tunic to hold these firm globes of soft flesh, but stopped myself – knowing it would sully the gallantry of the moment.

Even so. I wish I had.

In the afternoon of that same day, two familiar faces came into sight as I was trying, yet again, to saddle Tempest. It was Clemence and her servant Humbert. Thankfully Clemence was not in the humble cart in which she had left for the convent, but was riding a pony. Humbert held the pony's reins as if he were Sir Lancelot and she were Guinevere.

I ran to Clemence and she allowed herself, briefly, to be pleased. Her face softened into a smile that suddenly reminded me of Richard, our dead brother. The spread of her mouth and the dimples that dented her cheeks were exactly his. Tears formed in my eyes.

'I hope you're not crying because I've returned, little brother,' she said. The face hardened again and my glimpse of Richard was lost.

'I'm just pleased to see you.' She nodded in acceptance of this obvious truth. 'You heard the news?' I said.

'That de Caburn is dead?'

I nodded.

She shared a sly smile with Humbert. 'Of course the good news reached me, you foolish boy. Why do you think I'm back?' Then her face clouded. 'How's Mother?'

'Never mind Mother. How are you?'

Her face darkened further. 'We won't speak of it, Oswald.'

'But—'

'No.'

Humbert inhaled loudly and glared at me as if to underline Clemence's command. Then suddenly my sister smiled and the tension dissipated. I helped her from her pony and for the briefest of moments she hugged me.

* * *

I ran ahead to tell Mother of Clemence's return, only to be confronted by her angry face on the stairs to the solar.

'Where's that girl?' Mother was carrying a piss pot, though this one was not as full as the pot Mirabel had been assigned earlier. 'I've had to use your father's old chamber pot, and you know how I like to have my own. The girl is useless.'

'Mirabel has returned home for a day.'

'I did not excuse her. You should get on your horse and retrieve the wilful slattern, Oswald.'

'Forget that for now, Mother. Clemence has returned.'

'Clemence?' Mother seemed confused, as if I had just mentioned a rarely seen cousin.

'Your daughter.'

'What's she doing here?'

'She's returned from the convent, Mother.'

'Has she taken holy orders?'

'No.' I now felt exasperated. Her memory could not be so mercurial. 'She was forced to visit the hospital there. After de Caburn attacked her. Remember?'

She pulled a face. 'Oh yes. That. Clemence should return to Versey now she's killed her husband. I don't want her disturbing my peace here.'

'Clemence didn't kill her husband, Mother.'

She laughed. 'No. Of course not. It was that beast you burnt in the village.' She sighed. 'It's such a shame I missed it. Did any demons escape from his skull? I'm told they dislike smoke and will burst out through the eyes.'

I groaned, took the piss pot from her, and led her to the hall – where she and Clemence embraced as warmly as two lead dolls.

I found Brother Peter in the chapel, standing on a stool and cleaning the Madonna and child with a small brush. The whole place seemed cleaner, with dust removed from the painted panels and the altar chalices arranged into ascending sizes.

'See how much life there is in her eyes,' Peter said, when he realised I was standing behind him. The Virgin's eyes still looked dead to me. 'It's disgraceful that Our Lady was allowed to become so dirty. She watches over us all, Oswald. She is able to forgive.' The words hung in the air.

'I need you to bless a marriage,' I said.

Peter stepped down from the stool and replaced the brush behind his belt, alongside other cleaning rags. He looked more like Ada than a monk.

'Who's getting married?'

'I am.'

He hesitated. 'To whom?'

'To Mirabel,' I said with all the confidence I could muster. I would not apologise for my choice of bride.

'Does your mother agree to this?' His eyebrows tensed as if he did not believe me.

'Are you saying I cannot choose my own wife? When I am lord here?'

'No, Oswald. Of course I'm not.' He bowed his head to me. 'I was just questioning the wisdom of such a marriage, that's all.'

'Do not speak to me of wisdom.'

He bowed again. 'Very well, Oswald. When do you wish the ceremony to take place?'

In my haste I had given the matter no thought. But I did not want Peter to see this oversight. 'The day after tomorrow,' I said with authority. 'After that, you will return to the abbey.'

He opened his mouth to object, but shut it again. No amount of cleaning the chapel would cleanse his sin. It was better if we parted. He knew that, as well as I.

'Oswald,' he said softly, as I reached the door. I stopped, but did not turn to look at him. 'Do you love the girl?'

'Of course I do.'

'Then I am truly happy for you.'

* * *

As soon as Clemence was refreshed, I asked to speak to her alone, but Mother suddenly became difficult about allowing us some privacy. 'Am I no longer the lady of this hall?' she said. 'Your father would not have sent me to my bedchamber like a naughty child, when family matters were being considered.'

Clemence rolled her eyes. 'Father never allowed you to stay at any important discussion.' Then she glanced up to the squint from the solar. 'Not that it stopped you listening anyway.'

'Do you see how my peace is disturbed, Oswald?' said Mother, pointing at Clemence. 'How my own daughter agitates my humours.'

I took Clemence's arm and suggested we take a walk in the orchard, allowing Mother to take her Melissa Water and then rest for the afternoon. After feigning a sudden headache, Mother announced she would no more walk around the orchard with us, than she would sleep in a plague pit. And it wouldn't matter how many times we might try to persuade her to join us, she would not change her mind.

The afternoon was warm and cloudy, and the air was heavy with water. As we walked between the apple trees, the house moved in and out of the mist – its windows seeming like the eyes of the Colossus. We were shadowed by Humbert, who kept a steady twenty paces behind us at all times.

'Does he think I'm going to attack you?' I asked, looking over my shoulder to watch his pond-like eyes staring back at me blankly.

She picked a ripening apple from a tree. 'He's protective of me. That's all. I find it reassuring. He's sworn never to leave my side.'

'You will allow that?'

'Of course.' She bit into the apple and a little of the pink juice dripped down her chin. 'He has the strength of a bull.'

'But the temper of a lamb.'

She wiped the droplet of juice with her forefinger and put it to her lips. 'I have enough courage for the two of us.'

We walked on and I took her arm. For once she did not reject me. 'Do you know how de Caburn died?' I asked.

She smiled. 'I do. He was attacked at the throat and laid upon the Virgin Mary.' She suddenly took a little skip. 'And it's no more than he deserved.'

'Tell me, Clemence.' I paused. 'Did you write a letter to him? Asking him to meet you at the convent?'

'Are you questioning me, little brother?' She slowed her step.

'It's just a couple of matters are still troubling me.'

'You don't believe he was murdered by a dog head?' She growled playfully, making claws of her left hand as if to attack me. I was conscious of Humbert moving closer, but she waved him away. I had rarely seen Clemence in such good humour, and in truth I found it slightly disturbing.

'No. I don't,' I said.

'Or perhaps you killed him? I heard they put you on trial. But then Brother Peter found the deformed boy.' She squeezed my arm. 'Wasn't that lucky?'

I looked away. 'Cornwall is the guilty one. I have him locked up in the gaol house. Awaiting trial by the royal judge.'

'Cornwall?'

'Yes. But I need proof about the letter.'

'I will answer your question then.' She poked me in the shoulder like a small girl teasing her best friend. 'I did not, nor would I have written an invitation to that man. I hated him. And I'm pleased he is dead.'

'So there was definitely no letter?'

'That's what I've just said.' She pulled her arm away from mine. Suddenly the playfulness was gone. In its place was the bad-tempered sister of old. It came as something of a relief.

'It's just that Cornwall claims to have seen it,' I said.

'Then he's lying.'

'Or he wrote it himself.'

She cleared her throat. 'Maybe so. I can only tell you I didn't write a word to my dear, dead husband. And I don't care to be questioned further.'

I offered my arm again by way of apology and we carried on walking to the hedge and then double-backed towards the house. The floor of the orchard was thick with windfall apples. I noted that we should collect these up as soon as possible, and then do something with them. Exactly what, I did not know.

'When I've recovered my strengths,' said Clemence, 'I shall return to Versey.'

'You intend to go back there?' This surprised me since I had assumed that Versey would hold such bad memories for her.

'Of course I do. I'm still Lady Versey. There must be some reward for having married such a monster.'

I coughed and took a deep breath. 'The earl has asked me to take over the Versey estate. You can't have heard?'

She stopped dead in her tracks. 'You?'

'Yes.'

She pulled her arm away from mine. 'What about his daughters? What about me?'

'You can't manage the estate alone, Clemence. And Mary may take over when she marries.'

She produced a howl that seemed to rise from her belly and caused her teeth to clench. Humbert was at her side within moments. 'You're making this up,' she snarled. 'Do you have an official notification?'

'The earl will return soon with the papers.'

'And what exactly am I supposed to do?'

'Stay here at Somershill?'

It was a mistake to make such a suggestion, and I should have known better. She picked up an apple and threw it at my head, hitting me soundly on the temple. When I went to retaliate, I felt Humbert's enormous hands about my wrists, and though I struggled, it was impossible to shake him off.

Clemence regarded me scornfully. 'You? As Lord of Somershill and Versey?' You could barely steer your own shit into a sewer.' Then she clapped her hands and Humbert dropped my wrists as if they were covered in nettles.

'We'll see about this,' said Clemence, as she strode away towards the house. 'You will not have everything.'

Chapter Twenty-One

My day did not improve. Following my argument with Clemence, I decided to break the news of my intended marriage to Mother. It had to be done quickly, since I had made a commitment to break with tradition and hold the ceremony only the day after tomorrow.

I was hardly expecting Mother to be pleased at my news, but I had not expected such a visceral reaction. There were no threats or insults regarding my choice of wife. In fact, Mother was unable to form any words at all, since her response to my news was to vomit. The blood left her face and she became so grey and ashen that Ada and Gilbert had to carry her to bed, from where she could still be heard heaving for the next half an hour.

Absenting myself from Mother's bedside, I walked to the fields to see how the harvest was progressing. When I reached the demesne I met an old woman struggling to gather the cut barley into sheaves. Her face was drawn and tired, and she repeatedly stretched, clutching her back and groaning before starting her work again. Her skinny dog tried to nip at my ankles until I kicked him away.

Featherby ran over to greet me from the other side of the field. 'This woman is too old to be working in the field,' I told him.

He shrugged a little. 'But there's nobody else to do it, sire. And she works steadily enough, if we allow the dog in the field.' The dog barked as if chastising us for allowing his mistress to be worked into her grave.

'She looks half-dead, Featherby. Couldn't she be doing something a little less arduous? Some weaving maybe?'

He screwed up his face. 'Old Beatrice? No, sire. I wouldn't let her loose on the spinning. She distracts the other women with her gossip. And her hands are like twisted willow. She can hardly hold a carding comb.'

'How old is she?'

'Forty-five, sire.'

I turned around to look at Beatrice, and she curtsied to me with a toothless grin. She was thirteen years younger than my own mother, but looked as wrinkled and ugly as a baby bird.

I would take Mirabel away from this life, and was pleased of it.

'Make sure the water carrier sees to this woman first, when he comes into the field,' I told Featherby. 'And don't let her feed it all to her dog.'

'As you like, sire,' he said, beginning to loom.

I could see that compassion was out of place here, so I added, 'Keep your workers fed and watered, and they will work harder. That's what Father used to say.' He used to say nothing of the sort, but my statement seemed to reassure Featherby that he was not working for a simpleton.

Featherby joined the others across the field, and I watched them for a while. Two men bound the cut stems of the barley into sheaves and then tied them with cords of straw, whilst another picked up the sheaves and carried them to the corner of the field where they were neatly stacked like a pile of Roman bricks.

I looked at my large field and wondered if all the barley would ever be harvested, given the lack of hands and the threat of rain. I could not find any extra men to do the work, and could hardly squeeze any more labour from the likes of old Beatrice. Also, the villagers were keen to leave my land and return to their own small strips where they would harvest what they could before the autumn. I had every right to force them to stay in my fields, but they might starve this winter. Then who would plough, sow, and harrow next spring?

When I returned to the house, Clemence demanded an audience with me in the great hall. She shooed everybody away, apart from Humbert, who hung around behind her as ever, like a silent reflection.

I was weary from the heat in the field and did not feel like the next plateful of arguments. 'There's nothing I can do about Versey,' I told Clemence. 'It was the earl's idea. Challenge him on the matter.'

'This is not about Versey.'

I sighed again. 'So, what's the trouble now?'

'I hear you intend to marry Mother's maidservant.'

I should have foreseen this. Mother's outline was visible at the squint. 'I can do as I please,' I said loudly, so Mother might hear my words.

Clemence scowled. 'And bring shame to this family? You stupid little fool. You are Lord of Somershill and Versey now. You cannot marry such a lowly girl and expect to go to court.'

'I don't want to go to court.'

'But I do!' she said. 'And this ragged union will taint us all.'

'Mirabel will be a better marriage partner than you chose. At least there is some love between us.'

Clemence went to strike me, but I grabbed her hand and pushed her away – with such accidental force that she fell to the floor. Humbert jumped in front of me to shield his mistress, as if I were one of those rabid dogs that periodically roam the village in search of a victim to bite.

'Call him off, Clemence. I'm not going to harm you.'

'How can I be sure?' she said. Her voice was uncharacteristically nervous and thin.

'I'm sorry, Clemence,' I said, trying to look at her face around the bulk of Humbert's chest. 'I'm your brother. I wouldn't hurt you.'

She stood up reluctantly and waved Humbert away to the shadows, where he took up his station by the tapestry and fixed me with accusing eyes.

Clemence smoothed down her hair and patted her money purse to make sure it was still there. 'Now, let us conclude this business. You cannot marry this girl, Oswald. You must cancel the arrangement immediately.'

'No, Clemence. I will not. I love her.'

'Have you lain with her?'

'No. Not that it's any of your business.'

'That is a relief at least,' she said under her breath. She looked up, and cleared her throat. 'I had hoped to persuade you to behave correctly for the sake of our family honour. But it seems you won't listen. So I must tell you exactly why you cannot marry this girl.'

'What are you talking about?'

'It would be a sin. Her father is your father, Oswald. She is your half-sister.'

'No, she isn't,' I said, but immediately felt the first roll of my stomach.

Clemence looked to the roof. 'Why do you persist in being so naïve, Oswald? We talked about this before. Father has a whole set of bastards about the estate. She is one of them.'

I sat down on a bench, as my legs began to feel unsteady. 'How do you know Mirabel is his daughter? There's no proof.'

'Mother has a list.'

The blood was returning to my legs now. 'Mother has a list?' I scoffed. 'A list of what?'

'Of Father's bastards, of course.'

Now I laughed out loud. 'Mother could write anybody's name she cared to on such a list. I expect she wrote Mirabel's name this morning and sent you down here to stop the marriage. I admire your gall, but it won't work.'

Clemence pursed her lips. 'The list was written by Father,' she said.

'I don't believe you. Why would he do such a thing?'

She looked to the roof again. 'To prevent such an outcome as this, you fool.'

I stood up. 'Let me see this list then.'

Clemence bristled. 'It belongs to Mother. She won't show it to you. It's private.'

'Then I don't believe it exists. And I shall marry Mirabel.' I noticed Mother's shadow had disappeared from the squint. I hoped that she had gone somewhere to hide from me in shame. I had called her bluff on this pathetic little scheme.

Clemence faltered. 'Very well. I'll get it.'

I had rarely seen my sister appear as awkward as she did on leaving the room and climbing the spiral stairs to the solar. Humbert continued to stare at me. He neither turned his head nor blinked.

Raised voices reached us from the solar, as Mother and Clemence argued about how to produce a document in Father's hand from thin air. Soon I would be rid of them all. In fact, I decided at that very moment to send both of them to Versey. Then Mirabel would be Lady of Somershill, and we would have an idyllic life of love and contentment without the bickering and malice of these two de Lacy gorgons. The idea of it gave me a warm glow of hope, but it was soon to dissipate.

There was complete silence for a while, and then Clemence returned to the hall with a scroll of parchment. She unrolled it on the table and I could see immediately it was written in my father's hand. I could also see why Clemence and Mother had not been so keen to show it to me.

It was a list of names, under the title of *Filios meos*. My children. I counted twelve names. Some I recognised, such as

Godfrey, son of Rose the cobbler. Others I didn't, such as Clarice, daughter of Cissie Skippe. All but one of the names were crossed out, and against most my Father had written *Mortuus est. Pestilentium*, by which I understood them to have died of the Plague.

Running my finger down the column I soon came to the one name I had hoped not to see. 'Mirabel, daughter of Betty the ale-wife.' There could be no doubt. Her name was just above 'Alison and Matilda, daughters of Adeline Starvecrow'.

I sat down on the bench and once again my stomach rolled. 'Get Mother down here,' I said to Clemence, and for once she did not argue with me.

When Mother eventually descended to the hall, she had been crying and appeared more sheepish and discomfited than I had ever seen her. 'I'm sorry, Oswald,' she whimpered. 'I didn't want you to look at it.'

'I'm sure you didn't.'

Clemence tapped me on the shoulder. 'You understand now that you cannot marry this girl because she is your sister.'

I looked away and said nothing, but Mother took my silence as agreement and went to grab the document. 'Let's forget this nonsense, Oswald. We'll find you such a lovely girl to marry. Every bit as fetching as this silly Mirabel. These village wenches don't age well, you know. Show me a pretty foal and I'll show you an ugly—'

I seized her hand as she leant over. 'Thank you, Mother. But I'll keep hold of this list for now.'

Mother trembled. 'There's no need, Oswald.'

'But I intend to study it a little further. For I see some words written here in a different hand.'

'I'll keep it safe. You mustn't torment yourself.'

She tried again to wrest the document away from me, but I would not let go. 'Do you see these words, Mother?' I pointed to the parchment. 'This is your hand, I believe.'

She screwed up her eyes and rubbed her temples. 'I can't see anything, Oswald. My eyesight is as poor as a mole's.'

'Then perhaps you remember writing these words?' She remained silent. 'Do you?'

She trembled. 'I don't think so.'

'Really? You don't remember crossing out the names of Alison and Matilda Starvecrow?'

She let go of the parchment and backed away towards the stairs to the solar. 'I'm feeling quite disturbed, Oswald. There seems to be a noxious vapour in this room.'

'Yes, there is. It's you, Mother.'

She quickly shot up the stone steps, but I followed and shouted at her from the bottom of the stairwell. '*Lupae. Meretrices.* She-wolves. Whores. Those are the hateful words, Mother! To write against the names of two murdered girls.'

As a door slammed in the distance, I turned to face Clemence, who regarded me with her arms crossed. 'You can't expect Mother to like his bastards.'

I put my head in my hands. 'Just go away, Clemence. Leave me alone.'

She sighed. 'You'll get over it, Oswald. There will be other girls.'

I looked up again at her. 'Will there?'

For a fleeting moment, Clemence's expression changed. I think she might even have felt sympathy for me.

But then her old demeanour returned.

A face pickled in its own acid.

Chapter Twenty-Two

I crept into the chapel and sat on a small bench in the corner. The Virgin looked down upon me with her newly cleaned eyes. The serenity of her face and the velvet silence of the chamber wrapped me in a moment of peace, before Brother Peter shuffled into the chapel cleaning a silver chalice with a linen rag. He was so engrossed in his polishing that he didn't notice me at first.

I watched him for a while. His hair was now as white as the face of a barn owl, and his skin hung loosely from his skull. They say drink makes you fat to begin with, but eventually it sucks the flesh from your bones. It was true in Peter's case. He had been a corpulent man in younger years, but now he was little more than a breathing skeleton. I should have hated him for ever after his sins against Leofwin, but as he whispered words of prayer, I suddenly wanted to seek solace in his embrace. I coughed to let him know I was there.

'Hello, Oswald,' he said rather tentatively. 'I hadn't expected to see you until tomorrow. How are your wedding plans progressing?'

'They're not.'

'I see. Have you spoken to your mother?'

'The marriage is cancelled, Brother. I'm surprised you haven't heard. Mirabel is my half-sister.'

'What?' He seemed more surprised by this revelation than I had expected. Part of me had assumed he would already know the secret, after some revelation in the confessional. 'Who told you such a tale?' he asked.

'Mother and Clemence.'

Peter huffed. 'Those two harpies.'

'They have a list, written by my father.'

'What sort of list?'

'An inventory of his bastards.'

Peter sat down next to me with a thud, dropping the silver chalice into his lap as if it were nothing more than a piece of everyday stoneware. 'Have you seen this list?'

'Yes. It's written in Father's hand. With the title *Filios Meos.*'

'How many names were on it?'

'I counted twelve.'

Then he laughed. 'The arrogance of the man. Writing a list of his progeny for posterity. Who did he think he was? King David of Israel?'

'I suspect he wanted to stop any unfortunate unions.' I sighed. 'Such as the one I had proposed.'

'But you love this girl, Oswald.'

'What good is that?'

Brother Peter puffed. 'Don't let this ridiculous piece of paper ruin your happiness. There's no proof she's your sister.'

I snorted in disbelief. 'You can't give me such advice, Brother. Think of the repercussions? Think of the *sin.*'

'But I don't believe in the list, Oswald. The girl's mother was an ale-wife. Mirabel could be the child of any number of men from this village. Your father liked to think he could sire a nation, but his seed did not plant itself into every womb in Somershill. There were other men capable.'

'But what if she *is* my sister? Think of our children. Look at Leofwin. Son of his own mother and grandfather. I couldn't risk begetting such a poor creature.'

'Nothing is certain, Oswald.'

'Not certain, Brother? How would God suffer such ambivalence to His word?'

'I'm just being rational, Oswald. And do not quote the word of God back to me. Not when you are such an unbeliever.'

'But think of the words of Leviticus. Do not have relations with your half-sister, whether she is your father's daughter or your mother's daughter.'

'I only want you to be happy, Oswald.' The silver chalice then slipped from his lap and fell to the floor, making an ugly chime before rolling across the flagstones, circling, and coming to rest above the tombstone of my grandfather.

Peter quickly picked it up from the floor, before it offended any further member of my dead family. 'I didn't mean to upset you, Oswald. I'm sorry.'

'Then keep your vile suggestions to yourself!'

I rode to the village to speak to Mirabel, before my resolve softened and I began to countenance Peter's idea. Reaching her humble cottage, my heart sank down into my stomach and the urge to run away was strong. I tied my troublesome horse Tempest to a post and crept towards Mirabel's door and spied at her through a crack.

She was sewing a gown. It was not an ornate dress, but still beautiful – there could be no doubt it was for our wedding. As she pierced and drew the needle through the cloth, she sang a song. Its tune was melodic and mournful.

> Bird on a briar, bird on a briar,
> We come from love, and love we crave,
> Blissful bird, have pity on me,
> Or dig, love, dig for me my grave.

I knocked at the door and she jumped up to greet me – but the grimness of my face soon betrayed my purpose in coming here.

I did not possess the courage to share the true reason for my change of heart with Mirabel, but instead I gave her to believe our difference in station was to blame, and that she would be happier married to a village boy such as Nicholas Carpenter.

Mirabel took the news stoically, as if she had been expecting such an outcome all along – which only made me feel even more ashamed to have meddled in her life.

But if I wanted a regretful tear, she did not oblige. The door was shut firmly after me, and walking away I noticed a tall, red-haired boy sitting in a nearby tree. It was Nicholas Carpenter, and after I passed beneath his branch I'm certain he spat.

I was both heartbroken and morose, but had no time for the indulgence of self-pity, so following an afternoon of solitude in my bedchamber I resumed my duties. The barley and the rye were harvested, and the sheep were shorn. In the orchards, the plums were beginning to ripen in spite of the weather, though the apples were still green and hard. There were tithes to collect and rents to demand. I must soon hold a manorial court, and see to the administration of my estate. Both of my estates.

And there was still the issue of Cornwall's trial. After all the terrible events of this summer, I would secure his conviction. Though, in truth, I still felt I lacked enough evidence against the man.

I travelled to Versey to question two of de Caburn's servants about the night of their master's murder – though they added little to those facts already known. De Caburn had received a letter, said to have been written by Clemence, requesting he visit her at the convent. Both claimed to have overheard their master discussing the letter with John of Cornwall, but there was some disagreement between the two of them as to the existence of a messenger. One servant claimed not to have seen anybody, whereas the other servant, the dirty man who slept by the fire, claimed to have let a mounted envoy cross the bridge.

The only detail on which they could both agree was the extensive mutilation they had witnessed upon de Caburn's corpse. Particularly about his face and hands – where the skin had been scored and flayed so badly it was difficult at first to identify the man. It interested me to hear that they had also noticed a strange odour to the corpse. Not 'cooked', as Mirabel's young brother had told me before. They described the smell as 'burnt'.

I recorded all my findings onto a roll of parchment and analysed them nightly. But, for all my scrutiny, I could not read their story.

During this time plans were made for Clemence and Mother to move to Versey Castle. After months of their bitter company, I was pleased to be rid of them. Mother claimed the dampness of Versey would thicken her lungs and blacken her bile, but Clemence was glad to be leaving Somershill. Her only complaint was having to take Mother as her companion. Brother Peter still remained. I kept meaning to demand his departure for the abbey, but somehow I never quite got around to it.

I rode out one morning to Versey to oversee the preparations for the move of the de Lacy women, and took a diversion to Joan Bath's cottage. It was a visit I had been putting off, as we had not met since the burning – but I wanted to return Leofwin's silver knife to his mother. It would not go to the abbey as Brother Peter had proposed. I did not care to see it sold to finance more vestments and chalices.

I arrived just as Joan was slaughtering her pig. Her apron and skirts were covered in blood, as were her strong arms. Two blood-soaked boys hovered in the background, staring with wonderment at the pale entrails of the gutted beast.

Joan was as pleased as ever to see me. 'What do you want? I've some butchery to attend to.'

'Isn't it a little early in the year to be slaughtering your sow?'

She shook her head. 'Her last litter was too small. I'm swapping her meat for two ewes.' She wiped her hands on her apron.

'I'm moving the family to my father's cottage next week. Will you let me all his fields?'

'That's a lot of land for one woman.'

'Not if she has a herd of sheep.'

'As long as you can pay the rent.'

She forced a smile. 'I'm moving into wool. Of course I can.'

I dismounted. 'I've something that belongs to you.' She shooed the boys to attend to me, so they took Tempest's reins and tied him to the apple tree that shaded her door. The horse cooperated quite willingly with these two urchins, causing me to dislike him more than ever.

When the two of us were inside the cottage, she removed her apron and washed her hands and arms in a large caldron of water scented with sage and lavender. The smell blotted out the cloying odour of pig blood.

I reached into my belt pouch and took out the knife, the horn handle now re-attached. 'This was Leofwin's. It was found in his cave.'

She took the knife from me and eyed it sadly. 'You mean it was stolen from his cave.'

I didn't try to contradict her. 'It's yours now.'

She sighed deeply and wiped the blade of the knife across her cheek. Then her face crumpled into tears. I went to touch her, but she shrank away from me. 'Thank you,' she whispered.

'Perhaps you could sell the knife? It would command a good price at the market. Enough to buy a ram even.'

'No. I won't sell it. It belonged to my son.'

She placed the blade upon the stool, alongside the dusty corn maiden and a wooden crucifix. 'Do you still have the red coral beads?' she asked me. 'The ones you found under Matilda's bed?'

'I do. Why?'

A sly smile now crossed her lips. 'Matilda has no living relative. But she was betrothed to my father. So, by rights they should belong to me.'

'They were pulled from Cornwall's throat as he attacked her.'

Joan's face hardened. 'So you will give them to Cornwall? The man who sewed my son inside a bull and burnt him?'

'Of course not. But the beads are part of my evidence against him.'

'Yes. But do you need all of them?'

I hesitated, looking about her small cottage at the poverty in which the family lived. Old Ralph's home might be larger, but it was even more squalid and derelict than this. Joan needed help and I could not condemn her for asking, so I bade the woman hold out her hand as I emptied the beads into her palm. They were such perfect spheres of red coral.

She studied them closely and then counted them from one side of her palm to the other. 'Eleven, twelve, thirteen.' She looked up at me. 'It's fortunate that I'm taking some.'

I smiled. 'How so?'

'Because it's bad luck to keep thirteen of anything.'

There was no point in arguing with such logic. Her son had been killed by superstition, and yet she would judge a simple number capable of harming her. I gave her seven beads and dropped the remaining six back into the bag.

My unwilling mount then carried me towards Versey, but as he ambled along the woodland path, his resentful trudge lulled me into reflection. Something bothered me about my last conversation with Joan, but I was unable to hear its subtle notes over the rattling clamour that echoed about my head these days. Should I do this? How will I do that? The never-ending circle of questions and problems pushed out even the most rudimentary of clear thinking. I couldn't remember the last time I had read my books. Not even Bacon's *Opus Minus*.

In the forest the blackberries were already ripening on the bushes, and the oak leaves had begun to deepen to that tired green that signals their last snatch at the sun before autumn. In a clearing, ragged, grey-faced men poked at the walls of a charcoal kiln. I could even smell the mushrooms beginning to grow from the muddy mattress of the forest floor. It seemed the long fade into winter was beginning early.

I dug my heels into Tempest's flanks to hinder such melancholy thoughts and we galloped towards Versey.

Then the jolt of the saddle once again revived the subtle melody. The tune that had been troubling my thoughts since my visit to the Bath cottage.

And then, suddenly it was louder. I stopped my horse. Removing the six beads from my belt pouch I looked at them closely.

Finally I could hear their song.

Ada was already at Versey to meet me, full of tales of the young de Caburn sisters, Mary and Becky. How reproachable was their behaviour and how dirty were their clothes. I ignored her complaints and asked her to seek out de Caburn's manservant without delay.

The elderly fellow crept out from the kitchen and shuffled across the floor in a crab-like motion towards me, clearly expecting a beating. When I asked to speak with him privately, two blonde heads threw pine cones at me from behind a screen. Ada dragged the eldest girl out by her earlobe. It was Mary de Caburn. Her tunic was soiled and her locks were tangled into a bird's nest of hair.

'Why are they so filthy?' I asked.

Ada pulled a face of despair. 'The little runts won't wash, sire. And they refuse to change their clothes.'

Mary's face was reddening in pain, so I told Ada to release the girl's ear. Mary went to escape, but I took her by the arm. 'Listen to me, Mary. My mother and my sister will be living here soon.' She tried to wriggle away, but I would not release her. 'You cannot live with ladies, dressed in such clothes. Now have a bath and put on a dress.'

'I don't want to live with them.' Mary then looked over her shoulder towards her younger sister Becky, whose puckish face peeped around the screen like a demon from a church doom painting. 'Clemence is a bitch.' Both girls laughed until Ada boxed Becky's ears.

'Don't use that language,' I said. 'And you will call my sister Lady Clemence and my mother Lady Margaret.'

'Why should we?'

'Because I would like you to.'

'This is my estate. You stole it from me.'

'How would you manage Versey, Mary? You're no more than eleven.'

'I'd do a better job than you!'

I leant into her face and tried to make contact with her eyes, but she wouldn't look at me. I spoke kindly. 'No, Mary. You wouldn't. You're too young.' Her bottom lip protruded and she fought back tears.

I loosened my grip on her arm and spoke soothingly. 'I'll make sure you're treated fairly. I haven't forgotten how you helped me to escape that day. But please, for your own sake, learn to be polite.'

She nodded as slightly as it was possible, then pulled herself free of me and ran up the stairs of the north tower with her sister. Ada shouted up the stairwell, telling the girls' disappearing feet that she would soon fill the bathtub with warm water – but once the water had cooled she would not reheat it.

They neither listened to Ada, nor cared.

Now left alone with de Caburn's servant, I asked the man to sit down next to me on the bench, though he hardly seemed to know what was being asked of him, giving me to suspect he rarely sat on anything other than the floor. He lowered himself onto the surface of the wood as if he were about to sit on hot tinder.

'What's your name?' I asked him, when he had decided once and for all that the bench was a safe place to rest his backside.

'John Slow,' he said. The reason for his family name soon became apparent.

'I want to know about the night Lord Versey rode to the convent.'

Slow looked at the floor nervously. 'I told you about it before, sire.'

'Yes. But I want to talk about it again. To see if there is anything else you can remember.'

He bit his lip and now glanced about the room. 'I'll try. But my memory's not so good. Sometimes I forget which month it is. Yesterday I even forgot to wash.'

I found it difficult to believe the man ever washed, so disregarded this excuse. 'You were the servant who saw the messenger arrive with the letter, weren't you?'

He nodded vigorously at this. 'Oh yes. That was me.'

'Can you describe him?'

'I'll try, sire. He was a messenger.' He paused. 'He came on a horse.'

'Yes. But what did he look like?'

Slow now wrung his hands as if I were accusing him of stealing some bread from the kitchen. 'I can't remember. I really can't remember.'

'Calm yourself. This is not a court inquisition.'

'Sorry, sire. Sorry, sire.'

'Think carefully. Was he tall? Built like an ox?'

Slow now held his chin thoughtfully. 'He was a man.'

'Yes.'

'And he was riding a horse.'

'Yes?'

'And he had a letter for Lord Versey.'

'Anything more? I need as much information about this person as you can give me.'

'He came here from the convent.'

'Yes?'

There was a long silence. 'And then he went away again.'

It was difficult not to throttle the man. 'And you don't remember anything else about him? It's very important.'

Slow stroked his chin again, and gazed with great concentration at the ceiling as if he were about to pick out a memory from the beams. I held my breath for his answer. 'He had a letter with him.'

'Did you see the letter?' I asked.

'Yes.'

'What did it say?'

'Can't read, sire.'

My frustration was obvious by now and Slow flinched away from me as if I might strike him. I relaxed my hands. 'You may leave me now.' The man struggled to his feet, his knees creaking like gateposts after years of sleeping on the cold flagstones of this dismal place.

He hobbled away, but then stopped in the middle of the hall and hobbled back. 'Sire?'

'Yes,' I sighed, wondering what great truth was about to be revealed now. That the messenger had a head atop his neck? Or that the horse had four legs?

'I do know where the letter is, sire. If that might be of interest?'

I stood up. 'Of course that's of interest. Why didn't you mention this before?'

He flinched from me again. 'Is it important, sire?'

'Of course it is!'

'Lord Versey did say to keep it in his chest.'

'Take me to it now.'

'But nobody's to look in the chest. That's what Lord Versey says.'

'Lord Versey is dead!'

I followed Slow to the south tower, a corner of the castle that
I had previously assumed had fallen into disuse. We climbed
some stone steps, avoiding a badly stacked log pile and a broken
roasting spit, until we came to a wooden door ornamented with
stud nails and iron bands. Slow felt inside his tunic and pulled
out the key, which hung from a chain about his neck. He fitted
this key into the lock and pushed at the heavy door.

The room on the other side was dark and damp, with only an
arrow slit for a window – so at first it was impossible to see
anything. But as light seeped in from the stairwell I could make
out shapes – not beds or benches, but instead the apparatus of
torture. A Judas chair sat in front of the hearth with polished
spikes covering its back, seat, and arm rests. In the corner was a
knee splitter, the metal cage of a head brank, and the long thongs
of a scourge whip.

'Was this Lord Versey's room?' I asked.

Slow appeared confused at my question. 'Yes.'

'And he tortured people in here?'

Slow shrugged. 'Oh yes. But just thieves or scolds. Though
only in the winter.'

'The winter?'

'Well, yes. He preferred to be outdoors when the weather
was fine.'

I wanted to leave. Evil drifted from the room like a foul
miasma. 'Find me this letter. And be quick.'

Slow shuffled over to a corner, pushing aside a table that
looked like a butcher's block to expose a black and dusty wooden
chest. Turning another lock he opened its stiff lid and then delved
around amongst the contents, soon revealing this box to be a
collection of very particular items.

As he searched for the letter, Slow passed me a succession of
objects to hold. The first was a silver mug engraved with the
image of a man copulating with a horse. The second a phallus

carved in stone. The last, an illustrated compendium of obsceni-
ties. I will admit to lingering over this well-thumbed manuscript
a little longer than I should have, for Slow had to cough to get my
attention.

I took the small parchment from him, feeling a little embarrassed. I then unrolled it and read the simple message written
upon its powdery surface.

And then I knew.

Chapter Twenty-Three

I found Brother Peter in the kitchen of Somershill, stewing onions and willow bark in the large copper-bottomed pan, his eyes watering as he stirred the foaming concoction. The air was heavy with the vapour of the brew, and the window dripped with steam.

Piers worked alongside him. Squatting on a three-legged stool, the boy scoured the fat from two meat skewers in a bowl of greasy water. As he ran a rag up and down the twist of metal, he sang about the Great Mortality – his song as melancholy as the call of the storm cock. When I requested the boy polish the silver spoons and not return to the kitchen for at least an hour, his young cheeks coloured. Dropping the skewers into the water as if they were made of hot iron, he ran out with a whistle – for he had cleaned these same silver spoons only the day before.

'Why such secrecy, Oswald?' Peter threw a handful of sage leaves into the pan, transforming the soupy mixture from grey and sharp-smelling to green and wood-scented.

'I need to speak with you privately, Brother.'

He smiled. 'What about?'

'Where's Gilbert?'

Peter prodded the sage leaves with the wooden spoon, making sure they remained beneath the surface of the water. 'I think he's milking the cows.'

'And Mother and Clemence?'

'In the solar, I expect.' Peter wiped his hands upon a linen rag and looked at me suspiciously. 'Is there something the matter, Oswald? Your cheeks are pink.'

'It's the murders.'

'Have you received a date for Cornwall's trial?'

'Not yet.'

'I visited the man in gaol yesterday. He pretends to have lost his mind and will only speak in Cornish. The fool is trying to feign insanity.' He smiled. 'As if that will spare him.'

'Cornwall isn't guilty.'

Peter cocked his head and frowned. 'Oh yes?'

'Just listen to me, Brother.' I opened my hand and held out a single coral bead to him. 'I found this under Matilda Starvecrow's bed. Do you remember?'

'Of course I do.'

Water from the pan began to bubble into the fire. Peter turned his attention from me and stirred the soup to release the heat. 'These onions are far too pungent.' He wiped tears from his eyes. 'They should only be used for pickling.'

'The bead, Brother?'

'And I think the tonic needs liquorice.' He gestured for me to smell the pan and give my opinion. 'It's for your mother's jaundice. She's been passing dark water.'

Ignoring this invitation, I held my hand out again – the bead sitting in the middle of my palm like a drop of new blood. 'Do you remember I once gave you more of these beads? To show to Brother Thomas?'

'Yes, yes,' he said, now irritated. He picked up the bead in his thumb and forefinger and studied it closely.

'I gave you ten beads, Brother.'

'Did you?'

'But when you returned them to me, you passed over thirteen.'

He frowned. 'Did I? They are such small things. You might easily have counted incorrectly.'

'I didn't.'

'Then they must have become mixed up with some others in my pouch. I do sometimes collect such items.' He passed the bead back to me. 'I expect I returned them to you along with the originals.'

'No, Brother. All the beads were identical and came from the same necklace. A rosary of red coral.'

Peter returned to stirring the pot. 'What are you suggesting?'

'I'm suggesting it was your Pater Noster.'

He laughed. 'I've never owned such a rosary.'

'You didn't. But the abbot did.'

He now stopped stirring. 'I see, Oswald. So it's my turn to be under suspicion, is it?' Then he smiled. 'But I suppose I shouldn't be surprised. You've pointed the finger at nearly everybody else.'

It was a clever argument and I felt my feet beginning to tremble and lose their grip on the floor. 'You stole the rosary from the abbot on his deathbed.'

'Whatever are you talking about?'

'But you did. Along with the many other items that found their way into our cart when we left the abbey.'

'That was just wine and some unused vellum. Hardly a crime.' Now he crossed his arms. 'I'm becoming insulted.'

Once again he was undermining my arguments. But I would not be discouraged. This was no hallucination, nor false accusation. This time I was certain of my facts. 'I've seen this rosary twice before,' I told him. 'Firstly, when I peeped into the abbot's bedroom to spy upon his buboes. And then, when I was delirious and dying of the Plague myself. You held it over my face and prayed for me. You hoped its rarity and value would save me.'

'What nonsense.'

'I've dreamt about it. Repeatedly. Though I couldn't see the meaning of the image, until now.'

'So I'm accused on the strength of your dreams?'

'Matilda pulled the Pater Noster from your neck as you attacked her, didn't she?' He laughed again. 'You thought you'd collected all the beads from under her bed.'

If I had assumed he was going to confess, I was disappointed, since he pulled the wooden spoon from the soup and pointed it at me. His expression had turned from amusement to pique. 'Be careful what you say, Oswald. These are serious accusations.'

'But it's what happened, isn't it?'

'No. It is not!' he bellowed.

Peter then resumed his stirring and we avoided looking at one another until the kitchen cat bounded onto the table and broke the silence. As we shooed her away I surprised Peter by beginning my second line of attack.

'I believe you saw Alison Starvecrow. The day she came to Somershill.' I tried to keep my voice level and calm.

Peter reached for the silver flask in his belt pouch. 'Leave me alone, Oswald. Go to the stables and pick on Piers. Since you seem in the mood for a fight.'

'You suggested a private meeting with Alison in the chapel, didn't you? After she failed to secure an audience with me or Mother. You wanted to know the purpose of her visit.'

He swilled the brandy about his mouth. 'The girl was sent home. You know that.'

'But she didn't go. Gilbert saw her a second time by the chapel porch. He had the impression she was waiting for somebody.'

He burped and rubbed his stomach. 'Well it wasn't me.'

'Who else would she meet in such a place, but a priest?'

He took another swig from the flask and this time pointed a finger. 'I want you to stop this now, Oswald. You're suffering from melancholia and a broken heart after that business with Mirabel. So I'll forgive you. But you must say no more.'

'You discovered why Alison wanted to speak with me. Then you suggested she intercept me on my way home from Burrsfield.'

'I told you to stop this.'

'You followed her along the drover's road. Gilbert saw her a third and last time. She was walking towards the forest. Not the village.'

He laughed. 'That hardly constitutes proof, does it?'

I took the letter from de Caburn's secretum and placed it in front of him. 'No, but this does.'

The kitchen cat slithered past us, rubbing her neck against Peter's leg and looping her black tail about his ankle until he kicked her away. Unrolling the parchment, he squinted in a pretence of not being able to read the writing. 'What is this now?'

'It's the letter from Clemence to de Caburn. She demands he visit her at the convent.'

'What of it?'

'She didn't write this letter.'

'Clemence might say so. But you can't trust a viper like your sister.'

'It's written in your hand.'

'Another delusion.'

He went to screw up the parchment, but I snatched it back before he had the chance to throw it into the fire. 'You've disguised your writing well enough, Brother. But you've been my tutor since I was seven. I would know your hand if I were half blind.' I pointed to the lettering. 'See the ascenders of the "t"s, and the tails of the "g"s. Nobody else writes in such a way.'

His face reddened and tears were forming again, although this time the pungent stink of the onions was not to blame. He turned his back to me and stared at the wall.

I took a deep breath. 'You followed Alison into the forest and murdered her. The fatal wound was the clean slice of a knife.'

'You don't know what you're talking about.'

'Then you buried her body. Only her grave was too shallow, and Gower's pigs were able to sniff her out.'

He began to rock from foot to foot. 'This is absurd.'

'What was the secret Alison wanted to share with me, Brother? So terrible you had to murder her?'

'Stop it.'

'Because Matilda knew the secret too, didn't she? You realised that when I recounted my conversation with the girl.'

He turned to me again, his face tear-stained and red. 'She was infected with demons, Oswald. You couldn't believe a word the girl said.'

'You gave me a sleeping draught, then went to the Starvecrows' cottage to murder her. And it *was* the abbot's stolen Pater Noster that she grabbed as you attacked her. I know it.'

He shook his head, though I'm not sure if it was in disagreement or despair.

'Then you buried Matilda. Only this time you dug a much deeper hole. This time you wanted to make certain pigs wouldn't sniff her out like a truffle.'

'That's enough now, Oswald!' Peter clenched his hands into a ball, his bony knuckles white and pronounced. 'Don't speak that way of the dead.'

'She's only dead because you murdered her!'

His hands clenched further into fists and I think he might have been considering punching me, but then suddenly thought better of it. Slowing his breathing, he recovered his composure and smoothed down his habit. 'I wonder, Oswald, how Matilda's head came to be dropped in the well of St Blaise? If, as you contend, I buried her? Does your gift for deduction have the answer to that mystery?'

I had no further evidence to rely upon, only my suspicions. Nevertheless, I would not admit defeat. 'I can explain that,' I told him boldly.

A smile curled across his lips. 'Please do. I would be interested to hear.'

'I don't believe you visited the bishop during the week Clemence was married.'

'You're ignoring my question, Oswald.'

'You hid in the empty Starvecrow cottage.'

'Is that so?'

'When I found the burning embers of your fire, you locked me inside.'

He flung his hands up in the air. 'Why would I be hiding out in a hovel, Oswald? Once again your imagination spirals off into fantasy.'

'You were taking advantage of the good fortune you'd been handed.'

He laughed. 'What good fortune?'

'Cornwall's monster. The dog-headed beast.' He made as if to laugh again. Only this time the tone was thin and tentative. 'At first you were as disgusted as I by such a tall tale,' I said. 'Maybe more so. But then you realised this ignorant invention could work to your advantage.'

The onions began to bubble over in the pot, and steam filled the kitchen. Peter went to stir the pan, but I took his arm and prevented him from moving. 'While you claimed to be visiting the bishop, you exhumed Matilda's body and removed her head.'

'Nonsense.'

'You mutilated her corpse so it would appear she had been gored to death by a monster with the teeth of a dog. That's why there were fresh maggots in the wound. You then put her head in a holy place. The well of St Blaise. Somewhere you knew everybody would visit after Clemence's wedding.'

He remained silent.

'With the dog head story established, it was easy for you to murder de Caburn. You lured him into the forest with the letter. Then you ambushed and murdered him.'

'And how do you imagine I killed such a man as Lord Versey?

He saved the king's son from the French at Cressy. He's a giant, and I'm nothing but a withered old man.'

'You shot him with your metal weapon.'

Peter drew back. 'I told you. The black powder was exhausted. I had no more.'

'You lied. You had enough for a second attack.'

He pointed at me. 'The weapon hasn't left your father's library.'

'Yes it has. I even helped you lift it into the cart with Clemence myself. When you left for the convent. Except I thought your heavy chest was filled with brandy.'

'Stop this, Oswald.' His voice was suddenly small and defeated.

'You cut away the skin on de Caburn's face and hands to remove the sooty residue from the blast. But you could not remove the scent on his body, could you? The scent of burning.'

'Please, Oswald.'

'You then draped his naked and mutilated body over the shrine of the Virgin. To make his death appear demonic. Everything had worked out, just as you planned. Except for one thing. A turn you had not predicted. Something you had not foreseen.' He held his hand out to me, but I ignored it. 'You never supposed I would be arrested for your crimes, did you? So you panicked. And in your haste, you led them to Leofwin, an innocent boy.'

He spoke into the cowl of his habit. 'You don't understand.'

'No. I don't!'

He looked up at me with bloodshot eyes. 'Everything was dangerous for you here, Oswald. You must see that. At every corner there was a mischief maker or rogue waiting to defy you or even take your place.' A waft of brandy fumes hit my nostrils as he attempted to embrace me. 'I had to stop them. Why can't you see that?' When I dodged his grip, he slunk back to the bench and put his head in his hands. 'Why can't you be grateful that I saved you?'

I stood over him. 'So you admit to murdering the Starvecrow sisters and Walter de Caburn?'

He took a deep breath and nodded.

'I want to hear you say it.'

He whispered, 'You know I did.'

'And you caused Leofwin to be murdered?'

Peter wiped his mouth clear of spittle. 'Yes.'

The fire under the pan had died down and the onions now floated at the surface like dead fish in a poisoned pool. The cat crept out of the shadows and lay on the flagstones near to the embers, stretching out her claws, seeming to have forgotten her kicking.

In the distance we could hear Piers singing another tune from the back porch, this song no more cheering than the last. *Bones in the black pit, can't sow barley in the fields.*

Peter held his hands together and stared into the orange glow of the flames. 'What will you do?'

'I don't know.' It was the truth. I had planned no further than exacting a confession.

'I should have told you before, Oswald.' His words seemingly directed towards the fire. 'You would have forgiven me.'

'I doubt it.'

He wiped the sweat from his brow. 'I presume you've asked yourself why I committed these sins?' He turned and studied my face for a few moments. 'No. I see my motive has eluded you.'

'You had a warped notion of protecting me,' I said quickly.

He watched me a while longer, his eyes scanning my face. 'But you don't know why, do you? I can see that. I thought perhaps you might have guessed?'

'Guessed what?'

He sighed. 'Then there is something I should explain to you.'

I tried to laugh. 'More lies and excuses, Brother? No thank you. Keep them to yourself.'

He took my arm and I was unable to shake him off. 'You asked me about the secret the Starvecrow sisters kept. Do you want to know what it was? Or will you send me to the gallows with it?'

I should have told Brother Peter to keep the lid upon his Pandora's jar.

But I have been granted curiosity by the gods.

And regretfully I asked to look inside.

Chapter Twenty-Four

The Great Mortality has not only shaped the land, it has shaped me. Since last summer I have cut down hedges to farm sheep and abandoned my fields of barley. My rivers have broken their banks to find new courses, and my chestnuts grow un-coppiced into a forest. But all of this could be restored. If I had the men.

However, no army could restore me to the boy I was.

When the Pestilence first crept over from the east, I hid in a monastery, until its small hand knocked at the door to be let in. Then I left for my estate, along with my priest, hoping its silent footsteps would not follow us. As we travelled we eschewed all others and thought only of ourselves. We were both men of God, but we passed the homes of the dying and refused to administer last rites. We rolled past corpses and did not bury them. We beat away a child who clung to our cart for his own dear life. Without another soul to turn to, we abandoned this boy to a village inhabited only by the dead.

We did all this. I did all this. Even though I had nearly died myself.

And when we reached safety, we could not speak of these sins. The Plague was to blame. It had warped us into something we were not. It had disfigured and corrupted us.

But we had not been dirtied by the Pestilence. The very opposite was true. It was the lye soap exposing us for what we really were — our morality no thicker than the paint on the face of a wooden effigy. Easy to rub off. Quick to reveal the coarse grain beneath.

Now the Pestilence sleeps and the world is left only with the strong, the lucky, or the selfish. Which of those am I?

Perhaps I am all three.

Peter motioned for me to sit next to him on the bench, but I remained standing — not wanting to be drawn into his intimacy. When I refused, he took another glug from his flask, licking the last drops of liquor from about his mouth. 'I'll begin with your birth, Oswald.'

'Why? I don't see how that's relevant?'

He ignored my objection and once again reached out to me. But I would not be his friend, no matter how many times he held out a hand. 'You were born in May 1332,' he said with a sigh. 'Your mother nearly died in labour.'

'This is no secret.'

His voice tightened. 'Please just listen.'

'No. Don't you think I've heard this enough times, Brother?' He went to interrupt me a second time, but I held up my hand and impersonated Mother's breathless manner of speaking. 'I was confined to my bed for many months after you were born, Oswald. Not sure if I would live or die. Thanks to you, my under-carriage now droops between my legs like the udder of an aged dairy cow, and my breasts swing like a pair of long woollen socks drying in the wind.' I reverted to my own voice. 'So I say to you again, Brother. This is no secret.'

'I'm not talking about my lady. I speak of your real mother. A woman called Adeline Starvecrow.'

'What?'

He stoked up the embers and rekindled the flames beneath the pan of onions. 'She was a girl of seventeen. A spinner. Married to a ploughman called William.'

I wanted to laugh. 'My father wasn't a ploughman!'

Now he looked me in the eye. 'No, Oswald. Your father was a priest.'

I was dumbstruck.

Peter turned back to the fire and pulled up the hood of his habit – the steam of the pan now shrouding him like a pall. His profile was as slack as the old nag's in the water meadow, the peak of his hood bearing down upon his thin and ugly head.

I stood up in some consternation and walked to the door. 'My name is Oswald de Lacy, son of Henry de Lacy.' I pulled up the latch. 'Get out of here.'

But Peter did not move. 'Close the door, Oswald.'

'Get out! You're not my father. How dare you even suggest such a disgusting idea?'

Still he would not move, so I left the door and grabbed at the wool of his habit to pull him from the bench. But Peter was a sinewy man – still strong enough to shake me off. When I rushed at him a second time he was able to push me against the sweating stone of the wall and clamp his hand about my neck. 'I've committed mortal sins and shall burn in the fires of Hell, Oswald. What do you say to that?'

I struggled to speak. 'I don't care.'

The hand tightened. 'You think I would turn my back on eternal life so easily? For the son of a greedy nobleman? A boy I taught Latin and Geometry?'

'Let go of me, Brother. You're hurting.'

He relaxed his hand a little, but not enough for me to escape his grip. 'I love God, Oswald. You know that. So ask yourself why?' I felt his breath, hot upon my face. 'Why would I offend Him in such terms? Who could I love more than God?'

'I don't know,' I stammered. My throat was bruised.

'Only one person, Oswald. My own son. You!' His face was red. His eyes were bulging. 'So do not accuse me of lying.'

He allowed me to escape – but only as far as a dark corner, where I crouched between a broomstick and a sooty shovel.

'Will you let me explain?' he asked. I didn't answer, so he took a step forward and leant over me. 'Don't you want to know the truth?'

'No!'

He groaned in frustration and then returned to the bench, flopping down upon its lath of oak. The room continued to fill with steam as the onions bubbled away in the pan. Peter closed his eyes and seemed to be praying, so I considered creeping out towards the door, until he began to speak again. 'I came to Somershill often in those days. To copy your father's manuscripts.'

'I said I didn't want to know.'

'I don't care.'

I shuffled further into the corner.

'Sometimes I took confession at St Giles. It's where I met Adeline. Your mother. I loved her instantly. But it was a sin.' His voice was suddenly anxious and faltering, and as he spoke the cat jumped upon his lap. She coiled herself into a circle of black fur on his knees and purred as steadily as a priest saying mass.

Peter stroked her back and spoke more evenly, as if the cat had calmed his nerves. 'When Adeline told me she was with child, I panicked. I found her a simpleton to marry. A man who was pleased to take such a beautiful girl as his wife.' He sighed. 'A man who wouldn't ask too many questions.'

'As long as he shared her with you?'

Peter shook his head. 'No, Oswald. We didn't repeat our sin. William accepted you as his son, and you were christened Thomas Starvecrow.'

Thomas Starvecrow. It was the name of a horse thief or a common bondsman.

I laughed derisively. 'And I suppose this simpleton also accepted Alison and Matilda as his daughters? Though *their* father was Henry de Lacy.'

'As I said. He didn't ask questions.'

I snorted. 'A sensible man. Since his wife was a whore.'

Peter screwed up his face. 'Adeline was poor, you arrogant little fool!'

'But—'

'You know nothing of these people's lives. What they must do to survive.'

I pulled my tunic about my neck and tried to hide my face.

Peter lowered his voice. 'The de Lacys had a child within days of your birth. A boy. Farmed out to Adeline as his wet nurse.'

'Where's this boy now?'

'He died as a baby.'

I groaned. 'This story improves with each disclosure. No doubt you will now tell me Adeline starved him to death?'

'Of course not. The boy was a sickly infant. The type often born to an older mother. Adeline did nothing to harm him.'

'So why did he die?'

'His mouth wouldn't latch as his tongue seemed too short to suck. He faded with each successive day.'

'Whereas, no doubt, I grew quickly at my mother's breast?'

Peter waved his hand at me. 'It's the truth, Oswald. As the de Lacy boy became weaker, Adeline became afraid she would be blamed for his poor health. Women can hang for such crimes.'

'So she put her own boy in his place?'

'It wasn't deliberate. My lady made an unannounced visit and assumed the fat baby at Adeline's breast was her own son. It was easy for Lady Somershill to dismiss the sickly little boy in the other cradle as the son of a tenant. With each further visit it became harder and harder for Adeline to reverse her deception.'

'She could have tried.'

'She hoped to nurse the de Lacy boy back to health and return him to his place.' The cat jumped down from his lap and stretched her front legs, flexing her claws and then slithering away into the steam and out through the kitchen door.

Peter now spoke to the flagstones. 'One day Adeline came to see me at Somershill. She was agitated because the de Lacy boy could not be woken. I returned with her to the cottage, but he was dead already.'

'So what did you do with his body?'

'We buried him, of course. As Thomas Starvecrow.'

I pulled a face, but he shook his head at me. 'I made him a small coffin and we carved a headstone. He was not treated poorly. And you should not be disdainful, Oswald. You've been raised and educated in his place. You're a lord. Be thankful for it.'

'But I'm not a true lord, am I?'

'Does that matter? At least some good has come of this tragedy.'

I sat up a little. 'Don't imagine these revelations will prompt me to treat you as my own father.'

'But I thought you might—'

'You're a murderer, Brother. De Caburn might have deserved his death. But you killed two innocent girls.'

He began to twist the silver flask in his hands. 'Those girls weren't so innocent, Oswald. They would have revealed your true identity, had you refused to help them.'

'They were too young to marry such a man as Old Ralph. I would have helped them.'

Peter pointed a shaking finger at me. 'But it would have ended in your downfall. The sisters could not be trusted. Such secrets are like dry leaves in a drought. They easily ignite.'

'So you murdered them. Just in case?'

'I did it to shield you. I thought only Alison knew our secret. But after you visited Matilda, I realised Adeline had told both her daughters.'

I thought back to my brief meeting with my half-sister all those weeks ago. 'Father, father. Eye of a lover. It was *you* Matilda spoke about.' I looked at Peter. 'But it wasn't a father I shared with Alison and Matilda, was it? It was a mother.'

'I'm so sorry.'

I put my head in my hands. 'I don't understand you, Brother. You encouraged me to investigate. Why?'

He snorted. 'Because I expected some standards from you, Oswald. Otherwise what had been the point of your education?'

I nearly laughed at this answer. 'So you were anxious for me to investigate a murder that you, yourself, committed?'

'I didn't imagine you would get anywhere. I just wanted you to try.'

'And Joan Bath? Why fight her cause?'

'I'm not a monster, Oswald. The woman was innocent.' He puffed out his lips and blew. 'She reminded me of Adeline. A poor woman, struggling to survive.'

'So you were being compassionate?' Now I did laugh at him. 'Is that what you're saying?'

Peter took a deep breath and then drained the last few drops of the bottle of brandy from the flask, shaking it as if it might emit a further supply. When nothing was forthcoming he stood up and began to search amongst the jars and spice pots, moving them aside like a child looking for a lost penny. 'There must be something else to drink around here. I'm sure Ada keeps a bottle of Madeira for cooking.'

'The Madeira is for the table.' The voice was new to our conversation, but not unknown.

'Who's there?' said Peter.

A figure materialised through the steam.

Peter gasped to see her face. 'Lady Clemence. How long have you been standing by the door?'

'Long enough to hear that a priest killed my husband. And that my real brother is dead.'

I scrambled to my feet. 'I didn't know any of this, Clemence. I swear to you.'

'That doesn't change anything.'

'You shouldn't listen at doors,' said Peter, 'my lady.'

'Then don't leave them open,' snapped Clemence. She swept away the veil of vaporous water with her hand. 'But, no matter. Once the truth is known, I'll be head of this family and you'll be sent straight to the gallows.'

Peter took a step forward. 'I don't think so, my lady.'

She laughed. 'More insolence?'

Peter threw his silver flask at Clemence. 'You meddlesome little bitch.'

She ducked, but lost her balance and fell over, only for Peter to catch her. But this was no act of chivalry. Pulling a knife from the folds of his habit, Peter held it to Clemence's throat – the blade soon piercing her skin.

'Let her go, Brother,' I said. 'Please.'

'Why? She means to destroy you.'

'Peter. Don't kill anybody else.'

He met my eye. 'I'm damned already, Oswald. I may as well burn in Hell for four murders as three.' The blade dug in deeper and a bead of blood fell from Clemence's throat onto the velvet of her gown. The vein in her neck now pulsated like the chest of a trapped hare.

I tried to appeal to Peter again. 'Remember your vows, Brother. The commandments. Please. Just let Clemence go.'

He only sneered. 'She'd never do the same for you, Oswald. She despises you.'

'That doesn't matter to me. I still care for her.'

Peter twisted the knife a little further, and though Clemence tried to scream, she emitted no sound whatsoever. 'Don't waste your time caring for this old goat,' he told me. 'Her soul is as barren as her womb.' A pool of water emerged from beneath Clemence's gown and spread across the floor.

'But she's not barren, Brother,' I said quickly. 'She carries a child.' Clemence's eyes widened at my lie and her mouth fell open.

Peter flinched. 'What?'

'If you murder Clemence, then you also kill an innocent.'

He began to tremble. 'I don't care about her unborn child. What sort of fiend would it be anyway?' He took the knife from her throat and now waved it about in the air. 'Conceived by this She-devil and de Caburn.'

But Peter did care. My words had distracted him, giving me just an instant to act. Running at Clemence, I was able to throw her to the floor, before attempting to wrest the knife from Peter's hand. But the priest remained stronger than me, and he threw me off.

Sweat trickled down his face as he brandished the knife. 'You fool, Oswald. You should let me kill her.'

'No, Brother.'

'She will destroy you.'

'I don't care.'

Peter stared at me without blinking. I saw both sorrow and fear in his gaze. Even regret?

But if regret existed, Peter didn't get the opportunity to express it. For a pan of boiling water was cast upon his face, burning the skin from his bone. He shrieked in pain, held his hands to his eyes and then fell to his knees, before coiling himself into a ball on the floor. I turned to see Clemence still holding the pan. Her face was white with shock. The pan slipped from her hand and she then ran from the kitchen, calling wildly for Humbert.

I crouched over Peter. This man who was my father. As he screamed and convulsed in pain, I tried to calm him. But my words of compassion were too weakly made, and when he held his chest and fought violently for his breath, I found some cold ale in the cook's barrel and tried to douse his face with its cooling liquid. This soothed him a little, but by now he was barely conscious and seemed, by his heaving and wheezing, to be on the point of death. When Humbert ran into the kitchen only moments later, I ordered the boy to lift Peter's body to the chapel, where the priest could pray, one last time, for forgiveness.

We laid Peter before the altar on the flagstones of the chapel floor. When he was settled, I left the chapel to find some brandy to ease his journey.

This was my last mistake.

I was gone for only a few minutes, but on my return I discovered Humbert wandering around the chapel and staring at the floor as if he had lost a ring.

'Where's Brother Peter?' I said.

The boy studied his hands and didn't answer.

'Where is he?'

Now he blushed and looked ready to cry.

I ran to the chapel door and looked out across the fields, but there was no disappearing monk to be seen in any direction. I went back inside and shook Humbert. 'What happened?'

Humbert sobbed, but I was able to gather through the boy's tears that Peter had begged for a cup of holy water from the font near the chapel door. Humbert had turned his back for only a few short moments, and then Peter was gone.

We had fallen victim to yet more of Peter's lies. He had shown me the tunnel from the library and claimed he knew of no others. But they existed. There could be no other explanation for his sudden and miraculous evaporation.

I walked about the chapel, pressing flagstones or poking at carvings in the wall, but found nothing. I then told Humbert and Gilbert to guard the periphery of the house to intercept Peter as he made his escape from the other end of whichever tunnel he had used. Nothing was seen however, not even after hours of keeping watch.

Then I came to the wearied conclusion that Peter was in the

forest by now, hiding in a cave or under a tree. Trying to treat the burns to his hands and face. To save his own life.

A small part of me felt sorry for him.

Then I remembered my two dead sisters, and I hoped he would die.

Chapter Twenty-Five

A day later Mother called me to her bedchamber. She had been closeted in this room for hours with Clemence, so I was expecting to face a double denunciation. But I entered to find Mother alone, apart from her dog Hector, who lay across the bolster as if it were his own bed.

Mother beckoned me to sit beside her on the bench. She looked exhausted and grey, and, for once, not about to discharge a torrent of chatter.

'I suppose Clemence has told you everything,' I said.

'About what, Oswald?'

'That I am not your son and that Brother Peter committed the murders.'

She suddenly coloured. 'Well, I was very surprised to hear about Brother Peter. I was most convinced by the Cynocephali story.' She pulled a sooty bone from her pocket. 'I even bought a saint's finger from John of Cornwall, and paid him to sing a mass for the family.' She tossed the bone to Hector. 'I would demand my money back. If the man would answer to English.'

'I've let Cornwall go. He's left the parish.'

She huffed. 'So I'll never get my money back.'

'Forget Cornwall.' I leant towards her to make sure of looking into her eyes. 'I'm not your son, Mother. Do you understand that?'

'Of course I do, Oswald.' Hector jumped off the bed with his prize, running into a corner with it.

I sighed. Had Mother been drinking? There was a large pewter mug on the chest, half full of some noxious-smelling brew. 'Mother, I understand this must be a shock for you but—'

She put her hand on mine and her face took on an expression I had not seen before, nor since. 'You must think I'm very stupid, Oswald. Do you imagine a woman cannot identify her own baby? The child she has carried for nine months, and then given birth to?'

I hesitated to answer. 'I don't know.'

'When I visited your nursemaid . . .' she paused. 'Isabel was it?'

'Adeline.'

'Adeline. Of course. Yes, as soon as I went into that cottage I knew the girl had swapped her baby for mine. You might have formed this impression of me, but I'm not a comprehensive fool.'

'So, why didn't you say something, Mother?

She laughed and squeezed my hand. 'Because I'm a practical woman, Oswald. My own baby, your namesake, nearly killed me in labour. I was forty in the year of your birth, and my womb was exhausted from decades of childbearing. Only three of my previous eight children had survived. And after Oswald was born I was confined to my bed for many months . . .' She squeezed my hand again. 'But you know the story, don't you?'

I nodded. 'Yes, Mother. I do.'

'The baby was a sickly child.' She sighed. 'But he was a boy, and that's all Henry cared about. We needed three to be secure of a de Lacy succession, so I agreed to bear him one last son. You were our spare, Oswald. Our extra boy, in case your older brothers died. And, as luck would have it, that is exactly what happened. Henry was right all along. The de Lacy family has needed you.'

'But I'm not a de Lacy, am I? That person lies in a grave marked Thomas Starvecrow.'

'You've been raised as a de Lacy. That's good enough.'

'I'm not sure it is.'

'I couldn't have borne any more children, Oswald, so it's good enough for me. I didn't care you weren't my own child. You were the third son we needed. That *I* needed. Now Henry would finally leave me alone. He had enough whores around the village to keep him company.' She waved her hand at me crossly. 'Don't pretend to be shocked. I was pleased to be rid of his sweating and grunting.' Then she looked to the ceiling and appeared to be holding back a tear. 'But why did so many of his bastards live? When so many of my own poor children had to die?'

'I'm sorry, Mother. I don't know.'

She took a deep breath and sighed. 'They say a woman's womb needs to be kept warm with hot seed, Oswald, but I was quite ready for mine to cool. Can you understand that?'

I nodded.

'The wheel of fortune always turns against a woman in the end. Particularly in childbirth. If Henry had known our son was dead, he would have had me in calf again by the next spring. Don't you see? My body couldn't have taken it. I'm not a breeding heifer.'

I looked into her face. It was lined and pale, but she must have been beautiful once. She took her hand away and gulped from the pewter cup. It left a deposit of grey foam on her upper lip.

'I'll return to the monastery tomorrow,' I told her. 'The abbey is short of brothers, so there'll be no problem.'

She wiped her hand across her mouth. 'No you won't. You are needed to run the estate.'

'But I thought you would want me to go, Mother.'

'Don't be so foolish. You will remain here as Lord of Somershill and Versey. I command it.'

'But—'

Now I caught a wildness in her eye. 'By the bones of St Anselm!
Stop arguing with me.' Hector began a steady growl from the
corner of the room. 'Why on earth would I want you to leave?'

I went to answer, but Mother wasn't waiting for my reply.
'Listen to me, Oswald. You have made a slow start to your duties.
But your work on the estate has not been without merit.'

'I'm not sure that's true.'

'Nonsense. You are a clever boy and will prove useful to the
family. I'm sure of it. Look how you solved the mystery of those
murders. Nobody else had the wherewithal.'

I blushed a little at these words, as Mother was rarely generous with her compliments.

'And you have added the Versey estate to our own. That is
something my husband never managed.'

'That was just luck, Mother.'

'But it is good to be lucky, Oswald. At least the wheel of
fortune is turning in somebody's favour.'

'But what about Clemence?'

She snorted. 'Clemence will keep her peace and let you
remain here as lord. I've made it plain that it's not in her interests to disobey me. She would bring dishonour on the whole
family.'

'But she might tell somebody.'

'She thinks she's so clever, but she has to be forced to think
ahead. If you were swapped as a baby, then why not her as well?
She could be the daughter of the farmhand and the dairymaid.
She would turn the de Lacys into a laughing stock. Her scheming
would rebound upon her before she could turn the milk sour.'

'I'll speak to her, Mother.'

'It's up to you, Oswald. But don't expect a warm welcome.'

I knocked at the door to the library, the room that Clemence had
now taken over as her private chamber, despite its previous life
as an exclusively male domain. She called for me to enter, but

didn't look up – preferring to keep at the destruction of the stitching on a tapestry that would never hang. Humbert held her yarn and watched me impassively.

'I understand you are to stay,' she said. 'And that I am to thank you for trying to save my life.'

'There is no need to thank me, Clemence. Unless you mean it.'

Now she looked up at me uncomfortably and seemed about to say something, but the words stuck in her throat. Instead she returned to her needlework, stabbing her finger and drawing blood. 'Look what you've made me do,' she said crossly.

'I wanted to make you an offer,' I said, as she sucked the blood from her finger.

'What sort of offer?'

'I know you cannot be Lady of Somershill. But return to Versey. I won't stand in your way.'

She kept her eyes focussed on the cloth in her lap. 'I thought the earl instructed you to manage my estate.'

'You could do it instead. As long as we kept the arrangement to ourselves.'

'And when my child is born? Whose estate is it then?'

'Your child?'

Now she looked up and flashed a smile. 'Yes, Oswald. You were correct when you guessed I was carrying a child. My son will be both a true de Caburn and a true de Lacy. What do you say to that?'

I couldn't be sure if she was telling the truth or merely taunting me. But I no longer cared. 'Then your son shall inherit both estates upon reaching maturity. What do *you* say to that?'

I would tell you I received an embrace at the generosity of my noble offer, but the reality was rather more muted. In fact, it was subdued enough to be described as a sigh. 'Thank you, Oswald. But you shouldn't make such a promise.'

'Why not?'

'When you marry you will change your mind. At least Mirabel will expect it for your children.'

'Mirabel?'

She cocked her head slightly and eyed me curiously. 'Yes, Oswald. You told me you loved the girl. I assumed you still wished to marry her.'

My mouth hung open.

'Goodness me. You hadn't worked it out, had you?' Now she laughed. 'And Mother calls you our great investigator.'

'Worked what out?'

'My father is not your father. Which means Mirabel is not your sister.'

I stood up to leave. 'Please excuse me, Clemence.'

Now an odd expression crossed her face. Neither a sneer nor a scornful grimace, it could only be described as a tender smile – though her mouth was unable to hold this unfamiliar pose for longer than a moment. 'Go quickly, Oswald,' she whispered.

'I will.'

The rain had fallen upon many secrets in the last few days, causing them to spring up like dandelions in a field of grain. We had cut their heads or trampled them down, but secrets have deep roots and will always grow again – only the next time they will set their seeds.

So, while I had the chance, it was time to lead my life. I rode to Mirabel's cottage, hoping to tell her the good news, but dismounting from Tempest I found the place to be eerily quiet. No smoke seeped out through the thatch of the roof, and the door was closed, though the day was warm. I called out Mirabel's name and tried to push the door open, but the wood was unyielding to my touch and soon I realised that it was jammed fast with a peg.

In the distance somebody shouted to get my attention. I turned, hoping to see Mirabel's sweet face, but instead it was old Eleanor, who was seated in the garden of the neighbouring cottage with her swollen leg resting on a stool. Her mute grandson was beside her, still bashing mindlessly at his cartwheel.

'Where is Mirabel Turner?' I asked.

'She's Mirabel Carpenter now, sire. She married young Nicholas.'

'When?'

'Two days ago.'

'And where are they now?'

'Up country, sire.' Eleanor laughed. 'Said she'd never come back.'

Epilogue

Somershill Manor, November 1350

My life has taken many turns in the last year. I am now Lord
Somershill — the keeper of more than a thousand acres in Kent.
The owner of a village whose inhabitants owe me servitude. And
the master of a grand house complete with hunting forests, cellars,
and a stable of fine horses. Mother was correct — the wheel of
fortune has turned in my favour. I have been blessed, considering I
am the bastard son of a lowly priest and a poor spinner.

But the wheel has also turned against me — for sometimes,
when I think of Brother Peter, Mirabel, or the Starvecrow sisters,
an orb of pain spins in my stomach and rises into my chest. It is
hot and biting, and eats away at my heart, making me miserable,
if I will allow it. It is then that I find my work on the estate most
appealing, for against all expectations, I have come to enjoy my
duties. There is solace to be found in routine. And I believe I will
make a good lord.

Still, for all the times I have tried to forget the murders and
put such troubles from my mind, there remained one stone in
this story that I could not leave unturned. My curious nature
would not allow me to do so.

A crypt lies beneath the Somershill chapel, where the skeletons of the de Lacy family lie for eternity. However, there was

one de Lacy not residing in this crypt. A boy whom Brother Peter had told me was buried in the village churchyard, with the name Thomas Starvecrow scratched into a square of stone above his grave.

At full moon, this September just gone, I rode Tempest to the churchyard and searched for Thomas's grave – for I had to know if Peter's story were true. He had told me so many lies.

The moon lit my path, but the weeds amongst the headstones had grown long while the parish waited for the bishop to send a new priest. Pushing aside the cornflowers and fleabane, I found the headstone at last, hidden in the corner of the churchyard, amongst the graves of the many other Starvecrows.

I then dug into the soil, hoping nobody would discover me at my grave-robbing, and after a short while I found the simple wooden box that Peter had described to me. I pulled this coffin from the earth, waited until the moon had passed a cloud, and then prized open the lid – looking inside to see a ragged length of cloth wrapped about a thing that was the size of a tiny infant.

And then I felt guilty for disturbing the remains of a child. A poor boy whose place I had taken. I went to replace the lid, but curiosity once again got the better of me. Reaching into the coffin, I carefully pulled back the cloth, but my fingers did not find the tiny, fragile skeleton I had expected.

Instead they touched something that was cold, hard and unyielding.

The missing wooden effigy of the Christ child.

Glossary

Braies

The medieval version of underpants for men. A loose undergarment — usually made from a length of linen that was wound about the legs and bottom and then tied at the waist with a belt.

Chief Tithing-Man

Medieval law enforcement was controlled at a local level by groups of men organised into groups known as tithings. Formed of roughly ten to twenty men, each man was responsible for the actions and good behaviour of the other men in his group. The Chief Tithing-Man managed this tithing, and answered for their conduct to the constable.

Childwyte Fine

A fine levied in the manorial court against female villeins who gave birth to illegitimate children.

Constable

The constable reported crimes to the bailiff at the Hundreds Court.

Coroner

A local government official whose duty was to protect the financial interest of the crown in criminal proceedings. Any death that was considered unnatural had to be reported to the coroner.

Cotehardie

A closely tailored jacket that became popular in the mid 1300s. Worn over breeches, it developed into a scandalously short and revealing fashion.

Cottar

The poorest class of villeins. A person with very little land, usually only the curtilage of their own cottage.

Crespine

A netted metal device for holding and styling a woman's hair.

Customal

A document listing the financial and legal arrangements between the lord and his tenants.

Dais

A raised platform at the end of the dining hall/great hall. Usually furnished with a table and benches, it was reserved for people of high status within the household.

Demesne

The fields on the manor estate that were reserved for the lord's personal use and profit. Local villeins would work this land in return for the ability to rent their own plots. Tenants were often expected to work in the demesne, although they received wages for their labour.

Destrier
A war horse. Used by knights in battle and at jousts.

Hue and Cry
If a dead body was found under suspicious or unnatural circumstances, every man in the tithing was required to join a noisy
search party to alert the local neighbourhood to the murder, and
to flush out the culprit.

Humours
Harking back to the teachings of Galen in antiquity, the human
body was said to be ruled by four humours, or bodily fluids,
which needed to be kept in balance. Yellow bile, phlegm, black
bile, and blood. The balance of your humours ruled both your
health and your disposition. So, for example, an excess of black
bile caused a person to become melancholic.

Hundreds Court
A court that dealt with serious crime, or cases that could not be
tried by the manorial court. This court was presided over by the
sheriff, unless the case involved murder – in which instance a
royal judge was summoned.

Indulgences
Taking the form of a letter or receipt, an indulgence was an
award for the remission of sin. It was earned by prayer and good
deeds, but increasingly in the later Middle Ages through a money
donation.

Infirmarer
The infirmarer managed the infirmary at the monastery, where the sick and elderly of the community were cared for. The position was a prestigious post, and the infirmarer was usually trained in basic surgery and medicine.

Kirtle
A tunic-like garment, usually made of wool.

Lay Brother
A monk of lesser status than the ordained members of the monastery. The lay brothers undertook much of the heavy agricultural and domestic work for the community.

Manorial Court
This court was overseen by the lord of the manor. It usually dealt only with minor issues restricted to the manor itself, such as disagreements between tenants, or infringements of the lord's rights.

Pardoner
A man who was authorised by the bishop to sell indulgences and relics for money. The funds were often used by the Church to finance special projects. The pardoner kept a proportion of his takings as payment.

Pottage
A type of soup often made with dried peas, grains, and sometimes meat or fish.

Purlieu

A deforested area on the edge of hunting forests, still subject to forest law – especially with respect to hunting.

Reeve

An officer of the estate, responsible to the lord for organising and overseeing agricultural work on the demesne fields. A position of status within the community.

Royal Judge

Royal judges, from the court of the king's bench, were responsible for justice with regards to cases of murder. Travelling to each county approximately twice a year, they tried the criminal cases, which had been referred to them by the sheriff.

Sheriff

The position held the ultimate responsibility to the king for law and order in a shire. Literally the 'shire reeve', he had the power to arrest, imprison, hold trials, and organise juries, but not the power to try and sentence a suspect for murder.

Solar

A room set apart from the rest of the household for use of the lord's family. This room usually had a large window, giving rise to the idea that it was named after the sun. However, the word may also have derived from the French word 'seul', which means to be alone.

Sumptuary Laws

A law passed in 1337 and strengthened in 1363, prescribing exactly what clothes each class of person was allowed to wear. For example a yeoman farmer and his family were forbidden from wearing furs other than rabbit, fox or cat. Only the most noble and wealthy person might wear ermine.

Surcoat
A tunic or outer coat.

Tenant
A person who rented farmland from a lord, but who received payment for working on the demesne. The status of the tenant was as a free man, meaning he and his family could leave the estate without the permission of the lord.

Villein
Villeins worked the lord's lands, but were not waged. Typically they worked for three days a week, with extra services required at certain times of the year such as at harvest. In return for their labour they were able to rent a small amount of land from the lord. Their status was unfree, meaning the lord had a great deal of control over their lives.

Yeoman
A richer tenant farmer, who had the means to rent larger areas of land, and could afford to employ both servants and farmhands. They often acted as officers for the manor, such as the reeve or constable, giving their family greater status. Often more prosperous than the lord himself, in the wake of the Black Death they were known to take over the management of whole estates in return for paying fixed rent.

Historical Note

The bubonic plague of the 1340s originated in the arid plains of central Asia and was the second pandemic of the same infection – the first having been in the sixth century. The fourteenth-century plague was known at the time as the Great Mortality or the Pestilence. The term 'Black Death' was not coined until later in the seventeenth century.

The plague was caused by the bacillus, Yersinia Pestis, which lives in the digestive tract of infected fleas. It has three forms – bubonic, pneumatic, and septicaemic, but the bubonic form is the one we most commonly associate with the Black Death. Certainly most of the eye-witness accounts would support this assumption.

The bubonic form is an infection of the lymphatic system, caused by the bites of infected fleas as they move from rat to human hosts. To begin with, the sufferer experiences a high temperature, sweating, and severe aches to the joints. After a day or so the buboes swell in the lymph nodes of the groin area and under the armpits. As these painful lumps, typically the size of an egg, turn from red to black due to internal bleeding, the body is overwhelmed by a bacterial infection that, during the 1340s, was usually, but not always, fatal. It was an excruciating and horrific death that caused mass hysteria.

More deadly however, even than the bubonic plague, is the

pneumonic form, which occurs when the same bacillus, Yersinia
Pestis, infects the respiratory system rather than the lymphatic.
It is likely that this form of the infection was also at work during
these years. Rather than being spread by the bites of fleas, it
relied upon airborne transmission and was probably passed on
by the coughing up of blood or by the inhalation of flea faeces.
This virulent and highly contagious form of the plague was rapid
in its onset and always fatal. Pneumonic plague was also less reli-
ant on the climate than the bubonic form, and would explain
why the plague continued to claim victims through the winters
of 1348 and 1349. Fleas need warm temperatures to remain
active, whereas the pneumonic plague could continue to cause
infection by human-to-human transmission during the colder
winter months.

A third form of the plague is the septicaemic, which affects
the bloodstream, once again causing an overwhelming infection,
ending inevitably in death.

The plague itself is believed to have originated in Mongolia,
and was confined to that area for many centuries before it moved
west in the mid fourteenth century. The reason for this new
outbreak was a perfect storm of circumstances that provided the
bacilli with the opportunity and conditions to spread.

Firstly, there was a resurgence of commerce between east and
west due to the opening of new trade routes in the years preceding
the plague. There was increasing demand for Eastern goods such
as exotic spices and silk – but these were not the only cargoes travelling west. The black rat was happy to live alongside humans,
particularly and crucially on ships. But even if the rats themselves
were not travelling, these new trading routes were able to trans-
port infected fleas. It is estimated that a flea can survive up to
eighty days without a host, which was time enough for these para-
sites to travel long distances in fabric and clothing.

Secondly, the population of Europe had grown rapidly during
the previous two centuries – the so-called Medieval Warm

Period. During this time of more favourable climate, the population of England had grown from somewhere around two million at the time of the Norman Conquest, to at least four million (but possibly as high as six million) by 1300. As the climate then began to cool in the little ice age of the fourteenth century, this larger population came under pressure, as inefficient farming practices and poor growing conditions caused a succession of famines. A weakened population was inevitably more vulnerable to the effects of the bubonic plague. The population of England did not recover to pre-plague levels until 1600.

Lastly, the medieval world was a dirty, smelly place where people lived cheek by jowl with their animals, their own waste, and their own animals' waste. They had little conception of sanitation – and where there is waste and dirt, you will also find rats. However, once the local black rat population had become infected, the subsequent collapse in rat numbers meant that fleas were suddenly in need of new hosts. And who better to have turned to than the humans who lived in the same streets and houses?

After the devastation of the plague, it is easy to understand how people searched about for a cause – if only to give some meaning to this catastrophe. The predominant belief in society was that God had allowed the plague to happen because of sin. The populace considered themselves guilty of all of the seven deadly sins, but the finger was particularly pointed at the sin of pride – with many commentators blaming the ornate, impractical, and revealing fashions that had become popular in the earlier part of the century.

But if sin were not to blame, there were plenty of other candidates – most notably the Jews, who were accused of poisoning wells. Some even looked to astrology for answers. The King of France commissioned an investigation that went on to identify an unfavourable planetary alignment back in 1345. It was not until much later that the link between rats and the bubonic plague was established, and the actual bacillus was not identified until the nineteenth century by the French scientist Alexandre Yersin.

The narrative of the plague played well to the medieval mindset, which was generally fearful and superstitious. Churches were not the simple, white-washed places of later years – instead they were theatres of high drama, decorated with doom paintings depicting hideous and terrifying images of hell and purgatory. Manuscripts such as the Luttrell Psalter of 1337 were illuminated with bizarre drolleries – grotesque creatures with the heads of gargoyles and the bodies of lizards or snakes. A popular book of the time, *The Travels of Sir John Mandeville*, tells the story of this man's journey across Europe and into Asia where he meets all manner of fearsome people. Some have horns, some have only an enormous eye in the middle of their head, and some bear the heads of dogs. His descriptions range from the tribe who fatten and eat their own children, through to the 'isle where the people live just on the smell of a kind of apple'. It is easy to smile at these ideas – but the fear of the unknown was very real and was played upon to great effect by the Church.

By contrast, the main character of *Plague Land*, Oswald, is a boy who leans towards rational thought. He is also a sceptic, even an atheist. This might seem a very twenty-first-century sensibility, but there is evidence of unbelief from those times – though it is difficult to gauge the true extent of this, as you were likely to have kept any scepticism to yourself. But even if doubts were rare, impiety certainly was not. One only has to read the *Canterbury Tales* to see this. The Middle Ages might have been an age of faith, but was not always an age of morality, and it seemed not everybody was willing to lead a chaste and blameless life, no matter how dire the visions of Hell and the vengeance of God.

Even amongst those who were pious, the Church itself often came under heavy criticism – mainly for corruption and the monetisation of faith. The unrestricted sale of mass-produced indulgences was used to finance the Crusades and the building of cathedrals. Cathedrals and shrines competed for pilgrims and the money to be made from the sale of souvenirs and relics. The rich could even pay for masses to be sung with the intent of hastening their passage through Purgatory. Chaucer satirises such practices in his *Canterbury Tales*, where the Pardoner claims to 'preach for money, and for nothing else'. In the poem 'Piers Plowman', written sometime between 1372 and 1389, the writer and cleric William Langland criticizes the amount of money that the Church exacts from the poor. 'Parish priest and pardoner share the silver' derived from 'preaching to the people for profit to themselves'.

The Great Plague not only had a lasting effect on the population size and psyche of English society, it also marked the beginning of the end for Norman-style feudalism. Landowners were suddenly and chronically short of labour, and were forced to offer more attractive terms to their tenants, or risk losing them to a neighbouring lord who would. For those tenants lucky enough to survive the plague, they suddenly found that better wages, better housing, and better land were available. Even the villeins, who were traditionally bound to the land and did not receive a wage for their labour, were empowered by the new circumstances, and started to question their status as un-free men vociferously.

The nobility tried to quash this new-found spirit of dissent with laws to peg wages back to their old, pre-plague levels. But these laws – the Ordinance of Labourers in 1349, and the Statute of Labourers in 1351 – were simply unenforceable. The plague had set the conditions for radicalism within the poorer strata of society, which led eventually to the Peasants' Revolt in 1381. Although this revolt was unsuccessful, feudalism had suffered a major blow and began its long decline —coming to a full stop around the time of the Reformation and the dissolution of the monasteries.

The bubonic plague persists to this day in the poorer regions of the world, especially in areas where the infection is endemic in the local animal population. It can be treated successfully in the early stages with antibiotics, but the infection still kills, and remains a serious public health concern.